Promised Soul

Promised Soul

Sandra J. Jackson

Dedication

For my husband, Perry, who supported me and never complained when I started this incredible journey. You are my soulmate. To my children, Melissa and Dylan, who, prior to my laptop, freely gave up the family computer whenever I asked. A mother's love is eternal.

Acknowledgments

I would like to express my heartfelt thanks to the many people who helped make this book a reality. First, to my sister, Lisanne and brother-in-law, Damian, the very first to read Promised Soul in its infancy. Thank you to my friend Yvonne, who read the novel in its entirety before editing. I would like to extend my gratitude to the readers on Wattpad. Your wonderful unbiased comments encouraged me to seek publication.

Prologue

Krista ran from her bedroom at the sound of her father's voice, leaving the picture she had been colouring on the floor, and jumped into his outstretched arms. She missed him terribly whenever he went away on one of his diving exhibitions. From her point of view, he was always gone far too long, though this last time it had only been three sleeps.

"Daddy!"

"Hello, my sunshine girl." Sid caught her up in his arms and swung her around as she squealed with delight before he carefully put her down again.

"Did you bring me anything?" Krista beamed. She reached up and tugged the back of her sundress down, smoothing it back into place. How her dresses always managed getting tucked into the back of her underwear, she wasn't quite sure, though that time she suspected jumping into her father's arms had something to do with it.

"You bet I did." Sid took off the backpack he had swung over his shoulder.

The two of them sat on the plush, grey-carpeted floor of the living room. Krista sat cross-legged and waited somewhat impatiently while Sid looked through the bag's contents. He found the box he was searching for, but before pulling it from the bag he carefully removed the cover and hid the object in his hand.

1

"Hurry up, daddy!"

"Patience is a virtue, Krista."

Krista rolled her eyes and thought to herself, what does that mean anyway? As Krista looked up, she saw her mother walking into the living room, a dishtowel in her hand. She sat, joining Sid and Krista on the floor.

"What's all the fuss?" Sheila asked.

Sid looked at Sheila, leaned in and brushed his lips gently across hers. "Hello, sweetheart!"

"Good to have you back home, safe and sound." Sheila leaned forward and returned his kiss.

"Eww! Mommy and daddy are kissing!" Krista giggled.

"You just wait fifteen years; it won't be so eww then." Sheila reached over and tickled Krista under her arm sending her over backwards in a fit of giggles. When Krista had contained herself, she sat up again, pulling her sundress over her knees.

"Are you ready?" Sid saw excitement as well as apprehension in Krista's eyes.

"Sid!" Sheila warned, "I don't think now –"

Sid interrupted with a smile. "It's okay." He reached over and patted Sheila's hand. After six years of marriage, his smile still managed to melt her heart.

"Now this. . . "Sid turned his attention back to his daughter, his hand still hidden in the backpack, "is something I found especially for you."

Krista felt that funny feeling in her tummy, Mommy called them butterflies, but Krista wasn't so sure.

"What is it?" Krista scooted a little closer, driving the back of her dress where it didn't belong. She squirmed a little, then finally reached under herself to flatten it out. All at once, she realized she had gotten too close for her liking. She stretched her legs out in front and inched back; her bare feet barely touched her father's crossed legs. Krista felt she was at a safe distance. She was still able to see what her father had when he opened his hand,

and at the same time, her outstretched legs would prevent him from moving too close, just in case he had something she didn't like. It wouldn't be the first time he'd brought something home that frightened her. She wiggled her toes and watched as the pink sparkly nail polish her mother had applied caught the light from a lone sunbeam shining in through the living room window.

Sid waited for his daughter to settle down. "Are you ready now?" He looked at Sheila; she wore a slight look of concern on her face. If there was one thing the two of them had in common, it was how easily their faces could be read.

"Yup, but open slowly," Krista said.

Sid did as his daughter asked and slowly opened his curled fingers to reveal a small starfish. Krista craned her neck to get a better look as Sid moved his hand toward his daughter.

"What is it?" she asked, pulling her legs under her so that she now rested on her knees. She inched forward. In this position, she could get up in a hurry and run to the safety of her bedroom if she had to.

"It's a starfish," Sid said, happy for once his daughter hadn't immediately sprung to her feet running and screaming to her room.

"Did it come from the ocean?" Krista folded her arms protectively against her body and scrutinized the small object her father held in his hand. She wasn't ever going to let anything from the ocean touch her.

Sid hesitated for a moment, knowing his answer would more than likely cause Krista to make a hasty get away. "Yes."

"I don't like it!" Krista whined and jumped to her feet, her arms still crossed and pressed tightly against her.

"But, honey, it can't hurt you." Sheila stood up and placed a protective arm around Krista's shoulders.

"I don't like it!" Krista yelled, stomping her foot for effect.

"But, Sunshine –" Sid moved to his knees, holding out the starfish.

"Mary says everything in the ocean is bad and to stay away." Krista pulled away from her mother's grasp and stomped back to her room closing the door behind her. As soon as she closed the door, she remembered that she wasn't allowed to have it closed. She quickly opened it again before plunking herself on the floor and resuming her colouring.

Sid looked at Sheila who reached out a helping hand. He took it and as he stood up, pulled her close to him while his other hand closed protectively over the starfish. "Who is Mary?" he said, brushing his lips over the top of Sheila's head.

Sheila pushed herself away in a playful manner and rested her hands on Sid's chest at arm's length. "Oh that! Well that would be, I guess, what you'd call an imaginary friend."

Sid's eyes widened, and he shook his head laughing, "Imaginary friend huh, since when?"

"Oh! About three days now, and you should know – she's having those dreams again."

One

The air was cold; she shivered and gathered her wool cloak pulling it tightly around her. Small daggers of ice formed inside her nostrils, stinging her with every breath she took. She brought a gloved hand to her face and cupped her mouth and nose trying to ease the sting, it helped – but not much.

"Pardon me." She pushed past the other passengers; ignoring the calls from her family to come back. With slow but determined steps she made her way to the front.

"Get back, girl," an annoyed man cried as she tried to push past him. The large and foreboding man glared down at her as she stood no taller than his armpits.

"P-please sir, let me p-pass," she stuttered as much from fear as from the cold.

The man looked at her and scowled.

Despite her fear, she stood her ground, determined to move to the front.

"John, let her pass, she's nay but a young girl," a frail woman said laying a gentle hand on his arm.

The girl looked at the woman whose kind voice and gentle touch seemed to soften the glare of the man she'd called John.

John looked at his wife and back to the girl; whose gaze clearly indicated the urgency she felt. "Fine, go ahead then, but mind who you're pushing against, they might not take too kindly to it."

The girl sighed with relief. "Thank you, sir; ma'am." The couple moved aside and let her pass.

At last, after what seemed like several minutes, the girl had made her way to the railing of the ship. She looked down at the people on the docks and strained her eyes for a familiar face in the crowd. The other passengers around her were shouting and crying as they waved goodbye to their families and friends. The girl looked to the sky as seagulls screeched under cover of the fog high above like invisible sirens warning of danger. Below, the waves lapped against the hull; icy fingers grabbing and clawing, like the hands of the starving.

The wind whipped the girl's long, dark hair into her face. Sweeping it away with her cold, aching fingers, she searched the dock one last time, hoping to find him amongst the crowd of well-wishers. Without warning, they slowly pulled away, the distance between the ship and the docks grew. For a brief moment she panicked, she was not going to see him; he did not come to say goodbye. She stared down at the icy cold water and shivered as a tear rolled down her cheek. The churning pattern of water and ice, held her gaze.

"Mary!"

Suddenly a voice freed her from her trance. "Thomas, Thomas, I'm here!" Mary called out towards the throng of well-wishers who stood waving on the docks. She leaned out over the railing, trying to find him. At last, she saw his arm waving above the crowd as he pushed himself to the front. "Thomas!" Mary waved her arms franticly, the people around her stared as though she'd gone mad, but she paid no heed.

The distance between them grew as the steam tugboat gathered speed, pulling the ship away from the docks and eventually out from London Harbour.

Thomas cupped his hands to his mouth. "Mary, I love you!"

The fog settled upon them, so that Mary could no longer make out the figures standing on the docks as the ship pulled further away.

"I love you, Thomas!" she cried out from the whiteness that swallowed her; the fog had taken over.

"I'll find you, Mary; I promise I will find you!"

As the fog lifted, sounds of waves and seagulls evolved into the sounds of rustling leaves, chirping birds, and squeals of delight from the neighbourhood children enjoying their first days of summer. Sleep and my dreams faded as consciousness began to take its hold. A breeze swept in through the open window, and my ears pricked to the sound of my lacy, white curtains fluttering in its path. I reached down and drew the sheet up under my chin; my eyes still closed. Rising from bed was not my preference, and it took great effort to fight the urge to open them. After all, it was my summer vacation, too.

"Just fifteen more minutes," I whispered, half smiling. My mother always said, 'Talking to oneself was just thinking out loud.' It seemed her habits were just as hereditary as her traits and that annoyed me.

Remnants from my dream lingered in my mind, tempting me to return to sleep; a state that was more than welcome to invade my body. Unfortunately, the noises from outside kept interfering with any attempt I made to remain asleep, so with much regret, I gave in and opened my eyes. Staring up at the ceiling, my mind continued pushing the smallest fragments of my dream to the forefront. Yet, there was nothing tangible to cling to. Eventually, I rolled over and checked the time.

"Seven thirty!" I groaned – not exactly my idea of sleeping in.

The sudden ringing of the phone created yet another interruption to my intended relaxing Saturday after the long week I had suffered. I reached over to answer it and inadvertently knocked a book off the nightstand. It landed on the hardwood floor with a thunk.

"Hello!" I said; my voice still groggy with sleep. I hoped the caller would get the idea and perhaps call back later.

"Did I wake you up?" The all too familiar voice on the other end admonished.

"Hi, mom!" Sounding more alert, I sat up in bed and placed a pillow behind me, confident that a quick conversation was not in my near future.

"I hope you're not planning to waste the day in bed."

I rolled my eyes and shook my head.

My mother continued in a much softer tone. "Would you like to join me for brunch this morning?"

If at that very moment my phone would have stopped working for some inexplicable reason, I would not have been happier. My plans for the day, already decided upon the night before, did not include spending the day with my mother. I tried to think of an excuse, but sadly, that was not one of my talents. I resigned to tell her the truth.

"Sorry mom, but I was planning on a quiet day, so I –"

"Honey, I hardly saw you at all last summer, and I'd really like for it to be different this time. Please join me for brunch, I'm not asking you to spend the entire day with me."

It was going to be a different summer; she wasn't going to be seeing me at all, and the guilt she unwittingly made me feel, changed my mind.

"Fine, when and where?" I closed my eyes and gently struck my forehead with the heel of my left hand. Relaxing would have to wait until after brunch.

"How about Jane's?"

"Sure! What time?" I asked with fake enthusiasm.

We discussed meeting times, and though I preferred later, my mother's preference prevailed; we would meet just before the restaurant opened. By the time our conversation ended, there wasn't much time to get ready.

"Yeah – brunch!" I said sarcastically, putting the phone back in its cradle. My stomach growled in reply, and I laughed. "Well at least part of me wants to go."

I swung my legs over the edge of the bed, stood up, and accidentally stepped on the book I'd knocked down earlier. I bent forward and picked it up. The image of an old sailing ship on the cover held my gaze as I turned it over. My finger traced over the ship's billowing sails. After a moment, I returned the book to the nightstand and began the process of preparing for my brunch date with my mother, the picture of the ship already out of my mind.

Stepping into the shower, I closed my eyes, welcoming the feel of warm water as it washed over me. My anxiety slowly ebbed with each breath that passed through my lips. I had not envisioned having brunch with my mother at the beginning of my summer vacation.

"Maybe it won't be so bad," I snickered, realizing as the words left my lips that brunch with Sheila Adams was never just brunch; there was always an ulterior motive.

Within half an hour, and still somewhat reluctant, I took a final look in the mirror and applied a small amount of make-up, tucked a loose strand of hair behind my ear, and smoothed down my floral print sundress. My shoulder-length, blond hair caught a sunbeam shining in through the window, and it glistened; reminding me of the pet name my father had given me. Examining myself closer, there was without question, a definite inheritance of my mother's height and slim build. However, it was always my father's bright-green eyes and pouty lips that reflected back from the mirror.

Satisfied with my appearance, I looked at the time. There was a call that needed placing but little time to spare. However, if it wasn't made, it most certainly would be forgotten.

"Where did I put that phone number?"

I searched my nightstand and the floor around it, before crouching down and looking under my bed. Nothing but a few dust bunnies greeted me. 'Housework' had now become next on my list, while pushing 'relaxing' to the bottom. Somehow a day planned for doing absolutely nothing was suddenly becoming a day full of everything.

Frustrated, I stood up and looked around my room once more. All of a sudden, I remembered the whereabouts of the missing notepaper. Picking up my book from the nightstand, I allowed it to fall open, and there between the pages lay the supposed missing piece of paper. With the page number committed to memory, I removed the notepaper and unfolded it.

It had always been a dream of mine to travel to England and that summer it was finally becoming a reality, but unfortunately, the trip would be alone. Originally, the plans had included my boyfriend, Brad, for the August trip. However, by the end of June, there was no denying that something was missing from our relationship. Thus, it was my decision to end it. More than ever, the inexplicable need to escape had grown stronger, and August had seemed too far away. My plans had to change.

After I had researched for some time, I found a tour guide agency that suited my needs and contacted them by e-mail. They had responded quickly, and fortunately, there was a guide available despite the short notice. His name was Aaron, and he had promptly let me know that under the circumstances he would only be able to fit me in between his other bookings. That idea had suited me fine, for I felt a great need, which couldn't be explained, for exploring on my own. All that week, we had exchanged e-mails, planning my itinerary for the dates he was available.

With my vacation quickly coming into shape, there remained only one other issue to take care of and that was finding accommodations. Not wanting to stay in a hotel for the next couple of months, I had intended on finding a place to rent. The task, after a few days of searching, proved to be difficult. Feeling discouraged,

I finally e-mailed Aaron and asked for his help. His reluctance was evident in his reply, but in the end, he had agreed. After several days of exchanging e-mails, Aaron had called to finalize my holiday plans, but sadly, that had not included accommodations. It was agreed that if he hadn't found anything before my arrival, I would stay at a bed and breakfast or hotel. Our conversation had been short, and I realized afterwards I hadn't told him my arrival time at Heathrow.

My call to Aaron would have to be quick. My eyes glanced at the clock again as my hand stretched for the phone. Just as I was about to pick up the receiver, it rang.

"Hello?" I half expected to hear my mother's voice again on the other end but prayed that it wasn't.

"Good morning, Krista, I hope I'm not troubling you."

As soon as the caller spoke, relief washed over me – my prayer answered. The tension released from my shoulders as I sat on the bed. Words, coated with enthusiasm, spilled from my lips. There was a moment of silence, and then I realized my exuberance had caught him off guard.

"Sorry, I thought you might be someone else. . . and quite happy you aren't."

"Oh, I see! Well I won't keep you; I just need to know your arrival into Heathrow and to let you know–"

"Just why I was about to call you," I interrupted. "I should be there by nine-thirty A.M. Should I just take a cab to my accommodations – assuming I have a place to stay by then?" I rambled as I opened the nightstand drawer and began rifling through its contents, searching for a pen.

"I can pick you up if you'd like and take you to your accommodations, save you the extra cost."

My muscles tensed a little and several thoughts bounced around my head. Should I take him up on his offer? The savings would be great, but is this really part of the deal? What do I do?

As though reading my thoughts, Aaron continued, "I have on occasion picked up clients and taken them to their lodgings, but if you prefer..."

"No, that's okay; I'll meet you at the airport. I just hope you'll have a place to take me to by then." I half joked, still counting on him to find me an apartment to rent.

"Well, I have good news on that matter. As of last night, I managed to find..."

Aaron's voice began to fade. My mind filled with swirling thoughts. Visions of England flashed in my mind as though I was leafing through a travel magazine. My dream trip was becoming a reality. My heart pounded and a wide grin spread across my face. It took all my energy not to start bouncing up and down. Another thought flitted through my head and suddenly my smile disappeared and was replaced by a stomach filled with butterflies. I ran my hand through my hair and bit my lip.

"...It's a bit of a drive..." Aaron's voice broke through my jumbled thoughts only to fade away again.

Would it go as planned? Would it be everything that I imagined?

Apprehension was building in the pit of my stomach; it was as if a spark had suddenly burst into flame. I closed my eyes tightly and snuffed it out, staunching any negative thoughts. I forced myself back to reality, fully aware that everything Aaron had said was lost.

"Is that alright with you?" he asked.

I scrunched my forehead, searching my memory for even a trace of what he had said. My preoccupation with my own thoughts and feelings had blocked out just about everything. Closing my eyes, I attempted to make sense of the bits and pieces that floated around in my mind, while the silence between us grew.

"Hello? Are you still there?" he asked.

"I'm so sorry Aaron I was looking for a pen to write down the information and... I'm sorry, what did you say about where I would be staying?" The heat rose in my ears from embarrassment as I abandoned my feeble excuse. I covered the mouthpiece with my hand and exhaled, happy he couldn't see me.

"Bourton-on-the-Water in Gloucestershire. It's a small village about an hour and half drive from the airport." There was no hint of irritation in his voice.

"So I guess that means you found a place for me to rent?" A wide grin crept across my face. The prospect of having my own place was exciting and it was all I could do to keep from sounding like a child on Christmas morning.

"Er... yes, as I said, it's a flat; I just hope it's what you are searching for."

"What do you mean?" I asked, narrowing my eyes. My hands stopped their hunt for the elusive pen, the drawer was so full of junk it was a wonder I could find anything at all.

"The thing is... you'll be staying at my aunt's," he blurted, just as my eyes spotted a pen.

I was silent for a moment. "Your aunt's?"

"Let me explain."

"Please do."

Aaron began to clarify that his aunt's home had a vacant apartment on the second floor, and she was quite willing to rent it to me for the summer at a discount. He explained that she was a kind and loving woman and assured me she didn't gossip or meddle, her only fault being that she could be a bit chatty. It sounded perfect.

"So you have no objection?" Aaron asked when he finished his account.

"No, not at all, it sounds absolutely perfect!"

"Right then, well I guess that's it. If you have any questions just send an e-mail or ring, you have my number?"

I looked at his number on the piece of paper still clutched in my hand and circled it with the pen I'd retrieved from the drawer. "Yeah, I've got it right here."

"Good, well I guess I will see you soon."

"Yeah, I guess so... thank you so much and I'm sorry for being distracted, my mind wanders sometimes," I confessed.

He laughed. "No worries, I too have that same affliction."

We said our goodbyes and hung up. I put my notepaper and pen down on the nightstand and flopped back on my unmade bed. I groaned, embarrassed for admitting to him about my wandering mind. The whole trip still seemed surreal to me. It wasn't often that dreams came true, most especially mine. I laid there for a few minutes listening to the birds chirping outside, closing my eyes, and allowing myself to drift in and out of consciousness.

"Oh crap!" I sat up on my bed and looked at the clock; it was ten after nine. I was undeniably late, and my mother was not going to be impressed. If there was one thing she didn't like, it was tardiness, and short of death, there was no excuse.

I made my bed, quickly throwing the pale yellow and blue comforter on top of the crumpled sheets.

"That'll have to do."

I picked up my book, returned the notepaper between the appropriate pages, and was suddenly preoccupied with the image of the ship on the front cover once again. As I stood there, I found myself immersed in memories from my dream.

Mary stood on the deck of a ship looking out at the people as they slowly pulled away from the docks. She searched the docks with her eyes, looking for someone. At long last, she saw him standing there; it was Thomas. Her heart sank when he waved and called to her. The ache in her chest grew stronger the further they drifted until eventually he disappeared under a thick blanket of fog. She felt sick to her stomach as tears slid down her cheeks. At that moment, Mary felt a warm hand on her shoulder. She turned and saw her father standing next to her. Without a word, he put his arm around her and gently guided her away, leading her to shelter.

I closed my eyes and shook my head, dislodging the image unfolding in front of me. When my eyes opened again, a single tear rolled down my cheek. I tasted its saltiness as it touched my lips, and I shivered. The tear dripped onto the notepaper, blurring Aaron's name.

Two

Being a private tour guide wasn't the profession Aaron Dyer had desired for himself; rather it found him when his lifelong friend, Peter, started the business. He had invited Aaron, who wasn't certain what he planned on doing with his life, to join him. The first five years went quickly, but now Aaron was beginning to find the job somewhat tedious. Though he enjoyed meeting new clients and showing them around the country he loved, it was becoming more difficult to show enthusiasm and appreciation for the same landmarks time and time again. He tried to make each tour unique, not just for the client but also for the sake of his own sanity.

Aaron hung up the phone and smiled as he replayed the conversation he'd just had with Krista. There was softness in her voice that comforted him, and he looked forward to meeting her.

When Aaron first received Krista's e-mail, he had assumed she would be no different from any of his other clients. He had even been prepared to decline her request for a tour guide. His schedule was busy enough, and on such short notice, he had thought it would be impossible to accommodate her. However, as he read her e-mail, he soon realized he had been mistaken. Though she had expressed some interest in a few of the usual tourist attractions, she was more interested in visiting smaller villages and the countryside. She wanted to explore, go on hikes, and spend time on her own. Moreover, unlike most of his clients who wanted to spend their entire vacation time in London, Krista had only wished to visit for a couple of days. Not all the tourist sites and landmarks seemed to excite her. After realizing what she had intended from her trip, Aaron knew that he could manage. He would fit her in amid his other clients during her extended stay, even if it meant he'd have to give up some of his own free time.

Aaron had responded to Krista directly, he felt thrilled by the challenge and spurred on by an almost instant renewed interest in his fortuitous occupation. There were, however, a couple of issues. The first was that he had a limited amount of time to spend with her. He would fit her in when he could, and when he couldn't, he wanted to ensure that she was staying somewhere interesting with plenty to do on her own. The second, and perhaps the most daunting task, was finding her suitable accommodations, a request she had made in a subsequent e-mail. Now he was not only tour guide, but estate agent as well.

Finally, after a week of planning Krista's itinerary, he was satisfied. It had taken up a lot of his time, and he'd spent every evening from both his office and home searching not only for destinations to take her to, but also for suitable lodgings – the latter being the most complicated. It wasn't until he'd spoken with his aunt that an idea occurred, and he'd finally found the perfect place for her to stay. He couldn't remember ever spending so much time on an itinerary, he was almost obsessed. With the planning stage finally over, Aaron could concentrate on his other patrons.

He sat at his desk and looked at his calendar to ensure that preparations were in order for his next clients. It would be a short excursion, and then he'd have a couple of days to rest. Before long, he was so absorbed in his work that when the phone rang, it startled him.

"Hello!" he said, his heart pounding a little faster than normal.

"Hello Aaron, it's Doc Broon," said the serious and very familiar voice on the other end.

Doc Brown was the family physician and had been since Aaron was a young boy. He remembered the first time he'd met Doc Brown, and how he'd had a hard time understanding the Doc with his strong Scottish brogue.

"Is it Mum? Is she alright?" He ran a shaky hand through his this dark hair, unable to contain his worry.

"She's fine, nae changes to her condition, but I am a wee troubled. I've just come from visiting with her and her emotional state concerns me. She says she hasn't heard from ye this past week, and she's beginning to fash that she's becoming a burden."

"What? Nah, I've just been busy with work, that's all. I'll come straight away and sort things out with Mum. I don't know why she would think that, she'll never be a burden to me." Aaron rubbed his cheek, the stubble rough on his palm.

"I ken Aaron, but sometimes... well she hasn't much time, perhaps six months, maybe a year at the most. We need to keep her positive, despite the prognosis."

"Yeah, sure doc. Thanks for keeping me informed. I'll come see her straight away. I'm done for today anyway, it'll be a nice drive."

"All right, Aaron, mind as ye go and don't droon yourself in your work."

"Yeah doc, I'll take your advice – for now anyway. Cheers."

Aaron hung up the phone and put his head in his hands. He had been so worried about his mother since her diagnosis and never missed a visit or a call until that past week. He felt badly that his mother would even think of such a notion that she was becoming a burden to him. He silently promised himself that he wouldn't allow work to come ahead of family again. Aaron lifted his head, shut down the computer, and gathered his things before rising from his chair.

"Hey, where are you off to?"

Aaron looked up to see Peter standing in the doorway. "Going to see Mum." Aaron pushed his chair back under the desk.

"Is she alright mate?" Peter folded his arms, leaned against the door jam, and looked intently at Aaron.

"Just a little depressed, I thought I'd go and cheer her up."

"Can I come? You know she's always been like a mum to me too."

Aaron remembered the many hours Peter had spent at his home when they were young boys. "Yeah, I think she'd like that, the more the merrier. Just give me a moment with her alone before you come and show your ugly face," Aaron said, forcing a smile.

"Yours is uglier; but sure, I can do that."

Three

Sheila Adams finally found a parking spot about two blocks away from the restaurant where she and Krista were going to have brunch. She looked at her watch; it was twenty-five past nine, she was ten minutes late.

"Damn," she said.

In so many years, Sheila had never been late, not once, especially not when meeting with her daughter. She'd spent too much time and energy trying to set the perfect example that the expression 'better late than never' didn't exist for Sheila. Still, she was late. She couldn't tell Krista about Jim, it wasn't the right time, yet she could not think of an excuse. She only hoped Krista wouldn't ask her why she was late, or even better, be late herself.

Sheila shrugged. "Oh well," she said and got out of her car.

When she reached the line-up, Sheila searched the small crowd of people waiting to get in and breathed a sigh of relief when she saw that Krista wasn't among them. She joined the others as the doors opened and filed into the restaurant. Sheila headed for a corner table at the back; she wanted to sit somewhere that was somewhat private. She had much to discuss with her daughter, and she didn't want too many ears to hear their conversation.

Sheila sat facing the window and looked at her watch again. Where is she? Before her overactive imagination came up with some horrible reason for Krista's lateness, a server approached the table.

"Good morning," the server said in a cheery voice. "Are you dining alone or is someone joining you?"

"I'm waiting for someone, thank you." Sheila smiled pleasantly at the young girl. She reminded her of Krista, only with darker hair.

"Can I get you anything to start while you wait for your guest?" The server returned the smile.

"Yes, a tea please."

The server nodded and walked away, leaving Sheila staring out the window once again, wondering where Krista was.

"Sheila!" A voice coming from a neighbouring table interrupted her thoughts. Sheila turned and saw a woman with a smile on her face approaching her.

"Grace! Please sit down." She motioned to the seat across from her. "How long has it been?" Sheila reached across the table and patted Grace's hand.

"Too long. Are you here alone?"

"Not for long, Krista is joining me." Sheila watched as Grace began to dig through her purse searching for something. At last, she found what she was looking for and she handed a small album to Sheila.

"Take a look at these; I'm a grandmother now!" A wide grin stretched across Grace's face as Sheila took the small album from her hands.

"Oh! They're beautiful, how nice for you, and twins even!" Sheila's voice tainted with jealousy. Grace, however, engrossed with showing off pictures of her new grandchildren, didn't seem to notice the change in Sheila's tone.

"And what about you?" Grace sounded haughty. "I'm sure Krista has, by now, given you some lovely grandchildren of your own?"

Always such a meddler, Sheila thought as she put on her best fake smile. If she thinks for even one minute that I am jealous of her, she'll take it as far as she can. No, I mustn't let on for even a second. She has always tried to 'one-up-me' but not this time though, I won't let her.

"Grandchildren! Oh goodness no, I am far too young looking to be a grandmother just yet, but it suits you. You fit very well into the grandmother role. Besides, Krista has a wonderful career as a teacher. No, I can wait a bit longer." Sheila smiled at Grace who no longer sat with a smug look on her face. "Speak of the devil, there's Krista now."

Grace turned to look out the window. "Yes, well," she said rising from her seat, running a hand through her silver hair. "I better go rejoin my husband. It was nice to see you again." Her pursed lips relaxed into a smile.

Sheila echoed the sentiment in words and tone. "Yes, you, too. Maybe we can have lunch some time. Old friends are hard to come by, especially as we get older." Sheila stood and hugged Grace. They smiled at each other one last time before Grace returned to her table.

Sheila returned to her chair and waited for Krista.

Four

Upon entering the restaurant, I spotted my mother seated at a table in the corner, looking out the window. Though fifty-two years, she looked much younger than most women of the same age did, and she painted the perfect picture of health. Most folks could hardly believe we were mother and daughter.

Her hair, like mine, was a honey blond but much shorter. She was holding a cup with one hand while tapping on the table with the other. It was hard to tell if she was upset that I was late or worried, either way she seemed to be deep in thought. I approached and slid into the bench seat across from her, an apology already on my lips. I was twenty minutes late.

"I'm so sorry I'm late. I was on my way out the door –"

"Don't worry dear, no need to explain," she said, taking a sip from her cup.

I narrowed my eyes and subtly shook my head in disbelief. She was far too casual, and there was no doubt in my mind that she was up to something. There was no way she would have ever been so relaxed about my being late. From where I was sitting, things did not look good.

Just then, a server approached our table, and I was glad for the momentary distraction. Whatever my mother wanted, it could certainly wait.

"Good morning! Would you like some coffee?" The server greeted me with a pot in her hand. The aroma wafting out led me to believe it was strong, just what I needed.

"Yes, please." I pushed my coffee cup toward her, watching as she filled it up.

"I'll be back in a couple of minutes to take your order." She walked away, and I watched as she headed towards another table, wishing that she had stayed a few seconds longer, anything to keep my mother from bringing up whatever she had on her mind.

We picked up our menus, and by the time we each decided on our order, to my relief, the server returned. I was sure my mother was soon going to divulge the true reason behind our meeting.

When the server left with our orders, I stalled my mother for as long as possible by talking about the previous night's firework displays, the weather, and anything else I thought of to keep her preoccupied. Unfortunately, she kept her answers brief, and after five minutes, an uncomfortable silence fell over the table.

"So," my mother began, "how's Brad?"

There it was. She wanted to talk about my relationship or rather my ex-relationship. I had just broken up with Brad last Saturday, and he'd had a hard time letting go. We had spoken almost every night at first until he finally understood me. I had loved him enough to know that he deserved better and more, even so it had been a difficult week. We had been together for one year, two months and five days – my longest relationship. I had cried myself to sleep every night after we spoke, worrying about him. Between speaking with Brad, seeking consolation from my friends, finishing the last week of school, and trying to change my travel plans, the week had been nothing but worry, stress, and tears. I did not want to relive it again with my mother.

"He's fine," I said examining the fresh daisies in the vase sitting on the table before me and avoiding my mother's gaze. I knew that she'd guess the minute she looked at my eyes that I was hiding something. The only person I hadn't told about my breakup was her. In the past, it only resulted in her disappointment, and I believed it would be far worse than any time before. Brad had been her favourite.

"Fine? That's not what I've heard."

I looked up from my distraction and found my mother staring at me. "What do you mean by that?" I didn't want to show any alarm, but suddenly I was worried about Brad, we hadn't spoken over the past three days.

"I ran into Brad's sister, and she told me you broke up with him." She folded her arms and leaned forward on to the table.

"Where exactly did you run into her?" My eyebrows raised. I was surprised that she'd even remembered Brad had a sister let alone recognized her, after all they'd only met once or twice. Alicia was never one to wear the same look for very long; even I had difficulty recognizing her on occasion.

"I saw her at the YMCA last Monday... when I went swimming."

I sputtered and almost choked on my coffee. "You go to the Y?"

The thought of my mother actually exercising was enough to stun me, let alone envision it, which of course I couldn't – at all.

"Yes, honey; I started last Monday. They have a great pool, and it's wonderful exercise."

"Sorry mom, I just never took you as the exercising type."

My mother ignored my statement. "Anyhow, I ran into Alicia, and she told me how you broke her brother's heart. I was quite shocked to hear the news and felt silly that I hadn't heard anything about it. So when were you planning on telling me?"

In truth, I did not intend to tell her. Certainly, it would have come out at some point in conversation, but as for calling her specifically for that reason alone – that wasn't going to happen. I shrugged. "I don't know." It wasn't really the answer I knew she wanted to hear, but I just couldn't bring myself to get into any details about my love life or rather ex-love life. We weren't like that, we weren't close. We used to be – once.

"You don't know?" My mother's eyes widened with disbelief.

I sighed, "I just wanted to get this past week behind me. Breaking up with Brad wasn't easy, but it was for the best." I was determined to show my mother that it was the right decision.

"Are you sure you breaking up with Brad was the right thing? You know by the time I was 27 years old I had been married for six years, and you were four." My mother folded her hands and placed them on the table.

If there was one thing I knew about my mother, my answer wasn't going to be enough – I had to give her more, enough that would make her understand, enough that we could both live with.

"Believe me; it wasn't easy for me either. I loved Brad, but not the way he deserved. I didn't want to hurt him, but it's better this way. Trust me." I blinked back the tears. My mother couldn't see me get emotional over it. It was over, and I was not going back to something that wasn't right. I sipped my coffee, hoping the warmth would take the edge off.

Seconds passed before she spoke again, and I could tell she was trying to choose her words carefully.

"I'm sorry. I just want you to be happy. I worry sometimes that... well, that you won't find someone special to spend your life with and selfishly... that I won't be a grandmother."

Shocked, stunned, surprised – that was not what I had expected her to say.

"How can you be so sure he wasn't the right one for you?" She looked me in the eyes.

It was a difficult question to answer, but fortunately, the server came back with our meals, giving me some time to think. The moment she left, I carefully began forming my response; knowing if I didn't, my mother would hound me with more questions until I did.

"I don't know Mom. It's like there was something missing."

"What was missing? I don't understand."

I squinted, unsure that there was an explanation, and then it came to me. "Mom, you and dad had something special. Something even strangers could see when they looked at you." My mother nodded, and I continued. "Uncle Brian said something about the way the two of you looked at each other. He said you shared a connection on a plain that was different from everyone else; like you belonged only to each other. That's what I want – that's what I was missing." I took a bite of my food, happy for the momentary silence, and quite proud of myself for my explanation.

My mother reached across the table and patted my hand. "I want that for you, too," she smiled.

I looked at her and for the first time, I really believed she understood me.

"Well, now that you're single again –"

"Mom I just –"

"Please let me finish. How soon do you think you'll want to start dating?"

I laughed. It wasn't funny, but I couldn't help myself. I looked at her in disbelief. "Geesh! Mom are you serious?"

She nodded, and I waited for her to finish eating so she could explain.

"I met some old friends of mine at the golf course and their son, Doug, has just ended a long relationship. It just occurred to me that you knew him back in school, and maybe you could meet him," she rambled.

I almost choked again on my food. Of all things, my mother was playing golf and trying to set me up.

"Wait! Since when do you play golf?" I hoped for a long answer to my question and a distraction from her matchmaking.

"Oh..., I started about three weeks ago. So do you remember Doug Saunders, and more importantly, would you like to meet him?" She finished her last bite of food, placed her cutlery and napkin on her plate, and pushed it all to the side.

Her answer wasn't the result I was hoping for, and my shoulders slumped in resignation. There was no way to get around the matchmaking thing.

"No." I shook my head. I couldn't believe what my mother was thinking. I finished my meal, pushing my plate aside. "God! I can't believe you're actually asking me if I'd be interested in meeting him!"

"Well no... Not right away, maybe in a few weeks when you're feeling up to it."

My heartbeat quickened a little and my cheeks warmed. My mother wasn't exactly aware of the change of plans I'd made to my upcoming trip. If she was upset about me not telling her of my breakup, she was definitely going to be upset about me leaving for the whole summer, especially if she heard it from someone else.

"Mom, there's something else I need to tell you." I leaned forward and clasped my hands in prayer fashion.

"What is it, honey?" There was a notable sound of concern in her voice. I had her full attention.

"I'm leaving for England a week from tomorrow," I blurted.

Though her face didn't quite betray her feelings, her voice certainly did. "You're still going?" she asked.

"Yes, I'm still going. You know how long I have wanted this; I've been saving forever. I've finally got my chance, and I'm not going to back out now." I was calm and sat back in my seat, my hands resting in my lap. My resolve was strong.

At that moment, our server returned, and my mother quickly asked her to bring our bill before she could even ask if we wanted anything else, sending her away a split second after she'd arrived at our table.

"So you're leaving soon. For how long?"

I took my time before answering. My mother was sure to be disappointed when she heard the news. I looked down at my hands and took a deep breath. "Ah... for the summer, I won't be back until the end of August."

She opened her mouth to speak, but I reached over and touched her arm, stopping her.

"Please, I know you're upset, but I need this... I need to find... me." I let out a breath and felt my shoulders relax as the epiphany struck.

She closed her eyes and nodded. "Okay," she said quietly. "Okay."

Her unexpected acceptance amazed me. She didn't try to talk me out of it instead she just sat there nodding, her eyes closed. When she opened them again, she looked at me and smiled. "Well I guess meeting Doug will have to wait for when you come home."

"Huh! Yeah, okay," I agreed shaking my head, what more was there to say.

I waited at the corner for the walk signal, realizing at that moment meeting my mother for brunch hadn't been too horrific. She had even taken the news of my plans for the summer better than expected, not to mention my breakup. My mind replayed our conversation, and I snickered a little recalling how soon she attempted matchmaking.

Our brunch continued playing in my head as I crossed the intersection and headed towards my car. My mother could have made things very uncomfortable, but she hadn't, and it was refreshing. She had changed somehow. It was as though we were beginning a new phase in our relationship, and that was appealing. There was definitely a sense of freedom and relief knowing that I could concentrate fully on my trip and not have to worry about anything else.

Just as I was about to round the corner, I sidestepped abruptly to avoid stepping in a rather large pile left behind by man's best friend. Shaking my head at the thought of the irresponsible owner coupled with my sudden movement – the collision was inevitable. I veered into the path of an unsuspecting pedestrian rounding the corner from the opposite direction and slammed right into him.

For a moment, we held each other's gaze, stunned by the impact, much like a bird that has flown into a window. His eyes were so penetrating that I had to look away, though there was something so familiar about them.

"Oh! I'm so sorry, I didn't mean to. . ." I blurted, bending down to pick up my purse.

"That's okay; I wasn't paying any attention and. . ." I heard him say as I bent forward and suddenly found my head knocking into his.

"Ow!" I stood up quickly and rubbed the top of my head.

"Ooh! Sorry!"

My purse dangled from his hand while his other pressed against his forehead. We stood for an uncomfortable second staring at each other in silence.

"Can I have my purse now?" I said annoyed, still rubbing the top of my head.

"Oh! Sorry!" He held out my purse.

"Thanks." I snatched it from his hand.

"Sure, no problem."

We stared at each other again, and again I had to look away.

"Do I know you?" he asked.

I tilted my head slightly to the side and narrowed my eyes. I considered his question as my mind sorted through my memories. My eyes moved over his face and scanned it, carefully searching for any little thing or quirk. I looked for anything, which might jog my memory, but there was nothing. His deep brown eyes seemed to be the only thing about him that was even the slightest bit memorable – familiar. Suddenly, I began to feel uncomfortable as his eyes locked with mine.

"No, I don't think so, thanks again," I muttered, finally pulling myself away.

"It was nice bumping into you, uh, I mean. . ." he called after me, but I ignored him and quickened my pace.

Once safely inside my car, I closed my eyes and rested my throbbing head on the headrest for a second. "That was very weird."

I started the car and looked in the rear-view mirror before signalling and pulling out. He was still standing on the corner staring after me, and I was still able to feel his eyes boring into mine.

Five

The two and a quarter-hour drive from London to Tockington was pleasant, though quiet, as Aaron and Peter shared little conversation. Aaron was glad for the quiet and the good sense his friend showed in keeping his usual talkativeness to a minimum. He was too concerned about his mother to be in any drawn out conversations, and the only time they spoke was to comment on the weather and the road conditions. Still, despite the lack in dialogue, Aaron was grateful for the company and the notion that while he was alone in his thoughts it was comforting to have someone with him.

Aaron pulled his car into the drive of his childhood home. The mature trees standing along the right hand side arched overhead, sheltering the driveway. Along the left, a multitude of gardens in bloom surrounded the nineteenth century, two-story, stone home. Aaron pulled up to the garage at the end of the drive, parked and turned off the car, but the two men remained where they sat.

"Well I guess we should go in," Aaron said after a moment with a somewhat halting voice, his hands still gripped the steering wheel. He wanted to see his mother – to reassure her, but at the same time, he was afraid.

Peter looked at his friend with concern but waited until Aaron made the first move to leave the car. Finally, after another moment, Aaron took a deep breath and opened the door, Peter followed suit. The two friends headed to the front door together. Aaron raised his hand to ring the bell, but before he could, the door opened.

"Aaron! What a lovely surprise, and you've brought Peter with you. Come in, come in, your mother will be so happy to see you; you're just what the doctor ordered!" A small, plump, older woman with rosy cheeks exclaimed, as she wiped her hands on the tartan apron she was wearing.

Aaron and Peter stepped into the house, closing the door behind them.

"Aunt Jane, what a surprise, I didn't expect to find you here." Aaron leaned over and kissed his aunt on the cheek. "Is Mum alright?"

When Aaron had seen his mother two weeks ago, she was getting by on her own fine. So, when Jane, his mother's only sister, answered the door, he quite naturally thought his mother had taken a turn for the worse. The look of worry was evident in Aaron's eyes, but Jane put him to ease as quickly as she could.

"She's fine, Aaron," Jane said, reaching over to her nephew and patting his arm. "I just arrived to keep her company this week."

Aaron nodded, a look of relief crossing his face, though he was still not entirely convinced.

"Hello, Aunt Jane, it's so nice to see you." Peter hugged Jane and gave her a peck on the cheek. "I must say, I'm happy that you remembered my name. It must be at least ten years since we last saw each other," Peter said teasingly.

"I should say, Peter, you still have that lovely ginger hair, I don't think I'll ever forget it, though it seems a lot less unruly now," Jane teased back as she looked at Peter's head.

Peter ran a hand over his very short, red hair. As a young boy, he wore it long, and the longer it grew, the curlier and more untamed it became. At times it looked as though the locks of hair were flames dancing on his head.

"Funny, I hated it as a child. Now that my dad's gone, well, it reminds me of him every time I look in the mirror."

"Your father was a fine man, and handsome, too, if I dare say. I think you have more in common with him then just your hair, lad," Jane said, winking at Peter and trying to lighten the mood.

"I love your aunt; she certainly knows a good looking bloke when she sees one." Peter looked at Jane and winked back, causing her already rosy cheeks to become slightly rosier.

"Will you two quit flirting," Aaron joked. "Let's go see Mum." Jane and Peter laughed, and the three of them headed into the parlour.

"Sit yourselves down boys. Your mum's upstairs. I'll let her know you're here." Jane turned on her heel and left the room quickly.

Aaron and Peter sat facing each other in the wing back chairs placed at opposite ends of the parlour. A small cream coloured couch sat between them. A large antique grandfather clock stood in the corner behind the chair Aaron was sitting in, its ticking the only sound in the room.

After a few minutes, Peter broke the silence. "You did hear your aunt say she was fine, right?"

Aaron smiled, "Yes, but I won't believe it until I see for myself."

Another moment of silence fell between them. Finally, after what seemed an eternity, it was Aaron's turn to break it.

"You know, Peter, I can't help but wonder..."

"What?" Peter looked at Aaron.

"Well you can always settle down with my poor aunt, I'm sure she wouldn't mind. I think you two would make a lovely couple," Aaron joked.

Peter picked up the small pillow tucked in beside him and launched it at Aaron. It was a bad shot that missed him all together, but managed instead to knock a picture frame over on the table beside him.

"Ahem... must you boys always resort back to your childish behaviours whenever you come home?" A woman chided as she stepped into the room, a smile slowly spreading on her face.

"Mum!" Aaron said as he stood up from his chair and walked over to greet his mother. He put his arms around her. She had never been a large woman and, in fact, was the exact opposite of her older sister, Jane, but now she felt frail in his arms. Consequently, Aaron was afraid to give her too much of a hug.

"Come now, Aaron, give your mother a proper hug. I promise I won't break," she whispered in his ear. Aaron carefully tightened his grip on his mother. She was right, she didn't break.

"See, I told you," Kate said after Aaron pulled away. Aaron could have sworn his mother was much taller when he'd seen her two weeks ago, now it seemed as though she'd shrunk.

"Your turn, Peter," Kate said with her arms outstretched as she looked at the young man standing beside her son.

"Hello, Mother Kate," Peter said as he hugged and kissed Kate on the cheek. "You look as lovely as ever."

"Ah Peter, how is it some beautiful, young woman hasn't stolen your heart yet?" Kate asked.

"To tell you the truth, Mum, I think someone has, although she isn't so yo –"

Peter delivered a sharp elbow to Aaron's side, cutting him off before he could finish his sentence. Aaron laughed, rubbing his side. Kate looked at both with a bewildered expression on her face.

"Don't mind your son, Mother Kate, he's just being facetious. I have, in fact, been seeing someone."

Aaron raised his eyebrows; it was definitely news to him. He looked at Peter, who gave him the 'I'll tell you later' look.

"Good for you. Does she have a sister you could introduce to this one?" Kate asked Peter, pointing her chin in Aaron's direction. Aaron looked at his mother, her eyes though a little duller, smiled at him.

Before Peter could respond, Jane came into the parlour and announced that dinner was ready.

"Shall we?" Kate said to the boys, linking both her arms through theirs and leading them to the dining room.

When dinner was over, the four retired to the parlour to catch up. Aaron looked at his mother with a discerning eye. They hadn't spent a moment alone, but he wanted to reassure her that the only reason he'd been away all week was due to business and not because of her illness. He hoped he would be able to find the time that evening. It wasn't long, however, before Kate began to show signs of weariness.

"Aaron, Peter, I'm so glad the two of you could come... " she sighed as she placed her hand on Aaron's knee, "but I am thoroughly exhausted and must retire for the night."

"Of course, Mum, I'm sorry we kept you up so late." Aaron looked at the grandfather clock. It was only half past eight, a full hour earlier than he thought. Last time he was there, she had stayed up with him until half past nine.

"You will spend the night of course?" Kate asked as an afterthought.

Aaron intended to spend the night; in fact he and Peter had discussed staying until Monday as they both were free, providing of course his mum was feeling up to the visit. In any case, they had each packed a small bag for the few days, leaving them in the car, just in case. Aaron wanted to spend as much time as he could with his mother and reassure her that he would be there for her. After all, there was no telling how much time she had.

"Of course we're staying; we're free the entire weekend. If it's not too much trouble, we'd like to stay until Monday morning."

Kate smiled and looked at Aaron and Peter. "Trouble! Of course not! I am thrilled that you will stay until then."

Aaron could see the relief wash over his mother, and it seemed her whole body relaxed. He could tell that she was worried about him, and he was glad he was there to put her mind at ease.

Kate reached over and hugged Aaron, her thin, arm reaching across his chest, pulling him near. Aaron leaned towards her. It was all he could do to keep his tears back. She was dying, and he felt powerless.

Six

Pulling into my driveway, I looked into my rear-view mirror, half-expecting to see the stranger behind me. Having spent the drive home thinking of him, imagining him following me; while at the same time trying to shake him from my mind – it was all a little unsettling. The bizarre thing was I could still sense his eyes on me, as though they left a mark. Despite my repeated attempts to push the encounter from my thoughts, something kept forcing me to reflect on it. After several minutes and still no satisfying answer, I gave up and finally got out of my car.

Housework was the next thing on my to-do list, and contrary to the appearance of my home, I despised it, avoiding it whenever possible. My friends, however, laughed at my complaints; instead, accusing me of being a closet 'neat freak'. They agreed that neither had ever seen anything out of place, even when dropping by unexpectedly. Of course, as a minimalist, there wasn't a great deal to put out of place. Knick-knacks weren't exactly my thing; the less stuff, the better. Unless of course you counted dust bunnies, for some reason or other that seemed to be the only thing I collected.

The cleaning occupied my mind, though occasionally, I found myself thinking of the stranger, unable to shake the feeling that there was something familiar about him. By mid-afternoon, my housework was complete, the memory of my encounter had faded, and the only thing on my mind was relaxing. Plunking down on my couch, a sigh of relief escaped from my lips, and my muscles relaxed. My mouth curled into a satisfied smile as contentment washed over me. My surroundings were finally clean and organized.

Before I could get too comfortable, the phone rang, startling me. It wasn't very often that it rang, my friends preferred to contact me on my cell, nonetheless, three times in one day was most certainly an oddity. I swiftly made my way to the kitchen before voice mail picked it up, as the possibilities as to whom the mysterious caller might be, ran through my mind.

"Hello!" I said pulling out a kitchen chair from under the table and hoping the caller wasn't a telemarketer.

"What are you doing tonight?" An enthusiastic voice asked.

"Hey, Amanda!"

Amanda and I had met in elementary school and since then we'd been best friends, and as such, supported each other in all matters of emotional state – good and bad. At the age of seventeen, my father died in a scuba diving accident, and Amanda was there for me. She was my confidant, who helped me through trying times with my mother and my failed relationships.

When Amanda married Jake almost two years ago, I was her maid of honour. Now she was six months pregnant with their first child, and she asked me to be the Godmother.

"Do you have any plans for tonight?" Amanda sounded as though she already had something in mind.

"No." I briefly thought of the book I'd been reading.

"Good, because Jen and Linz are free, too, and since it has been awhile, I thought we could get together. Please say you'll join us, it wouldn't be the same without you." I heard Amanda take a breath. When she was excited about something, she spoke so fast she sometimes forgot to breathe between sentences.

I laughed. "Okay, I'm good for tonight. When and where?"

"We thought maybe your place?"

"Sure, we'll order take-out. You can all stay over, too, if you want." I was glad I had spent the afternoon cleaning.

"Perfect. I'll call the girls and get back to you." Amanda hung up.

While I waited for Amanda's call, my friends came to mind. It would be nice to see them; it had been weeks since we were all together in one place. They were all so busy with their lives moving on, and I wondered how close we'd remain in the coming years. There was a time where we were inseparable. It had only been during our college years that Amanda, Jennifer, a close friend since high school, and I had gone our separate ways. Yet we made a point of seeing each other every chance we had and would often vacation together. Soon after graduation, I was fortunate and started teaching full-time, which was where I had met Lindsay. Amanda and Jennifer instantly fell in love with her, and our trio became a quartet.

Last May, Jennifer married, and in a few short months, it would be Lindsay's turn. With marriages and babies on the way, my life felt like it wasn't moving forward at all. Albeit, I had my career and a home, there was still that missing piece. I was happy for my friends, but envy tainted it.

The phone rang, and I grabbed it quickly. "Hi!" I said, anticipating Amanda's voice.

"Hey! It looks like we're all set. We'll be there between five and five thirty."

"Perfect, I'll see you when you get here." Amanda had already hung up.

Amanda was the first to arrive at 5:15 with chips in one hand and a gift bag in the other. She was a good four inches shorter than I was, and her blond hair, cut to a chin length bob, bounced along with her when she moved. She walked into the house, kicked off her shoes, and gave me a hug, which was a little difficult considering her protruding belly.

"What's that?" I asked.

Amanda pointed to her belly. "This is a baby," she said and laughed, "and these are chips." She held up the bag in her left hand.

"You're funny! I meant the gift in your hand." I reached for the gift bag, but Amanda snapped it out of my reach and hid it behind her back.

"Oh, it's nothing; here you can have this." She handed me the bag of chips.

"Thanks," I said taking the bag from her hand. "Seriously, did I forget something?"

"Don't worry, you didn't." Amanda winked.

Before I could ask any more questions about the gift behind her back, the door slowly swung open. Jennifer let herself in with Lindsay trailing behind. Each of them had their contributions, but they too had gifts in their hands. Jennifer tucked a lock of her long, dark hair behind her ear as she kicked off her flip-flops and hurried over to hug Amanda and me.

"Oh, it's so good to see you both at the same time," she said, handing the gift she'd brought to Amanda. She then proceeded over to the dining room table where she set down a bottle of wine and began searching for wine glasses.

I turned my attention to Lindsay, who was bent over unbuckling her sandals, her curly, auburn hair falling into her eyes. She swept it away with her free hand, then grabbed the items she'd set on the floor and stood up.

"This was such a good idea," Lindsay said, hugging me and then turning to hug Amanda.

"Yeah, I thought so, too. So what have you got there?" I asked pointing to the gift-wrapped package.

Lindsay ignored my question and handed over two movies. "I brought a romantic comedy and a drama; I hope there's at least one here you haven't seen."

"Thanks." I looked down at the movies in my hands, inspecting them and reading their brief descriptions. "No, I haven't seen either of these. So are you going to tell me. . . " I looked up before my question was finished; Lindsay was heading toward the dining room with Amanda waddling close behind her.

"Oh, I give up!" I sighed and joined the others. "So how does Chinese sound?"

I headed into the kitchen to place the order, suspicious of my friends' unusual behaviour. When I returned to join the group in the living room, they were all whispering, suddenly becoming quiet as they noticed me.

"Okay, what's going on? You are all being way too secretive."

The girls looked around at each other with smiles on their faces before looking back at me.

"We wanted to wait until later, but since you're being so paranoid, we'll do this now." Amanda was the first to speak. "We wanted to show you our support. Besides you're going to be leaving us for the entire summer." She pouted.

I looked around the room at each of my friends and smiled. "You are the best friends anyone could have," I said, trying to keep the emotion from my voice. "You all mean so much, but you didn't have to bring gifts, being here is enough."

"We know, so sit down and open them up," Jennifer said, patting the spot on the couch beside her.

Sitting among my friends, Amanda handed me the first gift. I reached into the bag, pulled out a wrapped object, and removed the layers of tissue paper, revealing a beautiful pewter picture frame. I stared at the photograph in the frame and gently traced a finger over the image, a thoughtful smile on my face. It was a picture of my father with Amanda and me standing on either side of him.

"Remember, that was the day we left for –" Amanda began.

"Hang on; hang on, everybody smile." Jennifer had placed her camera on the table, and all of us quickly gathered and smiled, while the camera flashed and snapped a picture.

"Okay, go on." Jennifer said, grabbing her camera.

"That was the summer we went to Colorado," I continued wistfully, the memory of that day becoming as vivid as if it was just a few months ago.

"It was the first time I went on vacation with you." Amanda interjected.

I chuckled at the memory that crossed my mind. "Your mother was so worried; she took this picture of us, just in case anything happened."

"Yup! Then she took about five more pictures of me while you and your parents waited in the car. I thought you'd just give up and leave without me."

I laughed. "Nah! It would have been a waste of a plane ticket."

"We had such a great time." Amanda briefly laid her head on my shoulder.

"We did. Thank you so much for this Amanda, the picture is great!"

"Sometimes remembering the past can be painful, but you can find a lot of joy there, too," Amanda said and gave me a hug.

"Where's Jen?" I asked as I noticed she was no longer in the room.

"I'm sure she'll be back soon," Lindsay answered with a strange look on her face. Before I could question any further Jennifer reappeared carrying her gift bag.

"Okay, time to open my gift," Jennifer said, holding her bag out toward me.

"Where were you?"

"Open it," Jennifer said, avoiding my question.

There was something suspicious about her smile as I took the gift from her hand. A tuft of pink tissue paper peeked out from the top of the bag and once removed, the gift came in to view. I reached in and pulled out another picture frame. I began to laugh, turning the frame around so everyone could see. Inside was the picture Jennifer had just taken of the four of us.

"Oh! So that's where you were." Her previous whereabouts had now become clear.

"Yup! As soon as I snapped the pic I went into your office, loaded the memory card into your printer, and voila, instant memory, nothing like the present."

"That's a great picture of us. Thank you! Okay, I sense a theme here. Lindsay, I am very curious, so hand it over."

Lindsay placed her gift in my outstretched hand. I tore off the wrapping paper, crumpled it up, and set it on the coffee table. Again, it was another frame, only there was no picture.

"This frame represents the future, and since we don't know what the future holds, I have left it empty. Maybe someday you'll put your wedding picture in it or..." Lindsay reached over and touched Amanda's belly, "your first child," she said and smiled at me. "Whatever you choose, I'm sure it will be great."

Tears welled up in my eyes as I looked at my friends. "Whatever my future holds, I know one thing for sure, the three of you will always be in it."

Throughout the evening, we took turns talking about our plans for the summer as we ate and drank. Listening to my friends, I was genuinely happy for all of them and their futures, but I couldn't help but feel a little sad that my future didn't seem as clear for me.

When my turn came, my trip and the excitement of it all was at the top of the list, followed by a recitation of my brunch with my mother, and her suggestion that I should go on a blind date when I returned. In recounting to my friends about the events of the day, my collision with the stranger came to mind once again.

"Something kind of weird happened to me today," I began. My friends looked at me with anticipation, as my words seemed to grab their immediate attention. "After brunch, I walked right into this guy while trying to avoid stepping in a pile of dog crap."

"Eww! I hope you missed it." Amanda scrunched up her face. "Who was he? Did you know him?" she continued.

I shrugged. "That's the weird part, I'm pretty sure I don't, but his eyes were so familiar. They were really deep brown, almost black, and our eyes locked for a moment and it felt –"

"What?" Jennifer interrupted, her eyes wide with curiosity.

"It felt like he was burning me with them. I had to look away, and then we smacked heads." I absently rubbed my fingers over the tender spot on the top of my head. "But then," I continued, "he asked if we knew each other, and I really had to look at him. I really don't think I know him, but it was like I knew his eyes, and it creeped me out. I spent the drive home afraid he'd follow me."

"My mother says 'the eyes are the windows to a person's soul'; maybe you knew him from another life." Lindsay shrugged. The hairs on the back of my neck stood up and goose bumps rose on my arms.

"You don't believe that past life stuff, do you?" Jennifer asked Lindsay.

"I don't know, I'm starting to believe anything is possible," Lindsay answered, draining the last drop of wine from her glass and placing it on the table.

"I believe in that stuff, my mother sees a psychic medium regularly and –"

"Hey, let's watch these movies before it gets too late." I interrupted Amanda before she could finish. My arms prickled, I didn't want to hear anymore.

When the movies were finished, I showed the girls to their rooms. Amanda and Lindsay shared the queen bed in the guest room while Jennifer slept on the day bed in the third bedroom that doubled as my home office. With everyone settled for the night, I slipped under the cool sheets of my own bed, closed my eyes and smiled. It was the happiest I had been in a week, and it felt good to be going to bed with such joy.

In the distance, there was a roll of thunder and a breeze picked up, causing the curtains to dance ever so slightly. The thought of getting out of bed and closing the window in case it rained was brief, and before long, I drifted off to sleep.

Seven

The ship tossed back and forth as waves crashed against the hull rocking the people within. Having left London a full week earlier, they had finally reached the Atlantic after passing by the Isle of Wight. Two days later, there was no land in sight and as they headed for New York, there seemed to be no end to the cruel winter storms. Chunks of ice crashed into the sides of the ship, the sounds of which sent shivers up the spines of the passengers and crew aboard.

"Mary, hang on to your brother and sister, I've got to find your mother." The man took his two younger children by the hands and handed them over to his eldest daughter. Two smaller bodies pressed into Mary's own. She wrapped her arms around them in the dim light. The ship tossed again and they fell to the floor.

"Father, don't leave!" Mary cried after him, but it was too late.

"Ann! Ann!" Mary heard him call.

Mary looked around. She could scarcely make out the faces of the people around her, but she could feel and hear their fear. There was a loud sound as the ship rolled back and forth, screams filled the air followed by a rush of cold water. Large chunks of ice battered against the hull, tearing it apart, sending splinters of wood careening through the air. Mary felt the sting as one such splinter slammed into her forehead inches above her right eye, and almost sent her over backward. Water rushed heavily through a large, gaping hole, passengers cried – there was panic on board.

"Hang on!" Mary cried to her siblings above the clamour. Rivulets of blood mixed with the spray of salt water ran down her cheek and into her mouth. The metallic taste of blood and salt assaulted her tongue.

Another wave forced its way through the ever-enlarging hole. Passengers scrambled, trying to get up the ladder and up to the deck above, each wave taking its toll on the side of the ship. Mary clung to her siblings as tightly as she could, but it was getting harder to hang on to them as the icy water crept up their bodies chilling them through to the bone.

Mary attempted to stand, pulling her brother and sister with her, but each time they fell back down. They tried crawling toward the ladder, but the other passengers and rushing water shoved them out of the way. An exhausted Mary began to lose her grip on her brother as her fingers became numb with cold. Another wave rocked the ship again, and as the water rushed back through the hole, Mary felt it pulling her brother with it.

"Hold on, John!" Mary yelled. She looked into his sad and scared deep brown eyes.

"I can't!" he cried; his icy cold hand slipped from her grasp.

"John!" she screamed. There was no answer.

Mary gripped her sister as tightly as she could, pulling her toward her body with one arm as she tried to make her way to the ladder again. Another wave grabbed them and dragged them back down toward the lower end of the sinking ship. The frigid water took their breaths. More waves crashed through, their long icy fingers clawing and pulling them closer to the opening. Sarah slipped from Mary's grasp, the waves claiming her and dragging her out to sea. The water receded from above Mary's head; she took a final breath of air and slipped out the hole. The freezing water enveloped her as she felt herself sinking towards the bottom. She struggled –

she wanted to breathe. Her lungs burned with the desire to inhale – she did and the icy cold water filled her lungs.

'Thomas' she heard her mind scream and then darkness.

"Hey, it's okay!"

Who is that? What's happened? My eyes burned and watered from the bright light. Cold and confusion enveloped me. There was a soothing voice in the distance. Where is it coming from?

"It's okay, it was just a dream, hush now, it's all right," the voice soothed again.

After what seemed like several minutes, I became more lucid as Jennifer offered calming words while she stroked my hair. The light on my nightstand burned brightly in the darkness. I sat up and looked at Jennifer, sitting on the edge of my bed, a look of concern on her face.

"What happened?" I asked as I wiped my hand across my damp forehead. "Why am I wet?"

Jennifer sighed. Her eyes looked upward for a moment as my awareness and clarity became evident. "You had a bad dream about your father. You were calling for him," she said.

"My father?" I was bewildered. It had been years since I had dreamt of him.

"Yeah, you called out 'Father, don't leave'. I came in as soon as you called. The storm was keeping me up anyway." Jennifer shrugged.

I looked around my room, still slightly puzzled. "Why am I wet?" I repeated.

"It was raining pretty hard, and the wind was blowing it in through your window. I closed it as soon as I came in, but it was already too late. The floor beside your bed is wet, too."

I looked down over the side of my bed and saw that a small puddle had formed under my window. The storm had reduced to distant rumbles in the night, and I shivered as bits from my dream resurfaced.

"Are you okay?" Jennifer touched my arm.

I nodded, though the dream had left me feeling uneasy. "Yeah, I'm fine. It was just one of those dreams that felt so real, you know?"

"Yeah, I've had those before. What was it about?"

I didn't want to relive the dream, but one thing that Jennifer was good at was deciphering them.

"It was kind of like the one I had before, but this one was more like part two. Does that make sense?" I looked at Jennifer, her eyes widened with intrigue.

"Yeah! Sure! What were they about? Maybe I can help you figure them out."

Without hesitation, I recounted my dreams, explaining how the first dream had woken me up the morning before, leaving a feeling of sadness in its wake. There wasn't much to tell about the second, the memory already faint, but one thing was certain, both dreams were about someone named Mary. I tried my best to describe how it seemed like I was Mary in my dream, but at the same time, it was as if I was watching the scene unfold from a distance.

"The strange thing is I don't recognize anyone. No one is familiar." I closed my eyes briefly, trying to conjure up images from my dreams, but none came to mind.

"Are the others familiar to Mary?"

I had to think about Jennifer's question. My dreams had never before felt or looked so real; it was almost like watching a movie unfold in my mind. Usually, my dreams were just a jumble of bits from the day's experiences, never really making any sense.

"Yeah... I think she knows them. But why do I feel like it's me sometimes?"

Jennifer had a thoughtful look on her face and I waited patiently for her to respond. I hoped she could offer some explanation.

"I don't know."

I ran a hand through my hair, caught my fingers in a tangle, and absently began working it out. I didn't expect her to know the answer and yet I couldn't help but feel disappointed.

"I'm sorry," Jennifer said reaching over to take my free hand in hers. "Was the dream you had tonight really frightening?"

"I remember being very cold." I shivered slightly at the faint memory.

"Do you remember anything else?"

I stopped untangling my hair, my fingers distractedly rubbing over the birthmark in my hairline. An image flashed in front of me.

"I'm on a boat, a clipper; I think." I reached over to my nightstand, grabbed my book, and pointed to the picture on the front. "I think a boat like this, only it was sinking."

Jennifer examined the picture. "Maybe this is the boat you're dreaming about, does it sink in the story?"

"No." I shook my head.

"Don't you have a friend from college coming to visit you soon?" Jennifer asked, sounding like she'd suddenly had an idea.

"Yeah! Why?"

"Isn't she a *Titanic* buff who wants to visit the Maritime Museum and the cemeteries?"

"Yes, she does!"

Gradually, I began to understand what Jennifer was getting at. Visiting the Maritime Museum had never been a desire of mine. I couldn't bear to read or see anything about tragic shipwrecks, the *Titanic* included. Now, a friend from college was coming to visit, and she wanted me to take her to the museum and visit the burial grounds for the passengers of the *Titanic* disaster.

"Do you think maybe your dreams have anything to do with that?"

"Yes, I do," I nodded. "But what about calling for my father?" That part was still a little puzzling.

"Maybe because you got a picture of him tonight, and it brought back memories and feelings." Jennifer shrugged.

I nodded. "It all makes sense now, most of it anyway. Some things aren't quite as clear."

"It's a dream, they don't always make sense." Jennifer laid her hand on my shoulder. "I think the storm is over, are you going to be okay?"

I nodded. "Thanks, Jen. Honestly, don't you ever get sick of coming to my rescue?"

"No," she yawned.

"Go to bed," I told her, "I'll be fine. See you in the morning."

Jennifer left my room and closed the door behind her. Brief memories from my dream came back, haunting me. I hoped she was right.

Eight

The night's storm cleared the way for a beautiful morning as the first rays of sunlight streamed brightly through my window. With my eyes still closed, I stretched and rolled towards it. The warmth of the sun soothed and embraced me; it felt good. A slow smile spread across my face as memories from the evening with my friends came to mind, my dream a distant memory. Fully awake, I opened my eyes, surprised to find the window shut, but soon remembered Jennifer had closed it during the night. Flinging back the blankets, I prepared to open the window for some much-needed air. As my feet hit the ground, the damp floor beneath them sent chills through my body, my lungs burned, and I gasped for air.

The icy cold water enveloped her, and she sank deeper into the sea. I shook the memory from my mind. It was just a stupid dream.

I opened the window and quietly tiptoed to the bathroom for a towel, throwing it on the floor and then making my way down the few stairs to the kitchen to start breakfast.

"Good morning, sleepyhead!" Amanda greeted me.

"Just in time," said Lindsay, grabbing a plate with a stack of pancakes and heading into the dining room.

"I can't believe you did this. I planned on surprising you with breakfast!" I walked into the dining room and saw the breakfast they had made.

"Too bad! We beat you too it." Jennifer smiled, already seated at the table.

By ten o'clock my friends had departed, each of us promising to keep in touch before my summer vacation. With everyone gone, the house grew quiet, and though I enjoyed solitude, it wasn't what I needed. Instead, I packed a picnic lunch, grabbed a few other necessities, and jumped in my car for the drive to the beach. The weather was nice, and it beckoned me to take advantage.

The beach was busy, but I found the perfect spot to lay out my blanket. With my plot of sand selected, my blanket in place, and my book in hand, the day showed signs of promise for a relaxing afternoon. However, before a chapter was even finished, a little girl, seemingly appearing from nowhere, interrupted me and found herself a comfortable spot on my blanket. Stunned, I stared at the child who returned my gaze with a wide grin on her face, a pretty girl, with brown, curly hair and deep blue eyes.

"Ah, hello!" I said, having gotten over my initial shock. I smiled at her and laid my book down beside me.

"Hi!" she giggled back.

"Where's your mom?" I looked around hoping to spot what would probably be a frantic mother searching for her child.

"Ovuh theah, sweeping." The little girl's Rs and Ls sounded more like Ws. She pointed to a woman sleeping on a blanket about 15 metres away.

"Is anyone else here with you?"

"My sister, she's playin' with her fwends." She pointed to an older child who was busily playing with some other girls. She looked to be about ten and didn't seem to notice that her much younger sister was missing.

"How old are you?"

"Four." She held up three fingers.

I laughed, "Four huh? What's your name?"

"You know silly, it's Sawah!" she smiled up at me and took my hand in hers. "I glad I found you."

The familiarity, in which she showed me, was shocking. I searched my memory trying to recall meeting her at some other time. She was not familiar to me, and so my eyes trained on her mother who still lay sleeping on the beach, but she was too far away, and it was difficult to see her face. Sarah's sister continued playing, oblivious to the whereabouts of her little sister. I watched the girls for a moment, thinking that perhaps one of them had been a student of mine, but soon realized there wasn't a familiar face among them.

"Why don't we go over and see your mommy? If she wakes up and sees you missing, she'll be very upset," I said, standing up and reaching for Sarah's hand.

"NO!"

Surprised by her loud voice, I quickly sat back down again, noticing that others were watching me. It was certainly not my objective to draw attention to myself; she was someone else's child. I didn't want anyone to get the wrong idea.

"Okay! You can stay awhile longer, but we're just going to sit here and as soon as your mommy or your sister comes to find you, you have to go right back."

"Okay," she mumbled and put her head down as though disappointed. Suddenly, she flung herself into my arms for a hug. "I missed you!"

My eyes widened as I tentatively hugged her back. After a moment Sarah sat back down on the blanket; she was beaming. Her apparent familiarity with me was puzzling and a little unsettling. I must know her from somewhere.

"Where you been?" Sarah asked folding her arms as her smile turned into a pout.

My answer had to be simple, there was no point in confusing her any more than she already seemed to be, so I responded with what I hoped would suffice.

"At home."

For a while, she asked no other questions, seemingly satisfied by my simple response. She continued to hold my hand, content to sit beside me and not do much of anything at all. It was a little strange; most children her age rarely spent a lot of time sitting that still without anything to occupy them.

"You know where Mummy is?" Sarah asked me, breaking the somewhat awkward silence. She looked up at me, and her deep blue eyes searched my face. I pointed to the woman still asleep on the beach.

"No siwwy, the other mummy," Sarah said, laughing at me.

What at first seemed to be a rather easy question to answer had turned into more confusion on my part. I didn't understand what she wanted from me. What does she mean?

"Oh, there you are," a voice interrupted my thoughts. I looked up to see a woman walking towards us.

"Emma, what are you doing over here? I told you to stay beside mommy." The woman directed her question to Sarah.

"Is this your mommy?" I looked down at the little girl sitting beside me. She quietly nodded.

"Of course I am." The woman sounded slightly annoyed.

"I'm sorry, but she told me her name was Sarah, not Emma," I explained to the woman who was now standing in front of us.

She looked down at the little girl, who remained seated beside me. "Emma, are you telling stories?" She put her hands on her hips.

The little girl looked up at me. "Sorry, name is Emma," she said sheepishly. She grabbed my arm pulling me toward her as she leaned in, cupping her hands over her mouth. I leaned forward and she whispered, "You can call me Sawah."

I looked at the little girl grinning at me broadly, her blue eyes sparkling. It was obvious to me now that she was just a four-year-old playing a silly game.

"Come on, Emma, let's find your sister, we have to go home now," the woman said before turning her attention back to me. "I'm sorry if she interrupted you, I hope she wasn't too much trouble."

"No, she was fine, she's very cute. How old is she?" I asked, suspecting Emma hadn't been quite correct when she'd told me.

"Three. Let's go Emma!" Emma's mother said, holding out her hand toward her daughter.

Emma reached over and hugged me again. "I glad I found you," she said for the second time since meeting. She grabbed her mother's hand and walked away. After a few steps, a beaming Emma turned around and looked at me. "Bye, Mary!" she waved.

The hairs stood up on the back of my neck as a thousand prickles crept along my spine.

Nine

I spent the next few days trying to forget about the encounter with the little girl and busied myself with shopping, packing, dining with my mother and friends, and catching up on my reading. By the end of each day, the exhaustion carried me into deep and dreamless sleep. My routine kept me occupied and so with each passing day, the memory of my bizarre encounter with the child continued to fade until it too seemed like just a dream. My life was slowly getting back to normal. My trip was in order, and my packing was almost complete. There was one more thing, however, that still occupied my mind and that was my upcoming visit to the *Titanic* exhibit in Halifax.

My eyes fluttered open as a distant ringing disturbed my sleep. I laid there for a moment trying to collect my thoughts. Realizing it was the phone, I jumped up quickly. My book, which lay across my chest, fell to the floor. I hurried to answer it but after a couple of steps, dizziness, which came from rising too quickly, necessitated in my grabbing on to the back of a chair to steady myself for a brief moment. Still not fully awake and with my heart pounding in my ears, I made my way to the kitchen.

"Hello!" I said, disoriented and shaky.

"Mary; I did not forsake you."

"What?"

"I said, it's Sherry, did I wake you?"

I closed my eyes, pulled a chair out from the table, and sat. I pressed the receiver to my ear with one hand while my other cradled my forehead. "Yeah. Sorry, I fell asleep on the couch; I'm still a little bit dazed."

"Oh! Not getting much sleep these days with your big trip coming?"

"Actually, I've been getting eight hours every night. I don't think I've slept that well since I was –" a surprise yawn interrupted, "a kid."

"Maybe you're not sleeping as soundly as you think. Anyhow, I wanted to let you know I get into Halifax Wednesday night. My meetings should be wrapped up by Friday morning, so I'll have the rest of the day before I have to fly out. I'm only sorry my visit is going to be so short."

I looked at the calendar on the wall and scratched my head. It seemed as if all the days in the past two weeks had blended. There was no telling what day it was.

"What day is it today?" I had to ask.

Sherry laughed, "Wow! You really have been on summer vacation. I'll be arriving tomorrow night, does that help?"

"Yeah, it does." My stomach rolled. The tour I'd feared a good part of my life, even feigning sick once for a class trip, was going to happen.

"Okay, good! So we're still on for the museum on Friday?"

I didn't want Sherry to hear any hint of unease in my voice, so my high school drama skills were put to use. Though I'm sure it wasn't very convincing, I did manage to speak with enthusiasm. "Sure! It'll be fun!"

"Good! I'll see you soon," Sherry said with equal enthusiasm.

My acting must have been better than I thought.

"Soon, bye." I hung up the phone, realizing as my eyes scanned the clock that it was past dinner, my stomach growled right on cue. I grabbed an apple from the bowl and bit into it.

By Friday morning, I had gotten used to the idea of seeing the *Titanic* exhibit and was actually looking forward to it, or at least that was what I told myself. In any event, the day was going to be spent with a friend I hadn't seen in a long time, so my irrational fears would have to wait.

I arrived at the museum at the agreed meeting time and five minutes later, Sherry joined me. Though we hadn't seen each other since graduation, we had kept in touch through social media and the occasional phone call. Seeing her again brought back fond memories. We hugged and talked for a brief moment before finally entering the museum. No sooner had we walked through the door, did a strange feeling come over me, and it felt like the room was rocking back and forth. It was how I imagined a boat ride on rough water would be like, imagined, because I'd never actually been on a boat for very long. My parents had given up taking me anywhere by boat for fear that my incessant screaming would get us all thrown overboard.

My eyes blurred and dizziness swept over me, I pressed sweaty palms against the wall to steady myself. A sense of passing out briefly washed over me, but just as suddenly, the dizziness left as it had appeared. The whole ordeal happened so quickly, in fact, that Sherry gave no indication she'd even noticed anything was wrong. We continued into the museum heading directly for the exhibit.

A chill coursed through my body, and the hairs on my arms stood at attention. All around me, in various showcases were recovered items from the doomed ship; it was all so tragic. A tremendous sadness fell over me at the loss of lives, and I empathized with the lost passengers. Sherry however, seemed to be enjoying every minute; reading every bit of information there was and snapping pictures along the way.

Finally after what seemed like a lifetime we moved on to look at what the rest of the museum had to offer. A full hour and a half later, we left, leaving the museum and its contents behind. Sherry was thrilled and couldn't wait to move on to the cemeteries. The prospect of looking at gravestones from such a tragedy, from my perspective, was not as thrilling. Trying to settle myself, I took a deep breath as we headed to the car.

We drove for a few moments before arriving at the first of three cemeteries where passengers from the fated *Titanic* had been laid to rest almost 100 years before. When we arrived, Sherry was the first to get out of the car, a map of the cemetery in her hand, she headed for the graves.

Why am I so scared? I sat in the car with both hands gripping the steering wheel, my knuckles slowly turning white as my grip tightened – motionless, paralyzed. A rap at the passenger window shook me from my apparent trance, and I jumped, biting the inside of my lip.

"Are you coming?" Sherry called to me through the closed window of the car.

I nodded and reached for a tissue to dab at my injury, the slight metallic taste of blood caused me to scrunch up my face in disgust. I exited the car, knowing Sherry would have some questions.

"Sorry if I scared you," she said. "I thought you were right behind me; what's wrong?"

"You caught me. I was daydreaming about my trip," I lied. "Let's go and see those gravestones." I smiled at her hoping that she wouldn't notice that it was the phoniest smile ever – she didn't.

Sherry marched a good fifteen steps ahead of me as we approached the headstones.

"There they are. It's so tragic!" she cried and quickened her pace.

I stopped, my feet unable or unwilling to move. My mind swirled, and it felt as though the ground rocked underneath me; the hairs on the back of my neck rose, and I trembled. Sherry's lips moved, but I heard no words, everything sounded muffled. I closed my eyes hoping the dizziness would pass.

"Oh, this is the saddest..." Sherry's voice broke through my confusion.

Finally, after a few seconds, the light-headedness that overtook me began to fade, and the world around me cleared. I took a cautious step forward. The dizziness returned, enveloping me, surrounding me with the sounds of screaming and crying. I pressed my hands tightly over my ears as the agonizing cries grew into a deafening din. I looked all around, yet there was nothing, and as suddenly as the noises began, they ended. Slowly, I pulled my hands from my ears. I feared I had lost my mind.

Sherry was at the last headstone in the row, but utter terror had prevented me from coming any closer. I stood there paralyzed, watching and praying she'd soon come back. Sherry pulled something from her purse, placed the small object on the ground, and wiped her eyes.

"This is so tragic," she called out, looking in my direction. I hadn't yet reached the first headstone of the same row.

"You've got to come and read this."

"I'm feeling a little dizzy, and it gets worse when I walk. I think I'll just wait here until you're done," I called back, my voice sounding shaky in my ears.

"Are you alright?" she asked, taking her eyes off the headstone and looking my way.

"Yeah, I'm probably just getting hungry," I lied to her again; I hated lying. "I get a little dizzy sometimes when I get hungry." That was far from the truth, or rather was true, except for the fact that I had eaten quite a substantial breakfast that morning.

"Are you sure?" Sherry asked. "We can go if you like."

I smiled another phony smile. "Yes, I'm sure. Can you read it to me?" I feigned interest.

Sherry turned back to face the headstone and read the touching epitaph. When she was done, I stood motionless watching her as she searched her purse, pulled out what looked to be a rather crumpled tissue, and used it to dab at her eyes.

My stomach rumbled. Hunger had replaced my light-headedness; my apparent illness seemed to dissolve. I waited a little longer, hoping Sherry would soon be done, as if reading my thoughts she walked away from the headstones pausing only occasionally to read their inscriptions.

"I'm starved, let's get lunch." She linked her arm through mine, turned me around, and we headed back to my car.

"I thought you wanted to go to the other cemeteries," I said, trying to keep my voice from sounding relieved.

"No, I think one cemetery is enough. I really just wanted to see the grave of the 'Unknown Child'."

I breathed a quiet sigh of relief, realizing that our *Titanic* mission was happily over. Each step we took away from the cemetery brought me more relief, and by the time we reached the car, I felt as good as I had earlier that morning. As for the nagging feeling that there was something seriously wrong, I suppressed it, resolving to deal with it later.

"You know," Sherry said as we reached the car, "the 'Unknown Child' really isn't unknown anymore."

"What?" I was preoccupied on a lunch destination. I unlocked the car doors, and we stood there as Sherry explained.

"The 'Unknown Child', they found him, they're pretty sure anyway. It's only the third time they've come up with evidence of his identity, but this time they're sure. I guess the third time really is the charm."

Sherry opened the car door and got in, leaving me to stand outside for a second longer looking back toward the cemetery and its markers. I was thankful, not only because we were leaving, but also for the child. I couldn't help wonder if he was too, knowing that he finally wouldn't spend an eternity being unknown. At least he had a place to rest – and a name.

I started the car and pulled away leaving behind the memory of déjà vu and the awful feeling it brought; more than happy to be out of there and happier still that I would not have to return. The rest of our afternoon went without incident, and we enjoyed each other's company for the little time we had left. When evening came, we headed for the airport.

"I'm so glad you could come for a visit, even if it was short," I said as we drove.

"Next time, I'll make plans to stay longer."

"I can always come and visit you next. We'll figure something out." We drove quietly for a moment as I tried to work out a plan in my head.

"Maybe we can get together between Christmas and New Year."

"It's not like I won't have the time off," I laughed.

"We could go to New York City, maybe for the New Year's celebration in Times Square; I've always wanted to do that."

The mere thought of going to New York City made my heart pound. The knuckles of my hands protruded and turned white as I held the steering wheel in a death grip. Small beads of sweat rose to the surface of my face, and I was grateful that Sherry was busy looking out the window and not at me.

"*It's the land of promise, Mary,*" a voice whispered from the deepest corners of my mind.

I eased the car over on to the shoulder of the road, opened the door, and threw up.

Ten

I was too afraid to fall asleep as I lay in bed staring up at the ceiling. It didn't matter anyway, my mind was racing, and it seemed the more I tried to push away the day's events the more they came back to haunt me. My sanity was in question. Hours passed before I eventually cried myself to sleep.

She sat on the cool grass, her legs stretched out in front with her hands behind her for support. Her head tilted back as she enjoyed the warmth of the sun kissing her cheeks. It was the end of summer, and they had just enjoyed a picnic lunch. She sat there basking in the warm sun while Thomas watched her, his hands absently picking at the grass and clover.

"Look, Mary, a four-leaf clover!" Thomas held the small clover between his fingers. Mary opened her eyes and looked at it.

"Let me see," she said and smiled. "I have never in my life seen such a thing. If only you were still a child; you could see the fairies." She examined the clover Thomas held between his fingers before returning to her sun bathing.

Thomas laughed, lay down on his back, and rested his head in her lap as he twirled the clover he held in his fingertips. "I'm crazy for you, Mary, absolutely crazy," he said looking up at her.

Thomas reached up and traced her jaw line with his finger. Mary looked down at his beaming face and smiled. She leaned forward, kissed him, and tilted her face back toward the sun again.

"What are you thinking?" he asked in all seriousness.

Mary sighed deeply. "Well, I'm wondering if I'll ever see you again; once they lock you away in the asylum," she laughed. She didn't like it when he was so serious.

"Oh Mary, you are always the jester. One of the many things I adore about you, but truly, tell me. Your eyes seem to hold so many secrets, and I have yet to find a way to unlock them." Thomas sat up and faced her. He reached over and tucked a loose hair along with the clover behind her ear. She sat motionless with her face still tilted toward the sun. He took her chin between his thumb and index finger and gently coaxed her to face him. She opened her eyes, and he looked deeply into them, trying hard to read her mind.

"Please tell me, Mary, tell me one of your secrets," Thomas pleaded.

Mary looked away for a moment and then back again. She loved him. She loved him more than she loved life, but how could she tell him that their time together grew shorter with each passing day. She adjusted her sitting position and curled her legs up behind her. She smoothed her skirts as she supported herself on one hand.

"I love you," she said, finally.

"That's truly not a secret, Mary, though I never tire of hearing it." Thomas smiled at her.

"I love you more than life."

"And my love for you is as big as the universe and all it holds," Thomas added.

"My love for you transcends death." At these words, a tear escaped from Mary's eye and travelled slowly down her cheek. Thomas touched the single tear as it tracked its way toward her lips, and then he brushed it away.

He looked deeper into her eyes. *"As does mine, but why do you cry?"* Her sudden show of emotion worried him.

"Because, Thomas, soon I will be leaving you and then my life will end," Mary blurted, losing herself in his eyes before turning away from him.

She knelt with her back towards him and buried her face in her hands. Her tears flowed more freely, and her shoulders began to shake as her sobbing overtook her.

Thomas became alarmed, he moved closer to her and wrapped his arms around her burying his face into her hair. He smelled the warmth of the sun on her long, dark hair mixed with the jasmine she used. They silently stayed that way for a while until Mary stopped sobbing. When she settled, she turned and faced him again. Still on their knees, they held each other's hands and looked into each other's eyes. Thomas was about to speak when Mary gently put a finger to his lips and stopped him.

"Please let me finish whilst I have the courage," she said. Thomas nodded and held her hands tighter. *"My father says we are leaving. We're leaving England and going to America; to... New York."*

Thomas nodded and closed his eyes. He knew many people who had left looking for a better and easier life. Some returned, some found what they were looking for, and some were lost at sea.

"Thomas, please say something," Mary said quietly, looking down at the strong hands holding hers.

"When?"

"February. Father said it is less costly then and –"

"And more dangerous," Thomas interrupted.

Mary didn't finish, she knew he was right.

Thomas grew angry at the thought of Mary leaving during the worst time of year. He held his temper and took a deep breath before speaking again.

"Is it because of me?" he asked looking at her; she was still looking at their hands.

He knew that Mary's parents didn't approve of their relationship, after all, she had only turned 17 that spring, and he was 26. He was the son of yet another struggling farmer with nothing more to offer, not even a place of his own. Her parents tried to keep them apart as much as possible by keeping Mary busy, but whenever she had a free moment, she would steal away, and they would meet. They had been doing that for almost a year, sneaking out even during the darkest of nights. Mary always believed that her parents would realize that their love was all that really mattered.

"I don't know. They say it's because the mines will be closing, and Father will have an easier time finding work in New York. He'll make more money," Mary answered.

"And..." Thomas said, knowing that there must be more.

Mary didn't want to say. She didn't want to hurt Thomas anymore, but she had to tell him what she overheard.

"I heard them say that once we're in America, I will see that there are far more choices in suitors. They feel that there aren't enough men here, and that's why I'm with you. They said I would be happier..." Mary's voice trailed off.

Thomas could no longer hold back what he truly felt. He let go of Mary's hands and stood up, unsure of what to say. Ideas and plans rolled through his mind until he settled on one. He hoped it would be enough to keep her safe.

"Did you tell them you didn't want to leave?" he said, not keeping the emotion from his voice.

His tone shocked Mary; she had never seen him so cross. She rose to her feet and faced him, reaching for his hands to calm him, but he pulled away.

"Of course, I did. Do you think I want to go?" she asked in disbelief, fighting back the tears, which sat just at the edge or her eyelids and threatened to spill over.

"It certainly doesn't sound as though you tried very hard to convince them."

His words stung her like a thousand bees.

Thomas turned his back to her; he couldn't bear the look of pain in her eyes. He had no choice. He clenched his teeth and with as much resolve as possible, he faced her again.

"Don't you believe me?" she yelled at him.

"If you really tried, you wouldn't be leaving. Maybe the prospect of other men does intrigue you," Thomas spat, the words were like acid on his tongue.

Mary couldn't believe what she was hearing. Only moments ago, they were professing how deep their love was for one another, and now they were in the throes of a heated discussion.

"What are you saying?" Mary cried, her tears escaping their confines.

Thomas wanted to take her in his arms and hold her, but he couldn't. The only thing he could do was to end their relationship. Perhaps if her parents knew their relationship was over, they wouldn't leave. At the very least, he could hope they would wait until summer when it would be much safer, and by then Mary would be 18 and able to stay behind should she choose.

Thomas took a breath. "I'm sorry, Mary – this is wrong," he said calmly.

Relieved by his words, Mary began to believe that Thomas had changed his mind, had come to realize he'd been too harsh with her – he was apologizing for his actions. She calmed herself and reached out to him, all would be well.

Thomas stared at Mary, uncertain as to why she was reaching out, and then it occurred to him, she'd misunderstood.

"No," he yelled.

Mary jumped back, startled.

"WE are wrong!"

Thomas's words shattered her heart. Mary's hand dropped to her side. She didn't understand, her head swirled as he spoke.

"I'm sorry, Mary. Your parents are right. We shouldn't be together; I see that now. You're still a child. I'm sure you can see

*the fairies." Thomas jutted his chin towards the clover still tucked
behind Mary's ear.*

*His harsh words struck her with such force that Mary's knees
began to buckle and she lowered herself to the ground before him,
as though she begged.*

*Thomas desired to reach out to her, to pull her up, to hold her
– but he resisted every urge.*

"No," her cries barely audible.

*Thomas turned and began walking away, his tears free to escape
the eyes that held them captive.*

*"My love for you will transcend death," Mary screamed after
him, and she curled up on the grass and wept, the clover still
tucked behind her ear.*

*Her agonizing words pierced Thomas's heart like a hot iron
through ice.*

"As does mine," he whispered as he walked away.

"Thomas, don't leave, Thomas, no. . . " I sat up in bed and wiped
tears from my eyes; my voice calling out for Thomas had awoken
me. It took a moment for my eyes to adjust to the dim light
shining in through the window.

Thomas left her, but he loved her. My mind raced as my
thoughts jumped back and forth between my dreams – the past
and the present.

"What the hell is happening to me?" I looked over at the clock;
it was three in the morning.

With great determination, I flung back the light sheet and
jumped out of bed. The desire to prove my sanity was strong.
More out of habit than cold, I pulled my silk robe down from
the hook on the back of the door and left my room crossing the
hallway to my office.

Once seated at my desk, I turned on my computer and patiently
waited while it came to life. It was a long wait. Finally, the familiar

welcoming sound greeted me, and there I sat with the screen lighting up the room.

"What am I doing?" I laid my head down on the cool desk.

Time passed before I finally found the courage to click on the internet. It loomed in front of me as the prompt on the search engine flashed – taunting me.

"Fine!" I mumbled under my breath, giving in to the relentless flashing. My fingers typed the words – Past lives.

What emerged was a deluge of websites. From fun little tests, to videos of people undergoing past life regression, to websites promoting those who claim they can help you find out who you once were. It was all very overwhelming and after a few short minutes, I shut the computer down and trudged back to my room – defeated.

My room was dark and cold. I shivered and pulled my robe tightly around me, exhaled and watched as my breath turned to vapour. I stood in the doorway, afraid to enter, unable to move. The room had changed, and it was no longer mine. In the darkness, nothing looked familiar not even the shadows and yet, it was all too familiar – hauntingly so.

The second my hand touched the wall in search of the light switch, I pulled it away, shocked by the feel of weathered old boards instead of the smooth, painted surface of drywall. As my fear abated and courage returned, I slowly moved my hand back. My fingers ran up and down frantically searching for a switch that no longer existed, while my eyes darted around in the dark, searching for a familiar object.

"Ouch!" I cried out, promptly pulled my hand away from the wall, and absently put the tip of my index finger into my mouth. The metallic taste of blood assaulted my taste buds, forcing me to remove it for examination instead. However, the darkness made it impossible to see anything. The distraction brought on by my injury was fleeting, and within seconds fear returned as the transformation of my room became evident.

Paralyzed by fear, I stood in the doorway searching the darkness with my eyes, waiting for them to adjust. Small shards of light seemed to filter in through what resembled cracks in the walls, casting unfamiliar shadows on objects in the room. I looked in the direction of my bed. The space appeared empty with only a few smaller objects in its place. Carefully stepping forward, the boards beneath my feet creaked unexpectedly, as though they were about to give way, and I jumped back. The room smelled of sweat and panic. Was it me?

A gust of wind blew in from where the window once was, and it smelled of the sea. A whimper from the far corner of the room made me snap my head in that direction. Again, there was nothing but strange shadows. Intense fear enveloped me – paralyzed me. I shivered again, a cold sweat pooled on my brow. My feet froze, as though I stood in icy, cold water. My head spun.

"Close your eyes," a voice whispered.

Who said that? Did I say that? Of course I had, there was no one else. I closed my eyes.

"Calm yourself, switch on the light." There was that whisper again.

I turned around, opened my eyes again, and faced the doorway. My heart thumped as adrenaline drove my every move. There was nothing left to do but listen to that oddly familiar voice in my head – mine, but not mine. My legs carried me a step forward towards the open door, and my hand reached for the wall; it was like watching someone else's body move. Slowly, my hand moved over the now smooth surface, found the switch, and turned it on. The brightness of the light stung my eyes, and my hands instinctively covered my face to shield them. After a moment, I turned around and faced into the room, slowly removing my hands from my eyes. Everything was where it should be; everything had returned to normal.

Sleepwalking! I breathed a sigh of relief. That was it. My mother told me I did it all the time as a kid. "That has to be it," I whispered as if saying it aloud made it true.

My eyes searched the room, making sure everything was in its place and finally rested on the clock on the nightstand; it was 3:33. I yawned, as a deep need for sleep fell over me; the strange experience had left me completely drained.

I peeled off my robe, and dropped it to the floor; too tired to hang it back up. Out of habit, I reached up the wall to flick the switch but thought better of it. I switched on the lamp on my nightstand first before switching off the overhead light.

My sheets were cold as I slipped back into bed, shivers coursed through me as the cold wrapped around me. I reached over and turned out the light, settling down into bed and pulling the sheets tightly up under my chin for protection. My muscles jumped as my body gave way to exhaustion and sleep overtook me, the night's events slowly faded.

The songs of birds woke me in the early morning. I laid there enjoying their melodies and hoped they'd sing me back to sleep. Suddenly, the night's events came to mind and the desire to fall back to sleep was no longer a priority. Questions needed answering, and there was only one person who could help me. I grabbed the phone and dialed. The sleepy voice that answered prompted me to look at the clock; it was five thirty in the morning – too late now.

"Amanda, I need your help."

Eleven

It had been another long week at the office for Aaron. He worried about his mother daily, although he felt satisfied that after spending some time alone with her, she no longer thought that he felt she was a burden. He also promised her that he wouldn't go as long as he had without calling or coming for a visit. In return, Kate promised him that should she feel worse, she would let him know immediately. Still, despite her promise, he couldn't get over the sense that she had indeed weakened in the past three weeks.

When Aaron and Peter had returned to London, the first thing Aaron did was call Doc Brown, who assured him her condition had not progressed. The reassurance was welcoming, so Aaron sunk himself into his work for the remainder of the week. By the time Saturday had come around, he was glad he had another free weekend. He needed the next couple of days to regroup for his next tours. Now that they were heading into the second week of July, they were getting busy.

Aaron threw a few things into his rucksack for the weekend and soon he was on his way to Tockington. He was more than happy to be going alone; he wanted to spend some quality time with his mother.

The day was beautiful and the sun shone as he made his way to the village of his youth. It seemed like no time at all when he pulled into the drive and parked behind a familiar vehicle.

Immediately upon seeing the car, Aaron's heart began to race. It was Doc Brown's, and it was unusual for him to be making house calls on a Saturday. Aaron climbed out of the car and hurried to the front door, but before he could grab the handle the door swung open, causing Aaron to jump back.

"Aaron! Ye gave me a bit of a fright; I wasn't expecting ye, but I'm glad ye're here," Doc Brown said as he pulled the door closed behind him. "Come, let's take a seat." He waved his hand toward a stone bench that sat in a small garden under the trees.

"What's the matter, Doc?" Aaron asked. He couldn't hide the worry in his voice as he followed Doc Brown over to the bench and took a seat beside him.

Doc Brown got right to the point, knowing Aaron well enough not to stall. "I'm afraid your ma has gotten a wee bit weaker."

Aaron put his head in his hands and pressed the heels into his forehead, the pressure briefly numbing the dread, which instantly fell upon him. "How long?" he asked afraid of the answer he might hear.

"It's difficult to say; maybe weeks; days. I've had patients hang on for months." He looked up at the second floor window of Kate's bedroom; it was obvious he couldn't look at Aaron at that moment.

Aaron nodded, unable to speak, his head still resting in his hands. After a moment of silence, Aaron removed his hands and placed them on his knees. He looked down at the grass in front of him, leaned over, and plucked an ordinary clover.

"I found one once, almost in this exact spot, when I was young." Aaron's voice was barely audible as he twirled the clover between his fingers.

Doc Brown, bewildered by Aaron's statement, looked at him. "Found what?"

"A four-leaf clover; right here." Aaron twirled the clover between his fingers. His voice becoming distant, like it wasn't his. "I found another one too, long before, in another place." The words came from his lips, but it wasn't Aaron's voice, it had changed somehow. "I gave it away, but it turned out not to be very lucky." Aaron's voice trailed off to a low whisper.

Some time passed before Aaron spoke again, more coherently, more like himself. "The one I found here, I pressed in a book until it was dry, and then I gave it to Mum for her birthday. She said she'd save it for when she really needed it." Aaron looked up towards his mother's bedroom window; he turned toward Doc Brown, his eyes brimming with tears. "Do you suppose she still has it?" he asked as the tears spilled from his eyes.

Doc Brown gently put an arm around the shoulders of the young man who suddenly was the charming boy he had met all those years before. They sat there quietly for a while, both scanning the ground.

"Do you think..." Aaron hesitated.

Doc Brown waited patiently for him to finish.

Aaron started again, trying to maintain his composure. "Do you think she'll make it to her birthday?"

It was a moment before Doc Brown answered the question, and Aaron suspected it was because he truly didn't know. His mother's birthday was in the first week of August, and right now that seemed so very far away.

Before Doc Brown could answer, Aaron spoke again. "Never mind; we'll take it day by day." Aaron stood up, mindlessly twirling the clover between his fingers. Doc Brown rose to his feet as well and faced Aaron.

"Are you on your way then?" Aaron asked.

"Aye, there's not much more I can do. She's comfortable enough for now, and your aunt has everything under control."

Aaron nodded and looked back toward the house. "I guess... I guess, I'll go see her." Aaron wanted to head towards the house but his legs held him glued in place – frozen.

"Ye'll be alright, Aaron." Doc Brown laid a reassuring hand on Aaron's shoulder. "She'll be happy to see ye." Aaron looked away from the house and back at Doc Brown. "Thanks, Doc."

"I only wish there was more I could do, Aaron. Let me ken if she gets worse. I'll come straight away."

"Thanks."

The two men stood there for another few seconds, Aaron still apprehensive.

"It's alright, Aaron, go ahead," Doc Brown said encouragingly.

Aaron turned and headed towards the house, feeling Doc Brown's eyes on him as he walked away. Aaron reached the front step, placed his left hand on the handle, and looked back at Doc Brown, who nodded at him encouragingly. He took a deep, steadying breath and turned the handle. Before he stepped across the threshold, he closed his right hand into a fist and opened it again. The crushed clover fell to the ground.

Twelve

I pulled into the cul-de-sac and circled around until I found the correct address. The house wasn't as foreboding as my mind led me to believe it would be, in fact it looked similar to the ones on either side. Before me stood a grey, two story, stone home that couldn't be much more than ten years old, complete with the proverbial white picket fence. My imagination seemed to have gotten the best of me again, and I half laughed at myself, shaking my head.

After apologizing profusely for calling Amanda so early on a Saturday morning, I explained everything and Amanda was eager to help. Never before had I ever even contemplated the notion of visiting such a place, but there I was.

Slowly, and with just a hint of unease, I emerged from the car and made my way to the front door. The small gardens on either side of the walkway comforted me with their normalcy. Just as my foot landed on the step of the small porch, a cat leapt from the rocking chair it had been occupying and ran down the steps. The sudden movement startled me, but I quickly recovered and reached out to press the doorbell. The door opened before my finger could connect.

"Hello! Please come in." A well-dressed woman, around the age of my mother, stood in the doorway and ushered me inside. Her piercing blue eyes met my gaze as I stepped over the threshold.

"Welcome! It's always so nice to meet new people," the woman said smiling eagerly at me and shaking my hand as we stood in the foyer. "Please, follow me." She turned away and headed down the hall. I was about to kick off my sandals when she called back to me. "Don't worry about your shoes, you can leave them on."

I did as I was told and followed her into the bright and welcoming kitchen. From the entrance, everything looked normal. The woman headed toward her cabinets and took down a couple of teacups. She turned and faced me, smiling.

"I'm sorry; I don't often have new clients. Please take a seat at the table." She pointed towards the round table, covered with a white lace tablecloth, which sat nestled in the breakfast nook surrounded on one side by windows.

I walked towards the table and stood there, undecided where to sit.

"Any seat is fine," she said.

I watched the woman who busied herself pouring two cups of tea, and I finally chose a seat that allowed me to look out the windows.

"Your gardens are absolutely beautiful," I said turning my attention back to the woman. My voice sounded funny in my ears, and I hoped she wouldn't think it strange.

"Thank you. It's my greatest passion."

The woman brought over a plate of cookies and set them down on the table. She turned away and headed back to the counter for the tray, which held the full teacups, cream and sugar, and a small pot with the remaining tea. She brought this over and unloaded it onto the table, setting the tray down on the floor.

"I hope you don't mind tea," she said. "I know it's a little presumptuous of me to fill your cup." The woman pulled out a chair and sat across from me.

"So, do you read tea leaves?" I asked with a little more enthusiasm than I had intended.

"Goodness no; I use tea bags."

Warmth rose up my neck and settled in my ears. "Tea is fine, thank you." I said quietly.

"Good." The woman smiled and reached across the table and patted my hand. "Don't worry, dear, a lot of my new clients are nervous at first, but they soon realize they have nothing to fear." The woman picked up her teacup and took a sip.

"Um... I thought you said you didn't get many new clients."

"What I meant was that I don't usually get new clients here by themselves. They usually come with my regulars for their first experience. It's not every day a client is willing to give up their regularly scheduled appointment for someone else."

"I hope you don't mind."

"Of course not, I'm always willing to help however I can. Besides, Maggie is more to me than just a client, she's a good friend, too, and when she called this morning to give up her appointment for her daughter's friend, I was intrigued and knew I had to help."

"What exactly do you know about my situation?"

"Nothing, really; just that she wanted to give up her spot for her daughter's friend."

"So, you have no idea at all why I'm here?" I was surprised; certain that Amanda would have told her mother everything.

"No." She picked up a cookie and took a bite.

"Well Madame Ze..." I hesitated. "I'm sorry, what should I call you?" I wasn't sure of the proper way to address the woman seated across from me.

"You can call me Ruth."

I was positive that the business cards on the table in the foyer said Madame Zenith. "Ruth?" I questioned.

"Yes, Ruth. Madame Zenith is just the name I use for psychic fairs and the like, gives everything I do a sense of mysticism." Ruth wiggled her fingers in the air for effect.

"Okay! So the reason..." Before I could explain, Ruth stopped me by holding up her hand.

"Please Krista, don't tell me anything."

"How did you know my name?" I hadn't told her.

"Well, Margaret did tell me that much about you," Ruth laughed.

We continued for a short while with our small talk. We discussed weather and Ruth's gardens and then back to the weather again. All the while, I made sure I didn't divulge anything about myself or my reason for being there. Before I knew it, half-an-hour had passed and I began to wonder when our session would start or if it already had.

"So, shall we get started?" Ruth asked as she finished her last sip of tea and stood up to clear the table.

"Okay! Is there anything you need?" I asked and placed my empty cup and the plate of remaining cookies on the tray.

"No, all I need is right here." Ruth took the now full tray over to the counter and returned to the table with a notepad and pen.

"Will you be taking notes?"

"No. I find that I need an outlet, so I sometimes doodle to keep my hands busy. But, if you brought paper you can take notes."

"No, I didn't think to bring any."

"Here take mine," Ruth said offering me her notepad. "I've got plenty. I'll meet you in the living room; it's much more comfortable in there."

I got up from the table and headed back toward the front room. It was an inviting room with pale olive green walls and cream coloured furnishings. The large comfortable looking chair in the corner of the room was my choice. It wasn't long before Ruth returned with a notepad and pen of her own.

"Is this chair okay?" I felt somewhat small in the large chair, but it was very comfortable, and I didn't want to relinquish it if it wasn't necessary.

"That's perfectly fine," Ruth said, smiling and taking a seat on the sofa. "Before we get started," Ruth continued, "I'd like to explain a few things."

I nodded and listened intently to Ruth as she began explaining her usual ritual as a psychic medium. Having seen the odd talk show with people who claimed to speak to the dearly departed, it certainly was interesting having it explained to me firsthand. I kept an open mind when she spoke of being able to see earthbound spirits, but could only hear those who had crossed over; nevertheless, part of me remained a little skeptical. By the time she had finished her explanation, I was more than ready to get started, particularly when she said that she would use specific names or nicknames. She was not like those I had seen on TV who'd say 'someone with a 'J' name wants to speak to you'. Scam was always the first word on my lips.

Ruth had definitely piqued my curiosity, and after what I'd experienced over the past couple of weeks I was ready to believe in just about anything.

"Can I ask a question?"

"Of course," Ruth replied. She set her notebook and pen next to her, leaned forward, and looked at me intently.

"Well. . . ," I hesitated, "I met this little girl several days ago who behaved as though she knew me. She told me her name, but it turned out it wasn't her real name. When she left, she called me by another name. I convinced myself she was playing a game, but now I'm not so sure. Do you think there was something more to this encounter?" I really hoped Ruth could help. Though Emma wasn't on my mind all the time, every once in a while thoughts of her trickled in.

"Sometimes the very young have memories from a past life. Usually by the time these children reach the age of four, the memories start to fade. How old was she?"

"Three."

"It's quite possible she was remembering something, but then again she could have been pretending. Without asking her key questions, I don't think you'll ever truly know."

I nodded in agreement, resigned that Sarah/Emma would remain a mystery.

"Let's get started, shall we? There are a few people who have been waiting patiently since your arrival."

I opened my mouth to speak but closed it again, shocked by her statement. From now on Ruth could do the talking.

"Did you have another questions?" she said, not missing a thing.

"No, please go on."

Ruth closed her eyes and began to scribble on her notepad as she mumbled seemingly to herself. She laughed then as if someone had told her a joke.

"Yes, yes you'll all have a turn," she said a little louder and continued mumbling for a few seconds longer. "We have some strong individuals here, but I think they're willing to take turns." Ruth opened her eyes and smiled at me.

I stared back at her with my mouth partly open.

"Sunny? Sunny girl..." Ruth muttered, staring at me.

I stared back blankly, confused by what she was saying.

"Sorry," she said, as if to someone else in the room, and then she turned her attention to me. "I meant 'sunshine girl', does that mean anything?"

My heart skipped. Yes, that most certainly did mean something. "Y-yes," I stuttered, my voice cracked. I cleared my throat and spoke again. "Yes," I said clearly. "Yes, that's what my father used to call me."

Ruth nodded and continued speaking again to the unseen entity. "He said there was a lot of water around him, he just couldn't get out – he tried."

My eyes filled with tears. Before I could wipe them away, Ruth handed me the box of tissues, which sat on the table in front of her.

"Happens all the time, dear, don't worry about it."

I took a couple of tissues and dabbed my eyes. "He drowned."

Ruth nodded as the bit of information I offered confirmed what I suspected she already knew.

"He says he was at your party the other night."

Astounded, I stared at Ruth who continued to have a quiet conversation with my father, her eyes closed.

"He remembered the picture, too, and how much fun you had on your trip."

My mind returned to that night and the picture Amanda had given me of the three of us. I smiled through my tears but remained quiet as Ruth continued.

"He doesn't want you to worry, you're not crazy. You're just remembering things from long ago and..." Ruth stopped mid-sentence, opening her eyes.

"What is it?" I was unable to contain my silence any longer.

"Sorry, someone else wants to speak."

I was a little disappointed and wanted to continue the 'conversation' but at the same time, eager to find out who else felt the need to speak to me. Ruth continued to scribble on her pad and spoke aloud to the unseen guests. Sometimes her words made no sense to me at all.

"Queen? The Queen?" Ruth looked at me as she spoke and scribbled on her pad. "No, no reaction... What? Oh, motion? No? Okay, what then?"

My eyes fixed on Ruth as she spoke to the new guest, her scribbling grew more intense.

"Oh, sorry... ocean; Ocean Queen." Ruth looked at me. "Does Ocean Queen mean anything to you?"

The words meant nothing to me, and I shook my head. "No, it doesn't. Should it?"

"That's what he keeps saying and that he drowned too."

I was perplexed. Who was she speaking to? Was it still my father? "Are you sure it's not my father, he's the only one I know who drowned."

"Who are you?" Ruth said plainly to the air around her, she shrugged. She closed her eyes again and continued to scribble and mumble.

"Mary? Do you know someone named Mary?" Ruth's eyes popped open again.

My arms began to prickle, and I shivered. "No, I don't." My voice wavered. Who was Mary? She not only occupied my dreams, but her name seemed to seep into my everyday life. "I have dreams about someone named Mary, and that little girl called me Mary. Who is she? What does she want?" I asked in frustration.

Ruth held up her hand. "I know you have questions Krista, but I truly can't help if you give me too much information." Ruth smiled sympathetically at me.

I took a deep breath. Still frustrated, but waiting patiently for the answers I hoped would soon come.

"He says he's her father."

"Who – Mary's?" I asked.

Ruth nodded.

My mind swirled with more confusion than ever before. I didn't know who Mary was and certainly didn't know her father. It seemed I had more questions than answers.

"Tell him I want to speak with my father again," I said, annoyed by the intrusion.

"He can hear you," Ruth said. "He says you are."

I ran my hands through my hair. "What does he mean by that?"

"Sorry, he's gone. Your father is back; do you have any questions for him?"

I was happy to hear that, but there were so many questions to ask. Is he proud of me? Can he see into my future? Does he watch over Mom? "I have so many, but I don't know where to start."

Ruth scribbled some more and mumbled. She laughed, "Okay, I'll tell her, indecisive, just like you. He says it's okay, you're just like him."

My eyes filled with tears again as I listened to Ruth.

"He's proud of you, loves that you're a teacher."

The tears slowly ran down my cheeks despite the smile on my face.

"He's happy for..." Ruth hesitated, "for Shirley? Sheila, sorry Sheila?"

"That's my mother."

Ruth nodded and continued. "He's happy she's finally moved on after all these years."

"What!"

"Your father is laughing; he says you'll understand soon enough." Ruth kept scribbling. "He says you'll be happy too, soon. You made the right decision."

Made the right decision about what?

"Oh! He's gone now."

"Gone! I didn't get to tell him I love him," I whispered, fresh tears coming to my eyes.

"It's okay, dear, he knows you do. He's always there watching over you. He feels your love always."

"Did he tell you that?" I said wiping my eyes with new tissues from the box.

"Well, not in so many words. It's more of a feeling, a warm and tender feeling, like a great big hug. It's the sense that remained when he left."

I nodded as I blew my nose. "Is anyone else here?"

"Oh yes, but they're all wanting to talk now and it sounds more like a hive of bees than any actual conversations. You see, just like those who are alive who are sceptical, there are those who have passed who don't believe I can communicate with them, and so they wait in the background awaiting proof. Once they see it actually works, they all want their chance to speak, but I can't make heads or tails out of any of it."

"So are we done?" I hoped we weren't done; there were still so many unanswered questions.

"Well as for talking with spirits, yes we're done. However, I think that some of what was said today might help you figure out what has been going on. You just need to put the pieces of the puzzle together."

I looked intently at Ruth, waiting for her to continue, and hoping she'd give me just a bit more. What she said next almost knocked me to the floor.

"As I mentioned earlier there are such things as past lives, and I sense that you have an old soul. If you look at your notes, I believe you were given some details today that might help you figure it all out."

I was astonished and looked down at the notepad that rested on my lap – it was blank.

Thirteen

"*You are by far the most beautiful creature I have ever had the pleasure to know,*" *Thomas said to Mary as he held her hand while they walked through the meadow.*

Mary stopped; she didn't quite know what she should say. She'd never thought of herself as beautiful. Before she could say anything at all, Thomas locked his eyes with hers. Mary felt his hypnotizing gaze penetrate through her, down to the depths of her soul. Heat rose from the pit of her stomach and settled in her face. She turned away before he could see her blush.

"*Don't turn away.*" *He placed his hands on her shoulders and turned her back around.* "*You're even more beautiful when you blush like that.*"

"*Thomas, please, I'm afraid I might stay this colour if you continue to speak to me this way.*" *Mary lowered her head not wanting him to see the colour deepening and taking hold. Thomas took her into his arms and held her, their hearts were beating in unison as they breathed in the scent of each other.*

"*These last few months have been incredible, Mary; I have never felt like this before.*" *Thomas released his grasp and looked down at her. He bent his head forward and gently brushed her lips with his. The blush that had only just left Mary's face returned in full force.*

"*I love you.*" *Thomas breathed into her hair as he pulled her back against him.*

Mary stiffened briefly only to relax again into his arms. She so wanted to say the words back. Inside her head, she screamed, 'say it, say it'. She hesitated; finally, the words came to her lips. "I love you, too, Thomas," she whispered.

They held each other for another moment. There, in the meadow, it was as though they were the only ones left in the whole world with only the grasses and flowers to bear witness to their love.

Thomas was the first to let go. "Kiss me, Mary," he said closing his eyes and waiting for her kiss. Mary leaned in but changed her mind at the last second.

"You'll have to catch me first," she laughed and gently pushed him away. Mary gathered her skirts and ran up the gentle slope of the meadow; she headed for what looked like the edge of the world.

Thomas stood for a moment and watched her run ahead before making his way toward her. He shook his head, laughed, and picked up his pace. It wasn't long before he caught up to her and as they reached the top of the hill overlooking the sea below, he wrapped his arms around her and pulled her close again.

"Have I earned my prize now?" he asked, looking down at her and smiling. Mary stood on tiptoe and gave him a quick peck on the cheek.

"Is that all?"

"I should think it would be unladylike to throw myself at you," Mary replied, a hint of laughter catching in her throat.

"Well then, shall I take the lead?" Thomas didn't wait for her to respond, instead he gathered her into his arms and kissed her. Mary melted in his embrace and her body became limp. Her reaction was all Thomas needed as consent and gently, he lowered her to the ground.

The air around them filled with the roar of crashing waves from the sea below as if it questioned the gulls soaring overhead, and the gulls screeched in reply. Their reply summoned a gentle salt breeze causing the meadow to stir. The grass and flowers began to whisper; Thomas and Mary had become one, and they were not alone in the world.

"Ladies and gentlemen, we are about to begin our descent..."

No! No! Not yet!

The outside world interrupted, slowly pulling me back to consciousness, while my desire to dream pulled me towards sleep. I was teetering on the edge, very much hoping that sleep would win. I turned my head to my left, hoping the change of position would send me back to my dream before the outside world got its way. It worked, slowly I felt myself begin to fall.

"...Please make sure your seat backs and tray tables are in their full upright position..."

Oh shut up! Come on Mary, where did you go? I replayed the dream in my head, tuning out the irritating outside voice as I attempted to lull myself back to sleep.

"Excuse me, Krista. Sorry to wake you, but we're going to be landing soon," a voice whispered in my ear just as sleep had begun to win the battle.

My eyes fluttered open briefly; I looked at the man speaking to me before closing my eyes again. I needed to get back to my dream.

"Krista!" the voice said again, a hand on my arm gently shook me. I opened my eyes and stared at the man, attempting to make sense of it all.

"We're landing soon; you'll have to put your seat up."

"Oh, sorry, sorry!" I said groggily, finally aware of my surroundings.

I searched my memory for the name of the passenger beside me, remembering we'd exchanged names and some other details during the long flight. Finally, as the fog from my sleep slowly receded, my memory returned.

"Thanks, Jason," I said, returning my seat to the upright position and fastening the seat belt.

"I don't mean to pry, but that must have been some dream," Jason smiled amusingly, as he fastened his own seat belt and pushed his tray up.

The tips of my ears began to burn. "Oh God! What did I say?"

"Don't worry, you didn't say anything incriminating. You just laughed out loud a few times and smiled a lot."

I remembered my dream quite vividly and was thankful that laughing and smiling was all I'd done.

"Really! Is that all I did?"

"Yes. Well you did –"

"Ladies and gentlemen, we have just been cleared to land at the Heathrow International Airport. Please make sure one last time that your seat belt is securely fastened –"

"What did I do?" I whispered to Jason, ignoring the rest of the flight attendant's announcement.

"Nothing really, I think you called out Thomas."

"Was I loud?" I tried not to sound too concerned.

"It's okay," Jason reassured me. "You more or less just whispered the name. I don't think anyone else heard you."

Soon after, the plane touched down and taxied to the gate. With the last of the announcements over, I unbuckled my belt, and with Jason's help, retrieved my carry-on bag. After waiting patiently for several minutes, I was exiting the plane to begin my new adventure. Butterflies danced in my stomach as I headed into the terminal.

Fourteen

Aaron shut his computer down and glanced at the neatly stacked papers on the desk one final time to make sure everything was in place. He had returned late the night before after having been home with his mother, and now he felt a deep sense of urgency to get back. The only reason he was even at his office was to take care of some unfinished business. Now that he had, he was ready to get on the road as quickly as possible. Though his mother's condition hadn't worsened, there was no telling how much longer she had. With one final sweep of his eyes across his desk, Aaron rose from his chair quite satisfied that everything was now arranged, and he was free to leave, though he still couldn't quite shake the feeling that he was missing something. Aaron pushed his chair back into place.

"Ah, there you are. How's Kate?" Peter asked as he stood in the doorway of Aaron's office, a great look of concern and sympathy on his face for his friend.

"No change really," Aaron said wearily.

"Well, that's good then, right? Perhaps she's not as bad as Doc Brown first thought."

Aaron knew Peter was just trying to be positive for him and though at times it drove him nuts, he knew how much his mother meant to Peter as well. He wouldn't be selfish in his feelings as there were others in his life who had been touched by his mother's warmth, sincerity, and kindness.

Aaron looked at Peter and forced a smile. "Thanks, Peter. I'm sorry I've unloaded much of my work and worries on you this past week. I really couldn't have done it without you. I owe you."

"Look no worries. I have others taking over some of your clients the next couple of weeks. Your mum is family to me, too. You know I'll do anything to help. When are you planning to head back?"

Peter's question caught Aaron off guard. He thought for sure Peter understood that he'd be going back as soon as possible. "I promised Mum that as soon as I left here, I'd be on my way."

"Right now? Aren't you picking up a client at the airport?" Peter asked with surprise.

Aaron rubbed a hand over his face as he remembered Krista. "With everything going on, I completely forgot. Though didn't you just say you'd taken care of everything?" Aaron crossed his arms. He was annoyed both at Peter for leaving his client unattended and at himself for forgetting. He was mostly annoyed at himself though as he never expected to forget about a client, especially one who had kept him so busy.

"She was the only client I didn't bother with. Since she's staying at Jane's, I assumed you would be taking her. Sorry, mate." Peter rubbed his brow.

Aaron noted his friend's exasperation and effort to remain calm. He returned the favour and took a breath before speaking; arguing about it wouldn't solve anything.

"No, it's not your fault. I should have... Ah well, it doesn't matter." Aaron looked at his watch. "Her flight should have just arrived and..."

"I'll take your place; your mum will be fine 'till you get there."

An unspoken understanding came between them as Aaron sat back down at his desk, grabbed a pen and notepaper, and wrote hastily. When Aaron finished, he stuffed it in an envelope and sealed it.

"Here take this to her, it explains everything," Aaron said handing the sealed envelope to Peter. Peter took the envelope and put it in the pocket of his shirt.

"Thanks, mate." Aaron rushed out the door.

Fifteen

Having landed on time, I hoped that when I at last made my way through passport control and baggage claim, Aaron would be waiting for me. Finally, after forty minutes, I followed the signs leading the way to the official airport meeting point. It was a short walk to the arrivals hall, where a small crowd gathered and waited for their travelers. I scanned the crowd looking for my name among the few cards still held up by strangers. Slowly, people began leaving with those who had come to pick them up, friends and strangers alike. Ten minutes had passed when I finally noticed someone holding up my name on a piece of cardboard. As I approached, the man holding the cardboard smiled broadly.

"Krista Adams?"

He was a handsome, young man with a gleaming smile, full of perfectly white teeth. He had beautiful, bright blue eyes and very short, red hair, not at all, what I'd imagined Aaron to look like. Nonetheless, he was very pleasant looking.

"Hi, Aaron, it's so nice to finally meet you!" I excitedly extended my hand.

Within seconds of speaking, I knew I'd been a little overenthusiastic with my greeting as Aaron's eyes widened briefly, before he smiled. He took my hand in his, the warmth and softness surprised me as my hand disappeared into his much larger one.

"Nice to meet you too, but you should know I'm not Aaron. I am his very good friend and business partner, Peter."

I was surprised and a little disappointed. I truly wanted to meet the person who helped make my dream a reality, not to mention he'd promised to pick me up. My feelings reflected in my expression as Peter quickly began explaining the situation, putting my mind at ease.

"I'm sorry to say that Aaron was not able to meet you due to unforeseen personal circumstances. Rest assured, as Aaron and I are business partners and childhood friends, I am very well acquainted with your situation and know that you will be staying at his aunt's home in Bourton."

I stood there; mouth agape, listening to Peter's animated explanation. Realizing he was now staring back at me, I quickly closed my mouth.

"I see." No other words came to mind. We stood there awkwardly for another moment before Peter spoke again.

"Shall we go now or..." His voice trailed off as he stared at me. Finally, he averted his gaze and pointed towards the exit. I instantly snapped out of my trance.

"I'm so sorry, it's just all so new and exciting and you know, unexpected. I'm a little overwhelmed by everything."

Peter nodded, reaching down and taking the handles of my two large suitcases. He mumbled something under his breath as he started to walk away pulling my bags behind him. The bags looked as though they were bursting at the seams, ready to spew out their contents. Puzzled, I continued to stand where he left me, my feet still firmly planted in place. Solicitously, he turned around.

"Shall we?" he asked me again directing me with a nod of his head towards the exit.

"Yes, of course," I said as I adjusted the carry-on bag on my shoulder and hurried to catch up to Peter as he led the way out of the airport, and I quietly followed behind.

"I must tell you," Peter began, turning to look back at me, "I am a bit at the back of the car park; I hope you don't mind the short hike."

"No, after flying for so long I am glad for the chance to stretch my legs a bit." We walked along quietly before I felt the need for small talk. "So what kind of car do you drive?" I looked around the parking lot at the seemingly equal amount of familiar and unfamiliar makes and models. I was not one who was very well skilled in the recognition of car makes and models, unless of course the name appeared on the car. I hoped he drove something I could spot from a distance, such as a Volkswagen Beetle.

"It's a Peugeot 508."

"Oh!" It was definitely not anything I'd ever heard of before.

We continued to walk toward the back of the parking lot. Rather, he walked while I almost had to jog to keep up with him, his stride being much longer.

"I take it you've never heard of it before," Peter said, walking slightly ahead of me.

"Nope!" I said breathlessly as I slowed down my pace and fell a good five steps behind. Suddenly, Peter stopped ahead of me and turned around.

"Sorry, I didn't mean to walk so fast." He waited for me to catch up. When I did, we continued making our way to the back of the lot. He wasn't joking when he said it was a hike. We continued our walk in silence.

"It's French."

"What is?"

"The car, it's a French make."

"Oh! What colour is it?" I looked around as we neared the back of the lot where there were fewer cars, and I hoped his was some uncommon colour that would stand out.

"Blue, and it's right over there." He pointed to a metallic blue car about 10 metres away.

"Perfect, let's get out of here." Finding a boost of energy, I hastily walked past Peter towards his car. He chuckled behind me, but it was of no concern, I wanted to get out of there and begin my adventure.

When we had both reached the back of the car, Peter unlocked the trunk with a click of his key fob. He lifted the largest piece of my luggage and placed it in the trunk, a pensive look on his face. He looked at me, and I smiled.

"I don't think that other one will fit in here, it'll have to ride in the back." He reached up and closed the trunk, as I started around the side of the car.

Peter laughed behind me. "If you're going to drive, you might want these," he said, holding out the keys towards me.

I was baffled. Why would I drive? I soon realized what he meant as my eyes glanced at the car.

"Sorry, I forgot your cars are backwards here," I laughed, walking towards him.

"Backwards! I'm afraid you have it wrong, your vehicles are the ones that are backwards." He smiled and winked at me as I walked past him, headed to the other side of the car, and climbed into the passenger side. It felt odd being on what would be the driver's side back home. I jumped slightly at the sound of the driver's door closing. If Peter noticed, he said nothing.

"All set then?" Peter asked as he buckled his belt, turned the key in the ignition, and began to back out from the parking spot.

I took a minute before answering, taking it all in as I settled down in my seat.

"More ready than you'll ever know. Oddly enough, I feel as though I'm home."

Sixteen

It was strange riding in a car on what felt like the wrong-side-of-the-road, but I soon adjusted. Despite my exhaustion from travelling, the exhilaration of finally being in England was enough to keep me awake as we drove towards Bourton. We travelled out of Greater London on a busy four-lane highway and within minutes, we were outside of the city heading northwest. Aside from driving on the opposite side of the road, the scenery didn't look much different from home. I laughed at myself for being so ridiculous.

"Something funny?" Peter asked; his eyes glued to the road ahead.

I waved my hand dismissively. "Nothing, I just thought things would look... different." Not exactly, the word I was searching for, but the only one that came to mind.

"Different – in what way?"

"I don't know, maybe I've seen too many movies or pictures or something." I turned and looked back out the window.

"Well, I suspect all motorways look similar. I am quite sure you're bound to find places that look nothing at all like home." Peter said, still staring at the road in front of him.

We drove in silence for a few more minutes while I took in the sights. Dense bush followed alongside the highway, held back in places by wooden fencing. Occasionally, a farmer's field would come into view. I paid close attention to the road signs as we travelled, eventually spying a sign for Oxford. My interest piqued.

"Are we driving through Oxford?"

"Actually we're traveling around. Do you know of Oxford?"

"Some, only what I've read about and the university, of course."

"So, what do you know?" Peter asked testing my knowledge.

"Just that it's famous for its university. I mean I don't remember what I've read about the city itself."

"You'll see a bit of the city as we drive around." Peter took the next exit. A few moments later, a red double-decker bus passed us from the opposite direction.

"Now I feel like I'm in England!"

"Ah! The red-double-decker bus." Peter looked at me with an amused smile.

"Well yes, they are kind of iconic, you know."

Peter shook his head and continued to drive down the tree-lined, two-lane highway as we ventured further in toward Oxford.

"This is really pretty!" My excitement was becoming more difficult to contain.

"Yes, I suppose it is."

I looked at Peter, but his eyes never left the road. He certainly was handsome, yet it was difficult to have any sort of real conversation with him, small talk was all we managed. I'd never experienced such awkwardness speaking to someone of the opposite sex before and wondered if it had anything to do with coming from different cultures. He was pleasant enough and except for his long-winded explanation at the airport, he really didn't have much to say. At the very least, I expected he'd explain the sights along the way. Granted, so far there wasn't a whole lot to see on our road trip. Nonetheless, he was a tour guide after all, surely he could tell me about something; maybe even give me a history lesson.

We drove in silence. My eyes focused on the road ahead while my ears attuned to the quiet hum of the air conditioner. Topics for discussion swirled around in my mind. I opened my mouth to speak but stopped myself. I needed to talk as the silence was becoming uncomfortable. Peter was Aaron's business partner and friend. We were bound to meet again and I didn't want this awkwardness to follow us.

My mouth opened and I spoke the first words that came to my mind. "So... I meant to ask earlier, how long of a drive is this anyway?" I kept my eyes glued to his profile – studying him.

"It's about an hour-and-a-half from the airport to Bourton."

"That's right, Aaron told me that."

"Hmm." Peter grunted; his gaze firmly attached to the road and both hands glued to the wheel. I was in part glad that he was such an attentive driver – I was relaxed.

I turned and looked back out the window, resigned that the rest of the trip would be in total silence. Minutes passed, and as I stared at the passing scenery, my eyes began feeling heavy. The hum of the air conditioner was hypnotizing. No sooner had my eyes closed when Peter's voice startled me awake.

"We're here!"

"What? Bourton?" I asked a little surprised and dazed, unsure how long I'd actually been asleep.

"No, Oxford, or rather the outskirts. The 'Welcome to Oxford' sign is just ahead, see there," he said pointing out the sign as we drove past. I caught a glimpse of it and was delighted to find out that sleep hadn't taken over for very long.

Within moments, we were entering the city outskirts and finally there were things to see. My eyes absorbed as much as possible as we drove along; drowsiness no longer an issue. My brain adapted to my surroundings as it finally sunk in. My heart thumped with joy at a dream finally realized. My throat clenched, for fear I might squeal like a child. My thumbs twiddled, excited and nervous. My stomach rumbled, loud and embarrassing. My thumbs stopped. My throat opened letting out a small gasp. My heart skipped. My brain distracted. My eyes looked down. Instinctively, my hand flew to my abdomen as if to staunch the embarrassing noises, but it was too late.

"Are you hungry? We can stop somewhere along the way," Peter asked, this time he turned to look at me. I felt my ears begin to burn and sensed the redness taking over.

Great! Why is he looking at me NOW? "No, I'm fine."

"Are you sure? It's really no trouble."

"No, I can wait till we get to Bourton. I would sooner have something to eat there... so I can get used to the town." I added quickly as an afterthought.

Peter nodded. "Fine, that sounds reasonable; it's not much further. I don't think you'll fade much between now and then." His blue eyes quickly scanned over me as if trying to gauge whether or not I could last the rest of the drive.

"Yeah, I'm good." I turned and looked back out the window just in time, as a sudden warmth washed over my cheeks.

As we drove along, Peter easily managed the first of six traffic circles that we would encounter, or 'roundabouts' as he called them. Seeing the first one reassured me that I had made the right choice in not renting a car and driving to Bourton myself. It would only have resulted in my driving around in endless circles, no doubt eventually heading off in the wrong direction.

The dense shrubs and trees sandwiched the road as we left Oxford behind, and a bicycle path followed along escorting us out until it broke away and merged with another road that headed elsewhere. Once more, we were travelling through the countryside, and for a short time, the two-lane highway merged with another road – three lanes heading north. The southbound lanes were only visible wherever dense shrubs and trees were sparse. The landscape continued to change as did the road. Peter and I drove in silence, apart from the few times I asked him about the things I saw.

Soon after the final roundabout, we made a right hand turn off the highway we'd been travelling on, and Peter announced that we were on the final leg of our journey. The quaint, narrow road seemingly transported us back in time, the pavement being the only thing that gave the true century away.

Just as I was about to speak, my stomach rudely interrupted with another cacophony of growls, indicating that it would not wait much longer. Peter, who seemed unable to control himself, laughed aloud. I was mortified at first, but soon joined him, especially when Peter's stomach started in on its own rebellion.

With the resulting giggles finally under control, I returned to paying attention to my surroundings. A small, stone wall covered with what looked like ivy, led the way on the right hand side of the road while trees followed along on the left.

"I wouldn't want to meet another vehicle in the dark on this road; it doesn't seem wide enough for two to pass," I said, trying to estimate the width of the road.

"It's not, but there's plenty of room for both cars to move over allowing each other to pass," Peter explained. The charming road continued to intrigue me as we made our way past old houses and farms.

"Is this the usual way to Bourton or a shortcut?"

"I'm not sure if it's much of a shortcut, but definitely more scenic and interesting, don't you think?" Peter turned and looked at me smiling. His smile was warm and infectious and again I was quite surprised when I felt the tips of my ears burning. I quickly turned away and looked out my window, hoping he hadn't noticed.

"Scenic and interesting – definitely; but as to more, I guess I will have to take your word for it."

We traveled along the road, hardly meeting anyone, but when we did both drivers cordially moved towards his or her respective sides of the road and easily passed.

In the distance, I could see what looked to be rooftops slowly emerging from behind the trees that lined the road. As we approached, a sign announced we were indeed in Bourton-on-the-Water; the small village erupted from out of nowhere.

"This place is beautiful! I feel as though I've stepped into a puzzle or a postcard."

"Yes, it is quite a quaint little village, I'm sure you'll enjoy staying here." Peter smiled at me, but I was too busy taking in the surroundings for it to cause any effect.

"Shall we get a bite to eat – I'm famished." Peter said laughing at me as my stomach growled right on cue.

"Yes, please."

He parked the car in a spot that had just opened up along some storefronts. I looked at the shops noting that they were definitely worth visiting.

"There's a footbridge over there we can cross." Peter pointed toward the river that ran through the village. Crossing the river was a stone footbridge, and on the other side of the river, a path led to a number of stone buildings, one of which was the hotel restaurant where we intended to dine. "We can sit outside if you like and enjoy the scenery," Peter said as we headed across the bridge.

"Yes, that sounds perfect." I could no longer stifle my excitement and grabbed Peter's arm. "I can't believe I'm here!" I squealed. My eyes were wide and there was an equally wide grin plastered to my face; it was all I could do to contain myself. I looked down at my hand clutching Peter's arm. "Oh! Sorry." I felt warmth growing in my cheeks and quickly withdrew my hand.

"Happens all the time," Peter said, smiling down at me.

"Really?"

"No. I mean people are generally excited, but I do sense a bit more enthusiasm with you."

"Sorry."

"Don't be, it's rather refreshing. Here we are... so outside then?"

"Yes."

We sat ourselves at a table with an unobstructed view of the river. From there, I watched intently as people strolled along the path and ducks made their way up and down the waterway.

"I can't remember the last time I felt so happy." My eyes suddenly filled up with tears surprising both of us.

Peter grabbed a napkin from the table and handed it to me.

I hastily took it and dabbed at them. "I don't know why I'm crying," I managed to say, overcome with emotion. "I'm so embarrassed."

Peter reached over and patted my hand. It was nice if not a bit awkward. "I'm sure it's just all the excitement and exhaustion getting to you," he tried to reassure me. "When we're done with lunch, I'll take you straight away to your flat to rest."

"Yes, I think you're right." I sniffed and felt myself beginning to settle down.

"All right now?"

I nodded, afraid that if I opened my mouth to speak the tears would start flowing again.

Lunch went on without further incident and by the end, I was quite sated with food and conversation. Peter had finally spoken in longer sentences.

I was excited to get out and tour my new surroundings but first, I wanted nothing more than to lie down and rest; there would be plenty of time to get to know the village. When we were ready to leave, we headed back to the car in silence.

"Are we far from the apartment?" I asked, trying to stifle a yawn but to no avail. I gave in and covered my mouth; my eyes watered.

"No, it's just a few streets away." Peter started the engine and backed the car out of its spot.

Within minutes, we parked out front of a small Cotswold cottage resting at the end of a cul-de-sac and surrounded by stone walls and beautiful gardens. I emerged from the car, stretching and yawning once again, and contemplated whether my body would even make it to the flat. Before I knew it, Peter had already retrieved both of my suitcases from the car and was heading up the walk with me wearily following along behind him, my smaller bag slung over my shoulder. When we reached the front door, I noticed the hanging baskets full of flowers adorning each side. Peter pulled a set of keys from his pocket; one of which he used to open the front door. We stepped into the small vestibule, Peter set down the luggage, and I closed the door behind us.

"This door here," Peter said pointing to a door directly in front of us, "leads into the main house where Aunt Jane lives, and your flat is upstairs." With that, Peter picked up the two suitcases and began lugging them up the stairs with me following behind. He reached the landing and opened the door, quickly entering the apartment and making room for me to follow along behind. "Well here you are, home-away-from-home," Peter said as he made a sweeping motion with his arm.

I stepped up beside him and looked around the apartment. Immediately to my left stood a small bookcase jammed with books while across to my right, tucked in the corner, sat a desk complete with computer. I was very glad to see it, as the first thing I planned to do, after my rest, was to send e-mail messages to my mother and friends notifying them of my safe arrival.

Directly ahead of me was the living room inclusive of fireplace, sectional couch, and flat screen TV. It was impressive. Peter then led me into the kitchen, which was to the left of the living room. Just like the living room, the kitchen contained all of the modern amenities. A door at the far end of the kitchen led out to a balcony and a set of stairs, which Peter informed me led out into the back garden, a place I was more than welcome to enjoy. Once inside the kitchen, Peter turned left again and opened a door revealing the bedroom with a beautifully made-up queen size bed that beckoned me to crawl in and enjoy its comfort. Across from the bed and to my left, a large closet promised to hold all of my belongings. I followed Peter across the room where just on the other side of the closet at the end of the bedroom was a door that led to the en-suite bathroom. The bathroom was large and contained a corner soaker tub, separate shower, as well as a washer and dryer tucked behind the bathroom door. We walked to a door at the other end of the bathroom, beside the shower, and as Peter opened it for me, I found myself once again in the living room area beside the desk. To my left again was the door to the apartment. We had made a complete circle around the entire apartment. It was perfect.

"So what do you think of your lodgings?" Peter asked grinning.

"I never could have imagined a more perfect place."

"Yes, well the old stone outside surely is deceiving. When Aunt Jane had this place converted a number of years ago, the builders did a tremendous job."

I nodded in agreement, trying hard to stifle yet another yawn. My eyes watered, as the yawn grew more intense.

"I'm sorry; I guess I'm more tired than I thought." I wiped the wetness from my eyes.

"I will take that as my cue to leave, so you can get some rest. Before I do however, I will give you my number should you have any problems." Peter crossed over and sat at the desk, he opened up a notebook he'd found sitting beside the computer, and began to scribble down some numbers as I looked over his shoulder.

"This is my home number," he explained. "This one my mobile, and this is the office. Aunt Jane will likely not be around for a while, but rest assured she has left word with the neighbour, a very nice couple I'm told, and should you have any trouble, you may call on them for assistance."

I nodded trying to take it all in between yawns.

"Do you have any questions before I leave?" Peter asked as he turned around in the office chair to face me.

"No, nothing I can think of at the moment," I replied; blurry eyed.

Peter stood up from the chair. "I'll bring your bags into the bedroom and then I'll leave." With that, he grabbed the two suitcases still sitting by the entrance and headed to the bedroom with me following at his heels. I stopped at the front door and waited for him to return.

"Thanks for everything," I said, part of me wished he would stay. I was beginning to feel quite comfortable with him and believed he felt the same way.

"It was no trouble, I had fun." Peter grabbed the doorknob and turned it pulling the door open. "Oh wait!" he said, turning around. "I almost forgot." He reached inside his shirt pocket and pulled out a somewhat rumpled envelope. "Sorry it got a little crushed. Aaron asked me to give this to you."

I reached over and took it from his outstretched hand.

"I'm sure we'll meet again," Peter said, and he slipped out the open door leaving me to stare at the crumpled envelope in my hands.

Seventeen

Mary quietly tiptoed down the rickety, wooden stairs of her family home, carefully feeling her way with one hand on the wall and the other on the railing. It was the middle of a very cold and moonless night, and she was being careful not to awaken her family. With thoughts of their impending emigration to New York in just a few short weeks, she could not sleep.

At the bottom of the staircase, Mary turned to her right and headed into the dining room. With no moonlight shining in through the window, the room was quite dark, and it took several minutes for her eyes to adjust to the small amount of light coming from the remaining embers in the fireplace.

When she reached the fireplace, she carefully felt along its mantle for the lantern she knew she would find. Then she searched for the tin box of matchsticks kept close by. With both of the required objects in her hands, she turned in the direction of the dining table where she carefully put the lantern down and removed its glass shade. She opened the tin and plucked from it one of the few matchsticks left inside, luckily she and her mother were heading into town the next morning for some much-needed supplies, matchsticks being one of them.

As she struck the match head across the surface of the dining table, it instantly burst into flames. Carefully, she lit the wick inside the lantern, replaced the glass, and moved it to the centre of the table. The glow from the lantern caused shadows to rise from the floor and dance across the room giving it an eerie feeling. Mary quietly moved toward her father's desk which sat in the corner of the room. After a quick search, she found what she was looking for, returned to the table and sat on her chair. She placed a few sheets of paper in front of her and set her pen and ink to the right. She laced her fingers as if in prayer, placed her hands on the paper, and closed her eyes.

What should she say? It had been months since she and Thomas had spoken or even seen each other, not since the day he left her crying in the meadow. She sat contemplating the words for a moment and then opened her eyes and picked up her pen; she dipped it in the ink and putting pen to paper, she began:

> *My dearest Thomas,*
>
> *I trust this letter finds you in good health. I intended to write you sooner, but I have just now found where to send this. I heard you had gone to help your uncle in Croydon (father says this is near London). I hope your uncle is feeling better; I remembered meeting him in the spring and thought him to be a gentleman.*
>
> *The past few days I have found myself unable to sleep. I am sure you are well aware that I will soon be departing for New York.*
>
> *Thomas; I do not wish to leave without a proper goodbye. I do not want my last memory of us, our last farewell, to be the day in the meadow. We will be leaving for London in a fortnight and as you are aware, it will be a long journey by coach and train. When we arrive in London, we will only have a day before we are to board our ship on the 15th.*
>
> *Thomas, I will not implore you, but I will leave it in your hands to come and say farewell if you wish. The*

name of our ship is the 'Ocean Queen' if this helps you any.

I hope you will come; I miss you.

Lovingly,

Mary

By the time Mary finished writing her letter, her eyes burned with tears and lack of sleep. As she waited for the ink to dry, a single tear fell from her cheek and landed on the letter, narrowly missing the spot where she'd signed her name, the ink still wet. She waved a hand over the letter fanning it to speed up the drying process, wiping at her eyes with the other.

Satisfied that the ink was dry, Mary neatly folded the letter and placed it in an envelope, sealed, and addressed it. Tomorrow she would take it with her on their weekly trip to town where she secretly intended to post it.

Mary returned the remaining paper to her father's desk, and set the pen and ink back in their proper spots. She blew out the lantern and returned it to the mantle; the darkness enveloped her. She waited a few moments for her eyes to adjust and as quietly and carefully as she had descended the stairs, she ascended and returned to her room.

Her sister lay in the bed they shared, snoring softly, undisturbed. Mary slowly lifted the blankets and climbed into bed shivering as her side of the bed was cold. With her head resting on her cool pillow, Mary closed her eyes and quickly felt the beginnings of sleep taking over. She sighed heavily, welcoming the drowsiness, the first she had felt in a long time.

My eyes opened to sunlight streaming in through the window. Lying there confused, it took me a few moments before remembering where I was. As the memories of my trip slowly returned and my dream faded, I sat up in bed and stretched. The sound sleep in a strange bed surprised me greatly as it usually took me a few nights to get used to different surroundings.

Suddenly, it dawned on me; just how long had I been asleep?

I threw back the duvet and climbed out of bed. There didn't seem to be a clock anywhere in the room, not even a clock radio, and I made a mental note that that was going to change. My unpacked suitcases still sat in front of the closet as I headed toward the bedroom door, remembering there was a clock out into the kitchen. Sure enough, I found it on the back wall by the kitchen table.

"6:30 – great! Is that A.M. or P.M.?" I couldn't tell if the light shining in the window was early morning or evening light. Confused, I headed to the desk, knowing that the computer would reassure me of the date and time.

I sat at the strange desk and turned on the computer. After a few seconds, the screen came up, but much to my dismay, it prompted me for a password.

My first thought was to look in the notebook where Peter had written down his information. To my pleasant surprise, the notebook contained instructions on the first five pages regarding everything from operating the computer, including the password, to emergency numbers. Once logged on, I quickly searched the menu bar for the correct date and time and was relieved to see that it was 6:35 P.M. on the day of my arrival; I had slept for four hours.

Eighteen

He pulled into the drive of his newly acquired home and shut off his car. Quietly he sat for a moment, content with his new dwelling. Granted, it wasn't a large home in any way, but it sure did beat the flat he once had right smack in the middle of London. Albeit, his once fifteen-minute commute to the office was now four times the length, but he didn't care because this was his home, and he was glad for it.

In the stillness, his mind began to recall the day's events. He smiled; he was smitten, certain he'd just met the girl of his dreams. He hoped she had an attraction for him and yet he was determined that if she felt the same way, he was going to take it slow, very slow. His proven record with women was less than stellar. He meant well, he just always seemed to dive headfirst before checking out the depth and ultimately ended up alone. That's what happened with his most recent relationship and the one before. He wanted nothing more than to find a partner to spend his life with and with whom to raise a family This desire that seemed so easy to others always seemed so far out of reach for him.

A beeping sound suddenly brought him back to reality; it was his cell phone stowed away in the cup holder alerting him of an incoming message. He picked it up and read; 'Call me when you get home, ASAP.' Thinking the worst he quickly exited the car, locked it behind him, and headed up the walk.

Once inside his home, he threw his keys into a bowl on a small table resting just inside the entrance, and he headed straight for the living room. He plunked himself down on the large, black, leather sofa, which was too large for the room but was comfortable all the same. Grabbing the phone he began to dial with a bit of apprehension; he was dreading the news he felt he was about to hear.

"Hello!" Aaron said after only one ring.

"Aaron, is everything alright?" Peter asked. He knew his friend would hear the worry in his voice and quickly let him know the matter; his fingers crossed.

"Oh sure, yeah. Sorry if my text worried you."

"Your mum's fine then?" Peter asked, feeling a bit of relief. He felt his shoulders drop as the tension eased.

"Yes, as fine as she can be... I suppose."

"So, no change then?" Peter questioned Aaron, wanting to be sure. It wouldn't be the first time Aaron would let on things were better than he would acknowledge.

He recalled the time when Aaron had hurt his ankle during a challenging football match. He hobbled off the pitch and rested during half time. When the game resumed, Aaron returned scoring two goals in the second half, sealing the victory. It was only on the following day did he disclose the pain he was really in and ended up going to the A&E. Luckily for Aaron, the stress fracture he'd suffered wasn't severe enough for a plaster cast, but it did mean resting his foot and no football for four weeks.

"No; no change."

"Well that's good then, right?" Peter asked, trying to sound upbeat and positive for Aaron.

"Yeah, I guess."

"So why the urgent message to call you?"

"Urgent? Not truly urgent, but I supposed that if I didn't say ASAP it might be some time before I heard from you; aye?"

"Perhaps, though I did just pull into my drive when you messaged me," Peter said, leaning back on his couch and putting his feet up on the table. If his mother were there and had seen he was still wearing his shoes, she would have cuffed him one.

"I just wanted to know how it went today; you know picking Krista up for me. I really appreciate you doing that." Aaron's voice lowered.

"No need to say it, I know."

"Yeah well, anyway how did it go?"

"Well. . . " Peter hesitated, "I must say she's quite stunning."

"Really!"

"Yes, really. Though I'm sure she must have thought I was a bit of a git at first, I scarcely spoke the entire drive." Peter thought back to the many awkward, quiet moments in the car.

"What – you! I'd have thought you would have talked her ears off, pointing out this and that along the way."

"I couldn't mate; she's lovely. You'll see." Peter flushed at the thought of Krista, he was glad Aaron couldn't see him.

"Yeah; anyway. . . " Aaron paused, "I hope so, I'm not scheduled to take her on any tours for almost a week and with Mum. . . "

"Well, your other clients have been taken care of and if you need me to see to Krista, I'm sure I can move things around." Peter sounded a little too eager even to himself, he hoped Aaron wouldn't notice.

"Steady, man, you've only just met her. Besides, I thought you were seeing someone."

"Humph, she decided to go back to her ex, she wasn't quite over him," Peter said somewhat irritated with the thoughts of his last love interest.

"That's too bad, I'm sure it was for the best. Anyhow, I should go, I'm sure you must be knackered. Thanks again mate."

"No. . . " Peter yawned mid-sentence, "problem, any time. Keep me informed about your mum."

"Yeah, will do."

"Have a good night mate," Peter said as he stretched, feeling more tired.

"You as well." Aaron hung up the phone first.

Peter laid his head back on the couch and closed his eyes; visions of Krista came to mind and he smiled; a few seconds later, he was snoring quietly.

Nineteen

Aaron chuckled quietly to himself and shook his head as he thought of Peter who seemed to fall in love every time he saw a beautiful woman. It was just too bad he always picked the wrong ones.

"Come in," Aaron called out to the unexpected knock at his door as he sat at the mahogany desk in his childhood room, of course it looked nothing like the room from his memories. It was now more sophisticated – adult.

Aunt Jane slowly opened the door and entered the room. She was dressed in deep purple and tied around her middle was a vineyard motif apron, the appearance of which made her look a bit like a grape; Aaron smiled.

"Supper's ready," she announced as she stood in the doorway. "Your mother will be joining us tonight." A slow smile spread across her face, knowing the news she delivered would make Aaron happy.

"She is! Is she sure she's feeling up to it?" He didn't want his mother to tire herself out needlessly.

"Yes, I think so; she's had a good day and she would like to dine at the table with us tonight. Would you help her down the stairs whilst I put dinner on the table?" Aunt Jane turned around and headed out the door.

Aaron stood and followed suit heading towards his mother's room at the far end of the hall. A few quick strides and he was at her door. He knocked and waited for his mother's reply; silence ensued. He knocked again, a little harder and pressed his ear to the door. Another moment went by but still nothing. He was about to knock a third time when he finally heard his mother call out.

"Come in." There was a slight tone of weariness to her voice, but it was nothing he hadn't heard before.

Slowly he opened the door. Kate sat on her bed with her hands clasped in her lap. Aaron looked at them and instantly noticed that they resembled the hands of someone much older. She had lost weight in recent weeks, and it had left the bones and tendons much more visible in her hands and hollowed out her face, her cheekbones and jaw becoming more prominent. She had never been a large woman, always on the slight side, so any amount of weight loss was too much.

Kate looked up at her son and smiled. "Come to help me down for supper?" she asked.

"Aunt Jane said you're feeling well enough to join us; are you sure?" Aaron asked looking at the dark shadows under his mother's eyes.

"Quite sure; I don't know how much more time I've got, but I'm going to make the most of it. Now come to my side and help me up." She smiled softly.

Aaron left his post at the door and went to his mother's side. He gently eased her off the bed and to her feet. He steadied her as her legs buckled a little.

"Are you sure, Mum?" he asked again, his arms securely around her, steadying her. He was afraid to hold her too tightly, she felt as though she would snap in two at any moment.

"Yes," Kate said with determination and patted the hand Aaron had wrapped around her waist.

For the first time since entering the room, Aaron noticed his mother was dressed. "What are you wearing?" he asked, not familiar with her clothing choice. Until she had become ill, Kate had been a very fashionable dresser, always wearing nicely designed clothing, even when at home by herself. He used to tease her saying that she looked as though she was ready for a visit with the Queen, should she stop by. Kate would fire back that the Queen just might and if she did, she would be ready. She always looked her best, no matter what.

"It's a jogging suit of course. Jane picked it up for me." Kate said, absently running her hand slowly over her thigh, feeling the soft material underneath.

"Oh, I see."

"Don't you like it?"

Aaron thought carefully for a moment. It certainly wasn't his mother's usual taste, but the royal blue colour suited her even though it hung from her ever thinning body Nevertheless, it did seem to please her. "Yes, I do Mum, it looks lovely on you." Aaron leaned over and kissed his mother gently on her cheek.

"Well, not really," Kate confessed, "but it is rather comfortable and does make me feel a little better to be dressed than wearing pyjamas. Now, let's head down for supper. I imagine Jane will be wondering what's taking so long."

Aaron stayed close by his mother's side as the two of them headed down to the dining room. It was a bit of a slow trip, but Kate managed. Her arms hooked through Aaron's for support as he led the way down the hall and then the stairs. Aaron wondered if there would be many more trips down these stairs together or if this would be the last. As if reading his mind, Kate spoke.

"I hope to be able to have dinner in the dining room as much as possible, especially when you're here."

"I hope so, Mum, it's not the same eating without you." Aaron choked back the lump he felt forming in his throat, hoping his mother didn't notice.

Kate suddenly changed the subject. "By the way, haven't you taken enough time off from work? I'm sure they need you back."

"Getting tired of my company already, are you?" Aaron teased.

Kate teased back as they entered the dining room. "Of course, what parent in their right mind wants their adult children moving back home again?" She smiled and winked.

Aaron pulled out a chair for his mother, helped her to sit, and then pushed it back into place. The chair slid effortlessly over the hardwood floor as though it had wheels.

"Thank you, love," Kate said as Aaron pulled out his own chair across from her and sat. Kate reached across the table with both hands and placed Aaron's hand between them. She looked at Aaron and smiled before a look of seriousness came over her face. "I love having you here, but I could be in this state for months, Aaron. I think it is time you go back to your life. You've already taken too much time away." She smiled again and withdrew her hands.

Aaron looked down at his plate. He knew she was right, but how could he possibly leave her. Granted what she said was true, she could be like that for the next six months, and yet she could die the minute he left. He wouldn't forgive himself if that happened. He was torn and on the verge of tears just thinking about it, but he had to be strong. He took a deep, though somewhat shaky breath. "I know you're right. Peter and the others have been fantastic taking over for me this past week. I promise I'll make a final decision after Doc Brown's visit tomorrow."

"Decision about what?" Jane asked as she entered the dining room carrying in a plate of freshly carved roast beef. The aroma filled the room, causing Aaron's stomach to rumble.

"That smells absolutely delicious, Aunt Jane." Aaron tried to change the subject, his mouth watering at the sight of the roast she'd placed in front of him. He hadn't realized just how hungry he was, and he felt as though it had been days since he'd last eaten.

Jane adjusted herself in her chair beside Kate, her vineyard apron still tied around her middle.

"Aaron's going back to work soon," Kate spoke up, answering Jane's question.

"I'm thinking about it," Aaron corrected.

Jane nodded. "Yes, I think it's time, Aaron. You're not that far should we need you."

"Well, I'll make my final decision after Doc Brown's visit." Aaron reached over and helped himself to a couple of slices of meat hoping to end that particular conversation.

"And what does Peter think about you possibly not returning until after I..." Kate didn't finish her sentence.

Aaron looked at his mother and aunt who stared back at him intently. "I haven't told him I might not be returning until..." Aaron paused, "anyway, he just told me not half an hour ago not to worry, he'll cover for me.

"All summer?" Jane asked.

Aaron hesitated before responding. "Well no, not exactly, but I'm sure –"

"I'm sure Peter will cover for you from time to time, but he can't possibly all summer, after all he does have his own clients to worry about."

Aaron knew his mother was right. There was no way Peter and the others could cover for him all summer. He would have to go back.

"Fine, I'll go back as soon as I can. Now can we end this conversation and eat?"

Without another word, Jane picked up Kate's plate and filled it up.

Aaron knew his mother would barely make a dent in it, but if left up to her, she'd barely put anything on her plate and eat even less.

The three of them sat and ate in silence. Aaron and Jane filling their forks while Kate slowly picked at her food, pushing more of it around on her plate then actually eating. It made Aaron worry more as he watched his mother take very few bites of the delicious meal.

"Speaking of Peter," Jane suddenly spoke up, "how are things with that new girlfriend of his? Are we going to meet her the next time he comes 'round?" she asked between bites.

Aaron swallowed the mashed potatoes he had on his fork before answering. "Well, Aunt Jane, apparently it didn't work out, they've broken up."

"Oh, what a pity," Kate said as she stabbed at piece of meat with her fork and stared at it.

"Yes, well don't worry," Aaron said as he placed a piece of tender beef in his mouth, chewed and swallowed, enjoying the flavour as it slid down his throat. "He's already got his sights on someone else."

"Really? So soon? Jane said.

"Anyone you know?" Kate put down her fork, the piece of meat still skewered on the end.

"My client." Aaron replied dryly, stabbing his fork into his green beans.

Twenty

It was eight o'clock when I finally arrived home, completely sated with dinner eaten at a local pub. I tossed my keys on the desk and plunked down in the chair, spinning around like an elated child. After a few spins, I stopped and waited a moment for the room to catch up. My dizziness was not just from the ride in my desk chair, but from excitement and complete happiness. Anyone seeing me now would certainly think I had gone nuts. I laughed aloud.

"Oh crap!" I said, pulling myself closer to the desk. I had intended to send out e-mails, apprising my family and friends of my safe arrival. However, in my haste to get out the door after my lengthy nap, I had forgotten all about my intentions. Sure enough, as I logged into my e-mail account, several e-mails from my mother and friends sat waiting for my reply. Instead of reading and responding to each of them, I sent one general e-mail to everyone, knowing they were all asleep and wouldn't read it until tomorrow morning anyway.

> *Hi all,* I began.
>
> *I'm so sorry for taking so long to respond to your e-mails.*

The prompt blinked at me, patiently waiting for me to type my next words. Each time I started a new sentence, I deleted it immediately.

*I just got in from a wonderful dinner. My apartment
is great and the village (so far) is spectacular.*

Again, I paused, re-reading what was written; somewhat satisfied,
I continued.

*I will send pics of the place later in the week. I'm
so glad I did this. It's amazing! Can't wait to explore
further. Take care and I will write to you again soon.*

Love Krista, xoxo.

I read the e-mail again; BCC'd everyone on my list and hit send,
shutting down the computer as soon as the message left the queue.
The screen went black as the computer fell silent.

Just as I was about to walk away from the desk, the corner
of what appeared to be an envelope, peaked out from under the
notebook of instructions and caught my attention. Sliding the
book over, I picked up the envelope and turned it over. Scrawled
on the front in black ink was my name. The memory of Peter
handing it to me came to mind.

I scanned the top of my desk for a letter opener and found
one hiding among the pens and pencils in a rather unique, what
looked like a ceramic, holder. Upon closer inspection, it revealed
itself to be made of clay, glazed and fired, with the impression of
a small, yet clearly visible handprint wrapped around it as if it
were holding the container. I smiled at the thought of the young
child who had made the container and placed my hand over the
imprint. Expecting it to be cool, it was surprisingly warm, so I
withdrew my hand. Regaining my focus, I pulled a letter opener
from the container and carefully opened the letter. Just as I was
about to sit back down in the desk chair, I changed my mind
deciding on a more comfortable location for reading, and headed
over to the living room. I sat in the corner of the couch and
switched on the lamp beside me, curled my legs up on the couch,
and began to read.

Dear Krista,

I feel that I must apologize for not keeping my promise to pick you up at the airport personally. I'm sure Peter told you I had a personal matter to attend to, but I feel as though I owe you more of an explanation.

My dear mother is ill. Her doctor tells me there is nothing else that can be done for her and so I wait to say goodbye. She's recently become weaker, so I have been at my childhood home to be by her side. It's not certain to any of us if this is the final stage or just a bump in the long road ahead. I apologize for being so candid, I hope you don't mind.

In any case, I'm sure Peter made you feel at home in your new surroundings. I hesitate to say that I will see you for your first "expedition," it depends on my circumstances. Rest assured you will be taken care of.

Yours Truly,

Aaron

I sat and examined the letter with its perfect penmanship. How long had it been since I'd read a hand written letter?

As a teacher, my young students submitted many pieces of hand written work, but a truly hand written letter from an adult, no less; I couldn't recall. It was much more personal, meaningful – it was romantic in a nostalgic sense; more so than the e-mails and text messages that we've become accustomed to writing and reading.

Charmed, I read the letter again. Though having yet to meet Aaron in person, seeing his handwriting gave me a sense of familiarity, the sadness he felt captured in his prose.

Carefully, I folded the letter and tucked it back into its envelope. Thoughts of my own relationship with my mother smouldered in my mind, and it paled in comparison. It was obvious that Aaron and his mother were close, something I wished for with my mother. There had been a time when we were closer, when my father was alive. It was at that moment that I decided that upon returning home, I would make more of an effort to get closer to her again. It wouldn't be an easy undertaking, but I would at least try.

My eyelids grew heavy. Tired and wanting to go to bed, yet so comfortable, I couldn't bring myself to move. I reached for the TV remote on the end table beside me and clicked it on. After some time of surfing, nothing caught my attention, and the TV returned to its idle state. With the resulting quietness, I rested my head on the large armrest of the couch, yawned, and closed my eyes for a few seconds.

"I've got to go to bed." I whispered to myself. There was every intention of getting up and going to bed as the words trickled from my mouth, but my body was already asleep, slowly my brain followed, the letter loosely clutched in my hands.

Mary turned the letter over in her hands. She hoped it would reach Thomas before she arrived in London.

"Well miss, are ye going to post that letter or are ye just going to stand there twirlin' it." The man's gravelly voice startled Mary out of her trance.

"Yes, sorry," she said handing the envelope to the shopkeeper along with a penny for postage.

The shopkeeper took the coin and the letter and turned toward the back counter where he placed the letter in a basket of outgoing mail. It was just in time too as Mary's mother was approaching with a basket full of supplies.

"Did you find what you were looking for?" she asked.

Mary had to think quickly, not a process she was very good at; nonetheless, she felt she had no choice. She had told her mother that she was looking for something; she didn't want her to know that she was posting a letter, it would lead to too many questions.

"No, it seems they're all out," Mary lied.

"Well, maybe next time," her mother said with a smile and a wink of her eye.

Mary instantly felt guilty for lying; she only hoped her mother didn't want details on the supposed item, for she hadn't exactly planned on any further explanation.

"I'll pay for these and we'll be on our way and back home in plenty of time to fix dinner. Now where's your sister?" she asked Mary as she looked around the store.

"She's waiting outside, I'll fetch her." Mary turned and headed out the door; happy for the excuse to leave her mother's side before she asked her any questions about the anonymous item.

Mary looked up the road and saw a small group of children playing. She took a few steps in their direction and spotted her sister instantly; she stopped and called out.

"Sarah, we must go now."

The young girl waved bye to her friends and hurriedly made her way toward Mary. Mary watched her bounce along, her pigtails swinging back and forth, as she came closer into view.

I sat upright on the couch and rubbed my face. "Sarah!" I whispered, the image of the little girl from my dream clearly in my mind, with Emma's eyes reflecting back.

Twenty-One

It took me a few minutes to understand exactly where I was upon waking in a strange bed, in a strange room. Even crawling into bed seemed a blur, much less falling asleep. The only thing I did remember was that Sarah was on my mind. Who is or was the girl that now haunted my dreams?

I laid there in bed, staring up at the ceiling trying hard to recall my dream from last night and all my other dreams since they had started. Bits and pieces came flooding back but there was no making sense of any of it. Throwing off the light sheet which covered me, I sat up, filled with anticipation. I had to understand what was happening, they were no longer dreams to me but messages from another time and place.

I grabbed my robe from the back of the bedroom door, pulled it on and made my way toward the desk. My fingers rooted through the handmade pencil holder jammed with pencils, markers, and the like and searched for a pen with which to jot down my thoughts. Finally, with a suitable pen in hand, I snatched the notebook from the desk and proceeded to the living room, plunked myself down in the corner of the couch, and opened the book to its first available blank page. I stared at the clean page, wondering just where to begin. Should I work backwards or start from when the dreams began?

It was better to start with the freshest; it was easier that way. I began writing furiously as if my life depended on it. Each idea, memory, and thought seemed to evoke a surge of others. It wasn't until my wrist began to ache and several pages were filled that I stopped – drained.

I closed the notebook and placed it on the coffee table in front of me, leaned back on the couch, and closed my eyes, still not sure where all the information was leading. The uneasy, gnawing feeling burned in the pit of my stomach just as the unanswered questions burned in my brain.

Slowly, I began going over what I knew for sure. First, at the meeting with Ruth just days before, she had contacted my father. I truly believed she had because what she'd said was too specific to have been a ruse. Then there was the other spirit who had wanted to speak to me; he was completely unfamiliar. I tried to recall what he'd said, unfortunately it hadn't been written down. Too engrossed with the whole experience, I had simply forgotten. Finally, the information Ruth had given me about past lives, telling me that my soul was old. Does that mean my life now is not the first? Had there been others? Some small part of me knew there had, but I kept pushing it down whenever it surfaced. There had to be another explanation.

I opened my eyes and stared at the notebook lying on the table in front of me, not wanting to go back through it to examine the information I'd just written down. Yet, I was compelled to do just that, too troubled not to. I leaned over and picked up the notebook, flipping it open to where my notes began. Carefully re-reading it, I added details left out the first time around. Still in the end, I had no definitive answer and began wondering if things shouldn't just be left as they were. Maybe all the recapping of my dreams was hurting more than helping.

I tossed the notebook back down on the table – frustrated. It was all too much for me, and my head ached. Leaning forward, my head cradled in my hands, I closed my eyes and shuddered, my lungs breathed in deep. I wanted to cry but thought better of it; it would only make my headache worse. Instead, I rose and headed to my room. My mind needed clearing.

The soothing, warm water ran down my scalp sending tingles through my body as it ran across my shoulders and down my back. With my arms stretched out in front of me and my hands pressed against the back of the shower for support, my muscles began to relax as the water seemingly washed away the tension; the pounding in my head began to ease. I tilted my head towards the shower and allowed the water to wash over my face. My eyes still closed, my hands reached down and slowly turned the cold-water off making it hotter. When it was as hot as could be tolerated, I turned away and let the water pound fully on my back; my eyes remained shut. Minutes ticked by as I stood there almost asleep on my feet.

My eyes popped open with sudden awareness that if I soon didn't get moving there probably wouldn't be enough hot water to wash with, and there was nothing I hated more than a cold shower.

I washed and conditioned my hair quickly, then poured a generous amount of jasmine scented body wash onto my loofah mitt and brought it toward my face, inhaling its scent and feeling my anxiety drift away. I rubbed the loofah over my body a little harder than usual, feeling its scratchiness wash and exfoliate. It was as though I were trying to scrub away that part of me that kept nagging the truth – pushing it away. When I was finished, my skin tingled; it felt good.

I turned off the slowly cooling water just before it took away the warmth that covered my entire body and stepped out of the shower. The steam poured out behind me. The white fluffy towel was soft and soothing on my body as it enveloped me. Wrapping a smaller towel around my head, I headed toward the mirror that hung above the sink; it had completely steamed over. I caught sight of myself in the mirror, and as I stared at the foggy image, I found myself unable to move. For a moment, it was not my reflection but that of another with long, dark flowing hair. I snatched the hand towel from the bar and quickly erased the image from the mirror, seeing only my own frantic look staring back at me.

I dressed quickly, all the while convincing myself the image was just the result of an over active imagination. What I needed was to get out and get some fresh air, and wherever my feet led me was irrelevant.

Once dressed, I grabbed my make-up and headed for the bathroom, but after a second thought decided on using the mirror in the bedroom instead, not wanting to conjure up any more images, real or imaginary.

From the sunshine that shone through the window, it looked to be a beautiful, warm day. However, goose bumps remained on my skin. I turned abruptly toward the closet and snatched a sweater leaving the hanger it had been hanging on to swing wildly back and forth.

I shut the red door behind me. The warmth of the sun greeted me as I stepped out from under the protection of the small overhang above the door. Closing my eyes, my head tilted briefly toward the sun, I enjoyed the way it caressed my face. An image from earlier dreams of Mary enjoying the sun flashed in my mind. Shaking my head, I tied my sweater around my waist and headed up the street toward the town centre, my small purse slung across my shoulder.

After walking for several minutes, I came across a tearoom. Its awnings and outside seating mirrored each side of the main entrance and presented as authentic and quaint. Deciding that it seemed to be a good place to calm my somewhat frazzled nerves, I entered.

Finding a recently vacated table by the window, I took my seat and awaited the server to clear the remnants from what seemingly was another satisfied customer.

"Hello, love; let me clear this away for you, and I'll take your order." I looked up to see the smiling face of a woman who was about my mother's age carrying a bus pan in one hand and a damp cloth in the other. She quickly cleared the dishes and placed them in the bus pan she'd set at the other end of the square table. "Is anyone joining you then, dear?" she asked while she busily cleaned the table of its bits and pieces.

"No, it's just me."

"Tsk, tsk," she clicked her tongue. "a pity such a lovely girl as yourself is here alone on such a beautiful day." She smiled warmly, stopping for a second to look at me.

I blushed. "Thank you. I'm here on vacation."

"Lucky you! So how do you like our 'Little Venice of the Cotswold's?" she asked. I stared at her for a moment a little bewildered by her statement. "That's how many refer to Bourton-on-the-Water," she clarified.

"Oh! Well, it is beautiful; though I only just arrived yesterday afternoon, so I haven't seen much of it yet."

"Well then, be sure to see the 'Model Village', it will give you a good lay of the land and show you where everything is."

"Oh thank you, I will." I smiled back, thankful for the information. The woman pulled out the chair beside me and picked up a newspaper that was lying there, probably left by the previous patrons. "Can you leave that please?" I asked, interested in looking at the local paper.

"Of course, love; I'll be right back with some place settings and a menu." She set the paper on the table.

"Thank you." I looked at the cover of the newspaper and read its aptly named title, The Bourton Times. Carefully, I thumbed my way through the pages taking in every article and advertisement. Working my way slowly through the paper, I found myself engrossed in its every detail. So much so, that I hadn't heard the server when she returned.

"Here you are, dear." She placed the menu on the table beside me. I must have jumped a foot out of my seat. "I'm so sorry, love; did I give you a fright?" The look on her face was one of concern and puzzlement.

"It's fine; I guess I was just really into this story."

She looked over my shoulder at the short story I had been reading. "Hmm, I don't think I read that one," she muttered under her breath. "I'll be back to take your order." Before I could say anything more, she left and headed to the back of the restaurant.

I perused the menu for a couple of minutes unable to decide what to order. My stomach rumbled and it seemingly decided on the bacon, egg, and toast. When my server returned, I placed my order along with a pot of Manuka honey tea. The server graciously explained that the tea I'd ordered came from Cornwall and was made by the only successful tea growers in the country, even the type of honey that was used to flavour my tea was produced there. Cornwall sounded like a place I needed to visit.

I picked up the paper and resumed reading, awaiting my breakfast.

"Hello there, would you mind if I joined you?"

I put my paper down and looked up. "Peter!" I said, happy to see a familiar face, "of course." I gestured to the empty chair across from me. He walked around, pulled the chair out, and sat clasping his hands in front of him. "What are you doing here?" I didn't think I'd see him so soon.

"Well..." He reached into the pocket of his khaki coloured shorts and held his hand out in front of me. I stared at it somewhat perplexed; when I looked back at Peter, he was smiling.

"I don't understand." I watched as the smile disappeared from his face.

"It's not yours?" he asked. I shook my head, examining the bracelet he held in his hand. He closed his fist and withdrew it as he put the piece of jewellery back into his pocket. He leaned forward and laced his fingers, resting his hands on the table in front of him, his arms noticeably strong. "Well then, I guess that's a mystery I'm just going to have to solve on my own." His smile returned, his blue eyes sparkling somewhat mischievously.

"You didn't drive all the way out here for that did you?" I felt badly he'd made the trip for nothing.

"Well, it seems that I did. But no worries, I'm sure I'll find another reason for being here." He smiled at me again, and I felt my cheeks flush.

"How did you find me anyway?" I asked folding up the paper and placing it back on the seat beside me, making a mental note to take it with me.

"Find you? Well actually, this is a coincidence. I came for brekkie. I was going to head to your place afterward." Peter leaned back in his chair and stretched. I could just make out the outline of neatly carved muscle beneath his eye-matching blue, golf shirt. He was definitely in shape.

"Peter! How lovely to see you!" My server addressed Peter with my breakfast plate in her hands. I raised my eyebrows and looked at him.

"Hello, Liz, how have you been?"

"Never better," Liz answered as she placed my plate in front of me.

"And Sam?" Peter questioned our server who I now knew as Liz.

Liz laughed. "As grumpy as ever, but I do think he's starting to mellow in his old age." She winked at Peter.

"Well, there may be some hope after all for the ole codger." Peter joined Liz in laughter that seemed very much an inside joke.

Liz eventually turned her attention back to me as I continued staring at the two of them; it was obvious they knew each other quite well. "Well now, if anyone was going to join you, you picked a good one in this chap." Liz smiled at me. I didn't know what to say.

Sandra J. Jackson

"Actually Liz, Krista's a client of Aaron's. I just brought her to town yesterday, thought she'd left something behind, but alas it turns out not to be hers." Peter had rescued me from any explanation.

Liz nodded, pursing her lips. I thought she looked as though she were going to add something more to the conversation but changed her mind. Her face lit up again though. "How are Aaron and his poor, dear mother?" Liz asked.

Peter shrugged. "I spoke with him last night, and Kate seemed to have had a good day yesterday."

"Well, give them my love when you talk next. Now can I get you anything dear?"

I spread strawberry jam on my toast, quietly watching the exchange between them.

"I'll have the same as Krista," Peter said, pointing his chin in the direction of my plate. "A coffee though instead, please."

"Back in a bit," Liz said, turning back to me and winking.

"She's great, isn't she?" Peter asked.

I swallowed the piece of toast in my mouth and washed it down with a sip of tea. "Yes, very nice. You've known her for a while?" I picked up a fork full of egg and put it in my mouth. The yolk was slightly runny, just the way I liked it.

"Yeah, family friend." Peter reached toward the paper on the chair between us and picked it up. "Is this yours?"

I chewed, swallowed, and sipped again before answering. "No, I guess the person before me left it. I thought I'd keep it though, it's got a lot of ads and stuff in it about the area."

"Yeah, it's a good one; it'll give you a feel for the area." Peter put the paper back in its place.

Liz was true to her word and a few minutes later, she returned with Peter's meal. I still had about half of mine left, and as we ate in silence, my mind drifted back to the morning's events.

I certainly hadn't expected to be dining with anyone, much less Peter, yet there we were enjoying breakfast. With everything

135

that was going on in my life, I began wondering if it was merely coincidence or if it was something more. Reading into every little thing that happened to me was crazy, yet the idea of not exploring those coincidences seemed crazier. If my dreams were truly messages, I needed to figure them out.

"Is everything alright?"

I jumped a little at the sound of Peter's voice. He had finished his breakfast and was staring at me. "Yeah, why do you ask?"

"You seem a little... preoccupied."

I followed Peter's gaze to my teacup. Though still half full, I had absently taken up a teaspoon and was 'drawing' figure eight patterns, watching the tea swirl around in the cup. Embarrassed by my zoning out, I quickly pulled the spoon from my cup and laid it down on my empty plate. "Just some stuff on my mind." I took another sip of my tea just as Liz approached.

"Would either of you like anything else?" Liz interrupted.

"No thank you. It was delicious." I smiled up at Liz, very happy for her timely interruption.

"Sorry, Liz, that's all for me, too," Peter added.

Liz pulled out two bills from her apron and handed them to each of us. "It was very nice meeting you, Krista, and I do hope you'll stop in again soon."

"Of course, I'm here until the end of August."

"Oh lovely!" She clapped her hands together. "Well, you enjoy our little village, and if you need anything at all don't hesitate to drop by and ask; I'm always here." Liz winked and headed off to the back.

"She's so nice," I said, turning to Peter.

"That she is. So tell me what do you have planned for the rest of the day?"

Planned? I really hadn't thought any further than breakfast, but heading back to the apartment was not an option. My mind was obviously still too focused on the events of the morning. I needed some distraction for a while longer, anything that would keep my troubled thoughts away.

"No plans. Maybe walk around a bit, shop a bit. I need to pick up groceries today, I can't keep going out for my meals; I'd be leaving a lot sooner if I did that." I looked at my bill, not sure about the currency conversion thing, but I wasn't worried because the credit card company would do that for me. I reached into my purse and grabbed my wallet.

"Did you manage to exchange some money?" Peter asked while I opened my wallet to grab for a credit card.

"No, not yet; just getting the old plastic out."

Peter laughed.

"Ah, what's so funny?"

"This place doesn't accept credit or debit, not just yet anyway."

"What?" I was dumbfounded; apart from a Canadian five-dollar bill and credit cards, I had no other form of currency.

"Here," Peter reached out and took the bill from my hand, "my treat. See I told you I'd find another reason for being here."

"Yeah, well I've got a couple of others for you, too. Do you think you can take me to a bank and then to a grocery store?"

Twenty-Two

Upon opening the door, I moved quickly to my left to allow Peter, heavily laden with grocery bags, into the apartment. He moved swiftly toward the kitchen, one of the bags tearing with the weight of its contents, but he managed to get it onto the table just as it split open.

"That was close," I said as a number of cans tumbled out. One made its way to the edge of the table, but Peter snatched it quickly before it fell off, and he set it up right.

"I'll go get the last of the bags," he huffed, his face almost as red as his hair. He'd managed to carry six bags himself while I jostled only half as many.

I started unpacking the bags and organized the items on the table, apart from the refrigerated stuff; I wasn't quite sure where everything was going.

I had only just finished unpacking four of the bags when Peter came in with another haul and placed five more bags on the table, bringing the count to fourteen.

"Did you remember the three in the back seat?" I asked, not looking up but continuing to unpack the bags and sort through their items. Peter mumbled something as he walked out of the room. "I guess not," I quietly muttered to myself trying hard not to laugh. When Peter returned minutes later, I had emptied half of the bags.

"You could open up your own little market with the stuff you've bought today," Peter remarked as he placed the last three bags on the floor since there was no room left on the table.

I laughed, "Yeah, I don't think I've ever bought this many groceries before." I stood with my hands on my hips staring at the table filled with goods, with another ten more bags yet to be unpacked.

"Well, apart from perishables, this should last you the rest of the summer." Peter stood beside me shaking his head. "If you'd like, I can finish unpacking, so you can put stuff away."

"Sounds like a plan."

It took a good half hour to get everything sorted and put away, with cupboards and refrigerator full, it felt more like home.

"Meet you in the living room with a cold drink?" I smiled at him.

"Brilliant!" Peter turned and headed out of the kitchen.

I rummaged through the cupboards, grabbed a large, green, plastic bowl and filled it with chips, or crisps as Peter had called them, then set the bowl on a tray I'd found on the top of the fridge. After locating a couple of large glasses, I filled them up with ice and pop. Thankfully, Aaron's aunt had made ice prior to my arrival; one of the many entries she'd written in the notebook.

"The notebook!" I spoke quietly to myself, suddenly panicked remembering the notebook was sitting on the table in the living room.

Carefully lifting the tray, I walked swiftly into the living room where Peter was sitting, the notebook in his hand. For a moment, I felt anxiety beginning to build, but I managed to stop it before it controlled me.

Maybe he didn't read anything. I silently tried to reassure myself.

"Ah," he said, putting the notebook back on the coffee table.

I placed the tray into the centre. The room suddenly seemed to fill with awkwardness, and I sensed that Peter had indeed read my crazy writings. I tried to lighten the mood and figure out just how much he'd read.

"So, interesting read?" I asked jutting my chin out in the direction of the notebook on the table.

"Just reading all the instructions Jane left you." He didn't quite look me in the eye, but reached for one of the glasses from the tray and took a long gulp.

"Is that all?" I pressed some more. Though it was embarrassing, I needed to know exactly how much he'd read.

"Er, well no... I did sort of start to read, you know... something else, but I promise I just realized it was... you know... sort of personal when you came into the room, so I put it down, I'm sorry; I certainly didn't mean to pry into anything." His eyes told me he was being honest with me, and I relaxed a little and sat on the couch beside him. I reached for the remaining glass on the tray and took my own long sip almost drinking half of the large glass. "Look, I'm sorry. I didn't read more than the first little bit."

"That's okay. I've had a lot on my mind lately and thought it would help if I wrote it down."

"No need for explanations, I understand completely." He sipped again from his drink and grabbed a handful of chips as if to wave the whole incident aside; however, his actions still didn't manage to clear the air. We sat in silence, drinking and eating. Finally, Peter placed his empty glass down on the table and turned toward me. "So do you really believe in all that stuff; you know, past lives and ghosts and everything of that sort?" He looked at me with raised eyebrows and waited for my answer. When he put it that way, I just didn't know anymore, it sounded too incredible.

"I thought you said you only read a little bit?"

"Well, I may not have been entirely truthful; it was more like the first three pages."

My eyes widened. Three pages! I couldn't remember what exactly was written on those first three pages, but I did know that what he'd read was definitely enough for him to get the gist of the whole thing. I didn't know whether to laugh, cry, or just throw him out.

"You should blink or something before your eyes dry up and fall out of their sockets," he said smiling.

I closed my eyes and my mouth.

"I'm sorry, I truly didn't mean to pry but I wasn't sure what I was reading and then by the time I realized, it was too late. Can you forgive me?"

Peter's blue eyes sparkled, there was no way I could be mad at him. I nodded.

"Good. So do you?"

I crumpled my brow and thought a moment before finally answering. "I don't know." My response was almost inaudible; my eyes looked down at my hands resting on my lap. Finally, I gained just enough courage to look Peter in the eyes. "I don't know what I think. My dreams, my experience with a medium; it's all too much, and yet I keep coming back to one conclusion. I'm just not sure I'm prepared for it." It was strange talking about this with someone I'd just met and yet, it was a relief, like keeping a big secret that had been nothing but a burden. "Do you believe in that sort of stuff?" I asked even though I already suspected what his position would be on the subject.

"No." It was emphatic.

Not surprised, I nodded.

"What makes you so convinced this sort of thing is even possible?"

I leaned over, picked up the notebook from the coffee table, and handed it over to him. "Keep reading." I held the notebook out to him.

"Are you sure?"

I nodded, and he reached over taking the book from my hand. He read and I watched, hoping that there'd be something in my written words that would convince even the most rigid of skeptics. My eyes scanned his face for any readable expression, but there was none, his face remained unmoved. It wasn't long before he finished, and then he closed the notebook and handed it back to me.

"Well?" I asked cautiously, drawing the notebook toward my chest and folding my arms protectively around it.

He sat there straight-faced – quiet. He stretched and leaned back against the couch closing his eyes as if in meditation. Patiently I waited.

"Look," he began, his blue eyes stared into mine, "I'm not quite sure what to make of your experiences. I'm sure they've been quite... " he paused, "unsettling. Personally, though, I still don't believe in that sort of thing. Though in truth, it does all seem quite... odd, for lack of a better word." He scratched his head. "I don't know."

Instantly, I regretted opening my mouth and encouraging him to read what I'd written. The whole thing was rather embarrassing and for a moment, tears threatened to make an appearance. I took a deep breath and resolved to put the whole thing behind me, or at least not talk about it with Peter.

"I know someone who is not as skeptical, mind you he doesn't like to talk about it much, but perhaps he'd be willing to help."

"Who?" I was a little thrilled that someone might be able to help me.

"Aaron."

"Aaron?" I scrunched my eyes in confusion. "Yeah, well seeing as we haven't quite met... besides telling you was awkward enough, I'm not sure I want to start that conversation again." I picked up my glass and drained the last bit of pop.

"I suppose you're right. I could maybe speak to him about it first. That is if you would like me to." Peter looked at me.

Goose bumps rose on my arms, and the hair stood up on the back of my neck. I didn't know whether it was from the way he looked at me or if it was just the idea of telling someone else. Whatever it was, it passed quickly.

"I don't know. I have to think about it."

"I understand. I won't say anything unless you ask." Peter stood up and looked at his watch. "Well I should be going."

"Oh!" I was a little surprised by his sudden urgency to leave. I stood up and walked with him to the door. "Well, thank you so much for taking me around town and helping me with my groceries and everything." It still felt awkward between us.

"It was my pleasure. Thank you for the drink."

I waved my hand as though it were no big deal. Peter reached up and gently touched my chin. Before I knew what was happening he kissed me, the shock of it all caused me to jump back.

"I'm sorry, I didn't mean –"

"No, no it's okay," I interrupted. "It's just that. . . " I paused trying to find the right words, "I just ended a relationship, and I'm not ready to. . . " I let my voice trail off.

"I understand completely. Don't even worry about it. I just. . . anyway don't worry." He reached for the doorknob.

"Peter!" I said placing my hand on his arm stopping him. "Thanks for understanding. . . everything." I turned and looked at the notebook on the coffee table before looking back at him.

"Like I said 'no worries'. You have my word that I won't say anything, unless of course you want me to. He really might be able to help."

"I'll think about it. Who knows maybe we'll hit it off, and I'll be brave enough to once again tell my strange stories to a virtual stranger." I smiled.

Peter raised his eyebrows but said nothing, the matter dropped. "Have a good evening," he said as he opened the door to my apartment and headed out.

"Yeah thanks, you too," I called after him, watching him head down the stairs. He raised his arm in acknowledgement.

I closed the door to my apartment and leaned back against it. My lips still tingled from his kiss, my fingers absently rubbed over them. His kiss left me confused; it was all so sudden. Peter was handsome and our time together was enjoyable. Could there possibly be something more than a new friendship? It was certainly too soon to tell and in any case, I was not ready for anything more, at least not yet. My trip was for one reason and that was to regroup, to find myself, so to speak. I laughed aloud about the double entendre that statement seemed to make in my life. Which 'self' was I trying to find?

Twenty-Three

Peter pulled into the drive of his home and turned off his car. He rested his head on the leather headrest, closed his eyes, and let out a small burp as he rubbed his stomach. He had eaten far too much, and now he was paying for it. He loved the food at the small diner he stopped at on his way home, but it never seemed to like him. He was tired from the day he'd spent with Krista and just wanted to spend a nice quiet evening at home, maybe even go to bed early.

Finally, he opened the door of his car grunting and groaning as he got out, his hand still rubbing his expanded gut. He reached down and unbuttoned his shorts, it helped a little but still didn't give him the relief he was looking for. He closed the door and pressed the door lock icon on his key fob, the beeping sound giving him the security that the doors had locked as he headed up the walk. Peter burped again, that time more loudly.

"Always biting off more than you can chew, hey Peter?" He scolded himself under his breath as he unlocked the door to his home. The expression he aimed at himself was meant both literally and figuratively.

Peter took off his shoes, pushed them over into the corner out of the way with his foot, and unzipped the fly on his shorts to loosen them up even more. He needed to get out of them and into something more comfortable, something with elastic. He headed into his bedroom, taking his shorts off as he went along and threw them into the laundry hamper in the corner of his room. He was a bit of a neat freak and nothing ever was out of place. Though it was still quite warm outside, his home was comfortably air-conditioned. With that in mind, Peter found himself a nice, baggy pair of jogging bottoms and pulled them on.

He headed into the washroom, flipped on the light, and rummaged through the medicine cabinet looking for the antacids he kept on hand. Finding the ones he was looking for, he swallowed them down with water he drank directly from the tap. Peter turned off the light, headed toward the living room, and flung himself on his big, oversized couch landing with a flump.

He laid there for a moment, but soon realized that lying down wasn't a good idea, at least not until the antacids kicked in. He sat up, leaned his head back on the couch, and closed his eyes. Flashes of the day's events bombarded him as clearly as if he were watching them play out on a screen. He shook his head as though to erase the images and opened his eyes. He sat forward and rested his face in his hands, rubbing his eyes with his fingers.

"Argh!" Peter grunted in frustration. "Why do I always manage to ruin things?"

He had spent a good part of the drive home going over the day and the signals he thought he had received from Krista. He was so sure that she was interested in him, but apparently, he'd been wrong. At least not enough to make her forget about the relationship she'd just left. In any case, she had stated it plainly. Then of course, there were all of those strange occurrences she had been having, and the thoughts she'd had about possibly having a past life. It was always the same thing. Whenever he was interested in a girl, she always had baggage of some sort to deal with, never mind his own. Nevertheless, the women he fell for always seemed to have much more.

"That's it," Peter told himself, "from now on it won't be me making the first move." It wasn't the first time he'd told himself that, and it probably wouldn't be the last.

He grabbed the remote from the table and sat back on the couch as he turned on the TV. After a few minutes of flipping through the channels, nothing caught his attention, so he turned it off. His stomach gurgled, a good sign that the antacids were working.

Peter thought back again to the last few minutes with Krista. He had told her that he had a dinner to get to, which wasn't exactly true. He wanted to get out of there quickly given that things were getting awkward. Then he thought of his kiss. It was nice, though much too short. She had jumped back with such shock that he'd been embarrassed, and all he could think of was to get out of there as quickly as possible. He hoped that if they ever saw each other again, a prospect he was quite sure was in his future given the turmoil in Aaron's life, they could overcome the unease they both certainly felt and move on.

The phone rang and Peter jumped, his heart raced. He'd fallen asleep on the couch and hadn't realized it. Reaching across the armrest, he grabbed the cordless phone from its cradle on the end table.

"Hello!" Peter said groggily.

"Hey, did I wake you?" Aaron asked.

"It's alright, mate. What time is it?" Peter rubbed his free hand over his face.

"Quarter past ten. Are you feeling ill? I'm surprised you're even at home. I tried your mobile, but it just went to answerphone."

"Yeah, I turned it off earlier today; I didn't want to be disturbed." Peter sat forward and scratched his head.

"Now I'm interested, what have you been up to all day?"

"Before I answer, how's your mum?" Peter asked putting up a hand to his mouth and stifling a burp, he was feeling much better.

"Not bad. She's had a good couple of days."

"That's good. So I take it you'll be back soon?" Peter didn't know how to feel about that. On the one hand, he needed him back. Right now, they were managing but in the next week or two, it wouldn't be quite as easy. On the other hand, he wanted to see Krista again, even if it was awkward.

"Yeah, I think so, barring any turns for the worst. Now are you going to tell me what you've been up to?

Peter scratched his head searching for the right way to tell Aaron exactly what he had been doing.

"Well, I found a bracelet in my car. I thought maybe it was Krista's, so I headed to Bourton to bring it to her."

"You drove up to see if a bracelet in your car belonged to Krista?" Aaron asked incredulously. "Wouldn't it have been easier to just ring her?"

Peter was a little embarrassed, the thought had crossed his mind, but he wanted to see her again and it was a good excuse. He rose from the couch and paced around, something he was in the habit of doing when he wasn't quite sure of himself.

"Yes, I could have, but I wanted to see her again."

"So was it hers?"

"No. But we did spend the day together."

"Really!"

"Showed her around, took her shopping." Peter shrugged as if it was no big deal, images from the day flipped through his mind.

"And. . . ?"

"And nothing really, it just got a little awkward."

"Awkward – how?"

Peter thought about telling Aaron about Krista and her belief that she was dealing with past life memories but remembered his promise to her.

"I kissed her."

"You what?" Aaron said loudly.

"I know, I know." Peter's ears burned, he did not need nor want chastising from his friend.

"So what did she do?" Aaron's tone was back to normal.

"She jumped away, and told me she'd just ended a rather serious relationship and wasn't looking for another one just yet."

"Ah!"

Peter knew his friend well enough to know that had Aaron not been going through a bit of a rough spot, he would be rebuking him, especially since Krista was a client.

"Yeah, ah!" Peter repeated.

"So I suppose you would really like for me to be back in the next few days?"

"Yeah well, I'm a little torn about that. I'd like to see her again, but I don't want it to be strange. If I don't see her again, I don't want her to think I'm avoiding her." Peter paced back to the living room and flopped back down on his couch.

"She's expecting me anyway, so you won't be avoiding her. I'm sure you'll meet again, she's here for quite a bit of time." Aaron sounded reassuring.

Peter stretched and yawned. "I've got to go; I can barely keep my eyes open anymore." He rubbed at his watering eyes.

"Yeah, me too," Aaron yawned back. "We must be getting old, it's only half past ten," he laughed. "Have a good night and see you soon."

"Same to you." Peter hung up the phone. He stretched again and wearily headed off for bed, crawling under the cool sheets.

His lips tingled briefly at the memory of his kiss, and he slipped easily out of consciousness, a smile on his face.

Twenty-Four

"Do you trust me?" Thomas whispered.

Mary lay on her back staring up at the millions of stars twinkling overhead. She turned her head and faced Thomas. He was lying on his side, propped up on his right hand while his left traced lightly up and down her stomach, her skin prickled and she shivered slightly. "You're giving me the chills."

"That's not an answer to my question." Thomas replied flatly.

"I'm sorry. What was your question?" Mary turned and looked back up at the stars again mesmerized by their twinkling.

"I asked if you trusted me."

Mary turned, facing him again. The full moon was high and lit up the meadow. Mary could just make out his face in the moonlight; he was sullen. She reached up and laced her fingers with his, mostly to help make her point, but it also resulted in him being unable to continue tickling her; a sensation she was growing tired of feeling.

"Of course, I trust you. Do you think I would be out here with you in the middle of the night if I didn't?"

Thomas lay quiet and unmoving, reflecting on Mary's question. Then he unlaced his fingers with hers and rolled over onto his back, his features clearly visible in the moonlight. Mary desired to say something more but thought better of it. Instead, she remained quiet, awaiting his answer.

"*I suppose trust isn't the right word.*" *Thomas finally said.*

For a moment, they laid in silence, the only sound coming from the chirping crickets and waves crashing in the distance.

"*Why do you hide me from everyone?*" *Thomas broke the silence once more.*

"*I don't hide you,*" *Mary said, slightly annoyed.*

"*Don't you? You haven't introduced me to your parents and when your friends draw near, you're full of excuses as to why you must go. It seems as though this meadow is the only place where we can be together. I know it's only been a few short months, but I would think by now...*"

Mary cut him short. "*It's not a matter of trust; you're a perfectly wonderful man. It's just that...*" *Mary paused. She didn't know quite how to put it.*

"*What then?*" *Thomas demanded sitting up and drawing his knees to his body, and then resting his chin upon them.*

Mary sat up, too, curling her legs behind her and supporting herself on one hand while she reached over with the other and placed it on Thomas's leg. She took a deep breath before speaking. "*I'm afraid my parents won't approve.*"

Thomas looked at her. Mary couldn't quite make out his features as the moon shone down behind him casting shadows across his face, but she heard the disbelief in his voice. "*What is there about me that needs approval?*" *he asked. Before Mary could explain further, Thomas continued.* "*I work hard, I can read and write, my father's farm is doing well enough...*"

"*But that's just it, don't you see?*" *Mary interrupted,* "*it's your father's farm. You're 25 years old and still living on your father's farm with nothing of your own. You don't even know if you want to be a farmer.*" *Mary tried to be gentle with her words but knew she had failed when he pulled his leg out from under her hand.*

"*Do you want me to go in to mining and work for your father – is that it, working long, dirty hours. Have you not noticed that mining isn't exactly very prosperous these days, not to mention*

*those men don't seem to live very long after spending years under-
ground?" Thomas spat back, he was already sorry at the mention
of a shorter lifespan.*

*Mary knew he was right of course, working in the mines was
never a job to envy, but it supported her family, her father was the
mine manager. Mary spoke more gently. "Thomas I don't want
you to be a miner. I don't care what you are as long as we're
together. I'm happy with you and doubt I could ever be happier.
My family only wants to make sure that whomever I marry, he
will be able to provide for me, that's all." She reached out her
hand and gently touched his leg, Thomas didn't pull back.*

*"I can provide for you." Thomas said, lifting his chin from his
knees. "I will provide and care for you no matter how. You believe
me – don't you?" He sounded childlike.*

*Mary sat up on her knees and drew closer to him. She rested
her hands on the top of Thomas's knees as he looked up at her.
"Fine," she said, "come to my home tomorrow, I'll introduce you
to my family. Now, please stop talking." Mary reached up gently
and placed her hands on Thomas's chest pushing him backward.*

*Thomas caught her arms and pulled her down on top of him
as he lay back on the ground. Mary could hear his heart beating
as she rested her head on his chest, and Thomas held her in his
arms staring up at the night sky. The sound of the rhythmic beating slowly hypnotized her, and she closed her eyes, drifting off
to sleep.*

The sound of his heartbeat in my ear was soothing as I listened
to its rhythmic beat, slow and steady. I smiled and bent my outstretched arm, wanting to feel his chest under my hand. My left
hand slowly moved up over his shirt, searching for the buttons
that held it together. "I love you, Thomas," I whispered, still half
asleep.

Slowly I began to regain consciousness, realizing it was my own
heartbeat bouncing off the mattress and into my ear, the revela-

tion caused me to open my eyes. My left hand stilled as the shirt I was rubbing suddenly became a sheet. My right arm prickled, trapped underneath me. When it was free, my hand felt five times its normal size. I rolled over and sat up, shaking my arm, trying to bring life back into it. Finally, the prickles subsided and memories of my dream came back to me, which resulted in my need to write everything down.

Reaching over to the nightstand where the notebook casually rested from the night before, I flipped it open to where the pen held my last entry. My back-to-normal hand picked up the pen and diligently wrote out the memories from my dream, knowing it wouldn't soon be forgotten. It was now very evident that my dreams didn't occur in any specific order. However, it seemed as though certain events of the day triggered particular dreams.

When my notes were completed, I closed the notebook, set it back on the nightstand, and climbed out of bed. My feet landed on a cool softness that turned out to be my pillow. Tossing it back in its rightful place, I snatched my robe from the hook on the back of the door and padded out into the kitchen.

Each morning it was as if my body was on autopilot, first putting two slices of bread in the toaster and then brewing a cup of coffee. I stared out the kitchen window and looked out over the garden below; coffee in the garden seemed a good idea.

Before long, my toast was finished and with coffee in hand, I headed out the back kitchen door and down the stairs to the garden. Sunlight greeted me as I stepped out from the shadow of the house and sat on a weathered, stone bench already warmed by the sun. The bees and butterflies visited the flowers around me, and I wondered if they ever dreamed.

With each dream, my mind convinced me more that the dreams were memories, and yet to say it aloud or even to admit that to myself seemed crazy. Suddenly, an idea came to mind. I needed one final bit of reassurance and knew just where I was going to find it.

"Well, it seems like now is a good time." I drained the last drops of coffee from my mug. Several minutes passed as I sat on the bench procrastinating, before finally rising and heading back up the stairs.

Without further hesitation, I dressed quickly and pulled my hair up into a ponytail, grabbed my purse and headed out the door. My deep desire for answers was the driving force behind my quest, the exact plan unclear.

It wasn't a very long walk and in no time my feet brought me to the small cottage with the sign in the front lawn. I had seen the house yesterday when walking into town and gave it just a passing glance, at the time it was the last place I wanted to go.

I stepped purposefully up the walk, and just as my hand curled, preparing to knock, the door swung open. The small figure of an elderly woman stared up at me with an almost toothless grin.

"'Ello my dear, I've been expecting ye, won't ye come in." She smiled and stepped back, waving me in with a frail hand.

Oddly enough, I wasn't frightened and stepped into the dark entrance hall of the old woman's home, the door clicking behind me.

"When you said expecting. . . " I hesitated, following her down a dimly lit hall and stopping at a closed door at the end.

"'T'is only that I knew ye were on ye're way here, but I had to be patient aye?"

She opened the door to an office, and I was happy for the sunlight that streamed through the window since the rest of the house looked dark and almost ominous.

The large office had floor to ceiling bookcases along all four walls. Even the wall with the window right in the middle of it, had bookcases along each side; each of the bookcases filled with a multitude of books.

The old woman took her spot at her desk and motioned for me to sit in the chair across from her. I was surprised to see a monitor, though old, for she surely didn't look as though she'd be the type to even own a computer.

Sitting in the chair, I scanned the room and the bookcases. My eyes perused over the vast assortment of titles. Romance novels, children's fairy tales, biographies, and even books on the occult lined the shelves. I didn't think there was a single genre missing.

"Any titles you find interesting?" she asked as she busily searched the drawers of her desk.

"Well, I..." I stopped when she pulled a ragged looking book from one of the drawers and set it on the desk in front of me.

"What about this one then, I'm sure this will pique ye're interest." She smiled as she slowly pushed the book toward me. I felt small prickles trail up my back and stop as it reached the top of my head. My eyes locked on the cover too afraid to pick it up. "Go ahead, love." The old woman gently patted the top of my hand encouragingly. "It won't bite ye."

Slowly I raised the book and stared at its title 'Promised Soul'. The old woman watched me carefully as I picked it up. "I don't understand." I stared at her.

"Ye have questions, don't ye?"

"I do, but..." I waved toward the book I had set back down on the desk.

She smiled at me knowingly. "Ah well, I saw ye yesterday when ye walked by, and I knew then ye were troubled, and ye'd be comin' by."

"Yes, well I do have questions but I –"

The old woman held up her hand and interrupted me. She closed her eyes. "Ye've been having some troublesome dreams."

"Y-yes." My voice quivered, my hands clenched together.

"T'wasn't a question." She looked at me with piercing blue almost white eyes.

"Sorry."

She closed her eyes again. "Ye are not mad, but ye need to know that ye and the one ye dream of are one-and-the-same."

It really didn't come as a big surprise when the old woman spoke the truth aloud, I already knew deep down; Ruth had eluded to it. In fact, it was a relief. Finally, I could admit it to myself; Mary and I were the same. But why? Why now did she inhabit my dreams and sometimes, it felt, even my thoughts.

"There's a reason she's coming to ye." The old woman said, seemingly reading my thoughts. "Ye must complete her circle."

"I don't understand, what do you mean?" I looked at the old woman. Even though she'd clarified what admittedly my mind and body felt, there was still confusion on my part about what to do about it.

"Take the book and read it." She pushed it toward me. "It may help. Bring it back when ye're finished. There's someone else who'll need it soon." She winked.

My eyes narrowed. I was about to ask who, when the old woman stood up from her desk and headed toward the door.

"Ye can see ye'reself out." She stopped and turned to face me. "One more thing, listen to ye're dreams, Mary will show ye what she desires."

Twenty-Five

The walk back to my apartment was unmemorable. My thoughts clouded, and it seemed my body and mind were completely different entities acting independently of each other, while my eyes only observed. Only two things stood out in my mind, walking out of the old woman's house and walking back into my apartment, every moment in between was lost.

My hand threw the book down on the kitchen counter and grabbed a can of pop from the fridge, my eyes watched every move. Still disconnected, my body made its way into the living room, while my mind sifted through the evidence – cataloguing, disposing, and storing. My body worked on autopilot, my eyes an innocent bystander to her actions as they watched my hand place the can on the coffee table and my body flung herself down on the couch.

So... I had lived before – now what? "I was Mary." Saying it aloud didn't help me overcome the strangeness of it all.

All those weeks, and in fact perhaps all my life, there had been a feeling that there was something more to my dreams. Finding out that those feelings were valid didn't make it any easier to accept.

If I was going to move on – go back to just being me – I had to accept that there was a mission to complete and in order for that to happen, research into Mary's life was necessary. Sadly, there wasn't much to go on. Furthermore, spending an inordinate amount of time trying to research who I had once been, given the limited amount of information I had, seemed impossible. Living with what I already knew was easier, but I couldn't get over that nagging feeling, tugging at me. What were the dreams telling me or not telling me? The decision was final. I needed to sort through the information I had chronicled, listing only the vital clues, but first I was taking a shower.

My body felt more like a whole organism again. My eyes were no longer spectators, watching my body perform. My mind was no longer sifting through episodic memories. The hot water relaxed me, and I began to get lost in its warmth – I was putting off what I needed to do. Finally, I shook myself free from the bonds of procrastination and climbed out of the shower.

When I was re-dressed, I grabbed the notebook from the night-stand, but hesitated before heading out the bedroom door. Is this really necessary?

Yes. A voice responded from within, startling me. I shook my head, clearing my mind and proceeded toward the desk, determined to find answers and no thoughts or hesitations were going to stop me.

When the computer was up and running, I started by typing up all the strange occurrences and dreams that had transpired over the past few weeks in chronological order, after that – I was stuck.

At some point, while I was staring blankly at the screen, the thought occurred to me to put down all my fears. I began with anything to do with the *Titanic*, or any shipwreck for that matter and moved on from there. It soon became quite clear that all my fears related to each other in one form or another; such as being cold, drowning, swimming, boats – the ocean. A torrent of information came to mind, and I typed it all out.

Ocean Queen – unexpectedly, I remembered probably the most important detail given to me yet. It was during my session with the psychic medium, Ruth. She had mentioned, or rather the spirit that she was speaking with had mentioned, something about the Ocean Queen.

I reread my lists attempting to put the pieces of the puzzle together. After several minutes, I formed two conclusions. One, I had some inkling about how Mary had possibly died, and two, I had no idea where any of it was leading me, if in fact, it was leading me anywhere at all.

With the memory of the words Ocean Queen still fresh in my mind, I called up my favourite search engine and stared at the flashing prompt. Part of me so desperately wanted to know, while another part almost begged me to drop the whole thing. The two sides wrestled with each other for what seemed a long time until finally the winner guided my hands on the key board. It was quick and effortless. When the list of possibilities came up on the screen, it was the second entry that caught my attention, and it looked as though it pointed me in the right direction. Uncertain at first, my hand eventually moved the mouse and guided the cursor over the link.

"Well I've already gone this far, might as well go on." I clicked.

My eyes skimmed over the short paragraph about the Ocean Queen. Where she left from and how she was lost at sea. The memory from my dream of Mary slipping through a hole in the side of a ship came back full force and I closed my eyes, wanting to shut it out, instead it became more vivid. I shivered, tiny prickles traveled up and down my spine. When it was over, I opened my eyes again and scrolled down the page. A list appeared of the crew and passengers from the ship. It was almost too much to bear. I carefully skimmed over the names and searched for ones that were familiar. It didn't take long, for at the bottom of the first column of names were the names from my dreams; Charles, Ann, Mary, John and Sarah and beside them a bit further to the right, their ages; Mary was 17.

I stared at the names, wanting to remember that family – that time. Memories of my dreams flashed before me, confirming that

I had once been Mary and that the names on the list were my family from 1856.

"No wonder I've always wanted to visit England, it had been Mary's home."

I scrolled down further, but there was nothing. I kept searching, hoping to find more information but found nothing save for a picture of the ship Mary and her family perished on. It looked very much like the one on the cover of the book I was reading. At that moment, the thought occurred to me that my dreams began about the same time I'd started reading. Had that picture triggered my memories? Perhaps it was the planning of the trip itself. Truthfully though, it wasn't really the how that mattered, but the why. What was the purpose? The only other constant was Thomas. He had been in every dream, and if he wasn't actually in my dream, he was still a part of it.

I was getting weary thinking about it, trying to make sense of it all and my head began to hurt. "No more." I groaned. Just as I was about to shut the computer down, a last minute thought occurred to check my e-mail. My initial e-mail earned responses of good wishes for a great trip from family and friends, but as I was finishing with the last one, a new message arrived in my inbox from my mother.

Hello Krista,

Thank you for the update, I'm glad you arrived safely.

I have something to tell you. I wanted to tell you when we had brunch together and on the few occasions that we spoke on the phone before you left, though in truth, telling you over the phone seemed inappropriate, and I'm pretty sure it's inappropriate in an e-mail, too. Anyhow, I'll just get to the point. I've met someone. He's a wonderful man that I've recently reconnected with (we actually first met in high school) and well... last night he proposed to me.

"WHAT!" I yelled at the computer, my headache made worse.

*I know you must be shocked but I'm so happy, I hope
you can be happy for me too. Anyway, I just thought
I should let you know before you meet him, which will
be soon.*

*We are leaving for Paris in the next few hours for a
couple of weeks, and then we plan to stay in England
for a week. I'll contact you when we arrive in London,
and we can make arrangements to meet.*

Take care and see you soon.

Love,

Mom

I stared at the screen in complete and utter disbelief. My mother, engaged to be married, and she was coming to England! I didn't know which was more shocking. I buried my face in my hands and cried.

Twenty-Six

It was still dark out when I opened my eyes, my body and mind were well rested for the second time in as many days. It had been a long time since sound sleep was able to grab hold of my consciousness and send me into a dreamless state. Closing my eyes at night and then suddenly waking up completely rested, it was wonderful. Yet, I found myself wondering when it would all end.

I rose from bed and headed to the kitchen, my excitement was already beginning to build as Aaron would be arriving shortly to take me on my first sightseeing trip.

As my coffee brewed, I stared at the sky through the window and watched as it lightened with yellow, pink, and purple hues. A tremendous feeling of peace fell over me.

Two days ago, I had spent an entire day in front of a computer researching until my eyes had grown blurry, wasting my time and energy with very little to show for it. What little information I had gleaned about Mary and her family would have to suffice. There seemed to be no reason for knowing about my past life. Though it felt to me like Mary, who seemingly lived in my subconscious, was happy with my acceptance of her.

With my coffee in one hand and a muffin in the other, I made my way to the living room and sat on the couch. I was tempted to turn on the television, but quickly shook the thought from my head. I had had enough of technology, especially the computer. I looked over at the desk; my blue sweater still covered the monitor, tossed over it in frustration days before. The computer sat in silence, and for now it would remain in that state.

With breakfast over and nothing else to do but sit and wait, I made my way back to the bedroom and dressed. Though it was still early, I did not intend to make a bad first impression by not being ready when Aaron arrived, especially since I wanted to talk about making some changes to my itinerary.

Once ready, I sat back in the living room and picked up my book to pass the time. Before long, there was a knock at the door, and it startled me.

I put my book down on the table and jumped up from the couch, heading toward the bedroom for a quick glance in the mirror, calling out toward the door as I passed. "Be there in a second."

Satisfied by my appearance, I returned to the front door and placed my hand on the knob, hesitating for a split second before taking a breath and opening the door. For some odd reason, I was nervous.

"Hi!" I pulled open the door with a friendly smile on my face, which quickly disappeared, replaced by my gaping mouth.

"Disappointed?" he asked, his red eyebrows rose accentuating the question.

"Peter! What are you doing here?"

"Well, it's nice to see you again, too," he said as he entered and headed to the living room. He made himself comfortable in the oversize chair and left me standing there staring after him. Our last encounter had ended in an awkward parting, and it was obvious that tension remained. I closed the door and made my way over to him.

"I'm sorry..." I started, finding a place on the couch. "I didn't mean to sound disappointed. I'm just surprised that you're here. Did something happen to Aaron's mother?" I asked, not hiding the concern from my voice.

"She's fine. Still alive if that's what you mean." Peter's tone sounded a little cold to me, but under the circumstances, I understood. He'd shown me that he had feelings for me, and I hadn't exactly responded the way I'm sure he had wanted.

"Then why isn't he here?" I was feeling annoyed and beginning to doubt there was even a problem. I wondered if Peter was just trying to spend more time with me.

"He's sick."

"Sick!"

"Food poisoning or something. Anyway, he called me last night to explain and asked if I could find a replacement, so I rearranged my schedule." I must have worn an expression of distrust for he put up his hand. "I assure you I have nothing untoward planned, I promise to be completely professional and on my best behaviour."

I felt the need to settle things before we went anywhere. "Listen, about the other day, I really didn't mean to upset –"

Peter waved his hand interrupting my apology. "No need for you to apologize. I'm the one who acted inappropriately. Let's forget about it, alright?" He smiled, his blue eyes reflecting warmth.

I smiled back and nodded. "Okay. Friends?" I asked.

"Friends," he agreed. "Ready to go?" Peter rose from the chair and walked toward the door.

"Yup, just got to get my pack." I reached down and grabbed the small backpack sitting near the door, slinging it over my shoulder, and keeping the idea of changing plans to myself. I would enjoy whatever was in store for me.

As we headed toward Peter's car, I followed closely behind, suddenly remembering I had to get in on the other side, not before, of course, following him to the driver's side. We both laughed at my mistake.

"You'll get it by the end of the day," Peter said as I climbed into the passenger side.

We drove out of town, the streets only just beginning to show signs of life. We drove in silence, awkwardness still polluting the air, despite the apologies and the promise of friendship. I was resolute to put it all behind me, and the only way I knew how to do that was to start over. A new beginning meant pretending as though Peter and I just met and forgetting what we'd shared, erasing his kiss and the unease that followed, and overlooking Aaron's failure to show up – yet again.

"Where are we going anyway?" I asked, breaking the silence and pulling my gaze away from the window long enough to look at him while he answered.

"To Portsmouth, it's about 2 hours south from here." Peter looked briefly in my direction – it was a start.

"Oh! What's in Portsmouth?"

"You'll just have to wait until we get there." He looked at me and smiled.

Somehow, his smile melted away any remaining discomfort, and I knew then that I could push our little misunderstanding to the back of my mind and forget about it.

The two-hour drive went quickly with Peter explaining the sites as we drove, and in no time, we arrived in Portsmouth. Peter pulled into a parking spot alongside a park and handed me a list.

"What's this?" I asked taking it from his hand.

"That is a list of all the attractions and places to see here in Portsmouth. We can go to whatever spot catches your eye."

I flipped through the extensive list; so many places grabbed my attention. Finally after several minutes, I made some decisions and chose a number of attractions. Peter examined my choices and using his GPS plotted out the most practical routes to get to each of the attractions. It was decided we would get at least two destinations in just before noon and then we would decide on where to go next. By the time 11:30 rolled around, we had finished the second attraction of the day and made our way back to the car.

"Well, where do we go next – lunch?" My stomach rumbled, answering my own question.

"Do you think you could hold on for another couple of hours or so?" Peter asked.

"I guess so. Why?"

"There is somewhere I'd like to take you, but it will take some time to get there, then we can stop for lunch."

I was slightly disappointed, not having seen as much of Portsmouth as I'd wanted. Peter seemed to read my mind; my face always gave my thoughts away.

"Don't worry, we're not leaving quite yet, in fact we're just going on a bit further south. We'll have more time to explore later this afternoon."

I nodded as we headed toward the car. This time I remembered to get in on the left side.

"You're learning," Peter said with a laugh.

We drove south for a few minutes and came to the end of the road – literally.

"We're taking a ferry?" I tried keeping my voice steady.

"Yes, we're going to the Isle of Wight, there's a... "

My head swam as he said Isle of Wight everything else he said after that was lost.

"Are you alright?" Peter stared at me with a look of concern.

I didn't want him to know what I had discovered about myself, especially since he had already told me he didn't believe in the possibility of having a past life.

I wiped my sweaty palms on my shorts, pretending to smooth them out and forced a smile.

"Yeah, sure!" I didn't sound convincing even to myself.

"Are you sure? We don't have to go."

"No, I want to." I needed to get over my fear of boats and water and the best way to do that was to face them head on. Maybe that's why Mary had revealed herself to me. I could tell by the look on Peter's face that he didn't believe me, so with every bit of courage I could find, I steadied my voice and smiled as convincingly as possible. "Yes, I'm sure. It will be fun. It's been a long time since I've been on a ferry." My fists clenched as I dug my nails into the palms of my hands. The smile on my face didn't waver, and it must have worked because the next thing I knew we were embarking onto the ferry where an attendant directed us to a spot and we parked.

"Let's go." Peter said to me as he opened his car door.

"What!"

"Well, it's about a forty minute ride. You can't spend the trip in the car."

I thought about that for a minute. If the ferry were to sink, the last place I wanted to be was inside a car. I exited quickly and followed Peter.

Finally after some time, we climbed back into the car and began to disembark. As we slowly made our way off the ferry, I felt my shoulders begin to relax.

"You're looking a bit better," Peter said as we rolled off the ferry.

"What?" I was busy concentrating on relaxing.

"You looked a bit peaked. Were you feeling seasick?

"No."

"Don't much care for boats then?"

"No." I stared out the window, hoping Peter would get the hint from my one-word answers. He did.

We drove silently for another forty-five minutes while I recovered from the ferryboat ride. My body relaxed and I was content that Peter had given up on finding out what the matter was. Finally, he parked the car.

"Where are we?" I asked. Looking out the window, the ocean stretched out in front of us in the distance.

"We're going to visit a lighthouse. Now, I'm sure you've seen one before, but this one is particularly beautiful, and the walk is breathtaking."

"Walk?" I asked, spotting the lighthouse.

"Yes, well there is no access to the lighthouse by car, so we have to walk. Are you all right with that?" Peter looked at me with a discerning eye. I supposed my apparent seasickness made him question my health.

"Yes, perfectly fine." My stomach rumbled noisily.

"It's also a great place for a picnic." Peter walked around to the back of his car and opened the trunk. He pulled out a soft cooler, and slung it over his shoulder.

"Ready?" he asked closing the trunk. He looked down at my feet. I was wearing sandals. "Ah, those might be a problem," he said.

"Don't worry, I always come prepared." I set my pack on the ground, rummaged through it and pulled out a pair of running shoes. Once on my feet, I returned my sandals to my pack and sealed it up. "Okay, let's go." I flung my pack over my shoulder and waited for Peter to take the lead.

Peter was right, the walk wasn't too long and the views were stunning. When we arrived nearer to the lighthouse, he stopped and set the cooler on the ground.

"How about we get a bite to eat first, and then we'll visit the lighthouse."

I was quite happy to agree to his plan, so we sat on the cool grass and enjoyed our picnic lunch.

When we were done, I leaned back and placed my hands behind me for support as I tilted my face toward the warm sun. A flash from a dream – memory – of Mary doing the same thing crossed my mind, flickered, and was gone.

"You do think of everything, don't you?" I asked.

"I try," he said. I could tell by the sound of his voice that he was smiling.

We lingered for a few minutes more enjoying the sounds of the waves on the shore and the gulls in the sky, before walking over to the lighthouse.

"Do you think we can go out on to the deck?" I whispered to Peter as our lighthouse guide was explaining the mechanisms of the light to our tour group.

"I hardly think so," Peter whispered back. "I don't think it's meant for visitors."

"Well, can you ask? It's not like you don't know the guy." Peter seemed to know just about everyone we ever encountered.

"Fine, but only after these other people leave." He sounded exasperated.

We patiently waited and listened to our guide for a few minutes longer. Finally, it was time for us to leave the tower, but Peter and I hung back as the other couple made their way down the stairs.

"Hey mate," Peter said, clapping the lighthouse guide on the shoulder. "Do you think it'd be alright for us to go out on the deck? She'd like to snap a photo." He pointed at me.

I smiled and held up the camera clutched in my hand.

"Well. . . " our guide, I never did catch his name, hesitated, "it's not really allowed, but I suppose. . . so long as you're careful and not out there long. I'll go down and keep the other two distracted for a bit, but be quick about it."

"Sure thing," Peter said, grinning widely.

We followed our guide down the first bit of winding stair and then as he continued down the rest, Peter and I snuck out across the catwalk to the door that would lead us out onto the deck at the back of the tower. The salt air hit me as soon as we opened the door, and we carefully made our way to the front of the deck overlooking the ocean. I looked down at the ground below, immediately getting a little dizzy. I stepped back and pressed up against the tower.

"Are you alright?" Peter asked gently laying his hand on my shoulder.

"Yeah, just higher than I thought; here you'll have to take the picture." I handed him my camera.

"What exactly am I taking a photo of?" he asked taking the camera from my hands.

"Just the view out there." I pointed to the ocean ahead of us. I couldn't possibly tell him the reason, I wasn't even sure myself, it was just a need.

"Just straight out there?"

"Yes, please."

"Right then," he said, turning away from me.

A gust of warm air charged into me – pushing me back up against the lighthouse. It felt as though something slammed me hard and knocked the breath from my lungs. The salt air stung, and I closed my eyes for a moment. My head began to swim, and I felt myself sway. The sounds of the ocean and seabirds mixed into an ear-piercing din, and my hands instinctively covered my ears. All the while I leaned back against the tower, steadying myself. Just as quickly as the wind and noise appeared, it disappeared, leaving nothing but my confusion in its wake.

"There, I hope this is what you're looking for." Peter turned toward me. "What's the matter?" he placed both his hands on my shoulders and stared into my still tearing eyes. I sensed his alarm as the look of horror I must have worn on my face registered in his own.

"I – I..." I stammered. "Did you not see that – hear that?" I looked at him, not believing my own ears or eyes.

"What?" He turned around and searched the horizon.

My senses fooled once again by ghostly memories, as I was the only witness to whatever oddity had occurred. "Nothing, I guess I was still a little bit dizzy from looking over the edge. We better get out of here before that friend of yours comes looking for us." I forced a smile, took the camera's strap off his wrist, and turned to leave.

"Wait!" he said, grabbing my arm.

I stopped, not wanting him to ask me any questions about what had happened, or supposedly did. I wouldn't know how to answer him anyway.

"Is the picture I took alright?"

"What?" I asked taken aback, he seemed already to have forgotten about it.

"The picture, is it alright? You'd better check before we leave."

"Yeah, sure." Taking out my camera, I looked for the picture he'd taken. It was hard to see outside and at that point, I didn't much care anymore. "Yeah, it's fine. Let's just go, okay?" Again, I forced another smile.

"To the mainland?" he asked, as we headed into the tower of the lighthouse.

"Back home," I said as we made our way down the tower stairs.

I slept deeply the entire, uneventful, ride for it wasn't long before Peter was waking me up to inform me that I was home. I turned to get my pack from the backseat when Peter touched my arm.

"I'll get it," he said; the look of worry on his face kept me from arguing.

I led the way up the stairs and into the apartment. Peter followed me into the kitchen and put my pack down on the table.

"Thanks for the great day," I said smiling, that time it wasn't forced, I genuinely enjoyed myself, despite that one event.

"Just doing my job," he informed me.

"Yeah, well it was nice spending the day with a friend."

He blushed. "Friend, huh? I'm sure I can handle that. I should go." He turned to leave and I followed. As he reached the door, he faced me again, a look of worry still on his face.

"Get yourself something to eat and then to bed. I think you might be coming down with something." He leaned over and gave me a quick peck on the cheek. It was my turn to blush.

"Thanks again," I said as Peter left closing the door behind him.

The last thing on my mind was eating, and I quickly headed back into the kitchen to search my pack for my camera. The bright sun had made it difficult to see the picture Peter had taken but not so difficult to make out what I was sure I had seen, but when I looked again, there was nothing but a picture of the ocean. Maybe it was just my mind playing tricks on me, but I was certain there had been a ship on the horizon, and not just any ship but the Ocean Queen.

Twenty-Seven

The sun had set when Peter left Krista, but instead of driving home, he headed in the opposite direction toward Tockington. He needed to speak with Aaron in person.

When he finally arrived at his friend's home, he sat in the car collecting his thoughts. He didn't know what he was going to tell him and though he'd had over an hour to work it out, nothing suitable came to mind. A rap on the car window startled him. Peter opened the door and got out.

"You scared the crap out of me, brother," Peter said, lightly punching Aaron in the arm.

Aaron laughed. "I know, you should have seen yourself jump. I thought it was rather brilliant myself."

"You would. Feeling better then?" Peter asked remembering his friend's illness.

"Yeah, I think I ate something that didn't agree with me. What are you doing here anyway? I thought by now you'd be on your way home or at the very least trying to romance Krista again," Aaron teased.

"Yeah, well that ship has sailed. She and I have agreed to be friends, and frankly, I'm glad for it." Peter knew the news would stun Aaron as last time he'd talked to him about Krista, he was quite smitten with her and hadn't hidden his feelings.

Aaron cocked his head. "What happened?" he asked as he pointed towards the stone bench where they both took a seat.

"Well, I'm not quite sure," Peter began. "There's something a bit – odd."

"Odd?"

"Yeah, I know – just your type, right?" Peter quipped.

"She sounded quite normal to me when we spoke."

"It's just that... Look, I promised not to say anything, but well, she sort of has this whole past life issue she's struggling with."

Aaron furrowed his brow.

"I know what you're thinking," Peter said. "I accidentally read her journal and –"

"You accidentally read her journal?" There was no mistaking the sound of dismay in Aaron's voice.

"It's not what you think. I was reading the notebook your aunt left her, but Krista has apparently turned it into her journal. When I realized what I was reading, I couldn't pull my eyes away. Anyway, after the first few pages, I came to my senses and set the notebook down."

"But..." Aaron prodded.

Peter took a deep breath. He was disappointed in himself for breaking his promise to Krista, yet he needed to speak to someone about what he'd witnessed.

"She knew I'd read some of it and started explaining, then asked me to finish reading it – I shouldn't have, but I did. I told her I didn't believe in that sort of stuff, so we dropped it." There was a moment of silence before Peter continued to profess what had occurred between him and Krista. "I wound up telling her that you sort of believed in that stuff – sorry mate."

"Oh."

Peter sensed Aaron's aggravation. Unlike Peter, Aaron had always been a very private person, and the only one he confided in was his family or Peter. He wondered now if his friend would ever confide in him again. Peter quickly tried to resolve it. "Don't worry Aaron, I told her I wouldn't speak to you about it. She won't mention it to you."

"So why are you telling me this now?"

"It's just... I thought she was seasick on the ferry ride to the Isle of Wight. Then at the lighthouse, she said she was dizzy and wanted me to snap a photo... I think she saw something. Something frightened her, but she wouldn't tell me what, though it was obvious by the look on her face. But that's not the creepy part; it was on the ride back home." Memories from the drive home filtered through Peter's mind.

"What do you mean by creepy?"

Now that the words were out of Peter's mouth, he wasn't exactly sure how he was going to explain what had happened. "She slept in the car the whole drive home."

"What's so creepy about that?" Aaron asked.

"It's not the sleeping that was creepy, it's the conversation she was having whilst she slept that was creepy. I mean, I couldn't get her home fast enough. I'm likely to have nightmares about the whole thing."

"I'm sure it was nothing. She just talks in her sleep," Aaron said reassuringly.

Peter only wished Aaron was right, but he hadn't been there. Peter knew what he'd heard – what he'd seen.

"This wasn't your ordinary mumbling in your sleep. This was clearly a conversation between two people."

"Maybe she was just excited."

"No!" Peter shook his head emphatically. "It was like listening to a telephone conversation between Krista and someone else. She mentioned seeing a ship on the horizon and that it frightened her. There was no ship, yet she looked absolutely ghastly when I handed back her camera."

"Look, she was obviously just dreaming," Aaron said, sounding a little frustrated.

Peter thought how funny it was for Aaron, who claimed to believe in some of the things Krista had spoken about, to be so quick in finding a logical explanation. That job belonged to Peter.

"Well, she sounded pretty convinced about the ship, so I had to take a look."

"Look at what?" Aaron's frustration was growing.

"When we stopped for petrol, Krista was still asleep. So I went through her pack to get her camera."

Aaron rolled his eyes and covered his face with his hands as though trying to rub frustration away. "Ah!" he muttered disappointedly.

Peter held up his hand to stop Aaron from saying anything further before he finished. "I found the photo and of course, there was no ship. However, I must have snapped another photo by accident when I'd turned around to give her back the camera." Peter looked away for a moment, recalling the event. He struggled as he tried to think of the best way to explain. "It was a photo of Krista's face, only her eyes. . . " Peter hesitated, the memory of that picture still clearly in his mind.

"What about her eyes?" Aaron demanded as his frustration mounted.

"They were most definitely brown."

Complete confusion registered on Aaron's face as he listened to Peter's ramblings.

Peter sighed, "Krista's eyes are green."

Twenty-Eight

It wasn't necessary to look at the time when my eyes fluttered open, I knew it would be the same time as it had been every morning for the past several days. And just like every morning, I rose from my bed and padded out to the kitchen waiting to catch the first glimpse of daylight spread across the sky as the sun crested over the horizon.

I had never felt more alive – more at ease – more at home. However, that morning, dark clouds greeted me as I looked out, and instead of cheery streaks of light, streams of rain burst forth and beat against the window. Coffee in the garden was definitely out of the question, thus I resolved to take it in the living room.

Sitting silently, I watched the rain come down as I sipped my coffee; feeling the warmth spread through me. After some time, I turned on the TV and searched for the latest weather report. To my satisfaction, the rain was to end by mid-morning, giving me hope that my intentions for the day would go as planned. In the meantime, while the rain kept up its steady pace, I decided that it was time to lift the ban on technology.

I removed my sweater from the monitor and turned on the power, waking the computer up from its weeklong slumber. My first plan of attack was my very full inbox, in view of that I flagged the e-mails that needed answering.

At first consideration, I planned sending out the same general message to everyone on my list but thought against it, opting for a more personal touch. Finally, after responding to several e-mails, there was only one more to deal with, that one being from Aaron. It had been sent almost a week earlier and was yet another apology explaining his sudden illness and that he wouldn't be taking me on our outing. I laughed at myself, had I read that last Thursday it wouldn't have been a surprise when Peter showed up at my door.

When ten-thirty rolled around, the rain had all but stopped, and I spotted a beautiful rainbow crossing the sky as the sun burst through the clouds. Quickly, I headed to my room.

By the time I was showered and dressed, most of the clouds were gone and the sky looked promising. I headed out the door, grabbing my umbrella as an afterthought and tucked it into my purse.

The walk into town was refreshing, and the light from the sun glinted off the raindrops which stuck to the leaves on the plants and trees. I felt like a child and had to control the urge to jump into puddles I encountered on the way.

I met few people, but to those I encountered, my greeting was heartfelt with a smile and a jovial 'good morning' or 'it's turned out to be a lovely day, hasn't it?' It was as if with each passing day, I belonged in Bourton and was no longer just a visitor. In fact, the mere thought of leaving was depressing, so I pushed those thoughts to the farthest corners of my mind, resolving to deal with them when the time came. For now, I was content pretending that Bourton truly was my home.

I returned home later that afternoon, completely sated with food, drink, laughter and my purchases. So much so, that I decided a late afternoon nap was not completely out of the question.

After gently tossing the bags with my latest purchases on my bed, I returned to the living room and plunked down on the couch – weary from my day's adventures, but elated. My bare feet tingled as I propped them up on the coffee table, and then I leaned back against the couch closing my eyes. Within minutes, I was sound asleep.

"You have to find him," she whispered.

"Who?" I didn't understand what she meant.

"Him, of course." She showed me his picture drawn from her memories – my dreams.

"How? No – it has been too long. It's not possible."

"Yes, it is. He's in here," she said at the same time as I raised my hand and covered my heart. "What's that?" She sounded startled.

I looked around trying to find what she was talking about, yet only whiteness greeted my eyes.

"What?" I asked her.

"Are those bells?" she whispered.

"Bells?"

"There's ringing, I hear bells."

I listened carefully, and then I heard them, too. They sounded so far away at first, but then the sound moved closer and closer.

My eyes fluttered open, and it took a moment for them to focus on my surroundings. I grabbed the cordless phone that was lying on the coffee table in front of me, surprised that it worked, as it hadn't been in its cradle since the night before.

"Hello!" My voice was gravely; I cleared my throat. "Hello!"

"Hello, Krista?"

"Yeah."

"Have I woken you? I'm so sorry."

It took a second for me to place his voice and then it registered. "Oh! Hi Aaron." I knew I sounded standoffish, but I really didn't care.

Either Aaron didn't catch the aloofness in my voice or he ignored it, either way he began asking me question after question on how I'd been enjoying my stay.

"It's been great!" I couldn't hide my enthusiasm.

"Glad to hear it. So are you ready to head out tomorrow?" He sounded eager.

"Tomorrow?" I tried to remember the itinerary he'd planned, but every day seemed to have melted into the next since I'd arrived.

"I know the plan was to pick you up on Friday, but I happen to be free tomorrow, and I thought a day earlier would be better, besides..." he sounded sheepish, "I've got to try and make up for all my absences."

"Okay sure, tomorrow is fine. Should I bring a small bag for the day or..." My voice trailed off, I really wasn't sure where we were going.

"You can't see London in a day; you better pack for the weekend."

Now I remembered it was the weekend in London, I didn't know how I could have forgotten. "Right, London – I forgot."

"No worries. You don't have any other plans do you?" Aaron asked suddenly sounding concerned.

"No, of course not. I knew I was doing something this weekend and was planning to check my itinerary later," I lied. I did forget all about it and as for that itinerary; my eyes hadn't seen it since I'd unpacked my suitcase.

Beep! The cordless phone reminded me it was running out of battery power.

"Sorry, Aaron, but the phone I'm on is starting to die. Was there anything else?"

"No. Just pack for the weekend, and I'll get you bright and early in the morning say around six-thirty or is that too early?"

I smiled to myself. By six-thirty, I would be more than ready.

Beep!

"No, that's fine. I'll be ready."

"Good."

"Ah Aaron?"

Beep!

"Yes?"

"It will be you picking me up this time, right?" I almost hesitated in asking but I had a right to know.

Beep!

"Yes, of course, unless –"

"Aaron?"

I placed the now dead cordless phone back in its cradle and leaned back against the couch closing my eyes. It was then that my mind began to recall the dream I'd experienced before Aaron called. I wasn't sure what it meant, if anything at all. One thing was certain, there was a part of my soul that I shared with Mary and because we were connected, she shared her memories with me freely, no longer dreaming of her past, instead our memories intertwined. I began to understand what she desired more than any one thing, and it was the same for me, too.

The search was on, but with whom or where we would find that connection seemed so far out of reach. For now, we – it was hard for me to think of myself without having her be a part of me – would be happy in knowing that we would work together to find our soulmate.

Twenty-Nine

It had been a long night, and not because dreams interfered with my sleep, but because the excitement of spending the weekend in London roused me every couple of hours. Every time my eyes popped open and looked at the clock, disappointment followed. There was still plenty of time for sleep.

Finally, by four-thirty, I climbed out of bed, tired of waiting. However, instead of heading out to the kitchen for my ritualistic cup of coffee, I headed into the bathroom and took a hot and longer-than-usual shower. There was plenty of time to waste since I'd packed my bag the night before.

I stepped out from the shower stall, allowing the steam to billow out behind me, as apprehension began to build. Though I had grown used to seeing a different and distorted reflection of myself, it was still unnerving. Slowly, I made my way toward the steamed over mirror knowing that the moment it was wiped clear, my own recognizable image would materialize. However, I had a different plan in mind. My curiosity had taken over, and somehow I found the courage to take a moment and study the reflection, leaning merely inches away from brushing the tip of my nose against it.

The face that stared back was undoubtedly mine, but the eyes and the hair were brown. I picked up the hand-towel resting on the vanity and slowly wiped the steam from the mirror, erasing the reflection that was not me. With each stroke, my own image became clearer until the only steam that remained was where the eyes reflected back. Carefully, I removed the remaining steam, first from the reflection of one eye and then the other. Like magic, my eyes went from brown to green.

By six o'clock, I was fully prepared and waiting for Aaron's arrival, though part of me was skeptical that he'd actually show up. In any case, the excursion to London was exciting. I had mixed feelings though about finally meeting Aaron. In one way, part of me hoped Peter would show up instead, after all, we had become friends. Yet if Aaron didn't show, my frustration with him was sure to grow, and if that should happen, I didn't think I would want to meet him at all.

At six-fifteen, I locked the door behind me and carried my bag down the stairs, deciding to wait outside, as my eagerness got the best of me and made me feel like a small child on her way to Disney World.

Using my small suitcase as a bench, I plunked myself down, imagining what the weekend would be like, what we would see and do.

It wasn't long before an all too familiar blue car made its way down the street and pulled into the drive, there was utter disbelief in what I was seeing.

Irritated, I jumped up from my perch and headed toward the driver's side, ready to take my frustration out on Peter. The door suddenly swung open, and I had to jump back to avoid an unwelcome collision.

"Sorry," he said. "I didn't get you, did I?"

I looked at the tall, handsome man standing in front of me, looking me up and down for any signs of injury. At least that's what it looked like he was doing, the dark sunglasses he was wearing prevented me from seeing just exactly where his eyes were focused.

"No, I'm fine, quick reflexes." I smiled awkwardly.

"That's good to know. I'm Aaron." He thrust his hand out towards me.

"Hi Aaron," I said a bit too enthusiastically as I pumped his arm up and down. My hand disappeared into his and a strange, yet comforting warmth enveloped it. Though having never conjured an image of him in my mind, he certainly didn't come close to anything I could have imagined. For instance, he was quite tall, towering over me a good eight inches, with an athletic build and thick, dark, brown hair. His eyes, however remained unseen, protected by his dark sunglasses, though I imagined they would be nothing less than spectacular. He certainly was an impressive sight. "Well, let's go!" I said with so much zeal that I made a mental note reminding myself to take it down a notch – or five. I headed around to the passenger side.

"Ah, forgetting something?" Aaron asked, pointing his finger toward my bag, which had toppled over when I jumped up from it.

"Oh!" I laughed. "I guess I'm just a little bit excited."

"Don't worry, I'll get it." It took him only a couple of strides before he reached my bag. He picked it up and brought it back to the car, tossing it in the trunk he'd opened with the key fob. I felt a little guilty watching him, but he moved so fast that I didn't even get the chance to do it myself.

"Thank you!" I said as we climbed into the car. Plenty of questions ran through my mind as we pulled out of the drive, but I kept them to myself for the time being. My actions already seemed a little over the top and I wanted to show him that I really wasn't always so excitable. I patiently waited for him to speak first.

"So, are you excited about going to London?"

I took a moment before answering, slowing my heart rate and my breathing, wanting him to see a calmer side of me. "Yes, very. Couldn't you tell?" I made fun of myself.

He smiled as he turned his attention toward me. My heart skipped, and I silently scolded myself. I was on a mission with

Mary and couldn't allow myself to become distracted by every good looking guy that happened to smile at me.

"Not at all," he said.

I laughed nervously, though I'd begun to feel a bit more like myself and not like some pre-pubescent girl.

We fell silent for a moment, and it brought me back to the first time I'd met Peter and our seemingly awkward trip from the airport to Bourton, I hoped that the trip to London wasn't going to be the same.

"I'm sorry I –"

"Why are you driving –" We both spoke at the same time and started laughing.

"Go ahead, you first," Aaron said.

"I was just going to ask you why you are driving Peter's car."

"Well, that's a bit of a tale. When I woke up this morning my car was gone."

"Gone?"

"Yes; nicked, pinched, purloined. . . "

I stared at him blankly.

"Stolen," he said, chuckling.

"Sorry, I'm still getting used to some of the –" I paused, "well, for lack of better words; terminology."

"Right," he said, nodding. "Needless to say, Peter wasn't quite thrilled about having to bring me his car at such an ungodly hour."

"No doubt." I laughed, imagining Peter's reaction.

"Anyhow, after having stood you up twice already, I couldn't possibly do it a third time. I asked him to stay behind and report it to the police." He shrugged.

"I'm sorry, but I would have understood."

Aaron looked at me incredulously. "Would you?"

I laughed. "Probably not, but then I guess I would have thought that we just weren't destined to meet."

"Do you believe in that?" Aaron asked in all seriousness, almost a little too serious for our first meeting.

"Yeah. . . " I hesitated, "I think so." We drove on silently for a moment, while I contemplated the idea of destiny. I wasn't so sure that all outcomes of choices made were predetermined; after all, there was free will to consider. Would my choices eventually lead me down the path that the greater power – the universe – had in store for me? There definitely could be a wrong turn along the way, a distraction that might prolong the eventual result. I might even go as far as to ignore the signs – still if it was meant to be. . . But, if I ignored my dreams, the strange occurrences, what then? Would they eventually go away or get worse, eventually forcing me to do something? Would the higher power give up? I shook my head. My thoughts were too much and they didn't matter, I'd already made my decision. "What were you going to say?" I asked, remembering he'd started to say something earlier.

The muscles in his arm flexed as he turned the wheel. I began to imagine what those arms would feel like wrapped around me. Stop it! I silently reminded myself.

"When?" he questioned back, turning to look at me briefly.

"Back there," I said pointing behind me, "when we both spoke at the same time."

"Ah! I was going to apologize for causing you frustration when I showed up with Peter's car."

"What makes you think I was frustrated?"

Aaron looked at me and smiled again. "It was written all over your face."

"Am I that transparent?" I asked, knowing the answer to the question. My emotions were easily discernible; anyone who looked at me instantly knew what I was feeling. It was just the reason why I wasn't very good at lying or making up excuses.

Aaron shrugged. "Maybe just a wee bit," he said demonstrating with his thumb and index finger as he pinched them together.

I suddenly felt the need to ask Aaron about his mother but quelled the urge, afraid he'd think it intrusive. After all, we'd just met – in person anyway. Strangely though, it felt like I already knew him. Maybe it was the phone conversations, the e-mails, his hand-written letter, and of course, Peter, who spoke of Aaron quite a bit. In any case, this was a business relationship, even so it felt like we could also be friends, I didn't want to jeopardize my vacation plans by injecting myself into his personal life. Instead, I asked him questions about London and his plans for my visit, most of which he gladly expanded on. Some plans, however, were vague and I wasn't sure if that was intentional and meant as a surprise or reserved for last minute, spontaneous sort of side trips. By the time we'd reached London, I had begun to wonder if we'd ever run out of things to say to each other.

"If you don't mind, I need to stop by my office for a moment, it shouldn't take long; traffic doesn't actually look too heavy." Aaron smiled as we drove through one of the many districts of London.

I was too busy staring out the window taking in the sights to look at him. "Sure, not a problem." It didn't matter where we were going. He could have taken me to the most boring place in town, and it still would have been interesting.

"My office is just across the street." Aaron pointed to a building, which seemed to house a number of different businesses. "I don't normally drive in to work, so we might have to ride around a bit for a spot." After a few moments, we luckily found a nearby parking spot, exited the car, and made our way across the street to his workplace.

"Aaron, it's so good to see you. When did you get back?" asked a beautiful, blonde-haired woman seated at one of two desks placed on either side of the large foyer and sitting area. She looked close to my age and a grin stretched across her face as she stared at him; her eyes twinkled. There was no doubt in my mind she was infatuated, particularly when her eyes left Aaron's face long enough to spot me following along behind. She immediately jumped up, making her way around her desk to stand directly in front of him. She wrapped her arms around Aaron, stood on tiptoe, and gave him a quick peck on the cheek. The show of affection upset me for a fleeting moment, but my reaction upset me more.

"Just last night." Aaron said, seemingly unfazed by her attention, and then he turned his focus back to me. "Krista this is Cat, she's been with us for just a little over a year. Isn't that right?"

Her smile was so broad that each one of her teeth was visible. As a result, she reminded me of a carved pumpkin with its wide grin. I feared that if she continued smiling in that manner, her face would freeze that way forever. The momentary vision brought a laugh to my lips that I stifled before it escaped. Fortunately, her hair wasn't red as that would have made it impossible to remain sober. I silently reprimanded myself.

"Absolutely!" Cat radiated bubbly to the nth degree, at least where Aaron was concerned. She turned her eyes from Aaron for a brief second, acknowledging me and extending her perfectly manicured hand. Her eyes gave me a quick once over. "Catriona." She held out her hand, her fake smile was more than obvious.

I took her hand in mine only to find she was one of those limp-handed shakers. Either she lacked confidence or she was feigning interest. Whichever, it was clear she didn't want to make my acquaintance, but I didn't care; I didn't like her either. Thankfully, there was no need for any small talk as Aaron whisked me away to his office with Catriona calling after him something about getting together for drinks sometime.

Aaron's office was at the end of a hall that housed four offices, two on one side and two on the other. Each office had glass front walls with blinds in varying degrees of openness. The doors of the first two offices, which faced across from each other, were wide open as well as the blinds, and their occupants sat at their desks busily scanning their computer screens. Each looked up briefly as we passed, calling out hello. We stopped in front of a door on the left side; Aaron searched his pockets, finally producing a set of keys.

"This should only take a moment," he reassured me as we entered.

I sat in one of the chairs in front of his desk as he went around to the other side and turned on his computer. The modern, black furniture stood out cold and harsh compared to the soft grey walls of the office, and the space lacked that personal touch seen in many workplaces. There were no pictures of family, trinkets, or any other artifacts, which would suggest he spent little time there. Even the walls were bare save for a few framed black and white travel posters. In fact, the room was quite stark and devoid of any real colour, except for a small rack of very colourful brochures that stood in the corner.

Aaron removed his sunglasses and placed them on the desk in front of him. All the while keeping his gaze averted from me as he looked through the files on his desk waiting for his computer to come to life.

"Sorry, I've been away and just need to check a few things." He kept his focus on his work.

I shrugged. "So, you just got back then?" I regretted the question the moment the words spilled from my mouth and hoped he didn't think I was prying.

"Yes, well with my mother being ill..." His voice trailed as he busied himself with his search. The tone of which alone was enough of a hint for me to drop the subject of his mother.

I shifted uncomfortably in my chair, noting the growing silence as Aaron worked away busily at his desk while I patiently watched. Part of me hoped he'd stop and look up at me while another was quite glad he didn't.

There was a light rap on the door, and I turned around to see a familiar face smiling at me.

"Hello, Krista, did you enjoy the drive?" Peter asked as he stood in the doorway.

"Yes, I did." I stood up and hugged him. It was comfortable, like old friends greeting each other. Whatever tension there had been between was gone. We pulled away from our embrace, and I looked back toward Aaron, completely oblivious by Peter's interruption and our embrace.

"Aaron, could I see you in my office for a second?"

Aaron held up a finger indicating he'd be there shortly, without another word to Aaron, Peter turned away, and headed to his own office across the hall.

Not wanting to sit and twiddle my thumbs, I grabbed some brochures from the rack to flip through while I waited.

"I'll be back in a moment, and then we'll get going."

I looked up briefly as Aaron headed out of the office and then turned my attention back to the article I had been reading.

"Ready to go?" Engrossed as I was in the travel magazine, I jumped slightly as Aaron's voice interrupted. The beat of my heart quickened for a moment, but just as quickly resumed its normal pace. Aaron stood in the doorway, ready to leave; his sunglasses already back on his face.

"Yup!" I jumped up and began replacing brochures and magazines back in the rack.

"You can keep those if you want."

"Oh, well maybe this magazine." I grabbed the travel magazine back from the rack and followed Aaron out the door.

"Have fun," Peter called from his desk.

I waved and followed Aaron out front.

"Have a good day, Aaron!" Catriona almost gushed as we walked past.

Aaron gestured goodbye and as I walked past, Catriona's smile turned to a sneer as she glared at me.

"What's with her?" I asked Aaron as we crossed the street.

"Who? Cat?" Aaron almost snickered as if I'd discovered some private secret.

"Ah Yeah! Didn't you see the look she gave me?"

"No, but I'm sure she meant it as a compliment."

"Compliment?" I barked, surprised by his aloofness.

We stopped at Peter's car and as I headed toward the passenger side, Aaron stood by the trunk and opened it. I noticed this time he used a key instead of the fob.

"Yes, compliment." He tried to assure me as he pulled my bag from the trunk and locked it again. I watched, confused.

"What are you doing?" My attention briefly diverted from the conversation.

"Peter picked up a hire car for me. It should be just... " Aaron stopped as he scanned the nearby parking lot for the rental. "Ah, there it is. Come on."

I followed him down past the row of cars to a dark grey one, slightly larger and definitely fancier than the one Peter drove. Aaron opened the trunk and put my bag in. Then he unlocked the doors, opening mine for me; I got in and waited for Aaron to climb in on the driver's side. "What do you mean by compliment?" I fastened my belt and watched as Aaron did the same, not wanting to drop the subject until I got an answer.

Aaron sighed, "I believe Cat feels threatened whenever she's in the presence of other beautiful women. So, take it as a compliment." With that, Aaron started the car and pulled out of the parking space, the conversation on that particular topic, apparently over. Not knowing how to respond, I sat quietly as we headed down the street.

"Where are we going?" I asked, finally breaking the silence.

"I've arranged for you to stay at a bed and breakfast that a friend of mine runs. Since we're a day early the first night is free of charge, and she's given you a very reasonable rate for the rest of the weekend. Though, I'm sure it will cost me something." Aaron laughed as we made a right turn.

It wasn't long before we pulled up in front of a large, old home turned into a bed and breakfast. The exterior of which was so stunning I could only imagine an equally beautiful interior. Excited by the prospects of staying in such a place, I got out of the car as soon as Aaron had parked it and started heading up the walk.

"Aren't you eager?" He called out. I turned to find him staring after me. He was still standing by the car and flashing a wide grin.

I laughed, "I guess so. Sorry!" I headed back toward the car realizing I hadn't even retrieved my bag.

"I'll carry your bag." Aaron said as he pulled it from the car.

"That's okay." I reached over and took the bag from his hand.

"Suit yourself." Aaron led the way up the walk and rang the bell. A dark haired woman somewhere in her early thirties opened the door, a small child resting on her hip. The smell of freshly baked goods wafted out the door.

"Hello, Aaron, come in." She smiled at him, stepping back to let us into the large, bright foyer of her home.

"Hello, Anne." Aaron leaned forward and kissed the woman on the cheek. "Hello, sweetheart," he said as he patted the small child on the back. The child, who was no more than two, grinned in response.

I was glad Aaron had his back to me as a sudden surge of what felt like jealousy, coursed through my body. I quickly shook it off, again perturbed with myself.

"Anne, this is Krista." Aaron turned and introduced me to the woman.

"Hello, Krista." She smiled genuinely. "It's so nice to meet you. I must apologize, I'm sure I look a complete mess," she said as she pushed a lock of brown hair off her forehead.

I couldn't help but think that if she thought she looked a mess that I must look absolutely disastrous. She was very much put together even with a child on her hip. Her hair couldn't have looked more perfect albeit for the stray piece she'd tucked back behind her ear. She was well dressed and wore little make-up; she was a natural beauty. Though I tried to look fashionable and up-to-date, I had nothing on her.

"I just pulled a pie out of the oven when Christina here woke from her nap. It's been a bit hectic this morning." She leaned over and kissed the top of her daughter's head.

"Don't worry," I said reassuringly. "You look absolutely fine and the pie smells delicious."

"Sorry ladies, I have to take this." Aaron pulled a vibrating cell phone from his pocket and stepped outside, his sunglasses still glued to his face. I began wondering if he would ever take them off long enough for me to see his eyes. Why that was so important to me I couldn't guess, though I suspected it had something to do with Mary.

"Come, I'll show you to your room and give you a quick tour of the place."

I followed Anne as she turned and headed toward the grand staircase in the centre of the foyer. By the time we'd returned from our tour, Aaron had stepped back into the house.

"Is everything alright?" Anne asked him.

"Yes, fine." I saw something flash between Aaron and Anne that I didn't quite understand. Once again, I had to push down a jealousy that made absolutely no sense.

"You sure?" Anne pressed.

"Well, it seems my car has been found, but unfortunately, not in the same condition as it was taken."

"Oh yes! Peter told me your car was stolen."

"I'm sure he also told you about my waking him early this morning?" Aaron asked Anne.

"Of course!" Anne nodded. "He had breakfast with us this morning."

"You know Peter?" I blurted, immediately feeling stupid for asking such a question. Of course, she knew Peter, they were all friends.

"Peter's my brother," Anne clarified.

"He is?" I asked searching Aaron's face for confirmation but his sunglasses got in the way, so I looked back at Anne taking in her dark hair and still finding it hard to believe that she and Peter were siblings.

"Truly," she said touching her hair. "My mother was a brunette, but in the sunlight you can definitely see a hint of red. Now, can you stay for lunch?" Anne asked, changing the subject and looking at both of us for an answer. "Or do you have somewhere pressing to be?"

"Is it that time already?" I asked disbelievingly; finally understanding the connection between Anne and Aaron.

"Not quite, it's only half past eleven."

I looked at Aaron, waiting for his cue, not sure what he'd planned on, but happy to do whatever he suggested.

"Sure, if it suits Krista." Aaron turned and put the onus on to me.

"Yes, of course, I'd love to stay; as long as it's no trouble."

Anne waved her hand. "It's settled then." She smiled at both of us. "My husband, Paul, will be joining us. You two make yourselves comfortable in the parlour."

"Are you sure I can't help?" I offered.

"Aren't you sweet? No, I have it all under control." Anne turned to Aaron. "Would you mind watching Christina for me?" she said placing the little girl into Aaron's outstretched arms.

"Of course, come here you wee thing." Aaron smiled widely at the little girl. Christina happily climbed into his arms and nestled her head into his shoulder.

If there was one trait I found endearing, it was a man who adored children, and it was obvious that Aaron was one who did.

"Oh, and Aaron, take off those sunglasses. You're starting to remind me of that bloke on that American crime show, and he drives me crazy." Anne implored and turned back toward the kitchen humming a tune I did not recognize.

Almost on cue, Christina pulled away from Aaron's neck and snatched the sunglasses from his face, knocking them to the floor. Instinctively, we both bent down to pick them up, but as my hands were free, I was quicker and scooped them up, placing them into his open hand.

"Thanks," Aaron laughed. "Silly monkey." He tickled the child gently, and she giggled infectiously as only a child can.

For the first time since we met, our eyes locked and the smile faded from my face.

"My love for you transcends death," echoed in my ears.

Thirty

By the time lunch was ready, I had spent an almost unbearable half-hour in the parlour. Fortunately, Christina had kept me occupied playing and entertaining her, and I pretended that she had my complete undivided attention especially whenever Aaron spoke to me. It was much easier keeping my gaze fixed on Christina than looking at him. Soon though, we would be spending the rest of the day together and though the thought of feigning illness did cross my mind, it was short-lived.

Lunch was no better as the distraction of others was barely enough to keep my mind engaged. Each time Aaron addressed me, it felt as though my soul was going to jump out of my body. I avoided eye contact whenever possible, though it's certain he knew something was wrong, he'd already admitted to noticing my transparency.

The moment finally came when I saw an opening for escape and excused myself, heading directly up to my room, I desperately needed some time alone before we headed out for the afternoon. If spending time together was ever going to work, I needed a plan.

"It can't be." I said incredulously. "How is it even possible?" I questioned myself, pacing back and forth at the end of the bed. "How is any of this possible?"

I threw my hands up in the air and tilted my head up toward the ceiling waiting for an answer before finally throwing myself face down on the bed, exasperated. My jumbled thoughts raced in my head, trying to work out some sort of solution. My subconscious, or at least that's what I assumed it was, screamed unintelligible words at me. Rolling on to my back, I covered my face with my hands and waited, quieting my mind, hoping the part of me that was Mary would tell me what to do, but there was nothing. Frustrated, I sat up.

"Krista, are you alright?" Anne's voice called through the door as she knocked somewhat anxiously.

My absence had been far too long, and apparently, a waste of time too, as there still was no plan. I took a deep breath, smiling at myself in the mirror across from where I sat. So, this is how it's going to be. Apparently, I was on my own and somehow I would have to pull off the best acting I'd ever done.

I shook my head. Nope it's not going to work. I sighed quietly and rose from the bed, stepping toward the door. I closed my eyes and took a deep breath before pulling open the door and looking into Anne's concerned face. "Hi! I just needed to go through my bag to uh..." What am I going to say? "You know –"

Anne smiled and nodded. "It never fails to arrive when you have plans, does it?"

Yes! I celebrated inwardly. I lied without actually saying anything; Anne came up with a pretense for me. If there was one thing a woman could put blame on and get away with pretty much anything she said, did, or felt; it was getting her period – the almost perfect excuse.

"You're right about that." I smiled and pulled the door closed behind me.

"So are you ready for your adventure?" Anne said, leading the way down the stairs.

I smiled and followed along behind her, all the while my thoughts continued to roll through my mind. This was more than an adventure, it was turning into a journey of the soul. Somehow, I was going to have to complete it unscathed. As we reached the bottom of the stairs, Aaron and Paul stood waiting by the door, it was time for us to be leaving.

"All set?" Aaron asked. He'd put his sunglasses back on and a great sense of relief washed over me, it was much easier looking at him without seeing him looking back.

"Yes, good to go." I smiled; excitement and nervousness surged through my veins.

"Thanks for a fantastic lunch, Anne." Aaron reached over and hugged her, my heart lurched, and I cautiously shook my head, hoping no one noticed.

"Have a great afternoon," Anne said as she gave me a hug. "You'll have to tell me all about it when you get back this evening."

"Speaking about that," Paul said reaching into his pocket, "here's a key just in case you get in late." He handed me a golden coloured key, and I put it in my pocket.

"Thanks again for lunch." I turned to follow Aaron who was waiting for me on the walk outside. We both waved bye as Anne closed the door.

"What was that all about?" Aaron said as we headed toward the car.

Oh no! Has my face betrayed me again? I can't explain things to him now. I can't even begin to put into words what I can barely understand myself. He'll think I'm crazy. "What do you mean?" I felt my stomach turn with worry.

Aaron opened the car door for me and I climbed in, my mind racing. I couldn't take my eyes off of him as he walked around to his side of the car and opened the door.

"I mean with Anne," he said as he eased himself into the car.

Relief flooded over me, replacing my worry with confusion, Anne was someone I felt I could be friends with for a long time.

"I'm not sure I understand what you mean."

Aaron laughed at me as he started the car and pulled away from the curb. "I just meant you acted as though you've been dear friends all your lives. Anne's a fantastic girl, but she doesn't necessarily warm up to people that quickly. You must have said something to impress her."

"I guess I just have a way with people." I smiled as my heart rate slowed.

"I guess so." Aaron looked at me briefly and smiled back, warmth rose in my face. The blush, I was certain, covered me like a warm blanket as my blood pulsed through me.

At that moment, I wanted him to take off his sunglasses and look at me – through me – and really see me. I wanted him to understand what I was beginning to understand, and feel what I was feeling. Though what that was exactly, I wasn't quite sure since we'd only just met. If it was love at first sight, it wasn't something I ever dreamed would happen to me – that was reserved for fairy tales and Hollywood movies.

I stared at him as we drove through the streets, watching his every move, not caring if he caught me. Taking him in with my eyes was all I could do. My entire body tingled and I squirmed uncomfortably. The seat belt suddenly became too confining. My mind wandered, as did my eyes, scanning every inch of him. Good thing you're driving, because if you weren't... Whoa! What am I thinking? I silently questioned, surprised by my thoughts – if they were mine. At Anne's house, I had been beside myself wondering how to handle being alone with him all afternoon, and now I was ready to pounce. Maybe because his sunglasses shielded his eyes, it made me braver, unafraid of our eyes locking. It was all so confusing. One moment, I wanted our eyes to meet, for him to see through me – find out my secret, yet the next moment, the idea had me panicked. Isn't this what I want? Isn't this the whole point? How can I ever tell him without him thinking I'm crazy? The questions themselves were already driving me crazy, and it wasn't my intention to scare him away. Somehow, he would have to be convinced, and in some way, I was going to have to look at those eyes again. He wouldn't be wearing those sunglasses forever.

"So what would you like to do?"

I jumped, even though I was watching him the whole time. "What?" I asked, my heart thumping in my ears.

"Perhaps if your ear was turned toward me instead of your eyes you'd have heard. Why are you staring at me anyway – is there something on my face?" Aaron instinctively raised his hand to wipe away whatever phantom bits of dirt he thought lay on his cheek.

"Sorry, you're just really... " Oh God! Am I actually about to say what I think I am? "Handsome." Yup! I averted my gaze for the first time and looked out the window, completely embarrassed by my lack of formality.

He laughed, "You're not so bad yourself." Absently he reached over and patted my hand, sending shivers up my spine.

We pulled up to a traffic light and looked at each other, bursting out into laughter, the tension in the air disappeared. Once we settled down, the light turned green again, and we continued the drive.

I gazed at the sights as we drove along. "Where are we going anyway?" I asked.

"What would you like to see?"

It took no thinking at all to know where I wanted to go, I knew it exactly – it was almost instinctual.

"Can we go to the docks?"

Aaron looked at me briefly before turning his attention back to the road ahead. "The docks?"

I knew it was a long shot, but I had to try. "Yeah, I'm kind of interested in the whole emigration thing, you know back in the day." It sounded strange even to me, but there was no way to explain it. The desire to go there was strong, if not a bit unnerving.

"It's not exactly quite the same, you know."

"I... I know. I just want to see."

"Any particular one?"

I shook my head, I had no idea which one, but I didn't care, any would be fine. "No."

"The docklands it is then, but it may take some time getting there, we may even have to walk a bit." Aaron pulled out his cell phone as we pulled up to another traffic light.

"What are you doing?" I asked.

"Well, if you want to see the docks, then I'll have to book us a parking space."

"What?"

"If you haven't noticed, parking is a bit difficult." Aaron continued to search his phone. "Ah, got one." Just then, the light turned green.

We battled our way through the streets and traffic before pulling up to the gates. Aaron punched in a security code, the gates opened and we drove through.

"Here we are," Aaron said, pulling in to our spot and unbuckling his belt.

"Here," I said handing him a few pounds, "will this cover it?"

Aaron smiled, "For about an hour."

"That's fine; I don't need much more than that." I unbuckled my own belt, got out of the car, and closed the door behind me. Standing there, my eyes scanned the surroundings. We walked for a bit before coming to one of the docking areas. Aaron was right of course, it had changed. There wasn't a thing about that place that was even remotely recognizable. I thought being there might conjure up more memories, but there was nothing. It was as if I had never been there before, which of course was true, I had never been there – but Mary had. I only wish I knew just where exactly. My body turned in a small circle; still, nothing caught my eye.

"Do you want to keep looking around?" Aaron looked at his watch.

I sensed he was a little puzzled by my apparent indecision. Not knowing quite sure of what to say, I opted for the truth.

"You were right, it isn't the same. Can we go?" I'm sure my sudden change of heart caught him off guard. Of course, it was hard to tell since his sunglasses blocked me from at least attempting to read his true feelings.

"We can do whatever you like." Even his tone gave nothing away. If it were me, I would have been a tiny bit annoyed after driving out there only to leave moments later. However, not Aaron, he was indifferent.

We walked silently, for the most part, back to the parking spot. I took one final look around and got back in the car – somewhat disappointed in myself, and rather relieved. "Sorry," I said, buckling my belt. "It's just that... it's not what I thought it would be."

"No worries," he said starting the car. "Before we go anywhere else though, I should give you this." He reached into his pocket and pulled out a black, leather wallet. He searched it diligently before coming up with what he was looking for. "Here." He handed me a card.

"What is it?"

"It's your London Pass."

"Oh! I forgot you mentioned this." I took the card and put it in my wallet, still feeling a little disappointed and perhaps embarrassed about the docks. I so hoped that seeing the place where Mary emigrated from would help me to remember more about her life. We sat quietly, the only sound around us coming from the engine of the car.

"I have an idea that might help you to visualise life from the viewpoint of an emigrant."

I perked up a bit intrigued by his idea. The look on my face, of course, must have been all telling as he proceeded to explain in more detail.

"I know you're not very fond of boats."

"How did you –"

"Peter told me."

"Oh."

"If you want, we can take a boat cruise of the Thames. It's one of the best ways to get a glimpse of the sights we'll be visiting and some we won't."

"Yes," I said without hesitating, surprising even myself. Aaron was right; boats weren't my favourite, but it could be what was needed to finally get over my phobia. I needed to be where my dreams and memories began.

"Right, it's settled then." Aaron smiled at me as we pulled out from our parking space.

Before long, we were boarding a boat that promised great views of the city, yet I could think only of being on the water. As the boat pulled away from the dock, a flashback hit me. I gripped the edge of my seat, closed my eyes, and shuddered. An arm wrapped around my shoulder but instead of making me feel uncomfortable, I relaxed instantly.

"Would you like to change seats?" Aaron asked.

I had insisted on sitting at the open window seat, so I could look out over the water. I shook my head as Aaron released his grip.

My eyes were focused on the surface of the water, but occasionally, I looked away whenever Aaron's voice filtered through the echoes from the past that flooded my ears.

"Are you all right?" The concern in his voice was very evident.

I turned to look at him, surprised to find that he had taken off his sunglasses. "Yes, fine." I quickly looked away, unable to bear looking at him for even a second.

Aaron reached around, placed his hand under my chin, and gently coaxed me to face him. If it had been anyone else, I would have slapped his hand away. I closed my eyes.

"Why are you crying?" His hand gently stroked my cheek.

Surprised by his observation, I reached up with my own hand and felt moisture on my cheek. I opened my eyes and looked at my fingers and sure enough, they were wet with my tears.

"I don't know," I said staring at my hand. "Maybe dust or something blew into my eyes."

Aaron lifted my chin so that my eyes looked directly into his; quickly I closed them again.

"Open your eyes, and let me take a look."

"No, it's okay. I'm sure it'll be fine."

"Open them, please."

How can I possibly ever look into his eyes? However, his gentleness and concern made me brave, and I did as he said and opened them. Instantly, our gaze locked, and a whirlpool of echoes and memories encircled us. Flashes of sound and images spun around us in a dizzying fashion. Aaron held my face in his hands as he gazed into my eyes; my own hands clasped onto his and the heat between them almost burned. I struggled for breath as the air was sucked from my lungs. My heart pounded and I feared at any moment I was going to start gasping. The spinning of images and voices around us moved faster and faster until they became a blur, and the voices became a steady hum. Everyone and everything had disappeared, and it was just the two of us. I wanted to close my eyes, to pull away, but it wasn't possible, I was frozen. Slowly, the sounds and images began to ebb, and I began to become aware of my surroundings. My heart slowed to a near normal pace and my lungs filled with air.

"I don't see anything. I guess you were right, it was probably just dust." Aaron quickly removed his hands from my face.

I stared at him in disbelief. How could he not have felt that? Seen that? Heard that? He must have sensed something – anything.

"What's the matter?" he said staring back at me.

"Did you not just. . . " I stopped myself. What exactly was I going to say to him, anyway? Should I ask him if he heard the voices, saw our images, or felt our emotions? There were no words to explain what had happened. Nothing that wouldn't make me sound as if I hadn't completely lost my mind. Instead, I turned away from him and looked back out over the side. His hand touched mine, the heat still radiating between them.

"Yes, I did," he whispered.

Thirty-One

Aaron lay in bed, staring wide-eyed, yet as exhausted as he was, he could not fall asleep. The streetlight outside cast shadows of the nearby tree into his room, and he watched as they danced on the walls and across the ceiling. Krista was on his mind, and he couldn't shake the feeling that there was something about her that reminded him of someone. But what was it, he wondered, and more importantly who? Too many unanswered questions mulled around in his head. There was no going to sleep until he figured something out.

Slowly he began going over a checklist of possibilities as he tried to work out the connection, mentally crossing out each option as he went along. Krista, although attractive, wasn't his usual type, generally, he preferred brunettes. He was sure that she didn't remind him of one of his ex-girlfriends. It wasn't until he'd exhausted all avenues that a thought suddenly occurred to him. As farfetched as it was, perhaps she reminded him of a girl he used to dream of, a girl he hadn't thought about for a long time.

The girl was a nameless, faceless character that occasionally made brief appearances from as far back as he could remember, and though the dreams were never clear, she somehow left a lasting impression. For a time, he actually convinced himself she was real; he'd believed that if he ever found her, he would know it in his heart. Anne had once been the recipient of that belief, with her long dark hair that so looked like the girl's – the only true memory he had. As their relationship progressed, he began to realize that Anne wasn't meant for him. They had been together for almost a year, and in the end, their strained relationship had just about ended his friendship with Peter, especially when he had broken Anne's heart. It was then he decided to give up the search for the girl from his dreams, though he always felt a small part of him looked for her in every girl he dated.

His one true regret was that he'd once told his mother about the girl, and she had believed emphatically that she was not just a figure in a dream, but someone Aaron was destined to meet. She urged him to be patient, telling him that when the girl came along, he would know it the instant they touched. After his break-up with Anne, he made his mother promise never to bring it up again, eventually forgetting all about the girl as his dreams faded.

For the first time in his life, Aaron felt what his mother had meant. Each time he'd touched Krista, he felt electricity coursing through his veins, and each time it became more intense. Their initial handshake had just felt unusually warm, but when he'd reached out and touched her hand in the car, it was so shocking that he hadn't quite believed what he felt. He hoped for another chance to touch her again. Finally, the opportunity presented itself when he held her face in his hands. Her eyes burned into his own as he searched for whatever was causing them to tear. It had been hard to concentrate, particularly when he was sure the colour of them had changed. It happened so quickly that he doubted himself, blaming it all on his imagination. Especially after Peter's recounting of what he'd experienced. In any case, something had happened between them, something beyond his understanding, but definitely something worth investigating further. He didn't know or really believe that she was the girl from his dreams, he'd given up the notion that she existed years ago, but undeniably there was something about her that puzzled him.

Aaron rolled over onto his side tucking his hands under his pillow. He stared at the window, watching the patterns of light and dark. His eyes began feeling heavy and he breathed a sigh of relief as sleep finally took hold, pulling him under.

He heard a whisper and a slow, sleepy smile crossed his face – she was back.

Thirty-Two

It was without a doubt the worst sleep in weeks, if one could call it that. My eyes burned red from staring up at the ceiling for what seemed like all night. In any case, I was definitely going to need an entire pot of coffee just to stay awake.

Anne had been so interested in my day that she'd made a point of waiting up for me, though it was only nine o'clock when Aaron had brought me back to the bed and breakfast. At any rate, I had felt obligated to tell her about my adventure, apart from divulging anything about what had transpired between Aaron and me, although I truly felt she could be trusted.

As our conversation progressed, Anne had revealed that she and Aaron had dated a long time ago. The news had taken me by surprise and had caused a feeling of jealousy that I had never experienced before; I silently rebuked myself. By the time we'd finally decided to end the evening, it was eleven thirty, and neither of us could hold back our yawns any longer – it had truly been a marathon.

When I had climbed into bed, sleep had been the only thing on my mind. Unfortunately, the second my head had hit the cool pillow, my eyes popped open. No matter what I'd tried, sleep was not going to find me. There was no shaking what had happened on that boat; moreover, Aaron had admitted he had felt something, too. Although, he had never really made clear what exactly it was he'd felt.

After our boat ride, we had spent the rest of the afternoon walking around, visiting shops, and then dining at a pub. He'd not touched me again, and it had been difficult resisting the urge to reach out and touch him. I had begun to wonder if what he had felt had freaked him out; it certainly had me reeling.

I had spent a good part of the night trying to analyze what had happened between us, revisiting everything frame by frame. In the end, I still had no answers, only more questions. By the time one-thirty had rolled around, I had given up my futile analysis and only sought sleep. Unfortunately, my brain had had a different idea and appeared incapable of shutting down. An hour later, I had still not fallen asleep. Frustrated, I had jumped out of bed and searched my bag for the book the old woman had given me. After a few seconds, it had struck me that it hadn't been packed and that it was still sitting on the kitchen counter – untouched.

With the arrival of morning, I desperately wanted to fall asleep even if just for a little while, but the smell of breakfast kept rousing me, not to mention my ever-gurgling stomach.

"Okay, I'll get up." My stomach growled happily in reply. I pulled on my yoga pants and a tank, stuck my hair in a ponytail, and headed down the stairs.

"Good morning!" Anne greeted me cheerfully as I entered the dining room.

"Good morning," I said, trying to sound more awake than I looked.

"You don't look like you've slept very well."

I'd failed my attempt.

"Do I look that bad?" I said, pulling out a chair and sitting down at the perfectly set table, briefly taking note of the extra place setting.

"No, not bad, just tired."

"I guess as tired as I was all the excitement kept me awake."

"Well, here's some coffee. I'm sure you could use some," Anne said as she poured me a cup before leaving the room.

I bent forward, inhaling the coffee's aroma, the steam rising in my face. I grasped the cup with both hands and brought the energizing brew up to my lips. Blowing gently before taking a small sip, I closed my eyes as the warm liquid trickled down my throat leaving a path of warmth in its wake as it trailed down to my stomach.

"Good morning, Krista. Did you have a good sleep?"

I looked up to find Paul with Christina in his arms. At least, he didn't appear to notice the bags under my eyes.

"The bed was very comfortable," I said, hoping he wouldn't notice my blatant avoidance of his question.

"Ah, good. Christina here said she wanted to see the pretty lady this morning." Christina buried her head into her father's shoulder.

"Good morning, Christina," I said, managing a smile.

Christina smiled, rubbed her eyes, and turned her head back into her father's shoulder.

"I think someone is still sleepy," Paul said as he walked out of the room.

"You've got that right," I mumbled, taking another sip from my cup.

Moments later, Anne returned placing a plate of toast on the table. "Make sure you eat plenty. I hear you have a busy day ahead."

"Not that it's any of my business," I began, "but do you have another guest?" I asked jutting my chin in the direction of the empty place in front of me.

"No, that's for Aaron. He called this morning and asked if it would be alright if he joined you for breakfast." Anne smiled.

I just about choked on the piece of toast I'd bitten off. "Aaron's coming here – for breakfast?" I knew I sounded astonished, maybe a little overjoyed. Nevertheless, it was too late and no amount of backtracking could reel that emotion in. I saw it reflect back on Anne's face as her smile grew wider.

"Yes, he should be here any moment." With that, she left the room humming the same tune from yesterday.

As if on cue, the doorbell rang, and I heard voices coming from the foyer. I kept my head down and busied myself filling my plate with the foods on the table. By the time I finished, the voices had drawn nearer and gathered in the dining room.

"Good morning!"

I raised my head to see Aaron smiling at me or maybe it was more like beaming. It was impossible to tell, but whatever it was, I was sure that both Anne and Paul, who had followed Aaron into the dining room, saw it too.

"Good morning," I said, trying very hard not to blush, but it was too late as that all too familiar heat started rising. Quickly, I looked down and began eating, trying not to shovel the food into my mouth and choke.

"Thanks, Anne." I heard Aaron say while I busied myself with breakfast. There was no way I was going to look at him again, not until both Paul and Anne left the room, which couldn't be soon enough.

"If you need anything else, let me know," Anne said.

I looked up to see her smiling strangely at me. A grin that put the Cheshire Cat's to shame. A grin that said, 'I know your secret.' Moreover, if her grin wasn't telling enough, she winked at me as she left the room. I was mortified. Paul, on the other hand, didn't notice anything; he was the typical male that never seemed to pick up on unspoken words or subtleties.

Aaron and I ate in silence while awkwardness floated around the room dancing mockingly between us like an invisible fog.

"So, how did you sleep?" Aaron was the first to break the silence, and the fog began to ebb.

I stared blankly at him.

"Not too well – huh?" He answered the question for me, and it woke me from my stupor.

"Good Lord, do I really look that bad?" I picked up a spoon, trying to use it like a mirror.

"No, you look..." Aaron hesitated.

What – fine, beautiful, stunning, fetching?

"Lovely." Aaron smiled at me.

Well, that is certainly better than fine. I smiled. "What about you... did you sleep well?" I put a fork full of food in my mouth and stared at him. At least now, I could look into his eyes.

He stared back at me, finally answering. "Not at first, it took a while."

At least he's honest. "How come?" I asked, though it really wasn't any of my business, but more importantly, placed the focus on his lack of sleep and not mine. There was no way I was going to tell him that my entire night was spent thinking of him.

"Because, I couldn't get you out of my head." He took a sip from his cup, keeping his eyes glued to mine, his openness surprising me.

"So, why couldn't you sleep?" He turned the focus back on me.

Should I be as open as he is? I shrugged. "Because of you." I put another fork full in my mouth.

We stared at each other while we ate, seemingly unable to pull our gazes away. What his excuse was, I couldn't be sure, but as for me it was as though my body was made of metal and he was a magnet drawing me in.

"Really?" He smiled.

I put my fork down and replaced it with a napkin, wiping my mouth. What I really wanted to do just then was to throw myself at him from across the table. Of course, that idea completely shocked me; I really wasn't that type of person and had truly never experienced such a strong attraction for someone – ever. How is it possible to be so... in love, so quickly? Then of course, I remembered, we had always been in love. And at this moment in time, it was my job, somehow, to make sure that he realized that, too. Aaron was without a doubt my soulmate, my promised soul, and I didn't have to read that book to know it – not any more. I felt it in my bones and in every breath. He was my Thomas, and I was his Mary.

"Really." I smiled back.

Thirty-Three

After showering, I made my way to the mirror and carefully wiped away the steam. It had been a couple of days since I'd last seen Mary's reflection or at the very least, her eyes, and it left me wondering if it was because I wasn't at the apartment. In any case, her image had become somewhat expected and without it, she was missed. She hadn't even invaded my dreams and no new memories surfaced. It seemed I was all alone in my body again. Though I understood she wasn't another entity possessing me, it sometimes made it easier to think of her as separate from myself – less confusing.

I dressed quickly, knowing that in a few hours, I would be spending my last full day with Aaron before returning to my apartment, and I planned to make the most of it. Especially since it would be some time before our next outing, and I had a lot of questions. We had spent the entire day before visiting tourist destinations. He'd kept me so busy and involved that I never had the chance to find out exactly what he'd felt when we were on the boat. Apart from the occasional flirtatious gesture, there was nothing obvious about his feelings. At the end of the day, he assured me our last day would be slower paced. Somehow, I was going to find out what he felt or knew – if anything.

When breakfast was over, I waited in the parlour for Aaron. By nine o'clock, I was beginning to grow impatient, and when nine thirty ticked by, I started pacing and wondering what could be taking him so long. He was supposed to have picked me up at eight thirty.

"Is he not here yet?" Anne asked me as she walked into the room with little Christina tagging slowly along behind.

"Nope." I tried to keep my frustration to myself.

"Why don't I give him a ring?" Anne headed back out of the parlour, Christina in tow, before I could respond. I sat back down again and peered out the front window, yet there was still no sign of him. "I couldn't reach him, but I'm sure he's on his way. Can I get you something whilst you wait?" Anne said, returning to the room with a very tired-looking Christina on her hip.

She had been such a lovely host these past couple of days and had made me feel so welcomed in her home. I hated having her wait on me; it felt like I was taking advantage of her. "No, I'm fine."

"Well then, I'm going to put Christina down for a nap. She's not feeling herself today, are you, sweet pea?"

Christina shook her head as she rested against her mother's shoulder.

"If you need anything, let me know." Anne called back over her shoulder as she headed toward the kitchen – their rooms being on the other side.

I turned back to the window just in time to see Aaron's rental car pulling up to the curb.

"Well, it's about time." I muttered. I went to the door and opened it causing Aaron to jump a little.

"Hi!" he said sounding a bit surprised.

"Hi yourself. Is everything okay? I was starting to get a little worried."

"Yes, fine. Listen, I have a slight change in plans. That is, if you don't mind."

"Sure, what is it?"

"We'll talk about it in the car." Aaron turned away from me and headed towards the rental. Once we were in and our belts buckled, he turned and faced me.

"First, sorry I'm so late. This truly has been an extraordinary summer. I really don't make a habit of being late for clients or missing appointments. It's just this whole thing with my mother..."

"Is she okay? If you have to go, please don't let me stop you."

"No, it's not that. I mean she's fine."

"What's wrong then?"

"Well nothing – really. I don't know how say this, so I'm just going to start from the beginning." Aaron's eyes darted around before finally resting on mine. I was intrigued, but I couldn't begin to fathom what Aaron was about to say or why he was acting so strangely. "My aunt rang just as I was about to leave this morning."

"Your Aunt Jane?"

"Yes, she had a message from my mother about wanting to..." Aaron paused. He seemed to be struggling with what he wanted to say.

"Wanting what?" I encouraged.

"You're going to think this very strange, but you don't know my mother." I cocked my head completely baffled by the conversation and Aaron's strange behaviour. Aaron took a deep breath, "She would like to meet you."

"Meet me? Why does she want to meet me?" I was a bit shocked, to say the least. Had he mentioned me to his mother? We'd just met, or reconnected, or whatever you'd call it. Although, I knew my feelings, there was no telling how he felt, he surely didn't have the same insight that I did on our 'relationship'.

"I promise I never spoke of you to her, not really anyway. Not in any way that would suggest..." his voice trailed off. "The thing is my mother has this ability –"

"It's fine," I said abruptly. I'd been around enough people recently who knew things they couldn't possibly know. "I get it."

"You do?" His eyes widened in shocked amazement.

"You don't know the half of it."

"I guess it's settled then." Aaron turned the key in the ignition and put the car into gear.

"Wait, what do you mean it's settled'?" I asked nervously.

"Well... she wants to meet you now." Aaron smiled a crooked little smile, the kind that said, 'no time like the present'.

"When you say now, you mean like today-now?"

"Uh-huh!" Aaron started to pull away from the curb, stopping suddenly. "Unless, of course, you really don't want to, I would completely understand. I'm sorry if it's too strange, I shouldn't..."

I reached over and placed my hand on top of Aaron's; instantly feeling a sudden surge of heat between them, but I didn't pull away. It was comforting. "It's okay," I reassured him. "I would love to meet your mother."

He smiled, "Fine, let's go then."

It was a quiet trip to Tockington with neither of us saying much of anything, and it wasn't for a lack of trying on my part, either. Finally, Aaron spoke as we pulled into the drive.

"Well, here we are." He looked straight ahead as he parked.

I looked around at the beautiful flower gardens on either side of the drive, envious that my gardens back home were not as lush and colourful, no matter what I planted. A gardener, I was not.

"Wow! These are some of the most beautiful garden's I've ever seen. Green thumbs must run in your family since your Aunt Jane's are equally as lovely."

"Humph, it must have skipped a generation. I can't keep a cactus alive let alone ones that need actual caring." A small smile escaped from Aaron's lips, the first I'd seen since we'd left London.

I trailed behind Aaron as we approached the front door. Now that we were there, I was feeling a bit apprehensive but kept it to myself. Before Aaron reached the door handle, it swung open. A small, plump woman wearing an apron greeted us, grinning widely.

"Hello, loves, do come in, come in. Aaron, your mum will be so happy you're here." The woman ushered us into the foyer as she closed the door behind us.

"Aunt Jane, I'd like you to meet Krista, she's –"

"Yes, yes, I know." Jane turned her attention to me, taking my hand into her soft, plump ones. "Hello dear, it's so nice to finally meet you. I hope you've been enjoying your stay at my cottage. I'm so sorry that I'm not there to show you around, but as you know, I've been a wee bit busy."

"Oh yes, I've been having a great time. Thank you so much for renting your apartment out to me."

"Of course! I'm just glad to have someone staying there whilst I'm away. Have you found everything you need? I hope that note-book of instructions I left you has been helpful."

"More than you know."

"Sorry to interrupt, ladies, but how's Mum?" Aaron asked his aunt. Jane immediately withdrew her hands from mine and led Aaron away just out of earshot. I stood there waiting in the foyer not sure what to do. Thankfully, Aaron returned a short minute later.

"Sorry about that. Jane's gone to see if Mother is awake. We should wait in the parlour."

I followed Aaron to the parlour and took a seat in the middle of a small couch while he sat in the wing-backed chair to my right. We waited in silence, the only sound coming from the ticking grandfather clock in the corner. That billowing fog of awkward-ness had found us once again.

"Your aunt is very nice," I whispered.

"Why are you whispering?"

The beginnings of a blush crept slowly up my neck. "I don't know; it's so quiet here. I guess I felt I should whisper." I spoke a little louder.

Aaron opened his mouth as though to say something, but his eyes quickly averted to the entrance. I followed his gaze. Jane had just walked into the room.

"She'd like to see both of you in her room." Jane turned and left the parlour.

I turned back to look at Aaron. For a brief moment, a strange look crossed his face, one that I couldn't quite define.

"Ready?" He smiled, though more forced than genuine.

"I guess so."

Aaron knocked gently on the door before entering; I followed quietly along behind. It was very odd to be in the bedroom of a stranger, let alone a stranger who was dying. I stood by the door as Aaron approached his mother's bed. She was sitting up with two or three pillows tucked in behind her for support; her long, dark hair flowed out over her shoulders. Her beauty captivated me, for as sick as she was, her illness had just begun to make its appearance on her face, sharpening her features and making her skin more transparent.

Aaron leaned over and gently kissed his mother's forehead. She closed her eyes as though she were engraving the moment in her memory for eternity. Her hand reached up and gently stroked his arm. When she opened her eyes, she looked past Aaron and locked them on mine.

"Don't be shy, dear, I promise I won't bite." She smiled.

I smiled back and approached the bed slowly. I stood by Aaron's side, not wanting to take my eyes off her but not wanting her to read pity in them either. I finally broke our gaze and glanced at the floor. It was a little daunting being there.

"Krista, I'd like for you to meet Kate."

I looked up again and held out my hand to Kate. She took it in her own frail, though warm, hand and squeezed it gently.

"It's so lovely to meet you, Krista. I am so sorry my illness has kept Jane away from her home and greeting you properly. I hope you've been able to get along alright."

"Oh yes, it's been no problem at all, please don't worry about that." I couldn't believe that with all she was going through, she was worried about her sister not being there for me.

"I'll get some chairs," Aaron said, walking to the end of the bed and grabbing a chair from the corner of the room. He brought it over for me to sit on and then went back to get another for himself.

Once seated, Kate smiled at me again and asked me to tell her all about myself. At first, I just gave her the usual small details about where I lived, my career, the sort of things that only take a few minutes to tell. It wasn't long before it became apparent that when she asked me to tell her about myself, she truly wanted to know everything about me, like where I was born, grew up, went to school, who my parents were, and even how they met. She was so easy to talk to and such a good listener that before long I had given her my entire life story, everything but my past life memories, though it was very tempting. Then Kate prompted Aaron to fill me in on the details of his life and as it turned out, we both had lost our fathers earlier in life, a detail that I had wondered about but not asked.

"Aaron, dear, could you go to the kitchen and fetch us some tea and biscuits. I'm a bit hungry, I think." Kate said smiling at her son.

"Of course, I'll be right back." Aaron left the room leaving us alone.

"Could I ask you to do me a favour?" Kate smiled at me.

"Sure." Though having just met Kate, I would do just about anything for her.

"Open the doors of the armoire and you'll see a drawer. Pull it open and take out the Bible that's in there, please."

As I headed toward the armoire, a multitude of possibilities as to why she wanted her Bible ran through my head. Looking back at her, she smiled at me, not looking at all like she was about to pass away at any minute. It seemed such a personal thing to ask of a total stranger, granted she now knew as much about me as my friends and family back home did.

The Bible was just where she said it would be. It was a rather old looking book, but its black leather binding still held the pages together. When I returned to my seat at her bedside, I handed it over.

"Thank you," she said as she took the book from my hands and rested it on her lap. "When Aaron was very young," she proceeded to tell me, "he told me of places and people and things. Places he'd never been, people he could never have met, and things he could never have known." She rubbed her thumb across the cover of the Bible. "As he grew older, he stopped telling me his stories, no longer remembering – but I never forgot. Then one day he brought me a gift." Kate opened up her Bible to a page near the back that had been marked by the attached ribbon bookmark. She gently took out a pressed four-leaf clover from between its pages and twirled it between her fingers. "He gave it to me on my birthday for luck. Then he asked me if he'd ever found one before, for he had a memory of giving it to a girl with long, dark hair."

Thomas sat up and faced her. He reached over and tucked a loose hair along with the clover behind her ear.

I closed my eyes and shook the memory from my mind. Kate didn't seem to notice, she was almost trance-like staring at the clover she twirled slowly between her fingers.

"I said no, that it was the first one he'd ever given me, but I remembered his stories – all of them. Once he became very ill, and in his delirium, he began recounting tales, the same tales he told as a young boy. When he got well, the tales stopped, but every so often, I would hear him talking in his sleep. It was always the same dream, always the same girl. He never truly remembered – but I did." Kate stopped twirling the clover and placed it back in the book. Then she closed it protectively over her precious treasure. "Do you believe in a life before?" Kate asked quietly as she gazed pensively at me.

My eyes widened and the hairs on my neck rose as goose bumps travelled up my flesh. Without meaning to, I nodded.

"I believe that Aaron has lived before, as I have. I suppose that's why I'm not so worried about leaving this world – again. It's just that – well Aaron... " A flicker of sadness crossed Kate's eyes as she looked toward the closed door of her bedroom. "Give me your hand."

Without hesitation, I placed my hand between Kate's own. She closed her eyes for a moment, before opening them again.

"Do you know what I feel when I hold your hand?"

I shook my head.

"Life. Do you know what I see?" Her eyes burrowed into mine.

Again, I shook my head, too mesmerized to speak.

Kate closed her eyes again and kept them closed. "You are an old soul, Krista, but I don't think I have to tell you that." My hand stiffened in hers, though her hands were frail, they were still strong, and she held on tightly. I began to relax as she lovingly stroked the back of my hand with her thumbs. "You've told me all about yourself, but I sense there is something else"

Surprised and confused I gently tugged on my hand, finally withdrawing it from Kate's grasp; she opened her eyes. "What... what do you mean?" I stammered.

Kate opened her eyes and smiled. "Do your dreams ever leave you with a sense of longing?"

It wasn't enough that my face gave away my emotions to anyone who looked at me, but it seemed holding my hand gave away my secrets, too, at least to Kate. "How do you –"

"There are many things in this world that can't be explained, my gift is one of them."

After Ruth and the old woman, I'd given up trying to figure out just how these people had these extraordinary abilities. I accepted it as no different as someone with artistic talent. After all, dreaming of a past life seemed to be an ability in and of itself, who was I to be skeptical.

"I'm not quite sure I understand why I'm here."

Kate smiled. "Oh my dear, don't you?"

Maybe because I was so new to this strange phenomenon, environment – experience, I needed a clearer definition. I shook my head.

"I sensed something was going on with Aaron, so I asked Jane to call him this morning. I wasn't quite sure what it was but needed to meet you." She shrugged.

"That's all?" I asked in disbelief.

"When I took your hand, I saw flashes of your dreams – Mary, Thomas, they are the same from Aaron's stories and dreams, though I'm sure he no longer remembers. Once he told me of a girl from a dream, and I believed it was someone he was destined to meet, a girl in his future. He looked for her, but he eventually gave up. We don't speak of her anymore." Kate looked a little sad. My head began to spin as the reason for my being there was beginning to become clear. "Do you know what I believe now?" Kate asked smiling at me.

I shook my head.

"The girl wasn't his future, but his past. Do me another favour, Krista?" Before I could answer, Kate continued, "Help him to believe in that girl. Help him to remember you."

Thirty-Four

By the time we arrived in Bourton, I was exhausted, both physically and emotionally. It took everything in me not to fall back
to sleep as we drove through town. It had been an exciting yet
draining weekend, and I was sad to leave London and my new
friends. I promised to stay in touch before my holiday ended and
I returned home. Home – it seemed like being there was a dream.
If it weren't for my mother and my dear friends, there would be
no returning. In my mind, I was home.

My visit with Kate had affirmed my decision to help Aaron remember. However, I had no idea how that would unfold. It would
take time, but there was only a month left of my vacation and a
good part of it was on my own. Aaron and I weren't scheduled to
meet again until the fourth of August, and it would only be for a
couple of days – there really weren't many opportunities left.

"All right, sleepyhead, you're home." A distant voice whispered
through my thoughts and then a comforting heat fell on my shoulder. My eyes popped open to find Aaron gently shaking me awake.
"Sorry to wake you, but you're home now." He smiled.

"That's okay, I wasn't really sleeping."

"Oh no? What would you call it then?"

"Deep in thought," I replied, opening the car door up and climb-
ing out. I stretched up on tippy-toe and yawned.

"I'll get your bag." He called out to me as I walked up the walk of the cottage and fished the keys from my purse.

Oh yeah, my bag. If it wasn't for my exhaustion, I'd have turned back, but instead my feet continued toward the door. Once inside the foyer, my feet stopped and my eyes followed the staircase up to the door at the top. My shoulders slumped; the staircase lengthened in front of my eyes.

"Is something the matter?" Aaron's voice came from behind me.

"Don't those stairs look a long way up?"

He laughed. "Go on." I felt his warm hand gently press on my lower back as he encouraged me to take the first step.

Once at the top, I opened the door letting us in; grateful he was behind me, prodding me along. Otherwise, I would have spent the rest of the afternoon in the foyer.

"Can I get you something to drink?" It was far too early to go to bed, though the thought crossed my mind briefly as I stopped in front of my bedroom door on the way into the kitchen. Besides, it wouldn't be very hospitable considering Aaron had followed me in and didn't seem to be in too much of a hurry to be on his way. It had been a long day for the both of us, and I was sure he could use an energy boost as well.

"Yes, please," he said.

I set my bag down in front of the bedroom door and turned around; Aaron was still standing by the entrance to the apartment, a thoughtful look on his face.

"You can sit down." I pointed toward the living room.

"Sorry, it's been awhile since I've been here." He headed over to the couch and sat, still in a somewhat pensive state.

"Coffee?"

"Excuse me?" He stared at me blankly.

"Would you like some coffee?"

"Yes, please."

A slow smile spread across my face as I headed back into the kitchen; the more time we spent together, the better.

"Help him to remember." Kate's plea whispered in my ear.

When I returned from the kitchen, precariously balancing a tray in my hands and trying not to upset its contents, Aaron was standing by the computer desk. He seemed very much transfixed, and I wondered what caught his attention.

"I can't believe this is here." He spoke in a low voice, and I wasn't quite sure if he was addressing me or was inflicted with the same habit of talking-to-one's-self as I was.

Once I rid myself of the overloaded tray, my attention focused back on Aaron. In his hand, he held the hand-made pencil holder.

"That?" I asked walking toward him.

"Yes, I made it for Jane for Mother's Day."

"Mother's Day?"

"I felt badly that she had no children of her own, and since she spent a good deal of time looking after me, I had my mother help me make this vase, and we filled it with her favourite flowers. Only it proved not to be very watertight." Aaron placed the container back on the desk. "I had no idea she still had it."

"I think my mother still has just about everything I have ever given her. I'm sure your mother does too." I thought back to the clover Kate had pulled from her Bible.

"Oh that she does, indeed." Aaron smiled as he turned and looked at me. My skin prickled as our eyes met, and I felt a sudden flush of heat rise over me.

"I'll go check on the coffee." I started to head back to the kitchen when Aaron's very warm hand touched my arm, starting a new wave of prickles just as the first wave subsided.

"I'll go – if you don't mind." He smiled. I certainly didn't mind, despite the awakening of my skin when he touched me, my eyelids were beginning to feel heavy again.

Aaron returned seconds later with the coffee pot in one hand and a book in the other. My heart skipped a little. He set the pot down on the table and sat beside me on the couch, the book still in his hand. "Is this yours?" he asked sounding a bit excited as he held the book the old woman had lent me.

"No," I said, shaking my head and trying not to read too much into Aaron's expression. Grabbing the pot, I filled the mugs with the hot coffee, the aroma alone already giving me energy; it was either that or seeing what I interpreted as intrigue in Aaron's eyes that woke me.

"Can I ask where you got it from?"

"The old lady down the street gave it to me to read." I was trying to sound matter of fact, but at the same time, his apparent interest in the book had me quietly reeling. Peter had said Aaron believed, to some extent, in past lives. After meeting his mother, I understood why. Maybe it was just the thing we needed to start a conversation, but he was going to have to say something first.

"Do you think I could borrow it?" Aaron asked still holding the book out to me.

"I... I don't know, maybe." Suddenly I wasn't so sure if he should take it, having not read it myself. I took the book from his hands and placed it on the table. Though the desire to thrust it back into his hands was strong, a part of me needed to think about it.

We sat silently sipping our coffees and nibbling on cookies. That odd tension had returned – an awkward, invisible fog that swirled around us whenever silence filled the air.

"Would you like to go for a walk?" Aaron asked when we'd finally finished our coffee. I nodded, surprised, but quite happy he asked. "It's too nice of an afternoon to be wasted indoors, and truthfully, I'm not ready for the drive back home just yet."

"I would love to," I practically gushed, thankfully Aaron didn't seem to notice.

We headed in the direction of the town centre. I wasn't quite sure whether my sudden surge of energy came from the coffee or the simple thrill of walking beside Aaron, but I suspected it was the latter. In any event, the rush became stronger when his hand brushed against mine and even in that fleeting moment, it sent warmth, and I'm sure a glow, coursing through my body.

We approached the small cottage where the old woman lived and as we walked by I saw her peering at us from between her always drawn curtains. A knowing smile stretched across her face, yet another declaration that Aaron was indeed my soulmate – he was the only one that needed convincing.

When we returned home, hand in hand, the sun was setting in the sky as I invited him in again, and as before, he accepted. We were both giddy, and it was hard to tell whether it was from the dinner we'd shared, the entertainment we'd enjoyed, or the pure elation of being together. Whatever it was, I didn't want it to end, and I suspected neither did he. Once in the apartment though, things became awkward, as I truly wasn't ready for our relationship or whatever it was, to advance any further – not just yet, not until he knew everything.

"So..." I hesitated not knowing what to do next as we stood in the entrance of the apartment. "Can I get you a drink, something to eat?"

"No." His eyes burned into mine. We stood in the entrance staring at each other as if both afraid to make the first move. "Let's just sit a bit." Aaron grabbed my hand and led me toward the couch. I was happy he was taking the lead.

He sat down in the corner and patted the spot beside him. Obediently, I sat down. He put his arm around me, pulling me close, my head rested against him. I had never felt so warm and comfortable or relaxed, for that matter, in someone's arms. Closing my eyes, I felt myself begin to drift off as I snuggled closer, listening as he breathed slowly and rhythmically, his heartbeat so familiar in my ear.

My eyes sprung open and it took me a few seconds to realize where I was. "Aaron, Aaron wake-up." I whispered, placing my hand on his chest and gently shaking him.

"What? Where am I? Oh!" He pulled me closer, closing his eyes again.

"Aaron!"

"This is nice," he whispered.

"Yes, it is," I agreed, relaxing. "It must be really late." My own eyes closed as I felt myself drifting off in the comfort of his arms.

I felt him shuffle a bit and pull his arm free from behind me. Groaning I sat up, my eyes still closed. I knew he had to leave but despised the thought. I flopped back against the couch and felt him get up.

"I'd say it's pretty early."

I opened my eyes and found him looking out the living room window; golden streaks painted across the sky – it was dawn.

He was still looking out the window as I approached him and laid my hand gently on his back. "Breakfast?" I asked.

"Breakfast," he replied. My stomach rumbled loudly in agreement, and I padded into the kitchen, Aaron trailing close behind.

By the time we finished breakfast, the sun revealed a blue, cloudless sky, and it was time for Aaron to leave. He helped me clean up, and though I didn't want the moment to end, he finally announced the words I was dreading.

"I really must go."

"I know." In my ears, I sounded like a very disappointed child. "It's okay." I smiled, wiping the pout from my face. "You've got to get to work."

"Yeah." We walked out of the kitchen together and stopped at the door to the apartment. I sensed a moment of unease as Aaron hugged me quickly and briefly brushed his lips against mine. "I'm sorry. I need to go."

Though our first kiss was brief, it still left a burning sensation on my lips. I reached up absently and touched them, the confusion from his apology and his sudden indifference swirled in my brain.

"I know."

"Can I take that?" I followed the length of his arm down to his pointing finger and over to the object in question.

"Yes." I said. He left me and plucked the book from the coffee table, returning quickly to my side.

"I think I should read this."

"Yes, I think so too."

Thirty-Five

Time passed slowly with each day melting into the next. I'd practically become a shut-in. I was too afraid to leave the house in case he called – but he didn't.

I spent my mornings in the garden sipping coffee and my afternoons reading; the cordless phone always by my side. I checked my e-mail frequently, but there was nothing. On several occasions, my fingers frustratingly dialed his office number only to hang-up when it rang. Once I let it go as far as voice mail, but apprehension prevented me from speaking, so I hung up. Besides, what was I going to say – "I miss you"? It was the truth, but scaring him off was the last thing I wanted, though I was quite sure I had already done that.

Patience is a virtue, my mother's voice whispered inside my head.

"Screw virtue!" I yelled, trying to drown her out.

After four days of moping around, waiting for Aaron to call or send an e-mail, I finally decided to let matters be. In any case, I was sick of being bored, and I had a great need to get out of the apartment. Before leaving, however, habit prompted me to check my e-mail, and it was a good thing I did. I immediately opened my mother's message as it was already a day old.

Hello dear,

We just arrived in London yesterday. We've been having such a wonderful trip and can't wait to see you. We have rented a cute little car and have booked a few days at the Old Manse Hotel – Do you know it?

Of course, it was where Peter and I dined when I first arrived in Bourton. I continued reading.

If it's not too much trouble would you join us for lunch there tomorrow? They have a beautiful patio overlooking the river. The reservation is under James Houghton.

See you soon, Krista,

Love mom, xoxo

I shook my head in disbelief that my mother was getting married. "Great!" I growled under my breath. I checked the time as I headed to my room. I only had a few minutes to get ready.

As I walked down the now familiar street, I noticed a small crowd of people had begun to gather on the walk ahead of me; an ambulance and police car were parked on the narrow road. As I approached, the realization hit me that we were standing in front of the old woman's house.

"What happened?" I asked the nearest person who made eye contact with me.

"The old woman. . . " he paused and rubbed his nose, "seems she had a heart attack."

"Is she okay?"

"Don't know," he said and walked away leaving me standing there on the street amid a few remaining onlookers.

Minutes later, a plain, black van pulled up behind the police car. Its presence answered all of our questions, and the whispers from the small crowd suddenly stopped. We stood and waited in silence, some people noticeably praying, as they brought out the stretcher laden with a body bag and placed it into the back of the van. The crowd slowly dispersed as the van pulled away from the curb, leaving me alone. A single tear traced down my cheek. I wiped my eyes and turned to walk away – surely late for lunch, but not caring. I looked back at the window the old woman had peered from, remembering the approving smile on her face. For a brief moment, I imagined her standing there, and I froze in my spot as she waved. I closed my eyes and when I opened them again, she was gone.

It turned out I wasn't late; in fact, it was my mother who was late. I exhaled a sigh of relief. I was content that I had a few moments by myself. I sat and stared mindlessly out over the water, watching the people pass by.

"Krista!" I jumped slightly, woken up from my apparent trance by an overly, exuberant voice. It was one I recognized, but at the same time it did not seem familiar. "Krista!" My mother made her way toward me. A handsome man walked slowly behind her. He stopped when she threw her arms around me, almost knocking off my sunglasses in the process. "Oh Krista, I'm so happy to see you. I've missed you so much," she bawled, squeezing me a little tighter than she ever had before. The woman, who I called mother, was almost unrecognizable.

Finally, after what seemed like a very long hug, she released me, and I was able to get in a decent, deep breath. As if remembering she was not alone, she stepped back and linked her arm through the arm of the man who stood quietly behind her.

"I'm sorry. Krista, this is Jim – Jim, my lovely daughter, Krista. Isn't she beautiful?" she gushed.

I reached out my hand, which Jim engulfed in his much larger one. "Hi, nice to meet you," I said reservedly, looking him over. For the first time in my life, I felt protective of my mother – as if she needed protecting.

"The pleasure is all mine." He smiled and when he did, his whole face lit up. I could see why my mother was attracted to him, but still I was leery.

"Why don't we all sit down?" my mother suggested, taking a seat of her own. Jim took his spot beside her, and I returned to my chair with Jim sitting across from me.

"So, Jim, tell me all about yourself?"

By the time lunch was over, I had a good idea who Jim was, and I could tell by the way my mother looked at him that she truly was in love and happier than she'd been in a long time; at least, not since my father was alive. Who was I to stand in the way of that? Besides, I had my own love life to worry about, and from my point of view, it didn't look so great.

"So are you two ready to have a tour of this beautiful village?" I asked; having decided that after lunch, I would show them around before heading back to my place for dinner.

"Very!" my mother said and taking the last sip from her teacup, she set it back down on the table.

"Great! We'll go to the model village first; it'll give you an idea of where everything is."

"Sounds like fun, doesn't it, Jim?"

"Yes, very much." Jim said, smiling at my mother and patting her hand. I got the impression, at times, that the two of them were able to block everything out but each other.

"Should we take the car?" Jim asked my mother.

"It's only about a five-minute walk from here, unless..." I started to explain but quickly closed my mouth when I saw that my mother and Jim were in their own little world again.

"Oh, let's walk. It's such a beautiful day. I just need to go back to our room to get my purse," my mother said after a few silent moments.

"Don't worry, sweetheart, I'll get it for you. You sit and visit with Krista for a bit." Jim got up, kissed my mother on the cheek, and walked away leaving the two of us alone. No sooner had he left did my mother start in with her questions, and for once she wasn't, at least for the time being, questioning me.

"So, what do you think?" she whispered, reminding me of a lovesick teenager asking her friends about the new boy she was dating.

I couldn't help but chuckle a little as I looked at her. Her eyes darted back and forth, as she studied my face looking for any telltale signs. However, she wasn't going to see anything but my true feelings.

"Mom, I'm so happy for you. He's wonderful and I couldn't have asked for anyone better for you to get a second chance with." I reached over and took my mother's hand as tears welled up in her eyes.

"Do you really think so?"

"Yes, I do."

"Do you think your father... " Her voice trailed off, but I knew exactly what she was going to ask, and then I remembered what Ruth had said.

"I think Dad is especially happy that you've found someone. He wouldn't have wanted you to spend the rest of your life alone." I gave her hand a reassuring squeeze.

She wiped her eyes with her free hand. "I think you're right," she whispered.

My mother regained her composure and released my hand. It was nice to have a conversation that was all about her for a change. Unfortunately, it was fleeting as suddenly her attention turned to me.

"I have to tell you, Krista, there's something very different about you, I just can't put my finger on it yet, but I will." I didn't say anything. She was right, there was something different about me. "I almost didn't recognize you at first," she continued.

"I'm sure I don't look that different. I've only been away a little over two weeks." I shook my head as I sat back, giving a little chuckle at her scrutiny.

"I know, but you've changed, and you DO look different." She scrunched her eyes a little, as she studied my face.

I smiled. I could almost see her thought process as she tried to figure out what she thought was going on.

Just in time, Jim rejoined us carrying my mother's purse in his hand, thereby saving me from the inquisition that was about to take place. I was really going to like him if he kept that up.

"Here you go, honey," he said handing the purse to my mother and leaning over to kiss her on the cheek again. I couldn't help but laugh. They really were like lovesick teenagers.

I spent a good part of the afternoon showing my mother and her fiancé around town. We visited local shops, and I introduced them to many of the locals who knew me by name and who treated me as if I had lived there for years.

Time flew by and before we knew it, we were back at the hotel. I had suggested that we drive back to my place, although it wasn't too far, I didn't want my mother and Jim walking back in the dark. We all piled into the green rental, and minutes later, pulled up in front of the cottage.

I pulled a couple of weeds from the flowerbed as the three of us made our way to the door. The more time I spent there, the more it felt as if it was my home, and I had no qualms about maintaining it. I'd even spent time in the gardens out back, too, plucking weeds, deadheading plants and watering. I enjoyed the work despite Jane's instructions that her neighbour would tend to it.

"Make yourselves comfortable," I said as I headed into the kitchen after giving a brief tour of the apartment.

"This really is charming." My mother repeated for the fifth time.

I turned around to find her and Jim standing in the kitchen. "Yeah, I really like it," I affirmed for about the fifth time. "So, you're sure barbecue chicken is okay, 'cause I can make something else if you want?" I held up the bag containing the chicken we'd purchased at the local market before returning home.

"Yes, of course. Can we help?" My mother asked.

I looked from my mother to Jim and back again. My mind was busily searching for some chore to give them. "Sure," I said grabbing the tray from on top of the fridge and setting it on the table. "Would you mind setting up the patio table outside? The chairs are in the shed, and here's a cloth to wipe the table." I turned toward the sink and rinsed out a cloth, handing it to my mother.

"If you have paper plates, we could use those," she said taking the damp cloth from my hand.

My mouth fell open and my eyes widened with her suggestion. It wasn't the norm for her. If anyone had changed, it was definitely my mother. "Ah sure, I think I saw some around here somewhere," I said recovering from my momentary state of shock.

"Jim and I will get things set up outside. I'll be back for the plates in a bit." Jim held the door open and the two of them disappeared down the stairs.

Love: it definitely can make a person change – even if just temporarily. I shook my head smiling.

I busied myself with preparing the food when suddenly a loud uproar of laughter interrupted my focus and sent me to peer out the back door at just what had caused such hilarity.

"What's so fun...ny," I stammered as my mother, Jim and Aaron all looked up at me, huge grins spreading across their faces.

"Krista, you have a visitor," my mother called up to me with the strangest of smiles pasted on her face.

"I see that. What are you doing here?" I addressed Aaron from my perch at the top of the stairs.

"Work. I thought I would drop in for a quick visit. I heard voices coming from the back garden, so I introduced myself. Anyway, long story short, these lovely people have invited me to dinner. That is if you don't object."

Object! Why would I object? My heart was thumping and inside my head, I was doing the happy dance. "Sure, we've got extra. I'm just about ready to bring it down. Can you get the barbecue going?"

"No need, Jim already started it."

"Thanks, Jim."

"Sure thing," Jim nodded and turned my mother toward the gardens. They strolled over to the bench where I usually took my morning coffee and sat, their backs towards us.

"Let me help," Aaron called as he started up the stairs.

I wanted to throw myself into his arms, but two things prevented me from doing this. First and foremost, my mother, and second – it would probably only result in me knocking him back down the stairs since the landing at the top wasn't very big and as he reached it I had to step back into the kitchen to give him room.

"So, what can I do?" He asked, smiling sweetly.

What can you do? Well for starters... Many wonderful, lustful thoughts entered my mind, and I had to tell myself to stop. If we were to have a relationship, I couldn't pressure him. It was my job to help him believe – remember, but that would require careful and gentle execution. I didn't want to scare him away for good. "Here, you can take these down to Jim." I handed him a plate with the four prepared chicken breasts on it.

Aaron raised his eyebrows. "Were you expecting someone?" Holding the plate in his hands, he smiled at me. Every time he smiled, my skin prickled, and it felt like my legs melted away underneath me. I put my hand on the counter, steadying myself.

"No, I just have a habit of making extra. Don't you always make enough for leftovers?"

"Unfortunately, I spend more time dining out than in. Nature of the job, I guess." Aaron turned and headed toward the door. "Back in a moment," he called as he headed out.

Keeping my eyes off Aaron wasn't an easy task, but I endured, all the while hoping my mother's preoccupation with Jim was enough to keep her from paying any attention to me or Aaron. In any case, as dinner ended and the sun began to set, mosquitoes came out in full force. It was a welcome distraction for any peering eyes should they wander our way.

It wasn't long, however, before the bloodthirsty bugs drove us inside to the safety of my apartment. As we each grabbed an armload from the table, I convinced everyone that cleaning could wait. Once back in the apartment, I ushered them into the living room while I prepared a desert of berries and cream.

When I rejoined my guests, my mother and Jim were sitting on the love seat, of course, and Aaron had taken up his place in the corner of the couch. The very spot he'd sat in the night we'd fallen asleep. I set the tray of desserts on the table and sat beside him, my leg brushing lightly against his. Every touch, be it accidental or not, sent what I could only describe as an electrical charge coursing through my body, and I hoped he felt it, too.

"So Aaron, does business usually bring you here to Bourton?" my mother questioned.

I was interested in the answer myself. Apart from my situation, one he'd already told me was unusual, his tours usually focused on London and the surrounding area.

"No, not usually. My present clients are going on a walking tour of the Cotswolds, and it starts here in Bourton."

"A walking tour; that sounds lovely, doesn't it, Jim?" Mother turned and looked at her fiancé who nodded in agreement. "Are there many in this area?"

"Oh indeed, you can hike anywhere from a day to an entire week."

"Are you going on any?" My mother directed her question towards me.

"Uh, I don't know, I never thought of it. I might check it out." I really hadn't planned on going on any extended hikes.

My mother's focus on me didn't last long, and she resumed questioning Aaron. "If you don't mind me asking, do you usually visit clients on a social basis?

My mouth dropped open in shock, but no words came out. Leave it to my mother to be so blunt. I think even Jim was a little surprised by her question, but he didn't say a word, instead he sat there staring at me with a look as if to say – sorry about that.

Aaron laughed. Immediately, the tension in the room eased, and a slow breath escaped my lips. "Not at all," he said clapping his hands on his knees, a grin still pasted on his face. Even in that moment, I couldn't tear my gaze from him as I took in his profile. He looked nothing like the Thomas from my dreams, or rather from Mary's memories, but there was definitely something in his mannerism that was the same. My eyes might not recognize him, but my heart did.

"Krista is... a special case." Aaron's voice immediately brought me out of my stupor, and I once again looked at my mother, our eyes holding onto each other's.

"Oh? In what way?" She tore her gaze from mine and looked to Aaron for his response.

"Well for one, I've had to juggle and adjust to fit her tours in here and there. Usually, I see my clients for a few days and then it's on to the next. Not to mention, she is also renting this flat in my aunt's cottage."

I looked away from Aaron to my mother and then back again. Is that all I am – a special case? I wasn't sure if those were my thoughts or Mary's. Of course, my logical side certainly didn't expect him to declare his feelings for me in front of my mother, but still, I was a little disappointed. Don't you feel anything – some sort of connection – familiarity even? How can you not know it's me? How can you not know that I belong with you? I nervously wrung my hands as questions and feelings spun through my head – confused as to whose thoughts they were. At that moment, I realized that it was going to be a lot harder to convince him, and to make him remember.

"Yoo-hoo! Krista!" My mother called, snapping her fingers at me.

I blinked, realizing all eyes were focused on me. "Sorry, say that again?" I looked at my mother, guessing that she must have asked me a question.

"Aaron's aunt's house?"

"Didn't I tell you?"

My mother shook her head.

I shrugged and said, "It must have slipped my mind."

"Yes, I'm sure it did." My mother smiled at me, and my shoulders relaxed.

Jim, who had sat quietly the whole time, placed his hand on my mother's knee, a gesture that seemingly prevented her from attempting to ask any more questions. In any event, it didn't matter because it seemed it was Aaron's turn.

"So, have you set a wedding date yet?" Aaron asked.

Of all the things we'd talked about, that was the one question I hadn't thought to ask, and I silently waited for their answer.

"Well. . . " My mother looked toward Jim who reached over and took her hand.

"We'd like to get married at the end of September, with your blessing, of course." Jim said, smiling at me.

So soon? Can't you date for a bit longer? Two months, in my opinion didn't seem like a very reasonable amount of time. Of course, my face being like a book, it must have registered all the concern I had. Before I said anything aloud my mother began to counter my inaudible argument.

"You forget, dear, that Jim and I have known each other for a very long time, we even dated before I met your father. What we shared all those years ago resurfaced as if it was yesterday. And I believe to paraphrase you, 'You know it when you see it.'"

I thought back to our conversation during the brunch we had shared before my trip. Having my own words thrown back at me was surprising, especially, coming from my mother. I had no argument.

"Okay." I nodded. "I am very happy for you – both of you." I smiled, truly happy for my mother. She'd been alone for so long that it was time for her to have love again, even my father approved from the great beyond.

"Will you be my maid of honour?"

My mother's question took me completely by surprise. My eyes filled up, and I squeezed them shut for a second to keep the tears back. "Of course, I will!" Rising, I went over to her and hugged her.

"I hate to interrupt this moment, but I should be going."

I turned away from my mother and stared at Aaron who had already risen. For the first time all evening, I had forgotten that he was in the room. Heat rose up my neck and settled in my cheeks and ears. I hadn't expected to have such an emotional exchange with my mother in front of him and Jim. Neither man, however, seemed to mind as they both looked at ease. It was good for Jim if he was going to become my stepfather. It was good for Aaron too, should I manage the impossible and help him remember.

"I think we're going to head out, too." My mother was the next to stand with Jim following in suit.

I led them all to the door as we exchanged pleasantries. Hugging in group-like fashion, I planted a kiss on my mother's and Jim's cheeks. The corner of my eye registered Aaron standing patiently by the door, his hand resting on the knob.

"Join us for breakfast tomorrow?" Jim asked as an endearing smile spread across his face. I could see why my mother was so smitten.

"8 o'clock?" I questioned back, my own smile creeping across my face, my heart warming even more to the idea of Jim becoming part of our family. Suddenly, my heart quickened as my ears picked up the subtle sound of the knob turning, and I quickly focused my attention back to Aaron. I didn't want him to leave before I could say goodbye.

"Nice to meet you and enjoy your stay," Aaron said to my mother and Jim before turning his attention back to me. "Krista, I shall see you on the fourth." He pulled the door open.

"I'll be ready." It wasn't exactly what I wanted to say, and I secretly wished he'd hang back just for a moment, so we could talk privately. I attempted to convey my feelings on my face hoping he'd suddenly find a reason to stay. It seemed, however, that trying to be readable wasn't going to be successful as Aaron stared at me with an unrecognizable expression of his own before heading out the door with Jim following behind. I turned away disappointed, forgetting my mother was still behind me.

"I know what's different about you," she said, a huge grin on her face.

"What?"

"You're in love.," She said it so plainly, like she was reading it in print.

"What?" How the hell does she know that?

"Honey, it's written all over your face."

Oh sure – NOW my face is readable. I briefly looked past my mother at the mirror that hung on the wall behind her. There must be a way of being less transparent – plastic surgery maybe?

"Don't worry; it'll be our little secret, though in truth, I think he knows, too."

My eyes flitted back to her still grinning face. "Who? Jim?" My face must have evolved into yet another strange expression because my mother burst into laughter with tears streaming down her face. I'd never seen her laugh so hard in my life.

"Oh my dear, no wonder you have such a hard time finding true love. You don't see it when it's right in front of your eyes."

I was completely stunned, scared, overwhelmed, and in utter disbelief. How can she see something that I apparently can't? I stared at her, not saying a word, for there wasn't a clear way, in my mind at least, of expressing exactly what it was that I wanted to say.

"He couldn't keep his eyes off of you, and he jumped whenever you brushed up against him, it was almost electric. Not to mention the brief look of disappointment I saw in his eyes when he saw you had company. He definitely has feelings for you; he just might not be willing to admit it yet." She took me in her arms, hugged me tightly, and walked out the door leaving me staring after her.

Maybe it wasn't going to be so hard after all.

Thirty-Six

My mother had given me hope, and it was that hope that I clung to as each day passed. My anticipation grew as I waited to see Aaron again, and though it was difficult, I kept myself busy.

I spent a good part of the day on Saturday with my mother and Jim shopping and visiting museums. The time I spent with my mother was pleasant, and it reminded me of when my father was alive.

As a family, we had been close for the most part, but sometimes my father played the mediator and kept the peace in times of conflict. With just a look, he could stop my mother in mid-nag and keep me from insolence. He helped with compromises when my mother was being over-protective, and he let me know when I was being unreasonable. When he died a part of my mother died, too, I know because I saw it in her eyes. One day the light was there and then – Poof! Just like that, it was gone. No longer was there anyone to keep her from nagging and no one to keep me from talking back. That first year was tough, but as I matured, I realized that my mother wasn't the enemy, that she really did have my best interest at heart. So on the advice my father had given me a few years earlier, I learned how to compromise, to suck it up and take 'no' for an answer.

Over the years, we developed a mutual respect for each other, but we never regained the bond we had once shared. Now that she had found love again, that feeling of closeness began to resurface in just those few days together. When the time came for her departure, we said tearful goodbyes and as my mother and I hugged, I felt all the years of tension wash away with the tears that we shed.

The gloomy sound of rain tapping at my window roused me from my sleep – it was perfect funeral weather. My eyes fluttered open and scanned my dimly lit room, confirming what my ears suspected; the day was indeed dismal.

I burrowed under my blankets with the remnants of a dream nipping at my conscious, compelling me to remember. I gave in and laid there for some time, struggling to recall my dream. It had been awhile since dreams of Mary occupied my mind, almost as if they never existed, but of course, that wasn't true, the proof lived in my notebook. That same notebook rested patiently on the nightstand waiting for its next entry. Night after night, my sleep was silent, devoid of dreams, and morning after morning, the notebook remained closed.

An hour later, and still no recollection of my dream, I gave up, preferring the idea of a hot shower instead. My subconscious hoped the steam would conjure up an image from my past on the mirror, but unfortunately only my blurry reflection stared back from the steam-covered mirror. It seemed Mary no longer wanted to reveal herself to me, nor could I count on new memories to guide me – she had done her job, and now it was my turn.

I dressed slowly and trudged out into the kitchen for a light breakfast. The depressing day weighed heavily on me, my usual morning appetite diminished. Funerals weren't my favourite. I chuckled at the thought, shaking my head – they weren't anyone's favourite. However, as part of the community, and that was how I felt, it was important for me to pay my last respects to the old woman who had given me the clarity that I needed.

Fortunately, by the time I left the apartment, the rain had slowed considerably, and it was only spitting. The streets were relatively quiet as I trudged along slowly to the old, stone church. Whether it was because of the dreary day or the fact that I was going to a funeral, it was difficult to say, but the walk seemed much longer, and I feared I would be late. My worries, however, were unfounded, and there was plenty of time to spare as I walked into the church along with a large number of people. Inside, I found an equal amount of mourners had gathered, and I managed to find a seat at the back of the church in the last pew. I was happy to see that she'd touched so many lives and was important to so many. In my mind, there was nothing worse than dying alone, with no one to remember you.

I looked around at the beautiful, old church with its cheerful, blue carpeting, decorated ceiling, and stained glass windows. Other than weddings, funerals, and baptisms, it had been a long time since I attended a regular mass, and I made a promise to myself to try to go more often when I returned home.

By the time the service started, the church was filled to capacity, and as the pallbearers brought the casket in, an unexpected sense of envy came over me. I was envious of those around me who truly knew and loved the old woman. Suddenly, my stomach sank. I took a deep breath and slowly let the air out. I didn't have the right to be there – her name wasn't even known to me. The urge to leave was strong, but I couldn't find it in me to get up and walk away. I sat quietly, learning much about the old woman from the minister and all those who approached the altar and said a few words. When it was all over, I waited patiently for the entire congregation to follow out behind the casket. While the rest proceeded to the cemetery, I trudged back home in the rain under the protection of my umbrella.

The water sprayed off the tips of my shoes as I sloshed along the seemingly empty streets of Bourton. It was a ghost town, and in that moment, I never felt lonelier. Perhaps it was the distraction of watching my feet splash along the road, but when I finally looked up, I was approaching the old woman's house. I shook my head in disbelief, the trip back home always seemed much faster. With no conscious effort, my feet stopped, and I found myself staring at the window where I had seen the old woman smiling her approval at me. I found myself wishing to see her again. Suddenly, the front door swung open, startling me.

"Are you Krista?" A young man called from the front door. I nodded, surprised that the young man knew my name. "I have something for you. Please wait a moment." He turned and went back into the house.

I didn't move any closer, I only stood there on the walk staring back at the house, waiting for him to return. When he did, he'd pulled on a jacket and shoes. Opening an umbrella, he made his way out to me on the street.

"Here, my grandmother left this for you."

I looked at his outstretched hand. "Your grandmother?"

"I don't do well at funerals," the young man said, still holding the envelope out to me.

With some trepidation, I carefully plucked it from his hand, rubbed the creases from my forehead with my other hand, and stuffed the envelope into my pocket. "I'm Andrew." The young man thrust his hand toward me.

"Nice to meet you," I said, shaking his hand. "I'm really sorry for your loss."

"Thank you. Did you know my grandmother well?"

"Ah no, not really." I didn't want to get into my lack of familiarity concerning his grandmother.

Andrew nodded as though he understood. "Well, I should go. It was nice to meet you," he said abruptly and headed back toward the house, leaving me to stare after him long after he'd shut the door.

When I finally returned home, I shook out my umbrella and left it on the mat before making my way up the stairs. I shivered slightly, as the dampness of the day started to settle in my bones. Inside the apartment, I peeled out of my raincoat and hung it on the back of the door, becoming mesmerized by the rainwater as it ran in rivulets before finally dripping onto the floor mat below. My mind and body were numb from both the cold rain and the encounter with Andrew. After a few moments passed, I shook myself out of my stupor, reached into the pocket of my raincoat, and retrieved the slightly damp envelope. With shaky hands, I carefully opened it up and read its contents.

Krista,

I only wish we'd had more time.

Ann

P.S. When you get the book back, please keep it.

After two solid days of rain, the clouds began to clear just as the sun disappeared from the sky. The following day, I would be seeing Aaron, and we would be heading out on another adventure, albeit a short one for where we were going. It wasn't on the original itinerary, but I had the overwhelming desire to visit Cornwall, and Aaron being an ever accommodating guide, said he knew the perfect place. I had no idea exactly where we were going, only that we were leaving very early. So at nine o'clock, I crawled into bed. Although I was excited about my upcoming trip, the sound of chirping crickets lulled me to sleep.

Morning came quickly, and I was wide-awake just as the birds began their morning choir practice. I was undecided which excited me more – the trip to Cornwall or the time I would spend with Aaron. In either case, it only took me half an hour to get ready which left me with plenty of time to waste as the sun started to make an appearance.

By the time fifteen minutes had passed, I began regretting my decision to dress so quickly. As each additional minute slowly ticked by, my anticipation grew. Waiting became almost unbearable, and I needed a diversion. I made my way over to the computer where a new diversion came in the form of several e-mails from friends, and so I began replying to each one.

As I finished the last message and sent it on its way, a sharp knock at the door startled me. In my haste, I rose quickly, and had to grab the back of the chair as a head rush almost brought me back down again. I closed my eyes tightly and waited a moment for the dizziness to clear. Luckily, it did just as another rap sounded at the door.

"Just a second." I called out. My balance regained, I made my way to the door and opened it.

"Hi!" I said stepping back to let Aaron in. "I'll just grab my bag." It took everything I had not to stand on tiptoe and greet him with a kiss. I had turned and started to walk away when he took my arm and stopped me.

"Wait a minute, can we talk first?" He tried to smile, but I could see there was sadness behind his eyes.

"Is everything okay?" I asked, almost dreading his answer as we headed into the living room and took a seat.

"Yes, for now. I just wanted you to be aware that since our visit with my mother, she has gotten weaker."

"Oh, Aaron, I'm sorry. Look if you don't want to go anywhere I completely understand." I touched his hand gently, by now I was used to the almost electric-like feeling that passed between us whenever our skin met.

"It's fine, she's stable. I just wanted to warn you, just in case. Anyway, when we get back I'm heading to Tockington for the weekend." He looked down at my hand covering his – I withdrew it.

"You're sure you still want to go?"

"Yes, there isn't anything I can do. Anyway, every time I see her... well, I say my goodbyes – just in case."

No words could be spoken that would ease the pain so clearly seen in his eyes. Instead, I nodded in understanding and offered a sympathetic smile. After the weekend I'd had with my mother and the closeness we'd shared, I didn't want to imagine it.

"Are you ready?" He tried to sound excited as he clapped his hands on his knees.

"Of course, I'm always ready." I smiled back at him. I wanted nothing more than to take him into my arms. His pain resonated within me.

"Right then, let's go." Aaron rose from the couch and headed toward the door. "Are you coming?" He looked back at me; still seated in the living room.

It was a quiet ride for the first twenty minutes. I stared out the window watching the streets come alive as people made their way to work, or wherever they were going.

"Would you like to know where we're going?" Aaron asked.

I pulled my focus from the window and looked at him. My mind was so preoccupied with Aaron's situation that I almost forgot about the excitement that had enveloped me earlier.

"We're going to Cornwall, aren't we?"

"Well yes, but don't you want to know where in Cornwall?"

"Surprise me."

Half an hour later, I drifted off to sleep.

Thirty-Seven

Every so often, I became vaguely aware of music floating somewhere around me. Soothing melodies and lyrics lulled me back to a world of quiet, darkness, where no images flashed behind my eyelids, no dreams invaded my mind, and into a world where time advanced at an ever quickening pace. Each time the music drifted in, it tried to draw me back with it like a riptide. I struggled to break free, wanting to return to my peaceful darkness. Slowly, my body began its decent into the dark abyss again and my muscles relaxed, the music drifted away – unsuccessful. Just as I was about to make the final leap into peaceful darkness, I suddenly became aware that my mouth was wide-open, and drool pooled in its corners on the verge of escape.

I whipped my head forward, closed my mouth, and with the back of my hand wiped away the drool that had begun to trail down my chin – all in one fluid motion. Silently, I hoped Aaron hadn't seen the whole sordid thing.

"Did you have a good sleep?" Aaron smiled at me. By the look on his face, I was too late.

The thought of denying my state of sleep crossed my mind briefly, but then I'd have to explain the reason for the whole mouth-open-drooling thing. What I needed was to use a word that suggested my complete and utter depth of unconsciousness. A word that would describe a state where in no way was I accountable for the drool dripping from my mouth. "How long was I out for?" It was the best I could do.

"Oh, I would say about two."

"Two? Two what? Two seconds, two minutes, two hours... " I was still rubbing my eyes awake.

"Two hours. Actually, more like two and a half."

"Two and a half hours!"

"Yes, maybe even closer to three." Aaron chuckled.

"Oh! I missed the whole drive out here." I was disappointed.

"Not the whole trip," Aaron said optimistically. "There's still about another hour to go. Besides, you'll see it all on the way back. Are you hungry?" He changed the subject. Right on cue, my stomach rumbled in response to the mere mention of the potential for food, giving Aaron all the response he needed from me. "We can pull off at the next town and grab a quick bite; I need to stretch my legs, anyway."

By the time we got back on the road, I was wide-awake and quite certain that I would stay that way for the remainder of the trip. My stomach was now satisfied by delicious scones, of which I purchased a few more for the trip, and my legs felt well stretched.

Tall fir trees, forests, hills, and open fields lined both sides of the highway as we continued on our travels. Neither of us spoke, and for the first time it was not an awkward silence, but rather comfortable like we'd been together for so long that we didn't feel the need for constant conversation.

I stared out the windows watching the scenery go by, too pre-occupied by the view to worry about anything else. Occasionally we would pass a road sign, but I still couldn't figure out where we were heading. Each time we'd pass through a small town, I'd wonder if that was where our journey ended.

Strangely, and yet not so strangely, I felt connected to the area. Though not having any real clues from the memories that Mary had left me with, I couldn't help but wonder if Cornwall was where it all began.

It wasn't until I spied a large body of water out Aaron's window that my curiosity piqued and the silence that surrounded us was broken by my voice, startling not only Aaron, but myself as well.

"Oh! The ocean." I pointed, looking past Aaron to get a better glimpse.

"Surprised?" Aaron laughed.

"Yes, actually, I am. I thought, somehow, we were inland. Where exactly are we going anyway?" Finally, I asked the question I'd wanted to ask since getting back on the road. However, for some reason it hadn't sprang from my mouth.

"Bude."

"Bude! And why Bude?" I asked, saying the name with a poorly attempted English accent.

"Are you mocking me?" Aaron shook his head. "You should know that was a poor English accent." Aaron laughed at me again. He briefly looked in my direction and for that split second, our eyes locked, his eyes piercing through me as if he could see my soul. I quickly turned away and stared out the window as tiny, electric-like charges trailed from my head down to my feet, each one seemingly setting off the next, like a string of firecrackers.

"Well, maybe by the end of the summer I'll get the hang of it," I said quietly as my body recovered, my eyes focusing on the passing scenery. Several seconds passed before I finally turned my attention back toward Aaron and asked, "So why Bude?"

Aaron shrugged. "We had a holiday home there; I practically grew up on the shores of Bude."

"A holiday home! Well lad-di-da," I snickered, envisioning an opulent home overlooking the shoreline, Aaron playing on the beach as a child while his parents looked on.

"It wasn't all that glamorous, believe me."

"Can you show it to me?" I was curious to see any place where Aaron had lived; it made me feel closer to him.

"It burned down. Thankfully we weren't there at the time." I detected a touch of sadness in his voice.

"That's too bad!" The sound of my own disappointment surprised me. I sighed, I really wanted to know everything about him.

"Yes, but then they bought a much nicer place in Bridport." The corner of his mouth pulled into a smile as he looked at me from the corner of his eye.

"Would Bridport be nearby?" I wanted to keep the conversation going, talking only about him.

"It's not too far, a couple of hours away. In Dorset though, not Cornwall"

"Geography must have been a bitch to learn here." I laughed, shaking my head and looking back out my window.

"Yes, but history was even worse."

By the time we reached Bude, I had gotten Aaron to tell me as much as possible about the place and the summers he'd spent there. It was definitely his home away from home. He had made a number of friends during his summers, some of whom still lived in the area and with whom he still had regular contact. It was with one of these friends, I learned, that we would in fact be staying with for the next couple of nights. Aaron continued to recount his stories, and I listened quietly as we made our way through the streets, each story spurring on another memory.

His teen years of course were by far the most interesting as he recounted tales of mischief, beach parties, and of course, his first love, the details of which he didn't get into. Though Bude was where he found his first love, secretly I hoped it would help him to find his last. I made a mental note to make sure and glean some more information about Aaron and his summers in Bude.

"There is one place I must show you first before anything else." Aaron said excitedly, as if he had just remembered. I was happy to go anywhere he wanted to take me.

We drove along for a few minutes longer, finally stopping where the road seemingly turned into a trail with a stretch of beach at its end.

"You're taking me to the beach?" I asked as we got out of the car. I stood behind the open door staring out at the beach ahead of me.

"Not quite." Aaron closed his door and walked around to the front of the car. I reached back in, grabbed the scones, and put them in my bag before closing the door and joining him.

We walked down the trail that lay ahead of us, my eyes carefully watching my step as we picked our way along. Eventually the trail forked, and I found myself heading up hill rather than down toward the beach.

"Where are we going?" I asked trudging along behind him.

The waves crashed down on the rocks below as we continued our gentle climb, the long grass brushed against my legs, and every once in a while I had to rub away the tickling sensation it brought on.

"To one of my..." Aaron's voice was lost in the wind; it was difficult to hear him as he climbed ahead of me. There was no point asking again.

The short hike was getting steeper, and just as we neared the top, Aaron looked back at me, his face red from the climb and the heat from the sun. "Just one more step." He reached out his hand to me, and I was glad to take it as he pulled me up to the top.

It wasn't exactly the same, but so close that it brought back the memory from that night so long ago. We had run through the long grass and up the hill to the meadow. We stopped, just as we neared the edge of the cliff. Had we not, we would have run off the edge of the world and disappeared into the churning waters below. I couldn't be certain, of course, that it was the same place. Too much time had passed. It was another lifetime ago.

"Come on." Aaron grabbed my hand and pulled me after him. "You've really got to see this." I followed along happily, my hand in his.

Aaron let go of me, and I felt my heart sink a little as we stood at the edge looking down at the water and the rocks below.

"Isn't this a great view?" he asked, his eyes staring straight ahead at the open ocean.

"It is."

We stood there for a moment – silent, Aaron staring out at the ocean, me staring at him. Waves crashed below us as seagulls screamed overhead. It was déjà vu all over again.

"When I asked you before where we were going, what did you say?" I asked.

"It's probably very near, if not my most favourite place on earth. I came here a lot when I was younger, mostly by myself," he said finally turning to face me. "I don't think I have ever come up here with anyone else. Not this specific place anyway. There are plenty of others all along the coast line just like it of course, but I kept this one for myself."

"Oh, well I feel honoured then." I teased.

"And so you should." He smiled back. I so wanted for him to take my hand again as we stood there, but then suddenly he sat down. I stood for a moment looking down at him. "Are you going to sit or just stand there?" he asked looking up at me, his hand shielding the sun from his eyes.

Silently, I sat beside him. Time passed as we sat there listening to the sound of the waves and the gulls. The whole while Mary's memories flooded my mind, and I couldn't help but wonder if he felt anything. I absently picked at the grass beside me, feeling more awkward than ever. I didn't know what to do or say. Would this place make him remember?

"I finished that book you know." Aaron's voice startled me a little.

What is he talking about – what book? Then I remembered. "You did?" I held my breath as I worked to remain calm. I didn't want him to perceive the excitement in my voice.

He nodded, and I waited for him to say more.

"Was it interesting?" I asked finally, realizing he wasn't going to offer up anything more.

"It was." Before I could ask another question, Aaron beat me to it. "Hadn't you read it?" he said turning toward me.

"No – not yet." I looked down at the clover in my hand and tossed it away after counting only three leaves.

"Are you going to?"

"Maybe – I don't know." We sat silently for a while, both of us absently picked at the grass, occasionally looking at what our fingers had plucked.

Aaron let out a sigh and I looked at him. He opened his mouth then closed it again, like he wanted to say something but wasn't quite sure how to say it.

"What?" I asked.

Finally, for once, it wasn't my face being read like a book, and I was proud of myself for being able to read Aaron's face – a face that never revealed its secrets.

"I shouldn't tell you this, but Peter mentioned you sort of believe in that... stuff in the book."

I remembered the conversation with Peter after he'd read my notes. He'd told me that Aaron wasn't as skeptical about the whole notion of past lives, ghosts and the like, and that he might be able to help me. He also promised he wouldn't say anything – I made a mental note to be more careful around Peter.

"Yes, I do. Did he also tell you that he told me you weren't as skeptical about those sorts of things?" I thought it was only fair to divulge what Peter had told me since he'd already done the same.

Aaron laughed and nodded.

"Do you believe in the possibility?" I stopped plucking at the grass and stared at Aaron, his focus on the horizon.

"I did, or used to," he said. A sudden feeling of disappointment blanketed me, and I turned my gaze away, unexpected tears threatening as my fingers nervously plucked at the grass again. "But after reading that book, maybe I do again."

"Really!" I tried to keep my excitement back as my focus trained on Aaron. The threatening tears evaporating as I took a breath to calm myself down. "What in that book changed your mind?"

Aaron shrugged, his eyes still focused on the horizon. "It wasn't just the book."

"Oh?"

Aaron sighed rather deeply. He looked from the ground back out to the open ocean. Several minutes passed before he spoke and when he did, I wasn't prepared for his response.

"You did, too."

My heart pounded, skipped, and pounded again before finally slowing to a somewhat normal rhythm. Silence followed as even the crashing waves and the screeching gulls waited for further explanation.

I stopped picking at the grass and brushed the remnants from my legs before drawing them up and wrapping my arms around them. My chin rested on my knees. I didn't know what to say, and every time my mouth opened, I found myself closing it again. To put into words what my brain was thinking wasn't easy. The opportunity for conversation had finally presented itself, and I found myself mute.

"How?" I finally asked.

Aaron looked at me briefly before returning his gaze out over the ocean. "I used to dream about this faceless, nameless girl. She felt real to me, and I spent a lot of time searching for the essence of her in every girl I met. Even my mother had convinced me we were destined to meet – she was my future. I gave up after a while, but I think a part of me keeps looking for her." He fell silent for a moment, dug a small rock out of the ground and threw it out over the edge of the cliff.

It took all my self-control not to tell him what I knew. I battled with the part of me that wanted him to know that I was that faceless, nameless girl. I wanted him to know that the girl from his dream had been from his past – our past from another time. Yet, at the same time, that girl also held the key to his future –

our future. It was a continuous loop tying the past and the future together. I kept my mouth closed.

Aaron dug out another small stone and threw it even further. "It's been awhile since I've believed in... any of it." He waved his hands out in front of him for emphasis.

"And..." I prodded, keeping the conversation heading in the right direction.

"And now, I don't know," he said looking at me. "You are so familiar to me, like the girl from my dream. Though it has been a while, she's ingrained in here." He reached up and pointed to his head. "Your eyes though, it's like I can see into you and –"

"Me, too," I interrupted. A look of astonishment crossed his face.

"What do you mean?" he asked, turning his whole body and facing me. I did the same in return.

"When I look at your eyes it's like..." I hesitated, what was it like exactly?

"I know," he said, the corners of his mouth twitching a bit.

"When we touch, do you feel..." I didn't know quite how to explain it, but as I searched for the right words Aaron finished my sentence.

"Like an electric shock?" he offered.

"Yeah, only not... painful."

"No, definitely not painful, more like..." He stopped; his eyes squinted, as though he were trying to think of just the right words.

"It's almost..." I felt myself blush, "like a rush?" Not exactly the feeling I was going for but probably the closest I was going to get.

"Yeah, almost," he reaffirmed and smiled.

Again, we were silent before I broke it with yet another question. "Do you have any idea what's going on?" I asked.

Aaron looked at me, cocked his head to the side, and smiled. "Do you?"

I told the truth, telling him that I was sure that I had lived before. I spoke of my experiences with two psychic mediums, one of which had given me the book that he read. I told him about my dreams or memories of my past life. Finally, I told him I believed we were connected.

He sat there for a moment staring at me, and I realized then that I'd said far too much even though he admitted sensing there was a connection between us. He turned away and looked back out over the ocean, the sun still high in the sky.

"We should probably get going, I told Nate we'd be there by one o'clock."

Aaron brushed the grass from his lap and stood up, looked down at me, and stretched out his hand. I took hold of it feeling that familiar exchange of electricity, as he pulled me up a little too hard. I lost my balance and fell slightly forward into him, his arms instinctively wrapped around me for protection.

"Oh, sorry." I said trying to pull away from the now awkward situation.

"Don't be."

Aaron bent forward and kissed me. A kiss that was long, passionate, and gentle. A kiss saved for lovers who have been apart; a kiss that sent heat and shivers at the same time, coursing through my body. A kiss that made time stand still and yet made the world spin. A kiss that promised; a kiss that bound – for eternity.

My legs almost gave out from underneath, but his strong arms supported me while I regained my own strength. Suddenly he pulled away. "Sorry."

"Why?" I asked, remembering his other apology after kissing me in the apartment.

"Because it isn't right," he said straightening up and taking a step back from me.

"What isn't."

"Us. This isn't very professional of me. Not to mention Peter." He looked at me with an expression I couldn't read.

"Peter!" I was astounded. "What does Peter have to do with any of this?" I held out my hand and waved it between us.

"He told me he kissed you."

"So?"

"So he said you weren't looking for any relationship and now..."

I understood why the hesitation, the hot and cold responses I got from him, and the sense of turmoil. I laughed as it began to make sense. "Yes," I said when I finished laughing. "At the time, I didn't want a relationship and I wasn't looking for one. But then I met you, and I know that this connection between us is..." I watched his face for a reaction, but there was nothing. "You have to understand that..." You've already said too much. I silently warned myself. It's up to him. I looked down at the ground.

"Look," Aaron said, interrupting my thoughts. He reached over and placed his hands on my shoulders forcing me to look up at him. "I feel that there's something, too..."

"But you don't understand it's..." Enough! I warned myself again.

"This mightn't be anything more than... Look I don't want to misguide you, lead you in to feeling that this could be anything more than just a... a summer romance. Need I remind you that you are leaving in a few weeks?"

No, he didn't need to remind me. I knew all too well that my time was limited, but in that instant, I wanted to live in the moment and not worry about leaving. I shook my head in response to his question.

"I don't know if I've had a past life Krista. I don't have the memories or dreams like you. I don't know if that girl from my dreams means anything. All I know is that there is something between us that I can't deny – won't."

I leaned forward and hugged him, wrapping my arms around his middle and feeling him pull me closer. It didn't matter that he didn't remember, I had enough memories for both of us, and I would find a way somehow to help him or at the very least make him believe that we truly were meant to be together. It was a start, and I was taking it.

"And Peter?" he said whispering into my hair, he kissed the top of my head.

"We'll figure everything out."

Thirty-Eight

Bude; with its coastline beaches and cliffs, historic homes, pubs and so much more, was now not only Aaron's history but a part of mine as well. The two days spent there, were more than I could have imagined and if there was any possible way to make it last longer, I would have tried to find one. However, that was not the case and with sadness in my heart, I packed my few things back into my bag, preparing for the trip home. We wouldn't be leaving until the afternoon but as always, there was a need to be ready, just in case. Besides it was very early and by the sounds of things, or lack thereof, no one else was awake yet. Since my room had its own private bath, I showered and dressed, too.

While patiently waiting for the sun to rise, I thought back over the past couple of days, remembering every detail and etching it into my brain. I was afraid that when we left there, Aaron and I would go back to the same client/tour guide relationship – attributing everything we said and felt to a very short summer romance.

When Aaron and I had showed up at Nate's house we had decided to build a relationship, we would worry about my leaving when it came time. Aaron introduced me as Krista, leaving out the client part, and when we went for a walk after dinner, he held my hand. Later that evening, Nate and Gwen took us to a pub for drinks and music. Aaron sat beside me and despite the glances from both Nate and Gwen; he put his arm around me and pulled me close. At some point in the evening, Nate and Aaron disappeared, and I assumed they were talking about our relationship, as Gwen had had a few questions of her own. When we had finally returned home, Nate and Gwen went to bed while Aaron and I compared the interrogation we'd both undergone. Hours later, we headed to our own separate rooms. Saying goodnight wasn't easy, but we had decided spending the night together would not be a good idea, at least not in Nate and Gwen's home.

The next day, I slept in, and awoke only when a knock at the door, a rather impatient one, roused me from my sleep. I had been dreaming of Aaron and didn't want it to end. Reluctantly, I climbed out of bed and opened the door. Aaron whisked me off my feet, gently tossed me back on the bed, and climbed in beside me, pulling me close under the blankets.

"What time –?" I had started to ask.

"Eight," he replied, pulling me closer.

"What about Nate and Gwen?"

"Gone to work, I suppose." He nuzzled his face against me, and I felt his warm breath on the back of my neck and shivered; his arms tightened around my waist. "Are you cold?" he asked, sounding drowsy.

"No," I whispered and closed my eyes, drifting off into peaceful sleep, a smile pasted to my face.

When we finally awoke, it was to the sound of loud banging downstairs. Like two teenagers, we jumped up quickly; as though afraid someone would catch us. Fits of giddy laughter took hold of both of us, as if we were drunk. Slowly, we regained control of ourselves, stifling our giggles. Aaron kissed me quickly before heading back to his room, and left me standing there still feeling very much intoxicated. When I finally sobered, I jumped in the shower. The warm water washed over me, caressing me. I wrapped my arms around myself and closed my eyes, imagining Aaron's arms around me. I stood that way for some time before finally waking from the reverie and realizing that if I soon didn't make an appearance, there would be questions.

That morning, Aaron showed me around town, taking me to all of his favourite old hangouts, at my request, and together we found some new ones. We crammed as much as possible into what little time we had. Later that afternoon, we packed a picnic, headed back to his – and now my – most favourite place on earth and watched the sunset. I had never felt happier or more complete in all my life.

I sat on the bed with its floral bedspread, playing with the fringe on a matching throw pillow, a wide grin spreading across my face as I recounted the events of the past two days. When the sky lightened, I crossed the cool hardwood floor to the window, spreading the lightweight curtains apart to watch as the street came alive. In the distance, the vast Atlantic spread from shore to horizon. Oddly enough, I was no longer afraid of it.

A light rap at the door brought me from my trance, but I couldn't be bothered to cross the room to open it, instead calling out to the knocker to come in.

His reflection in the window caught my attention, and I smiled automatically as he approached. I continued to gaze out the window as morning brought life to the quiet street. He wrapped his arms around me, and I closed my eyes, savouring the moment.

"We have to go," he whispered, kissing the top of my head.

I could tell by his voice that he was upset.

"What's the matter?" I asked turning around. He wore an expression of deep sadness, one I'd never seen.

"It's my Mum," he choked. "Doc Brown says it's time. I'll give you a moment to pack-up."

"It's okay, I'm ready to go." I turned away from him, unable to bare the sadness in his eyes any longer and grabbed my bag from the chair by the bed. Quietly, we left the room.

We drove on silently, eating the breakfast Gwen had thought-
fully packed for us although Aaron left most of his untouched.
Finally, after half an hour had passed I broke the silence.

"You are taking me home first?" I expected as much as obviously, it was a time for family and close friends. However, knowing
that the drive from Bude to Bourton had taken us a little over
four hours, I had no idea where Tockington was in relation.

"There's no time." Aaron stated in monotone, staring straight
ahead at the road as he drove.

"Oh." Uneasiness fell over me as I realized what his words
meant.

"I'm sorry. I know it's not a very comfortable situation for you
right now." Aaron looked at me for a brief moment before focusing
his attention back on the road. "Tockington is about a two-and-
a-half hour drive from here," he continued. "We've got to head
straight there." He looked at me again and smiled, but I knew it
was only for my benefit.

"I promise I'll stay out of everyone's way. Maybe I'll go for a
walk or something."

"No! I want you with me, I need you." His voice dropped to
a whisper, his knuckles whitened as his hands tightened on the
steering wheel.

I reached over and touched his arm. He relaxed his grip and
the tension eased from his jaw line. He reached out his hand and
held mine, and there we remained for the rest of the trip. Neither
of us spoke, each of us locked within our own worlds.

When we pulled into the drive, behind two other vehicles, I
recognized one immediately as Peter's; my heart began thumping.
They weren't my family, and yet I felt as close to them as though
I'd known them for years; my heart was breaking, not just for
Aaron, but for everyone who loved Kate.

Before Aaron reached the door, it opened and Peter ushered
us in, a grim look on his face.

"Is she..." Aaron began to ask before emotion stopped him in his tracks.

"No mate, she's waiting for you, hurry!"

Aaron left immediately; his hurried footsteps reverberating as he quickly climbed the stairs. I turned and followed Peter into the parlour, each of us taking a seat on the couch side by side.

"Did you have a nice time in Bude?" Peter asked, though by his tone I knew he didn't really care. Kate was family to him as well.

"Yes." I reached over and took Peter's hand, trying very hard not to shed any tears. I was the one who needed to be strong for them. I squeezed my eyes shut and took a deep breath, maintaining my composure. "How are you holding up? I know this is hard for you, too." I squeezed Peter's hand.

He didn't speak, only squeezed my hand back as his reply. We sat holding hands for a few more minutes when Jane entered the room carrying a tray laden with teacups, cookies, and a teapot.

"Oh Jane, let me take that. I jumped up, taking the tray from her visibly shaking hands, and placed it on the coffee table. "Sit down, Jane, I'll get this stuff." Too upset to argue, Jane allowed me to guide her to a chair. "Is there anything else I can get either of you?"

Jane tearfully shook her head and dabbed at her eyes with what was left of a very tattered tissue.

Peter cleared his throat. "Tissue." Was all he managed saying.

Out of the corner of my eye, I caught Jane beginning to rise. "I'll get it." I said gently. Jane didn't argue only told me there was a box in the kitchen. I returned a moment later with the box of tissues in hand and held it out to both Peter and Jane before setting it on the coffee table beside the untouched tea.

"Can I pour anyone a cup?" I asked.

Both Peter and Jane shook their heads, and I took my place back on the couch beside Peter. The three of us sat quietly mesmerized by the sound of the ticking grandfather clock in the room. I jumped as the clock began to chime. Just at the last of ten chimes, a tall, grey haired man walked into the room. Peter jumped to his feet.

"Is..." Peter choked out.

The man shook his head, as though he knew what Peter was about to ask. Peter let out an audible breath before plunking himself back down on the couch beside me. The man took his seat in the chair at the other end of the couch.

"Hello, I'm Krista." I said standing up and walking toward the man with my hand outstretched.

He stood up in turn, took my hand and smiled. "Pleasure to meet ye, Krista. Basil Broon, I'm Kate's physician."

Dr. Brown's strong Scottish accent caught me off guard, though it was a pleasant surprise.

"Can I pour you some tea?" I asked pointing to the untouched tray.

"Nay, that's all right I'll pour it meself. Aaron has asked ye to join him."

My eyes widened and they flicked back and forth between Peter and Jane, their equally stunned expressions pasted to their faces. Never in my entire life had I felt more awkward or out of place as in that very moment. I wanted nothing more than to run from there and hide out in Aaron's car until it was over.

I looked back at Basil, who smiled somewhat knowingly. "It's all right, me dear, Kate asked for ye."

"What?" Peter said as I headed out of the room with Jane explaining to him that we'd already met. Their voices disappeared as I rounded the corner and headed up the stairs.

I knocked quietly at the closed door and waited for Aaron. His red eyes greeted me as he opened the door and stepped back to allow me into the room.

The frail looking woman on the bed was not the same person I remembered meeting only a short time ago. I approached and took a seat beside Aaron. Kate opened her eyes and offered a very week smile before closing them again. I smiled back, but instantly put my head down, my eyes filling with tears. My hand rested on the bed beside her, and as I worked to compose myself, I felt a very light and cold touch. My eyes instantly went to my hand, Kate's own hand rested by mine; a finger gently stroked the back for a brief second before dropping and joining the rest of her unmoving hand. Kate opened her eyes again and looked at Aaron. He moved closer to his mother and listened carefully, her lips barely moving.

"I think she wants to say something to you." Aaron rose from his spot at the head of his mother's bed and made room for me to get closer to Kate.

I leaned in as Kate painstakingly whispered the last words she would speak. "Take. Care. Of. Him... remember." Kate closed her eyes, her breathing laboured.

I moved out of the way, letting Aaron back in. He pushed his chair as close as possible to the bed. Bending his head forward he pressed his cheek against Kate's arm and closed his eyes.

"I'll get the others." I gently touched Aaron's shoulder and left the room. It only took a few seconds to get Jane, Peter, and the doctor, but it felt much longer.

I stood in the doorway as they encircled Kate's bed, turning to leave them in their moment of privacy.

"Stay, please!" Aaron's voice was monotone.

I looked around the room at the others who didn't seem to notice, their only focus on Kate. I nodded, but stayed in the doorway of the room, a thick silence filled the air. For what seemed an eternity, we watched as Kate's chest rose and fell with each breath, the pause between becoming longer and longer, until eventually, it stopped all together. Whispers and quiet cries of goodbye filled the air; I turned leaving the room, giving them their final moments.

Thirty-Nine

I returned to the parlour and sat quietly listening to the grandfather clock as it finished its last chime, thus signalling eleven o'clock. Peter silently joined me, his eyes red and watering. I handed him the box of tissue still on the coffee table. He plunked down beside me and rested his head on the back of the couch.

"I'm so sorry," I said. "Can I get you anything?"

Peter sat up and looked at me, his eyes full of confusion. "I have no right to ask you this, but what's going on?" His tone was even, but I detected accusation in his question.

"I'm not sure I know what you mean."

"I suppose I have to draw it out for you. What's going on between you and Aaron?"

I looked at him in amazement. Is he jealous? How does he know something is going on between Aaron and me? Are we that transparent? Of course, as I thought of it more, the very fact that I was with him during a most private time was enough evidence. Not to mention, other guides under the same circumstances would likely have arranged alternate means of transportation for their clients, should they need to leave unexpectedly. It was perhaps not that difficult to conclude that there was indeed a different nature to our relationship.

"Look," Peter's voice and manner softened, "believe me, I'm over whatever feelings I may have had – really. However, you said you weren't interested in any relationships. So why are you here? Aaron's a pretty private bloke, but to have... a virtual stranger at his mother's deathbed – obviously he has feelings for you. I want to be sure he's not going to get hurt."

Peter was right of course, I was a virtual stranger; with no right to be there, and could I have helped it, I wouldn't be.

"When I told you I wasn't looking for a relationship, it was the truth. But then I met Aaron and well..." My voice trailed off, I was not going to explain to him that I believed Aaron was my soulmate – Mary's Thomas. He'd read my notebook and told me he didn't believe in that stuff.

Peter continued, turning to face me. "So you admit it then, there is something going on between the two of you?"

I nodded and looked down at my hands.

"And what about when you leave? What then?" He waved his arm towards the world outside.

I sighed heavily. "I don't know," I whispered.

"Just don't hurt him. He's been through enough already." Peter got up and left the room, leaving me to sit and question whether the relationship was worth it or not.

"Anyone hungry?"

I looked up to find Jane and Dr. Brown joining me in the parlour. Jane plunked herself down in the chair before anyone could respond, and I sensed her question was merely out of habit and not the desire for feeding anyone.

"Krista, could ye help me for a moment?"

My eyes drifted away from Jane and up at Dr. Brown who was still standing in the entrance of the parlour. "Ah, sure," I said wondering how I could possibly help the doctor.

"Good, follow me please." Dr. Brown turned and left the parlour.

I rose and followed Dr. Brown out, but not before looking back at Jane, resting quietly with her eyes shut.

Dr. Brown led me across the hall and into the den, closing the door behind me. Dark panelling covered the walls of the room and a large bookcase took up an entire wall opposite to the door. A large window, framed by deep red curtains, allowed light to pour in from the front of the house, and anyone sitting at the desk across from it would certainly see any guests approaching from the road. Dr. Brown pulled a large chair from the far corner of the room and placed it in front of the desk.

"Please, have a seat." He pointed to the newly placed chair and made his way around to sit on the other side of the desk. I walked over and sat down, having absolutely no idea why we were in that office and what I could possibly do to help Dr. Brown. "Let me get straight to the point, shall I?"

I nodded and folded my hands on my lap.

"The funeral parlor will be here within the half hour to collect the body."

Again, I nodded in understanding, though still not sure where the conversation was leading.

"The problem is... I can't get Aaron to leave his mother's room in order to prepare her for transport. I was wonderin' if ye could somehow convince him to go. He shouldn't see his ma being placed inside a body bag. It isn't a pleasant spectacle."

"What makes you so sure I can get him to leave?" I asked, trying to reposition myself on the not so comfortable chair.

"I'm not. Peter's already talking with Aaron now, but just in case..." He sighed before speaking again. "I've known Aaron since he was a wee lad. The way I saw him looking at you; if anyone can get him out of the room, ye can." Just as Dr. Brown finished explaining there was a knock at the door. "Come in." Dr. Brown called to the closed door.

"Sorry, doc, but he won't listen to me, either." Peter glared at me before turning toward Dr. Brown.

"Thanks for trying, Peter."

Peter left closing the door behind him. He didn't look at me again and I felt a sudden sadness, like I'd lost a good friend.

"Would ye give it a go?" Dr. Brown looked at me pleadingly.

The closed office door made me feel safe, and I was very reluctant to step from out of that safety. There's no telling how the others would react, especially Peter, if they knew I was going to have my turn at trying to get Aaron out of his mother's room. Dr. Brown apparently was able to read minds too.

"Don't fash, I'll keep both of them in the parlour. I'll tell them you're out in the garden giving them their privacy."

I looked back at Dr. Brown and nodded. "Okay, I'll try, but really I don't know how much better of a job I'll do."

"Och, I suspect you'll do just fine." Dr. Brown smiled, rising from his chair. He made his way to the door and opened it.

I walked out of the office and headed toward the staircase. The walk up the stairs and down the hall toward the bedroom took longer than it should. All the while I thought of what I could say that would convince Aaron to leave. I approached the closed door with apprehension, lightly rapped, and waited. When I heard nothing, I knocked a little louder. The door flung open.

"Look I... Oh it's you, sorry." Aaron stepped back and let me into the room.

"I'm so sorry, Aaron," I said holding my arms out to him, my eyes filled with tears. He stepped forward, enclosed me within his large, warm embrace, and softly cried into my hair. After a moment, he pulled away wiping his eyes with his hands.

"Here." I handed him a tissue from the box on the dresser.

"Thanks. I'm sorry you had to be here for all this. I know this is so very awkward for you – for all of you." He blew his nose.

I reached out and rubbed his arm. "Will you stop worrying about me?"

I could see Kate's body from the corner of my eye as I stood there looking at Aaron. I'd seen plenty of bodies before, but usually only at funeral parlours. This was my first home death experience, other than witnessing the old woman's – Ann's, removal from her home back in Bourton.

"Here, let me. . . " Aaron turned and walked toward the bed and carefully pulled the sheet up over his mother. He hesitated as he neared her face leaning down to kiss her forehead before pulling the sheet the rest of the way up.

"So, come here to convince me to leave?" Aaron asked turning back to face me, a small, forced smile on his face.

"It probably wouldn't be a bad idea." I still hadn't figured out how I was going to convince him.

"I know I should, but if I leave her. . . " He didn't finish his sentence, but I had a strange feeling I knew what he was going to say.

"She's not alone, Aaron."

"No." He turned and faced her. "But I am." His head slumped forward and his shoulders moved, while uncontrollable silent sobs racked his body. My heart broke for him; I walked up and wrapped my arms around him resting my cheek on his back.

"You might feel alone, but you're not. I'm here, Aaron. I'm here," I whispered and he turned, taking me in his arms, his tears starting to ebb. "Hang on." I said pulling away and walking around the end of the bed to the armoire. I pulled open its doors revealing a small drawer inside. I opened the drawer, took out the book, and returned to Aaron's side.

"Your mother wanted to make sure you got this after she. . . " I couldn't bring myself to say the words, so instead I thrust the book toward him. "Here."

"A Bible?" he said taking the book from my hand.

"Open it."

Aaron opened the black, leather-bound Bible to the page where the ribbon held its place. He peered at the pages before him and then gingerly held up the four-leaf clover by the stem. His eyes filled with tears, but only one managed to escape and track down his cheek. I reached up and wiped it away before it fell on the pages of the book he held in front of him.

"I can't believe she kept this?"

"Haven't I already told you that mother's keep just about everything their kids give them?" I smiled and cocked my head to the side. Aaron reciprocated with a smile of his own.

"Yes, you did, but this?" He shook his head.

"Even that."

Aaron nestled the clover back inside its protective pages and closed the book. He looked down at me, his eyes shining. "She made it you know?" Aaron put his arm around my shoulders and began leading me toward the door.

"Made what?" I asked, as he placed his free hand on the doorknob and turned it.

"I hoped she'd live long enough to see another birthday." He pushed the door wide open and signaled me to lead with a wave of his hand. I walked out the door with Aaron following behind. I heard the gentle click as he pulled the door closed behind us.

"Her birthday?" I asked looking up at him. Aaron grabbed my hand and led me down the short hallway, stopping at the top of the stairs.

"Yes, it was today."

Forty

My eyes fluttered open in the darkness; my body still burdened by sleep. For a moment, I had no understanding of where I was, and then it became clear – I was home in Bourton. Rolling over, I nestled my head into the pillow and drifted back into a deep sleep.

Sunlight had already filled my room by the time my eyes popped open and my body began the ascent to consciousness. Blurry eyed, I rolled over rubbing away the last bits of sleep and focused on the alarm clock. I sat up in disbelief, staring at the numbers as they flicked to eleven o'clock. I'd slept the morning away, a consequence of returning home very late or rather, very early.

Back in Tockington, Peter had offered to drive me home, leaving Jane and Aaron behind. By the time we left, it was quite late. I was exhausted, but had managed to stay awake for Peter's sake, though we barely spoke two words. Finally arriving home, and far too tired to even bother getting out of my clothes, I'd kicked off my sandals and jumped into bed.

Sitting up in bed now, I regretted my tired-induced decision. I crawled out, kicking my sandals out of the way and looked at myself in the mirror. Streams of yesterday's make-up tracked down my face. Running my tongue over my gritty teeth, I remembered I hadn't brushed them, either.

"Yuck!" I scrunched my face. Going to bed with dirty teeth was not something I was in the habit of doing.

I turned to make my bed, but thought better of it and instead stripped it of its pale blue sheets. I carried the load into the bathroom and threw it on top of the washer, then stripped out of my clothes and added them to the pile.

Not being able to withstand the feel of my gritty teeth any longer, I brushed them vigorously. The minty freshness of my mouth put a smile on my face, but I wasn't done yet. I jumped into the shower to wash away the rest of yesterday's dirt. The moment the warm water hit my face, I melted into uncontrollable tears, the reason for which I could not explain. By the time the water started turning cold, I felt spent emotionally and physically. I dragged myself from the shower and dressed; thoughts of a large cup of coffee clearly on my mind.

If ever there was a time or a need for company it was at that moment. The thought of being alone for much longer was un-bearable. I wasn't in the mood for conversation, but the desire to surround myself with people was strong, even if they were strangers. I drank about half of my coffee and poured the rest down the sink, deciding to have breakfast in town.

I took my time walking into town, enjoying what was left of the morning air. I stopped when I noticed the 'for sale' sign on Ann's lawn. My eyes fixed instantly onto the house, half-expecting to see her in the window. I shook my head at the obvious absurdity, and continued to amble into town.

Delicious aromas wafted out from a local bakery as I passed. Invisible tendrils of scent reached out and grabbed me, pulling me back. Inside, the smells were almost intoxicating. I waited patiently for my turn at the counter, despite my stomach's com-plaints. Finally, with a scone in one hand and a cup of coffee in the other, I left the bakery. The lush, green grass on the banks of the river was inviting and I strolled over to an empty bench. A dozen or so ducks swam back and forth, dipping and diving for whatever bits of food they could find. I closed my eyes and listened to the sounds around me, wondering how it was possible to be both sad and happy at the same time. Taking the last bit of my scone, I split it in two and tossed it toward a pair of ducks who had just climbed ashore.

The rest of the morning and into the late afternoon, I spent my time walking around town, visiting just about every shop and garden there was, eventually making my way back home.

The cloudy sky began to turn dark and ominous, and the sudden change in the weather caused me to realize how unprepared I was. Though I had noticed the grey, cloudy sky upon leaving my apartment earlier, I was too absorbed in my thoughts to think of taking an umbrella. Of course, as I hurried home, the rain began to fall. First just spitting, but by the time I reached my street, it was coming down in torrents.

Dismissing the unfamiliar car that sat in the drive, I hurried up the walk; it was raining so hard there was no chance to examine it more closely. I pulled out my key, realizing as I placed it in the lock that the front door was already unlocked. For a second I hesitated, certain that I'd locked it behind me. A large clap of thunder and a bright lightning strike helped me make up my mind quickly, and I ducked inside the house, prepared to run up stairs to the safety of my apartment.

"Oh hello, sweetheart!"

I drew my breath in sharply and uttered a small gasp, placing my hand over my heart as it raced.

"I'm sorry, dear; I didn't mean to frighten you."

"That's okay, Jane. I wasn't expecting any one to be here." I felt my heart begin to slow back down to its normal pace. "I didn't recognize the car." Rainwater dripped from the top of my head and down my nose. "I thought you were staying until after the funeral." I combed my fingers through my damp hair, trying to untangle it.

"Why don't you come inside? I'll get you a towel to dry off." Jane turned around and headed back into her home. I kicked off my wet sandals and followed her inside.

Expecting to see very traditional and classic decor, I was surprised to find it was the exact opposite, not completely contemporary, but definitely more twenty-first century than I'd imagined. The living room boasted a burgundy, leather sectional and recliner set complete with a wide screen HDTV. A piece of metal wall art adorned the pale grey wall behind the back of the couch and reflected in the mirror that hung on the wall directly across from it. Some modern art prints and what looked like charcoal drawings, decorated the other walls in both the living, and the adjacent dining room. I followed Jane through her well-decorated living and dining area to her equally well-decorated bed and bathroom, appreciating all that I saw.

"Here you go, dear." Jane handed me a soft and fluffy white towel from the deep, cherry cabinet in her bathroom, which was the same layout as the one in my apartment, complete with soaker tub and separate shower, as well as a washer and dryer.

"You have such a beautiful home," I said gently as I squeezed my hair into the towel and then wiped it down my arms and legs, finally I draped the towel over my shoulders for warmth.

"Oh dear, you're shivering. Why don't you go upstairs, get out of those wet clothes, and then join me for supper. I'll explain everything when you get back." Jane led me from her bedroom back out into the living room. "I won't be heading back tonight," she said half to herself as she stopped to look out the living room window.

"I'll be back in a minute." I handed her back the towel and made my way quickly up the stairs, curious to hear her explanation.

Within seconds, I was wearing a pair of sweats and a tee shirt. I pulled socks on my feet and stuffed them into my slippers and then grabbed my sweater and pulled it on. The thought of blow-drying my hair was fleeting; I was in too much of a hurry to get back to Jane.

"That was quick," Jane said to me as she opened her door.

Upon entering her home once again, I soon realized what it was that I'd been searching for all day. It wasn't that I was looking to spend time around people, it was that I wanted to be around family. Though we'd only met a couple of times, and she wasn't exactly my family, she was the closest thing there was at that moment; before I knew it, I was hugging her.

"There, there, dear," she whispered in my ear as she patted my back. "What's this all about now?"

I pulled away and wiped the single tear that managed to free itself. "I'm sorry. I didn't mean –"

"It's all right, sweetheart. Come, let's sit down." Jane took my hand and led me to her couch.

I sat down and sank into its comfortableness. Jane sat beside me, and for a moment I thought the massive couch would swallow her up. Her small though plump frame, was definitely no match for that much larger piece of furniture. My tears had all but stopped as she handed me a tissue from the box on the glass coffee table.

"Thank you," I whispered.

"Now, tell me what the matter is." Jane reached over and patted the hand I had rested on my lap.

"I'm not sure I know." I said truthfully.

"Perhaps I can help?"

"Please do."

"Perhaps you're feeling a little homesick. Even if you're enjoying yourself, when you're without your nearest and dearest it does take its toll after some time."

I nodded in agreement. I really was missing my family and friends even though a big part of me felt at home here.

Jane continued her rather detailed and yet accurate and insightful description of my feelings. "I think the awkwardness you've recently experienced with Kate's passing..." Jane's voice broke for a moment, but she regained her composure and continued. "Anyway, I'm sure it was a very awkward situation for you."

I nodded again, my lips parted to speak, but Jane interrupted.

"You're also in love with my nephew, and your impending departure must be awfully difficult to deal with." She looked at me with sadness in her eyes.

I was completely stunned. Jane was either very intuitive or just like everyone else; she, too, could read my face. Either way, I made a mental note to study myself in the mirror and practice my poker face.

"If you don't mind me saying so," Jane went on, "my nephew is pretty smitten with you as well. Oh, I know love when I see it, and the two of you..." Jane clicked her tongue and shook her head.

Aaron had been right; his aunt was definitely chatty. However, at that moment it was of no concern. If I had to sit there and listen to her tell me a million times that Aaron was smitten, then I would sit and listen. By the time she had finished telling me stories about Aaron when he was a baby, a young boy, and a teenager, I felt like I'd known him for years – in his present lifetime anyway.

"Let's have a bite to eat." Jane wiggled her way off the couch and stood up just as a delicious and familiar smell wafted in from the kitchen.

"Would that be –"

"I had a lasagne in the freezer." Jane shrugged. "You do like lasagne?" she said turning to me. I had already risen to my feet and was following her to the kitchen.

"My favourite!"

"Wonderful! Mine, too!"

We sipped wine and ate the delicious home cooked lasagne at the dining table, occasionally making small talk, but nothing more. My mind was too preoccupied with thoughts of Aaron and my mouth too busy enjoying dinner.

As I placed the last forkful of lasagne in my mouth, I realized I hadn't quite found out the reason for Jane's returning home so early. It had been my understanding that she would return home only after the funeral. I fought with myself for a few seconds wondering if I should ask, when my mouth opened, making the decision for me.

"Weren't you going to tell me why you were home?" I put my fork down and picked up a napkin, dabbing at the corners of my mouth.

"I actually came home for two reasons." Jane sipped from her glass of wine before continuing. "First, I needed something decent to wear to the funeral. I hadn't planned that far ahead when I decided to stay and help Kate, I guess part of me was hoping..." Jane jumped up to clear the table.

I rose to help, but she asked me to sit back down. As lovely and giving as Jane was, when she asked you to do something, you did it with no argument. Not that she would ever argue back, but she did have a way of being convincing all the while using a very pleasant tone of voice. When she returned, she brought in a plate of cookies and set them down on the table before seating herself.

"The second reason?" I pressed curiously. If it weren't any of my business, she'd let me know.

"When Kate was first diagnosed and given her prognosis, she asked me to hold on to something until after she passed." Intrigued by that bit of information, I listened intently to Jane's every word as she explained. "Kate asked me to give it to Aaron after..." She didn't finish her sentence but I knew what she meant.

Several thoughts and ideas ran through my head. I battled with my conscious on whether or not to ask her what she was to give to Aaron. It really wasn't any of my business, but I was curious and it was my curious side that came up the winner. "Can I ask you what it is?" Now that the words were out of my mouth, I regretted asking, but held my resolve as I waited for the answer.

"It's a wooden box." Jane shrugged.

Once again, I fought with my curiosity and myself. I had already stuck my nose in further than it belonged, how could one more question hurt? "What's in the box?"

"I can't say." Jane said taking a bite from a cookie and wiping the crumbs that fell on the table onto the floor.

"I'm sorry; it's none of my business. Please forget I asked." I looked at my hands resting on the table as warmth travelled up my neck and began settling on face. My ears burned.

"No, dear, I didn't mean that. I meant I don't know. It's a locked box, and apparently, Doc Brown has the key."

Forty-One

All night long, questions buzzed through my mind regarding the locked box and its possible contents. When sleep managed to find me, strange kaleidoscope images of boxes and keys swirled through my dreams. By the time dawn arrived, I was glad to make my escape from bed.

Padding out to the kitchen in bare feet, I began my morning ritual and prepared the coffee maker. The bleak skies caught my attention and elicited a sigh. As I gazed out the window, I knew it would be another morning spent indoors.

With my coffee all set to brew, I made my way down the stairs just in time to catch Jane as she was leaving for Tockington. Though we had said our goodbyes the night before, I felt a need to see her one final time. There were so many questions on my mind, but as we hugged, I kept them to myself. If Aaron wanted me to know about the box and its contents, I felt sure that he would tell me, or at least I hoped. For now, I was going to be patient, there was no other choice; it would be some time before we saw each other again.

I dragged myself back up the stairs to my apartment, my disposition as dismal as the weather outside. I hoped my mood wasn't going to last as long as the dreary skies; it didn't seem like the sun was going to make an appearance.

Upon opening my door to the apartment, the aroma of freshly brewed coffee stirred my senses, boosting my mood somewhat, and I headed directly for the coffee maker. As I poured the coffee a wisp of steam rose from the cup. I closed my eyes and inhaled the rich scent. A small smile spread across my face.

Mug in hand, I returned to the living room feeling a little less depressed, and turned on the television for the morning news. Slowly, the slight elevation in my attitude began to trickle away as the forecast promised days of gloomy, rainy skies ahead. The rain began tapping at my window, tauntingly.

As each day passed, my mood continued to match the depressing onslaught of wind and rain. I watched as grey clouds swirled and undulated, mesmerized by how much they looked like churning, angry seas until they finally unleashed the rain that pounded at my window. The heavy streaks clawed at the glass like long fingers trying to drag me out. I was afraid, isolated – abandoned. déjà vu found me again.

With Jane gone and Peter's obvious disappointment, my only link with the outside world was the television and computer. I had become a shut in, the weather keeping me home – keeping me afraid. I hoped Aaron would come to my rescue, but I knew it wasn't possible. He had his own feelings to deal with and he had that box and its curious contents.

By the time the weekend arrived, I was determined to break free from my depression, determined to get out from under the clouds that followed me. With that in mind, I set my mug on the top of the bookcase and searched for something interesting to read. Finally I settled on a well-read romance novel. I retrieved my cup and headed into the living room. Just as I made myself comfortable on the corner of the couch, there was a knock at the door.

My heart beat with excitement, the first in what seemed a long while, as thoughts of Aaron and his rescue raced through my mind. A week had passed since we'd last seen each other, a week since we last spoke. I missed him terribly, but realized he needed his time. I crossed my fingers as my body seemingly floated over to the door.

"Hello, sweetheart! I hope I'm not interrupting?" Jane's smiling, plump face greeted me.

I deflated, feeling heavy on my feet, but I quickly recovered when she hugged me. "Not at all, come in." I stepped back allowing Jane to enter the apartment, closing the door behind her. "So, are you home to stay?"

"Ah yes, home to stay. You never realize how much you've missed it until you're back." She smiled as she walked over to the living room and sat on the couch. I felt a twinge in the pit of my stomach at her words.

"Can I get you anything?"

"No, dear, I'm fine. I just came by to see how you were doing, what with all this nasty weather we've been having." Jane motioned to the window as the rain fell in a light drizzle.

I glanced over at the window, something I'd avoided doing all morning. "Yes, I have been feeling a bit stir crazy," I said, joining her.

"Good!" She clapped her hands together.

My eyes opened wide at her apparent happiness with my discontent. My expression, of which I'm sure, was one of complete surprise. Jane immediately explained that she was inviting me on a shopping trip.

I jumped up. "Just give me a minute to change," I called out over my shoulder, Jane's laughter nipping at my heels as I headed toward my bedroom.

Before long, I was ready to go, realizing it had been a week since I'd stepped outside and left the apartment. For a moment I hesitated, the thought of stepping out into the rain froze me in my place.

"Good God, it's only rain," I whispered to myself, turning the knob to my bedroom door and heading out to meet Jane.

The moment we got into the car, my mind began racing with questions about Aaron and his whereabouts. I didn't want to come off sounding like some infatuated teenager or worse yet, a stalker.

My irrational fear of the rain was already a faint and almost laughable memory as I brushed the remaining drops from my jacket sleeves. "So how was the funeral?" I asked, easing into my questioning.

"The funeral? It was nice – as far as funerals go."

"So everyone's gone home?" We pulled to the end of the street and sat at a stop sign waiting for the traffic to clear.

"Yes, Peter went home the following morning." Jane turned the corner, and we headed out of town.

I sat quietly staring out the window wondering how to approach the subject of Aaron. For a woman who liked to talk, Jane wasn't offering any more information than direct answers to my questions. I needed to be cunning.

"What about Aaron? Did he have any clients this weekend?"

"He did, but Peter took care of them."

"So he's still in Tockington?"

"He is."

I nodded and turned to look back out the window, satisfied with his whereabouts. There was still some hope that he would stop by on his way home, even if it was out of the way.

"Have you not heard from him, dear?" Jane asked sounding surprised.

"Not yet." I tried to sound aloof. "I assumed he would be busy finalizing things, so I wasn't really planning on hearing from him for a while."

We rode quietly along, Jane paying close attention to the road while I tried to devise another round of questions regarding Aaron and his emotional state.

"So, how is Aaron anyway?" I asked directly, feeling that it was a legitimate question to ask about his well-being.

"He'll be fine. He just needs time."

I didn't know whether Jane was trying to reassure me or herself, but before I continued with anymore questioning, Jane finally started offering up information on her own accord.

"I hardly laid eyes on him after the funeral. He spent most of the time locked away in his bedroom, only coming down for meals before heading straight back up afterwards.

"Oh?"

"Whatever was in that box kept him quite occupied. For all I know, he's still locked away in his room pouring over its contents." Jane shook her head.

"Are you sure he's okay?" I asked trying not to sound too concerned, though I was deeply worried.

"Oh yes, he's fine, dear. He called me last night to make sure I'd made it home. No need to worry." Jane took her eyes off the road for a second to smile at me. A rush of relief flowed through my body, and I was glad that Jane had already turned her focus back to the road; I'd had enough of people, including her, reading my face. I turned my attention back to look out my window, glad Aaron was okay, but envious of Jane that she had spoken to him just last night. I wished he had called me, too.

"Ever find out what was in that box?" I tried to sound as if it didn't really matter if I knew or not.

"I can't say."

"That's okay, I understand." I felt my cheeks burn; still very glad Jane focused her attention on the road ahead.

"No, dear; I mean, I don't know. He never said, and well... we all thought it best to leave it at that. If he wants us to know, he'll tell us."

Jane was right of course. It was a personal matter between Aaron and his mother and it wasn't any of my business.

Forty-Two

August was turning into a wet and drab month, and having finally gotten out of the apartment, my uneasiness with the unsettled weather subsided. However, not hearing from Aaron was seemingly also becoming the norm, and that worried me.

Jane had told me that he was back at work, and I told myself he was too busy during the day with his clients and probably too exhausted by night. Around Jane, whom I saw rather frequently, I pretended that my lack of contact with Aaron didn't bother me, but something told me she knew it did. Luckily for me, she said nothing. In any case, we were soon due for another expedition.

With each day that passed, my anticipation grew as our tour date drew near and as I hadn't heard anything different, I suspected nothing had changed in the plans. Finally, the day arrived, the knock at my door startled me, and for the first time since arriving in Bourton, I wasn't entirely ready.

"Hold on," I called out to the front door as I made my way to the bedroom.

I was still in my bathrobe, my wet hair dripped down my back. Quickly, I threw on the clothes that lay on my bed and hurried back to the door, smoothing out my clothes with my nervous hands, before combing out my hair with my fingers. I hesitated, feeling somewhat nervous about seeing him again, it had been so long, and I wasn't quite sure what to expect. I opened the door. Aaron was more handsome than I'd remembered. I wanted to jump into his arms, but instead, stood on tiptoe and kissed him gingerly on the cheek.

"Hi! Sorry, I'm not exactly ready yet. I guess the time just got away from me," I rambled, my voice cracking a bit.

Aaron stepped into my apartment, his eyes locked on to mine and I found myself unable to look away.

"It's okay. I'm quite early." The way he spoke sent shivers down my spine, the good kind.

"Early?" I finally tore my gaze away and looked toward the kitchen. My mind wanted to know the time, but my body wouldn't move.

"Can we talk?" Aaron gestured to the living room.

"Sure." My stomach rolled as my feet led me over to the couch. Those three words weren't exactly my favourite. Nothing good ever came from those three words. I knew all about it; I had used that exact phrase on Brad before crushing his heart. A lump rose in my throat and I swallowed hard, driving it back down.

Aaron sat down beside me. My eyes concentrated on my fingernails, nervously picking away at them, keeping myself distracted from the words I felt sure to hear.

He sighed. "Please look at me."

I looked up and instantly felt tears beginning to well-up in my eyes. I blinked, forcing them back.

"I'm sorry I haven't been in touch with you since. . . " he paused, "well since everything." He gestured with his hands at an invisible vast expanse. "When I returned to London, I found myself very busy. I know that's not a very good excuse, but it is the truth."

I stared at him, afraid that if I opened my mouth the waterworks would begin.

"You must think I'm a real idiot."

I shook my head, casting my eyes back down at my hands. Where is this conversation heading? I felt him move and when

I looked back up, he was standing and pacing around the living room; looking at everything but me.

"Is that you?" he said distracted, walking toward the small table that stood under the window by the desk.

I rose from the couch and joined him. He had picked up a picture and was holding it out to me. I took it from his hand.

"Yeah, that's me, my dad, and my best friend Amanda just before we all went away on a trip. I was about fourteen." I placed the picture back down on the table.

"And this?" He picked up another framed picture and handed it to me.

"These are my friends; Amanda, Lindsay and Jennifer. It was taken just before I came here." I was about to put the picture back down when Aaron reached for it, taking it from my hands.

"Why is that photo," Aaron said pointing to the frame sitting on the table, "in this photo?" He pointed to the picture in his hands.

I explained to Aaron about the impromptu get-together I'd had with my friends before my trip and the gifts they had given me to offer moral support. I told him about the significance of the pictures, and their representation of the past, the present, and the future.

"They weren't here before. I mean, the last time I was here."

"They were in my room. I brought them out last week; I wanted them where I could see them..." I paused, "for comfort."

Aaron nodded. "And what were you given to represent the future?" he asked quietly, looking at me, his eyes bored into my soul.

"An empty frame." It was easy to read the puzzled expression he wore on his face. "I'm to put in a picture that represents my future." For the first time I knew what I wanted to put in that frame, but knowing that our conversation wasn't over, I didn't dare say.

Aaron pressed his lips together as though in thought as we stood at the table looking at the pictures. "Krista, I..." he paused, "you should sit down."

Four more words that didn't always mean a happy ending, unless followed by 'You won the lottery!' or something to that effect. I headed back to the couch, sat, and resumed the unattractive, yet seemingly necessary habit of picking at my nails. Aaron sat down beside me again, turning his body to face me.

"This isn't easy for me to say."

Oh, get it over with! I screamed inside, realizing as I waited, how Brad must have felt.

"I've been doing a lot of thinking, and I'm not sure..."

My mind started to wander for a moment, protecting myself from the words I didn't want to hear. I closed my eyes, both to keep any tears from escaping and to refocus my attention on Aaron, despite the pain.

"I'm not ready..." he began again. "I don't know if I can... I don't know if I can handle this. Us. You." His eyes filled with uncertainty. My eyes filled with tears, no longer able to hold them back. I kept my head down and blurrily watched as he reached over and took my now shaking hands from my lap. "But maybe... I'm willing to try," he whispered leaning over to kiss my forehead.

WHAT! I yelled silently inside my head. "What?" I asked looking up at him, the tears spilling from my lids.

"You were right." I looked at him bewildered. "I think..." he began, "I think we are meant to be together."

Does he remember something?

"The box my mother left," he went on to explain, "it was filled with notes. Her notes from when I was a child. Notes on how I used to talk about things. Places. People. All things that I couldn't possibly have known about when I was so young. She documented the dreams I recounted. Words I'd said in my sleep. Stories I told of places far away."

I stared at him disbelieving, my heart racing, and my mind spinning.

"Do the names Mary and Thomas mean something to you?"

My world went black.

Forty-Three

A thick fog encircled my feet and rose into the air above me; it was as though I were inside a cloud.

"You did it." Came the whisper of a voice, familiar, yet strange at the same time.

"Did what?" I asked, while turning a slow circle, trying to pinpoint the exact location the voice came from. There was no reply. "Did what?" I asked again, louder. I waited. I was about to ask for the third time when I heard the voice again.

"He will remember!" The voice exclaimed happily.

It was then that I realized the sound was coming from within. "Mary? Is that you?" I asked knowing with every bit of me that it was.

"Yes."

"Where have you been?" I asked, a bit more harshly than I had intended.

"Where I've always been; with you."

"Why haven't I felt you, or dreamed of you?" I said, stirring the fog with my hand and watching as it swirled up my wrist.

"You don't need me anymore."

I stood still and watched as the mist encircled me. It undulated as if a breeze was pushing it along, and yet I felt no movement of air. "What makes you so sure?"

Her voice fell silent. Was that the answer to my question? Silence?

"Don't worry. I will always be a part of you. I am you." She began to fade away taking the fog with her.

"Wait!" I called. "You haven't told me what I did?" I didn't want her to go. I needed her to stay.

The fog returned briefly and encircled my ankles; then it slowly made its way upward until it swirled around my head. "You found him. Now we can move on."

I followed the fog with my eyes as it retreated and when it reached my ankles it slowly drifted away. "Mary! Wait! Don't go. I still have so many questions."

"I'm a part of you." A faint whisper; a brief memory flickered across my mind. The fog receded, and I felt myself becoming more aware of my surroundings.

Dreams are strange. Sometimes so frightening that it is only upon waking that a sense of relief floods over the dreamer at the realization that the experience wasn't real. Other times, the dreams are so pleasant that the dreamer wishes to stay asleep. When I awoke from my dream, I wasn't really sure how I felt. Part of me felt complete while another part felt like I'd lost my best friend. Either way, it didn't really matter once I realized I was in Aaron's arms.

"Are you alright?" A mild look of concern showed on his face.

"I am now," I said reaching up and putting my arms around his neck, gently pulling him down so that our lips met. The heat and passion of a hundred and fifty-five years consumed us. Eventually, we pulled apart.

"I'm still confused, Krista," Aaron said as he sat up straight.

I was lying on the couch with my head resting in his lap. "I know." I sighed, and sat up too.

"Do you?" he questioned quietly and looked away.

"Yes." I reached over and grabbed his hands, drawing his attention back to me. A thought crossed my mind and in an instant, I knew what he needed. "Wait here." I jumped up from the couch, dizziness taking hold of me for a moment.

"You're not going to pass out again are you?"

I looked back at Aaron, concern flashed in his eyes again. "No, just a head rush." I smiled and headed to my bedroom. I returned seconds later with the notebook in my hand. "Here," I said, sitting back down on the couch and holding it out to him.

"Ah! This must be the famous notebook then," he said, taking it from my hand.

"You know about it?" I wasn't really surprised that he did.

"I may have heard something about it, though not a whole lot. I must say I was curious when Peter mentioned it."

I nodded. "Well read it... it might help." I got up from the couch. "I'm going to finish getting ready." I left Aaron sitting on the couch already engrossed in my writings.

When I returned, almost half-an-hour later, he was still sitting there, the notebook on the coffee table in front of him.

"So!" I said joining him.

"Well, that certainly does bring things into perspective. I just wish I remembered it."

"Why – would it help?"

It took a moment before Aaron answered my question. I supposed he needed to be sure. Finally, he turned toward me and took my hands in his, that familiar electricity coursed through us again – comforting.

"No. I know how I feel about you now – at this very moment. None of that matters." He pointed to the notebook. "It's just that I wish..."

I interrupted his words, placing my fingers gently on his lips. "Let's make a deal." Aaron cocked his head to the side. I continued, "From now on, we'll make our own memories; Krista and Aaron's. No more Mary, no more Thomas, just us."

"You are brilliant." Aaron leaned over, and we sealed the deal with a kiss.

Forty-Four

I didn't want to go back home to Bourton. Not after the weekend we'd had – not ever. The places Aaron had taken me to, and the things we'd seen and done had been extraordinary. Our itinerary now long forgotten as our relationship had changed from client/tour guide to girlfriend/boyfriend. I would like to have said lovers, but the fact of the matter was that it hadn't evolved into that – not yet. I wanted to stay in London with Aaron, but that wasn't possible. It was still summer, and he still had clients, yet I only had ten more days.

"Don't go." I pleaded.

Aaron had brought me back to Bourton, and I didn't want it to end. I pressed myself into his arms, and he held me as we stood in the doorway of my apartment.

"Believe me; I don't want to go, but..." I stopped him with a kiss and melted into his arms, hoping that it would be enough to make him stay. I heard the door close behind him and I smiled, not easily done while kissing. "Are you grinning?" Aaron pulled away from me; his eyes smouldered, a smile on his own face.

"Does that mean you're staying?" I grabbed him by the hand and led him to the living room, not waiting for his answer.

"For a bit," he said almost breathlessly. He followed obediently, not showing any signs of resistance.

"Good."

We collapsed in a heap on the couch, drunk with love and lust. Never had I ever felt a love so powerful, so strong, it was all consuming; it was whole; it was pure; it was true – it was unconditional. In each other's arms, we lay in it, wrapped in the comfort and the heat of it, and in that moment, I felt that our souls were joined by it.

"I really should go," he whispered in my ear. He did not attempt to leave.

"Uh-huh!" It was all I could say, I knew he wouldn't leave – couldn't.

Wherever his lips touched, it left a mark on my flesh. It was not visible to the human eye, only felt by the soul. His lips brushed across mine enticing me – tantalizing and teasing me. Slowly his mouth moved from my lips, followed along my jaw line to my neck, and sent a rush through my body so intense that I shivered beneath him.

"Really though. . . " He kissed back up my neck to my earlobe where his lips gently pulled, sending another wave of tingles down my body, his hot breath tickled. "I have clients in the morning," he whispered.

"Uh-huh." I drew my hands up his back, entwined my fingers in his thick hair, and coaxed his mouth back towards mine. "You should go then," I whispered mischievously, sealing his lips with my own before he could speak. I felt him shudder in my grasp.

"Okay," he said, releasing me, moving off the couch, and leaving me lying there. I was shocked by his abruptness and by the sudden chill that washed over me without his body covering mine. He stood by the couch staring down at me and held out a hand. Reluctantly, I reached out and grabbed it and allowed him to pull me up.

"Sorry, but I can't lie there anymore." He scooped me up in his arms, effortlessly.

"What are you doing?" I giggled as I swung my arms around his neck.

He didn't answer only headed in the direction of the door where he put me down. My shoulders slumped and my eyes looked down at the floor. The smile I had on my face instantly pulled into a frown. He leaned forward and kissed me on the forehead before reaching for the doorknob. I stood there, too shocked by the unexpectedness of it all, to even move, let alone speak. My brain screamed at me for my obvious muteness.

Don't let him leave! I cried inwardly all the while watching as his hand moved in apparent slow motion to the doorknob. I watched as he slowly turned the inner mechanism and locked the door.

"Wouldn't want Aunt Jane to disturb us now, would we?"

My eyes opened wide as his actions registered in my brain. A smile slowly crept across my face. "Does that mean...?" My voice had returned.

"You know perfectly well what that means," he chuckled as he scooped me up in his arms again and carried me to the bedroom door. I reached down and turned the knob opening it for him. He carried me in, pushing the door closed with his foot.

My eyes fluttered open just as scattered shards of light stretched across the predawn sky; it was the only thing I dared move. Eventually, enough light streamed in through the window showing me what I'd already suspected. A mass of tangled limbs stretched out before me, and in the dim light it was difficult to tell where I began and Aaron ended; the euphoria of it all was still very much alive.

I lightly traced my finger up his arm, watching as it left a trail of goose bumps behind, and yet there was no indication of his waking. I gently lifted his arm, placing it beside me and then slowly pulled my leg out from under his, gradually untangling myself. I held my breath as he rolled over onto his side away from me. I waited another second, and when he had settled, quietly slipped out of bed. I took my robe from the back of the door, put it on, and tiptoed out into the kitchen, pulling the door closed behind me.

Waiting for the coffee to brew, I watched out the kitchen window. Clouds began to roll in, but nothing was going to ruin the elation that encapsulated my body. When the coffee was ready, I poured a cup and ventured outside to the garden.

The air was cool, but I didn't mind, the hot mug in my hands warmed me up. I sat on the weathered stone bench, etched by wind and rain, and took my first sip, feeling the hot liquid run down my throat and pool in my stomach; it felt good. I closed my eyes and tilted my face towards the greying sky.

"Good morning!"

I jumped a little at the familiar and jovial voice. "Good morning, Jane," I said in an equally jovial voice, my eyes still closed and my face tilted toward the heavens.

"Well, you seem awfully chipper this morning." Jane's voice drew nearer, and I opened my eyes just as she joined me on the bench, her own cup of steaming tea in her hands.

"Do I?" I feigned ignorance and stifled the smile beginning at the corners of my mouth.

"Quite," Jane said staring at me. She took a sip of her tea. "So what time did he leave?"

I took another sip of my coffee. "He hasn't, he's still sleep – ing. . . " My voice trailed off.

A wide grin appeared on Jane's face as she drank from her cup. Warmth radiated up my neck and transformed my face into what I could only imagine an artist's pallet might look like. The slow, deepening heat of embarrassment that I'm sure went from a light glow of pink and gradually deepened to crimson. All my blood had seemingly left my extremities and pooled in my face and neck. My ears were on fire.

Jane giggled and patted my hand, but it did not ease the burning heat. "It's quite all right, dear." She tried to reassure me.

"How did you know?" I asked when I finally found my voice.

"You forget, dear, I do live underneath you – hmm?"

Just as I thought my ears couldn't possibly burn anymore, they did. I looked at my hands in my lap half expecting them to be ghostly white.

Oh God! I quickly looked back toward the house, somewhat relieved, as I remembered that her bedroom was at the back while mine was at the front, not one above the other, the heat began to ebb.

Jane however, was still staring at me and grinning. "I couldn't sleep last night, so I was up, oh 'till about two this morning watching the telly."

The heat returned as I realized my bedroom was above her living room.

"Oh, don't worry, love. I can't even hear you walking around up-stairs; good insulation." She sipped her tea. "I saw his car parked in the drive," she said as an afterthought.

I exhaled loudly, my shoulders relaxed, and I felt my blood returning to the rest of my body.

Jane stood up. "Looks like rain, dear, you should get inside before it starts up," she said looking around at the sky.

Just then, a small drop of water hit the top of my head, it tickled as it made its way down my scalp, and I idly reached up to scratch it away. I looked up and nodded, wanting to say something, but not knowing what. Instead, I rose and quietly followed behind Jane as we made our way back to the house.

When I reached the bottom of the stairs, and Jane reached her back door, I turned.

"Thank you." Was all I managed to say, but knowing how easily Jane read my face I was certain that she read a thousand words in just those two.

"Of course, dear." She smiled. "You better get back to him before he begins to wonder where you are."

With that, she turned and headed into her home, leaving me staring after her. Slowly, I climbed the stairs and just as I reached the top, the skies opened up; I had made it just in time.

Once back inside, I quietly tiptoed to my bedroom door and opened it; Aaron was breathing deeply. I sat on the bed facing his back and gently shook him.

"Hey! Aaron, you should get up now," I whispered close to his ear, gently rocking his shoulder.

"Huh!" he groaned.

"Aaron, you have to get up, you're going to be late for work." I said a little louder.

Aaron rolled over and faced me. Slowly he opened one eye and smiled.

"Good morning! Did you have a good sleep?" I laughed.

He stretched his arms above his head, the outline of his muscled body visible under the thin sheet that covered him. "Probably the best I've had in years or maybe ever." He smiled crossing his arms behind his head. He was now wide-awake with a wide grin spreading across his face.

"Well, I hate to disturb that great sleep of yours, and as much as I don't want you to leave, don't you have clients to see today?"

"I have time." Before I knew it, Aaron had reached over and grabbed me, pulling me on top of him.

"Oh you do? Time for what exactly?"

"For this."

Aaron easily flipped me over onto my back and covered me with the full length of his body, smothering my face with soft, warm kisses. He reached up and brushed the hair back from my forehead.

"What's this? A scar?"

I reached up and felt the mark just above my right eye in my hairline. "Nothing to worry about, I was born with it, just a strange birthmark. Don't let it distract you." I smiled.

Aaron grinned playfully. "Everything about you distracts me." He leaned forward, kissing my forehead and continued where he left off. I didn't resist as he worked his way down my neck. I felt him reach for the tie on my robe and before I knew it, he had it undone in one adept move. His hand, warm and soft, glided underneath, each feathery touch sent ripples of goose bumps as his fingers lightly brushed up my side.

"Wait!" I called out as much to his surprise as my own.

"What's the matter?" he asked. His face registered both concern and desire at the same time; I didn't even think that was possible.

"We can't." I reached under him and tried to pull my robe together. "I mean, it's not that I don't want to it's just... we shouldn't."

Aaron rolled over on to his side and looked at me, his arm tucked under his head and a crooked smile on his face.

"May I ask why not? You certainly didn't resist all those times last night... " He smiled seductively, tracing his fingers down my arm.

"You are making this difficult," I sighed and smiled at the memory.

"Yes, well you didn't make it very easy for me last night, as I recall. In fact, I'm pretty sure it was you who seduced me into staying." He propped himself up on his arm.

I reached over and ran my fingers through the front of his hair, brushing it back a little. He grabbed my hand and began to kiss each of my fingertips; he was trying very hard to distract me and it was working. I closed my eyes enjoying his light kisses as he traveled up my arm. When I opened my eyes again, he was hovering inches from my face.

"So are you going to tell me why," he whispered.

"I need to sit up."

Aaron moved out of my way giving me the room I needed. I sat cross-legged in front of him as he lay on his side, his body now completely exposed. Just another sly tactic to distract me; I kept my eyes glued to his face.

"We can't because we have no. . . " I hesitated. My face began to flush unexpectedly. We had a perfectly good reason not to, especially when we were still just getting to know each other – again. Luckily, for once, my transparency must have given away what I was thinking because Aaron saved me.

"Ohhhh!" He reached down and pulled up the crinkled white sheet, covering himself. "I guess you're right about that. We did use them all."

I laughed, relieved. "Not to mention your aunt."

"Oh! What about my aunt?" Aaron asked slightly puzzled.

"Well, I met her out in the garden earlier, and she knows you spent the night."

"Oh! Don't worry about her. She's pretty liberal minded, that one." With that, Aaron swung his legs over his side of the bed taking the sheet with him.

I laughed. "I thought people only did that in the movies."

"Yeah well, in light of things. . . Besides I don't want to make you feel bad knowing what you're missing." A sly smile spread across his face.

"UH!" I grabbed a pillow and threw it at him, hitting him squarely in the head. He laughed bending down to pick it up and tossed it back on the bed.

"I'm going to take a quick shower," he said as he moved toward the bathroom door.

"Don't use up all the hot water," I called out, as he closed the door behind him.

The door opened back up again, and he stuck his head out laughing at me. "Don't worry, I don't think I'll be using any hot water." He closed the door, leaving me rolling on the bed with laughter.

Forty-Five

Love – an emotion so strong it can make us feel invincible. It can drive every thought, make us do things we normally wouldn't do, and cloud our judgment. It can drive us crazy. We say 'love at first sight', 'madly in love', 'love is a drug', 'blinded by love', or 'love is blind'. It is not until we are truly in love that we can relate to any of those expressions.

For the first time in my life, I was truly in love. I knew it the moment I sat down at the computer, the minute Aaron left – as a result I changed my departure date. It wasn't by much, only a few extra days. The very idea of leaving terrified me, and yet it was inevitable. As much as Bourton had become a part of me; my family, my friends, and my career were back home – my heart, however, belonged to Aaron. I was torn, and every second that ticked by, brought me closer to leaving. I couldn't bear to think about it, and instead of figuring something out, something that could work, I chose to push the thoughts from my mind. I would deal with it when the time came.

I rose from the desk, content with my decision, and ready to spend the day in the apartment reading, or whatever else would occupy my time. By late afternoon, I was restless and anxiously waiting for the end of the workday – anxiously waiting for Aaron to call. Occasionally, my thoughts shifted to the inevitable, but as quickly as they emerged, I pushed them back.

When the phone rang, I jumped in anticipation, almost knocking the phone to the floor in the process.

"Hello!" I could barely hear my own voice over the sound of my beating heart.

We spoke for hours, neither one of us wanting to let the other one go. It was as though we'd been apart for weeks instead of hours. By the time our conversation ended, we made promises to call or e-mail daily, until we saw each other again. It was going to be a long five days without him, but I had no choice.

The days passed slowly, and after two days of longing for Aaron, two days of only hearing his voice, and two days of pushing away thoughts of my departure, my mind cleared. As much as I wished for time to stand still, it wasn't going to. Ideas circled around in my head, but no matter how I tried, the outcome was always the same. I had responsibilities that couldn't be overlooked. It appeared that being in love had completely clouded my judgement.

How could I be so irresponsible by falling in love with someone who lives in a different country? How do I say goodbye without destroying the one thing I was destined to find? How can I leave the one person I love more than anything in the world? How can this ever work? I repeatedly asked myself these questions both aloud and in my head. Even in my dreams, these questions and many more, haunted me. There never seemed to be an easy answer. I began to panic as I realized history was going to repeat itself once again.

By mid-week, I had made my decision and waited patiently for Aaron's call. My anxiety built as each minute passed. When the call came an hour later than usual, my head was about to burst. By the third ring, I reached for the phone with a shaky hand.

"Hello." My voice was monotone, my stomach churned. I plunked myself down on the couch, and tried sounding distant – aloof.

"It's me." There was something different in his voice – distraction maybe? Whatever it was the sound of his voice on the other end drove a knife into my heart. My promise to Peter was about to get broken. Not only to Peter, it suddenly occurred to me, but to everyone: Aaron, Peter – Mary.

"How come you're so late?" I whined. I didn't intend to sound that way, or maybe subconsciously I did. If I sounded bitchy, he'd be glad to be rid of me. Our relationship really only expanded one weekend – a few weeks – another life. We could chalk it all up to a summer fling, simple – nothing more. You can always come back! The thought flitted, once again, through my mind. It was true, but I couldn't ask him to wait. I didn't know how long it would take for me to settle things at home. He could come with you! I would never ask. His family, or what remained of it, was here.

"Sorry, but I do have a job." He sounded defensive.

"Well, you had one last night, and the night before that, but you managed to call on time those nights." I felt a pain in my throat as it tightened with emotion and my eyes began to well. What are you doing? I screamed silently, or was it Mary's voice? I rested my head back on the couch feeling its coolness on my neck and closed my eyes. What about us? He doesn't remember us, I replied silently.

"Look, I don't want to argue." Aaron's voice calmed to the one that made my heart melt.

"Sorry, me neither. It's just..." What am I going to say? "Can we talk?" Those three tell all words spilled from my mouth when I really wanted to say the other three words – I love you.

"Yes, I think we should." Was he going to make this easier? Easier, I almost laughed, nothing about it was easy. "About Friday..." he continued, "I think it's best that Peter take you on your last excursion."

My mouth dropped, and I had to cover the mouthpiece of the phone as an audible gasp escaped. I took a deep breath, unable to speak, the tears already pouring out of my eyes, the pain in my throat lessened as I gave in to the emotion.

"Krista! Are you still there?" His brittle, worried voice asked.

I cleared my throat and sniffed before removing my hand from the phone. "Yes," I managed to choke out.

It was his turn now to be silent. My chest ached as bits of my heart chipped away. Neither of us spoke for ten minutes.

"Krista!" Aaron cleared his throat, "Krista, I'm sorry. It's just that. . . " he paused.

"I know," I said quietly. "Please, don't say it okay." I let my voice break, wanting him to know that I was hurting too, that he wasn't alone in his pain.

"Okay," he coughed. More silence followed before he spoke again. "I'll get in touch with Peter. I'll tell him, don't worry."

I half laughed and cried at the same time. "He's really going to hate me now!"

"No, he won't," Aaron said quietly. "How could anyone hate you?" His voice broke again.

"He will." I paused. "I promised him I wouldn't – hurt you." The last words reduced me to tears again. I covered the mouthpiece as I tried to regain some sense of composure. All I wanted was to be in his arms.

"It's what you need to do." Aaron assured me.

I gave a slight nod. "It's just that I've never lo –"

Aaron interrupted, "Don't say it, okay? It'll only make it worse, but for the record – me too." His voice sounded raspier each time he spoke and he continuously had to clear it.

"Okay, I won't." I sniffed, wishing I had more tissue.

"Krista, I'm so sorry." I barely heard him.

"Yeah, me too," I whispered back. "Promise me one thing?" I asked, knowing that it was too much.

"Anything."

I wondered if he really meant anything. "Promise me not to blame yourself for any of this?" I was starting to blubber. I took a deep breath and contained myself again.

I heard him sigh and afterwards a long pause; dead air. Finally he spoke. "Only – if you promise me first." His voice was soft and so very sad.

I laid down on the couch, resting my head on the armrest and closed my eyes, squeezing out more tears. They slid down my cheeks and in my mouth; the saltiness of them no longer bothered me. I was a complete mess.

"But it is," I said. "It will always be my fault because I remembered. I didn't have to say anything and should have left things alone. If I had, none of this would be happening now, and you wouldn't be hurting." I raised my arm and crossed it over my eyes; the darkness was welcoming.

"You're hurting, too," he said, "and if you hadn't said anything, you would never be at peace."

"Neither of us is at peace now though, are we?" My voice had returned to its monotone state.

"Not now, no, but with time –"

"What, another one hundred years – in another lifetime?" I sat back up, crossing my legs on the coffee table in front of me.

"If that's what it takes, then I guess so. Perhaps next time, I'll remember too. Perhaps that's why this is happening" Aaron's voice sounded stronger.

"Maybe." I laughed nervously, though nothing was funny. "I've waited this long already, what's another hundred years." I wiped away the remaining tears from my cheeks and dried my hands on my shirt.

We sat in silence, listening to each other breathe, neither one of us wanting to let go.

"I should go," Aaron finally said, breaking the silence. "I'll talk to Peter, and don't worry he won't be angry."

"Hmph." I hoped he was right.

"Goodbye, Krista." Aaron's voice came as a whisper as he spoke my name.

"Goodbye."

The familiar click seemed louder than normal, thundering in my ear. It signified the end of our conversation, the end of our relationship, the end of our promise. I hated that click.

I crawled into bed fully clothed, makeup on, my teeth not brushed, and I cried myself to sleep. When I awoke the next day, it was two o'clock in the afternoon. Sleeping in so late was a good thing; it meant only having to endure the day for a short while until I climbed back in bed and allowed sleep to comfort me.

The day dragged on and by the time evening arrived, I was grateful. As I got ready for bed, earlier than usual, Peter called. I tried talking him out of taking me on the next day's outing. I didn't want to go – I didn't want to do anything but sit around and wait for the day I could leave. I regretted changing my departure date, but the drive wasn't in me to try and change it back. Instead, I considered it my punishment for being selfish or stupid, or both. If I had to wallow in self-pity for a few extra days than I would, after all it was my own fault; there was no one to blame but me.

Peter arrived on time the next morning, though I wasn't ready. I was still wearing my robe and drinking my coffee.

"We've got time," he said, as I let him into the apartment. Aaron had been right about one thing though, Peter wasn't angry with me.

"Yeah, sorry about that, I guess I slept in." There was nothing animated about me in any way. Though I was still breathing and moving – I felt dead.

"That's fine. Can I help you with anything?" Peter looked around the apartment. I saw the look on his face and for the first time noticed that I hadn't cleaned up after myself the last couple of days; a small stack of dishes sat on the coffee table. I turned, almost embarrassed, and started grabbing the dishes, tears immediately filling my eyes as I did.

"Here, I'll get that." Peter's hand was warm and comforting on my shoulder as he stopped me. "Why don't you go and get ready, and I'll clean this up. It's not that bad – really!" He smiled, but behind that smile, I could see the pity he had in his eyes.

I nodded and then headed for my bedroom. Somehow, I'd managed to get ready in a decent amount of time, though surely on auto-pilot for I barely remembered showering, let alone getting dressed. My wet hair was pulled up into a ponytail, either due to laziness or uncaring, I suspected the latter.

When I came out of my room, Peter was putting the last of the dishes he had washed away; the kitchen was back to a more recognizable state.

I smiled. "Thank you, Peter."

"Is that a smile I see?" he kidded.

I chuckled, shaking my head.

"Oh, and a laugh too – bonus points!" Peter took me by my hand and led me into the cleaned-up living room.

"Did it really take me that long to get ready?" I asked, looking around the now much cleaner room.

Peter sat on the couch and patted the seat beside him. "I told you it wasn't that bad." I sat, sinking into the couch. "Are you feeling any better?" he asked, the concern easily read in his eyes. I shook my head, knowing that speaking would be the end of my fragile composure. "I'm sorry you are both going through such a hard time," he said, his sincerity obvious.

I looked down at my hands. My nails were picked away as short as possible, they looked awful. I curled my fingers into my hands, embarrassed by their appearance. "I changed my departure date." I stared blankly at my hands. I hadn't told Aaron that, wanting to surprise him.

"You what?"

"My departure date, I was supposed to leave on the thirty-first, now I'm leaving on the fourth. Stupid – huh?" I looked up at Peter. Why am I telling him this? What does it matter anyway?

The next three days were the last of my sightseeing tours. After Sunday, I wouldn't be seeing Peter anymore either. I would have to spend an entire week waiting to leave. It wasn't that long ago when the thought of leaving left a heavy feeling in my heart, now I couldn't wait. It wasn't that long ago when it felt like the apartment was my home, now it was like a prison holding me back from where I belonged. Though in truth, I wasn't even sure anymore if Nova Scotia was where I belonged. In fact, it felt like I didn't belong anywhere. I only belonged with Aaron.

Forty-Six

My dreams were back, and each time a new memory or an old one surfaced; I forced myself to wake-up, not allowing the dream to take hold and sink me deeper into sadness. By mid-week, I was exhausted, but my ability to wake-up just as the dream began was almost perfect. Every memory I'd ever had of Mary and Thomas was pushed away as far as possible, never allowing them to get even the slightest grip. I was determined to go back to the life I had before the dreams began.

Each day seemed longer than the next and as the expression goes 'a watched pot never boils' the same holds true for the days of the week when checking the calendar every day. Though it was only four days away, Sunday wasn't coming fast enough. So on the eve of Thursday, I planned to get out of the apartment and get back to the routine I'd established. In doing so I hoped the time would go faster. Moping around certainly wasn't making the time pass.

My eyes fluttered open to a bit of sunlight streaming in through my window, the first in days. I hopped out of bed, putting my plan into action before I could change my mind. I grabbed my robe from the back of the door and headed out into the kitchen. With the last bit of coffee used up the day before, I settled on a cup of tea and the last English muffin, toasted with jam, and forced myself outside.

I slowly made my way over to the stone bench and silently hoped that Jane wouldn't see me and come running out. It had been sometime since I'd been out in the garden, not since I'd been with Aaron, not in the last week. It would be awkward if Jane were to come over, even if I did miss her. Right on cue, I heard the back door open, but I didn't bother turning around.

It seemed to take her a long time to reach the bench and so finally, after what must have been ten minutes, I turned around and faced the back of the house. At first she was nowhere in sight, but then her head popped up from behind one of her many shrubs covered with dead and dying flowers.

"Good morning!" I tried to say in my most cheerful good-morning-voice, but it was lifeless at best, just like those withered blooms.

Being the gracious person she was, Jane didn't let on, only smiled and continued working in her flower beds.

I finished my breakfast in silence. Wiping the crumbs from my lap, I stood and headed back toward the stairs.

"Hang on a moment would you, love?" Jane called from behind her shrubs.

I stopped and waited patiently.

"Ugh," she groaned as she stood up, "I am getting too old for this." She placed her hands on her hips and bent slightly back-wards, stretching out her back. When she was finished, she headed in my direction. "Would you mind coming in for a moment, dear? I'd like to wash the dirt from my hands."

I nodded and placed my cup and plate on the first step, where I could retrieve them later when I headed back up to the apartment.

Jane opened the door and waved me in ahead of her. I stood in her kitchen as she walked toward the sink to wash her hands.

"I do hope the sun stays out for a while and warm things up a bit. Hard to believe it's the first day of September isn't it?"

I nodded. "Yes." I was at a loss for words.

"Why don't you go make yourself comfortable in the living room? I'll only be a few minutes." She took off the brightly coloured apron she was wearing and hung it on a hook on the back door.

Before I could answer, she had already turned and headed back toward her bedroom. Reluctantly, I plodded into the living room. As much as I enjoyed Jane's company, being there with her hurt more than I thought it would. I plunked myself down on her oversized couch and waited for her to return.

If anyone could light up a room, it was Jane. Even though I was feeling low and close to tears knowing we soon would likely never see each other again, she still managed to make me smile.

"It's nice to see you smile," Jane said, smiling warmly herself and reaching over to pat my hand.

I looked down at my hands, her warm, plump hand with its neatly manicured nails, rested on top of mine. I curled my fingers under, still embarrassed by their ragged look.

"I have something for you!" she said, clearly enthusiastic.

I looked up at her smiling face, her brightly coloured wardrobe reflected her mood. For the first time, I noticed she had changed into a bright yellow blouse and a floral print skirt. She reached into the flowing skirt's pockets and pulled out a small green box neatly tied up with a silver ribbon. When I didn't move to take the box she used her free hand to take mine and pressed the box into it.

I looked down at the small box in my hand and back up at her smiling face. She reminded me of an excited child, I half expected her to bounce up and down on the couch, clapping her hands, and saying 'Open it! Open it!"

"Go ahead, love, open it." She gently pushed my hand back toward me.

I looked back down at the small gift and carefully untied the ribbon, lifted off the box cover, and placed it on the coffee table. I peeled back the layers of white tissue, finally revealing the box's contents. Carefully, I lifted the silver chain and watched as its small pendant swung back and forth. I reached up with my other hand and held the pendant still, examining it.

"It's a Celtic knot," Jane went on to explain, "for eternity"

"It's beautiful!" I exclaimed looking at the intricate detail as each knot circled and bound itself to the next, like a circle there was no end and no beginning. "It looks old."

"Oh it is, dear. It belonged to Kate and before that, Aaron's paternal grandmother."

I looked up at Jane's face with my mouth agape. I stretched out my hand toward her, the pendant swinging wildly back and forth.

"I can't take this," I cried, shocked that she would be giving it to me. Did she not know about Aaron and me?

"Yes you can, dear." Jane reached out and touched the pendant with her finger stopping it from its wild swinging.

"But it belongs to Aaron." I argued.

"No, love, it belongs to you. Aaron wanted you to have it."

She surely mustn't know about us. I opened my mouth to explain but Jane cut me short with an explanation of her own.

"Aaron asked me to give this to you."

I closed my mouth and pulled my hand back, relaxing it in my lap, still clinging to the chain. "You don't understand," I said looking down at my closed fist; I could feel the chain neatly tucked away in my grasp. Tears began to well up in my eyes, but I did nothing to stop them. Then when my lids couldn't hold them back any longer, I let them spill over the edge, not even bothering to wipe them away.

"Yes dear, I do." Jane's voice was kind and empathetic. "Aaron asked me to give it to you last night."

"What?" I said looking up at Jane's face, the remaining tears dripping from my cheek.

"I've been in London the past couple of days, visiting. He told me of your circumstances and asked if I would give this to you. He said it might mean something to you."

I opened my hand and looked at the pendant again. Eternity – I smiled. "Thank you." I leaned over and gave Jane a hug, by the time I finished; she too had tears in her eyes.

We visited a bit longer, neither one of us bringing up Aaron. By the time I got up to leave, I had agreed to join her for dinner on my last night.

I had waited impatiently all week for Sunday to arrive, but when it did I was sad to see it come. I wished that I had spent my last week saying goodbye to the friends I'd made in Bourton instead of wallowing in self-pity.

I crawled out of bed slowly, showered and dressed. Jane had invited me for breakfast, as there wasn't anything left in the apartment to eat. Grabbing what little groceries I had packed in bags the night before; I headed down to her place and quietly knocked on the door. Seconds later, the door opened and Peter greeted me smiling widely.

"Peter!" I exclaimed, "I didn't expect you here just yet!" I placed the bags in his outstretched hands and closed the door behind me.

"Since I was coming out to bring you to the airport anyway, I thought I might as well come out for breakfast, too," he explained as he headed toward the kitchen, the plastic bags dangling from his hands.

"Breakfast is ready!" Jane called from the dining table.

I headed into the dining room and sat beside Jane. When Peter returned from the kitchen, he seated himself across from me. Heaviness filled the air, surrounding us. Whether it was because of that heaviness or not, no one spoke a single word during breakfast. The only sounds came from the cutlery on the plates or the clunking of glasses as they were set back down on the table. Finally, I broke the silence, laying my knife and fork down on my plate.

"Ahem!" My throat felt thick with emotion. "I just wanted to say. . . " I cleared my throat again, and took a deep breath. "I just

wanted to say that I feel very blessed to have met you – all of you."
The tightness returned again. I picked up my cup and drank what
was left of my tea; the warm, soothing liquid coated my throat. I
could feel both Peter and Jane's eyes upon me. Neither of them
spoke as they waited patiently for me to finish. "I truly have never
felt more welcome by anyone in my entire life." My eyes burned
with tears, but I managed to blink them back before continuing.
"I will never forget your hospitality," I smiled at Jane and reached
out to grab her hand, "or your friendship." I reached across the
table with my other hand for Peter's; he met me half way with
his own warm grasp. "I hope someday I can return the favour." A
tear escaped. "Thank you, I will never forget it." I released their
hands as my voice broke and more tears fell from my eyes. Jane
handed me some tissues that she had in her apron pocket.

"Don't worry, dear, they're clean," she said dabbing at her eyes
with a tissue of her own.

"Okay ladies, I do believe it's time –" Peter smiled, though his
eyes looked a little wet.

"You're wearing it!" Jane interrupted.

"I don't think I'll ever take it off." I said, gently playing with
the pendant that hung from my neck.

"We really should be on our way." Peter reminded us.

I hugged Jane, and we said our tearful goodbyes. "Oh, I have
something." I reached into my pocked and grabbed a crumpled
piece of paper. "I never did get a chance to say bye to a few
people. Would you mind doing it for me?" I placed the list in
Jane's hand.

"Of course, dear." She smiled, putting the list in her apron
pocket.

"My contact information is there, too. I'd be happy to hear
from anyone."

Jane smiled and nodded. "Of course," she whispered. "You better get going." She ushered us to the door.

"Bye, Jane, thank you for everything."

Peter and I headed up to the apartment, grabbed my bags, and made sure I hadn't forgotten anything.

"Ready?" he asked my suitcases in his hands.

I took one last look around, committing my lovely home-away-from-home apartment to memory.

"Ready," I said my voice breaking; I cleared my throat.

The drive to the airport was long and quiet. I watched the passing scenery, towns, and villages and silently wished them all goodbye.

Forty-Seven

Peter and I walked silently from the parking lot into the terminal. It felt like a dream. People distorted, objects blurred, sounds muffled and memories faded. I felt sure I would soon be waking up.

"Well," he said, "I guess this is as far as I can go." He stopped abruptly and set my bags down on a nearby cart.

I shook my head and stared at him blankly, realizing I wasn't asleep.

"Yeah, I guess so." I nervously looked around.

Peter reached over and took me in his arms. "You take care of yourself."

"I will."

"He loves you, you know, and he understands."

I nodded, determined not to cry, but it was too late, the tears flowed freely. I pulled away. "I'm going to get your shirt all wet," I said, brushing his shoulder.

"I'm sorry, I didn't mean to..." Peter looked at me; it was easy to see the pity in his eyes.

"Don't be. It's okay." I absently rubbed the pendant that hung from my neck between my fingers.

"Okay, have a safe flight, and keep in touch." Peter leaned over and kissed my forehead.

I closed my eyes, remembering how Aaron used to do that, only his kisses left an invisible mark.

"I will. Take care." I hugged him once more and before the tears could flow again, I turned, pushing my bags towards the check-in area.

Once through security control, my luggage checked, I sat in the departure lounge and watched the monitor for boarding. Nervously, I looked around again. Finally, after about an hour, it was time to board the plane. I grabbed my carry-on and proceeded through the gate. Memories from another time flashed through my mind, a frightened and heartbroken Mary waiting to see Thomas one final time.

The attendant looked at my ticket and pointed out my seat. I waited patiently as passengers ahead of me placed their carry-ons in the overhead compartments and when I reached my seat, it was my turn to hold-up the passengers behind me.

I felt like I was in a fog as I sat in my window seat and made the necessary adjustments. I busied myself staring out the window at the ground crew below as they prepared the plane for take-off. I closed my eyes and rested my head against the window feeling the coolness of the glass. It felt good against my aching head.

"Excuse me; miss, would you like a pillow." A dark haired attendant, holding out a small blue pillow, interrupted my thoughts.

"Yes, thank you." I reached out, grabbed the pillow, placed it against the window, and closed my eyes. I sensed the other passengers had taken up their seats beside me, but I was in no mood for conversation. Within minutes, I felt myself drifting off; the sleep was both welcoming and threatening.

As my body and mind slowly drifted deeper into the abyss, the beginnings of a strange dream began trickling in. I tried waking before it took hold, but my exhaustion took control and a painful memory began playing through my mind.

Wake-up! My voice silently called from a distance, lost in a fog of swirling and intertwined memories.

The distant sound of a flight attendant going over emergency procedures briefly filtered through. The line between the conscious and the unconscious blurred, and I found myself teetering back and forth between one side and the other. I had to fight to stay awake, if sleep took hold; more memories would come flooding back. My exhaustion, however, was strong and kept me from breaking free, again I felt myself falling back. The dreams were getting stronger and becoming more difficult to push away.

Suddenly, my ears were filled with the muffled voices of passengers. There was snug pressure across my lap and I was reminded of the seat belt. I moved my head slightly and my cheek rubbed against the soft pillow. I had escaped. The warmth of a hand caressed my cheek and a smile stretched across my mouth. I stirred and turned my head toward the hand, my eyes wide open.

"Hello, sleepyhead." He smiled and his eyes sparkled.

"What are you doing here?"

"Shall I go?" he asked, moving to stand.

"NO!" I looked around as others stared at me. "No," I whispered. My heart pounded, and I was sure if I looked at my chest I would see it.

"I can't live without you."

I stared at Aaron in disbelief before finally finding my voice. "How did you..."

"Peter."

"What?"

"Peter told me you'd switched your flight. I guess fate really is on our side. Look, I'm even supposed to be sitting here." He smiled brilliantly, holding out the ticket to show me his seat number.

He couldn't look anymore handsome if he tried. My heart was melting, and all the sadness I was feeling melted away with it.

"Excuse me, miss?"

I knew I looked silly, a Cheshire grin pasted on my face, but I couldn't help it. Aaron was with me, and I was so happy. "I'm so happy you're here." I gushed.

"Miss?" I heard the voice, but chose to ignore it. I couldn't be sure if it was directed at me; I didn't care if it was. My focus was solely on Aaron. "Miss!" This time the voice sounded more impatient and came with the light shaking of my arm.

Startled, I raised my head and sat up, realizing for the first time that the voice came from the passenger beside me. My head had been resting on his shoulder.

"I... I'm sorry." I stammered, embarrassed and still dazed.

Confusion set in as I wondered if I was truly awake and if Aaron was a dream or was it that Aaron was real and the man beside me was a dream. I rolled my head back toward the window. Fresh tears rolled down my cheeks as my mind became clear, this was no dream.

Forty-Eight

The first couple of weeks of school went well enough, I had spent my first day back tirelessly working on a lesson plan and preparing my classroom. When I wasn't staying after school, working on the following day's lesson, I helped my mother with her wedding plans or visited with friends. Keeping busy was my newest habit, anything that kept me from going home until I had to – anything that passed the time. On weekends, I devoted my time to housework, and the moment it was completed, I left in search of other things to occupy my day.

I had become better at acting, lying – being poker faced. I kept my emotions in check when I spent time with my friends and family. I even managed to fool my mother, though she was busy with her wedding plans. I was doing a good job keeping up the façade of happiness.

Sleep had become my only refuge from the long days; I had given in to my memories. Whether new or old, happy or sad, dreams of Mary and Thomas filled my nights, even Aaron appeared occasionally, and I wished I never had to wake. They were all I dreamed of, all I wanted to dream of, and I couldn't wait to get back to them each night, even if waking saddened me every morning.

As the end of September loomed, I'd adapted to my new life. My mother and I grew closer as her wedding date approached.

Although I didn't share with her my true feelings about Aaron and the sense of loss I felt, I was able to share other feelings, including telling her that I had no intention of going on any blind dates with anyone. She was determined to find me a date for her wedding, even going as far as including a plus one for me on her guest list. I couldn't imagine being with anyone, not now – not ever.

"I didn't realize you were so talented."

His eyes widened and he smiled crookedly. "Oh! You didn't?"

I laughed. "You know what I mean."

"Do I?" He always loved teasing me that way and I didn't mind, it brought a light-heartedness to our relationship. I playfully slapped his arm."Be careful now, you might make the pencil slip and you'll end up with a wall where you don't want one." He sat back from the drawing on his desk.

I leaned over his shoulder and examined the floor plan he'd just completed. "It's perfect! When can we start building?"

"Right now." Aaron stood up and took me by the hand, leading me out the door.

We walked down a dirt road, trees lining the route as we strolled along. The air filled with the sound of chirping birds; a warm breeze gently blew through my hair. As we rounded a bend, the sound of hammering filled my ears, and the smell of fresh cut timbers wafted through the air.

"Is that ours?" I pointed to the frame of a house on a large treed lot.

Aaron wrapped his arms around me and kissed the top of my head. "Ours, forever."

The workers continued their hammering, unaware of our presence.

My eyes fluttered open, another night gone, another dream behind me, and another day to get through until I could return to the few hours of happiness sleep brought. I stared up at the ceiling trying to recall the dream, hoping to fall back to sleep and continue the story I'd written for myself. My mind had become very accomplished at making dreams go the way I wanted them to. I closed my eyes and drowsily rolled over, hoping the sound of knocking from outside would spark a memory and return me to my dream.

My eyes popped open again as I realized the knocking was at the front door. I slowly climbed from bed and grabbed my robe from the back of the door. The knock came again.

"I'm coming!" I called to the impatient knocker, knowing whoever it was probably couldn't hear me anyway.

When I reached the door, I peered through the peephole, only seeing the distorted back of someone as he began heading down the stairs. My first thought was to turn away and go back to bed, but I changed my mind. I opened the door, sure that the person leaving was undoubtedly another one of my mother's attempts at finding me a date. Despite having told her an emphatic 'no, not interested', she was still trying to set me up. I'd already turned down two of her previous attempts, and I believed if I didn't do it again, he'd be back. I couldn't help but smile at my mother's latest matchmaking as I pulled open the door.

"Can I help you?"

The man stopped and stood with his back toward me, turning slowly, until finally his eyes stared into mine, familiar eyes – eyes that burrowed into my soul and melted my heart.

"Hi." A slow smile spread across his face.

Paralyzed, I stood in the doorway, staring at him.

"Why... What?" My mind was swirling with so many questions that I didn't know where to start.

"Can I come in; it's a wee bit cold out here."

For the first time, I realized the temperature as a cool breeze fluttered my robe. I stepped back and let him in, folding my arms across my chest both for warmth and for protection.

"You have a lovely home," he said closing the door behind him.

I stared at him, unable to speak – catatonic.

"I'm sorry. I should have called, but I couldn't wait to. . . " His voice trailed.

I wanted to throw myself at him and would have, if I didn't think I was somehow still dreaming. It wouldn't be the first time I'd made a fool of myself by thinking I was awake when I wasn't. I remembered my flight home.

"What's that?" I asked, for the first time I noticed a large envelope in his hand.

"Can we sit down?"

I silently waved my hand toward the living room. He took a spot in the corner of the couch. I stood, my arms still crossed, still unsure.

"Would you sit, too. . . please?" He patted the spot beside him. I sat down, keeping a safe distance between us, my heart pounded. "It's for you. Here."

It seemed a long time before my hand moved to take the envelope and even longer for me to open it. Finally, I slowly opened the yellow envelope and pulled out a picture of the two of us taken in Bude. We'd asked a stranger to take the picture – the result was stunning.

"I thought maybe. . . . you could put it in that frame."

I knew exactly what frame he meant. It wasn't long ago that I'd had the same idea – the same hope. When I returned home, I considered throwing it out, but couldn't bear to part with the gift my friend had given me.

"This is real?" I asked, finally allowing myself to trust my eyes. "You're really here! Oh Aaron, you're really here." Happy tears spilled from my eyes.

Aaron took the picture from my shaking hands and placed it on his lap. He reached over and took my hands in his; little jolts of electricity flowed back and forth between them. "Krista." He looked into my soul. "I want to be your future."

I closed my eyes tightly to shut out the tears. I was done with crying. "But what about –"

Aaron finished my sentence for me. "Peter almost insisted I leave the tour guide business. He knew I'd never planned on staying as long as I did. Aunt Jane, she's met someone and never been happier. There is nothing for me over there. Everything I need is here. Everything I want to have is with you."

"But they'll miss you." My voice was shaking. My hands were shaking too, but he held them still in his own.

Aaron reached up, brushing the hair from my forehead and kissed the mark in my hairline above my right eye. "They'll be fine. We'll visit. They'll visit. We'll all be fine."

I shook my head in disbelief. I couldn't believe what was happening, he was really with me, in my home. I reached up and grabbed my pendant. "Eternity." I whispered searching his eyes.

"I promised I would find you." Aaron reached up and gently stroked my cheek.

"I'll find you, Mary; I promise I will find you!" Thomas's voice *echoed through the fog in my mind.*

"I remember Krista – all of it, every kiss, every laugh, when I chased you through the meadow – my promise to find you," he whispered as he leaned over to kiss me.

The moment our lips touched our memories combined as that familiar electricity ran through us. Our souls joined as one. I had found my soulmate – my one true love – my promised soul.

Epilogue

"Tell me again!" she whispered. It was obvious now that speaking was becoming more of an effort. Her small, thin, frail body was practically swallowed up by the bed they'd shared for so many years. Painstakingly, he had pulled the blanket up and tucked it under her chin, and if anyone were to look at her from above she'd resemble a disembodied head resting on a pillow.

He lay on his side watching as her chest rose and sank, and it reminded him of when he used to wake almost every night and lie just as he was now watching her sleep and breathe. It still amazed him now, even to this very day, that they had finally lived out their lives together, as it was meant to be.

It turned out Mary and Thomas weren't the first bodies they'd inhabited, in fact there were others before that – centuries before. Their lives were forever connected, but something always seemed to separate them. Finally, this last time around, they'd made it. No – Mary and Thomas weren't the first, but they felt certain that Krista and Aaron would be the last. They'd loved each other deeply, raised a family, and grew old together. Now, they were heading into the final phase of their lives; they had completed their journey.

Slowly he stretched his thin skinned, sun-spotted hand out to hers, the stiffness and pain evident to anyone watching. Gently, he held her thin, frail hand and slowly caressed the back of it with his thumb, the only digit that didn't hurt so much when he moved it. Behind him, their family stood in silence watching, waiting. Krista was too weak to notice, and Aaron had blocked them out.

"This time," he began, "we'll stay. We'll be together for eternity, young and beautiful." He looked at Krista's aged and frail face, she was still beautiful in his eyes, even more so now. He gently moved his finger toward the pendant and touched it. She'd never taken it off in all those years. "You'll go there first, but I promise I will be joining you very soon," he said, a single tear falling from his tired eyes.

Krista sighed, and with some more effort, she spoke, so quietly that only Aaron heard. "How do you know," she breathed, "that you'll be there soon?" Her eyes remained closed.

"I know," he said, "because I can't live without you." Krista opened her eyes. It took all her energy to turn her head to face him. She smiled and Aaron smiled back. "I love you," Aaron whispered; more tears escaped.

Krista smiled again watching her husband's face. He'll be there soon, she told herself. How happy she'd been over the years. How many now? She thought. Memories of their sixtieth anniversary and the party their family had given them slowly came to her mind. It seemed like it was only yesterday. Of course, she thought, as the images became clearer. It was just last summer, and then I got sick.

She wanted so badly to reach up to Aaron's face and touch it one last time, to wipe away his tears. Instead, with all the energy that she had left, she gently squeezed his hand; she only hoped it was strong enough for him to feel – it had been; he gently squeezed back. She kept her eyes focused on his face not wanting to see anything but him, but of course she did. She could just barely make out forms standing behind him, watching, and she knew it was their loving family. She was sad for them, losing both parents and grandparents wasn't going to be easy. They'll be fine, she told herself. She wanted to say 'I love you' one last time, but she couldn't, instead she stared at Aaron hoping he'd see it on her face and in her eyes.

"I know," he choked.

Krista watched her husband's face, not wanting to close her eyes for a second. She felt her heart begin to slow, and it seemed to take a long time before she felt the need to fill her lungs with air, each time taking longer and longer between breaths. She grew wearier as time went on, and she noticed her vision began to blur. Slowly her eyelids became unbearably heavy and with reluctance, she allowed them to close. She no longer felt the desire to inhale and finally sensed her heart no longer beating. In the distant fog, she heard the cries of her family and Aaron's final words.

"I'll be there soon, Krista, I swear I will."

Two weeks later, Aaron joined her, keeping his promise.

Dear reader,

We hope you enjoyed reading *Promised Soul*. Please take a moment to leave a review, even if it's a short one. Your opinion is important to us.

Discover more books by Sandra J. Jackson at
https://www.nextchapter.pub/authors/author-sandra-jackson

Want to know when one of our books is free or discounted? Join the newsletter at http://eepurl.com/bqqB3H

Best regards,
Sandra J. Jackson and the Next Chapter Team

About the Author

A graduate of a 3-year Graphic Design program, Sandra J. Jackson has always been creative, from drawing and painting to telling stories to her children when they were young. Her wild imagination lends itself to new and exciting ideas.

Sandra's debut novel, *Promised Soul*, was originally released in 2015 by her former publisher. A short story, *Not Worth Saving*, was published in New Zenith Magazine's 2016 fall issue. She also has had several sports articles published in a local newspaper. She holds a professional membership with the Canadian Author Association and is a member of Writers' Ink.

Sandra's second novel, *Playing in the Rain - Book 1 of the Escape Series*, released in September 2017 also by the same former publisher.

Sandra lives with her family in a rural setting in Eastern, Ontario. She is currently working on Book 3 of the *Escape Series*, her first trilogy.

Website: www.sandrajjackson.com

Promised Soul
ISBN: 978-4-86751-788-8

Published by
Next Chapter
1-60-20 Minami-Otsuka
170-0005 Toshima-Ku, Tokyo
+818035793528
12th July 2021

Lightning Source UK Ltd.
Milton Keynes UK
UKHW010920250721
387681UK00001B/103